A Tangled Web

Gwen Kirkwood

This first world edition published in Great Britain 2003 by
SEVERN HOUSE PUBLISHERS LTD of
9–15 High Street, Sutton, Surrey SM1 1DF.
This first world edition published in the USA 2003 by
SEVERN HOUSE PUBLISHERS INC of
595 Madison Avenue, New York, N.Y. 10022.

British Library Cataloguing in Publication Data

Kirkwood, Gwen
   A tangled web
   1.   Country life - Scotland - Fiction
   I.   Title
   823.9'14 [F]

   ISBN 0-7278-5986-2

Typeset by Palimpsest Book Production Ltd.,
Polmont, Stirlingshire, Scotland.
Printed and bound in Great Britain by
MPG Books Ltd., Bodmin, Cornwall.

My thanks to Padrayla Holdsworth of
Antiques Information Services Ltd, for her help and guidance.
Also to Elizabeth Morte for helping me convey a little of
the Welsh lilt in written word.

O what a tangled web we weave,
When first we practise to deceive.

Marmion,
Sir Walter Scott

One

B ridie stopped for a quick look in the newsagent's window.

'Bridie! Hey, Bridie Maxwell . . .'

She turned in surprise, scanning the passers-by on the
opposite side of the road.

'Oh . . .' She stared open mouthed as a tall slim figure ran
across the street, dodging between a horse and cart and the
butcher's van. 'Fiona! What a surprise! What are you doing
in Lockerbie? I haven't seen you for . . .'

'Years?' Fiona Sinclair prompted with a rueful smile.

'I think it is. Two at least. How are you? Are you on
holiday? Are you visiting your mother? How is she?' Bridie's
pleasure at seeing her old school friend was evident as the
questions tumbled out, one after the other.

Fiona's smile faded and the light died from the clear grey
eyes. Bridie remembered how expressive Fiona's eyes had
always been: tenderness, compassion, anger. They were like
a mirror reflecting her inner emotions.

'Have you time for a cup of tea, Bridie? I'd love to chat
for a wee while . . . That is . . . ?

'Of course I have time! I will make time,' Bridie said,
swiftly pushing out of her mind the million and one tasks
she had vowed to do. 'I've just been to the vet's for a drench
for a sickly calf, but so long as I'm back at Lochandee before
milking it will be fine. Shall we go into Stevenson & Wilson's
or do you prefer—?'

'Wilson's will be fine.' Fiona glanced at the baker's shop

with its upstairs restaurant only a couple of doors from where they were standing. 'I see they still make a lovely selection of cakes and scones. Oh look! Is that a Selkirk bannock I see? Mother used to love them. I'll buy it before anyone else snatches it up. It might just tempt her appetite. How many bread coupons do you think I shall need?' She fished in her handbag and pulled out a ration book.

'I don't think you'll need any.' Bridie frowned, puzzled. 'The government withdrew the bread units in July. Surely it must have been the same in Glasgow?'

'Oh, probably. I forgot. I shall have to get used to doing these everyday things again. I've been a bit spoiled with someone to do most of my shopping. Mrs Mossy seemed to know all the best places to register for things. She had three other households besides mine and her own.'

'Oh.' Bridie was at a loss.

'You go on up and choose a table and I'll follow as soon as I've paid.' The sweep of smooth, well-groomed hair hid her face.

Bridie made her way slowly up the stairs to the restaurant. It was quiet at this time, except on market days. Most of those who had been lunching had already left and it was still early for afternoon tea. She chose a table near the window, overlooking the wide main street of the little market town.

'I saw the waitress on my way up,' Fiona said, arranging her handbag and the neatly wrapped bannock on a spare chair. 'I ordered afternoon tea. Is that all right? I remember you always used to have tea before milking time at the farm.' She smiled across the table. 'Is it still the same routine?'

'More or less. I think we all assumed the rationing would go away once the war was over but some things are more scarce than ever. But never mind that, do tell me how things are with you, Fiona? I haven't seen your mother for ages, but she was so proud of you being a qualified accountant and working in the city. "Doing the work of a gentleman" she said.' Bridie grinned but she was dismayed to see a film of tears cloud Fiona's eyes. She blinked rapidly.

They had travelled together on the school bus each night and morning to the Academy and they had become good friends in spite of Fiona's two years' seniority and her brilliant academic achievements. Seven years ago Bridie remembered she herself had been desperate to leave school to help at Lochandee. As soon as she had finished the examinations for her School Certificate she had got her way, mainly because so many men were away at war and her mother was expecting Ewan and far from well. Fiona had been seventeen by then but she had passed her Higher School Certificate with distinction. Then, to Bridie's surprise, and Mrs Sinclair's dismay, she had become engaged to a boy she had known since they had started at Dumfries Academy together six years earlier. His name was Gerald Fountain, known throughout the school as Gerry. Bridie remembered him well. He had been tall, very fair, not exactly handsome, but his blue eyes had sparkled and everyone recognized his infectious laugh.

'Poor Mum . . .' Fiona said huskily. 'I'm afraid I have not been much comfort to her since Father died.'

'Oh, don't say that, Fiona. She was really proud of the way you . . . you picked up the pieces and made such a success of your career.'

'I know, but dedication to my work seemed to me all that was left after . . . . after Gerry was killed. I threw myself into studying and then work. I was blind to everything else, but the more I achieved the more time I spent away from home, and . . . and now it's too late. Mother is dying, Bridie . . .' Fiona's voice trailed away in a little choking sound, and Bridie guessed she was struggling valiantly to control her tears.

'Oh, Fiona . . . Are you sure . . . ? I mean, is there nothing the doctors can do?'

'No. They haven't told her, of course, but I insisted they must tell me the truth. I-I had guessed, b-but it seems so final when your worst fears are confirmed. They . . . they wanted to keep it to themselves, the doctors. She's my mother for goodness sake! I-I had a right to know.'

'I'm so sorry, Fiona.' Bridie reached out a hand and covered the restless fingers. She was rewarded with a wan smile.

'You were always so sensible, Bridie. So reassuring and full of good common sense. Mother always said so. Sometimes I used to feel you were the older of the two of us. I expect it is because you had a brother, or maybe because you lived on a farm and saw life and death in perspective. Right now it is exactly what I need. Someone who understands, someone to reassure me I have done the right thing.'

'The right thing? What do you mean, what have you done, Fiona?'

'I've given up my career in Glasgow. I had bought a house with the money Daddy left me. I've sold it . . . burned my boats.' She gave a faint, almost cynical smile.

'Given up your career? But you were . . . you had such great prospects. I thought . . . ?'

'Oh yes!' Fiona's tone was grim. 'I went up the ladder fast. But . . .' She gave a cynical laugh, totally unlike the girl Bridie remembered. 'It was not because I was brilliant, you understand. Oh no! I'm a woman! How could a mere woman be brilliant.' She smiled but it was a mixture of pain and bitterness. 'Our senior partner was at pains to tell me I had only gone so far, so fast, because there was no one else – a shortage of young men due to the war, he said. It would be laughable if it was not such a farce. Can you believe? Only five minutes earlier he had been telling me what a promising future I had. He had just offered me a partnership in the firm and several valuable perks to go with it.'

'I-I don't understand . . . ?'

'I didn't feel I could accept a partnership without being honest with him. I told him I should need time to spend with my mother. He almost exploded. He wanted – no, he

4

demanded – total dedication. Do you know what he said? "Get a nurse! You don't allow things like sickness to come between you and an opportunity such as I'm offering." I told him my mother was not just sick. She is dying. Dying. She may have only weeks to live – months at the most. "So?" he says. "Get two bloody nurses to stay with her then. You can afford the money for God's sake!" Money!' Fiona almost spat the word. 'It is God for half the men I came into contact with in my job. He had been so charming. Suddenly his voice was like ice, Bridie.' She shuddered. 'And his eyes . . . I've never seen such hardness. He looked utterly ruthless. I-I knew he would never listen to reason, or to pleading. Besides I was upset about Mum. I-I told him to k-keep his partnership.'

Bridie squeezed the trembling fingers. 'I understand. I do know how you must feel, Fiona.'

The grey eyes looked into Bridie's gentle blue ones. 'Yes,' she said at length. 'Yes, you are probably the only person who will, but I really believe you do understand. Mother is all I have left and the people you love have to take priority over everything else, haven't they?'

'Yes,' Bridie said quietly, 'they have.'

'I-I'm so glad I ran into you today. I've been feeling so low. It's silly, but you know, I feel like a stranger here. I was born in this area, went to local schools . . .' Her voice cracked and for a moment Bridie was afraid her control had snapped. 'It is where I fell in love . . . First made love. And . . . and where I went to the first funeral of my life – Gerry's . . .'

'I-I know. I was so dreadfully sorry. We all were. War is such a cruel thing.'

Fiona nodded and gulped hard. Then she took a sip of the tea, and another, striving to regain her usual composure. Bridie remembered Fiona had always envied her having a brother. She was an only child. Her father had been in the navy during the war and his ship had been torpedoed.

'Your Aunt Milly . . . ?' Bridie began tentatively. Fiona shook her head.

5

'She died just before the war ended. There's only Mum and me now. I have two cousins but they are in Australia. I only know them through photographs.' She reached for a girdle scone from the middle tier of the cake stand. 'Do you know, I feel hungry all of a sudden. It must have done me good talking to you, Bridie. I haven't been able to eat . . . or sleep. All hope seems to drain away once you hear the dreaded word cancer.'

'Well you mustn't bottle things up, Fiona. You are not so far away from Lochandee. You must come and visit us whenever you can get away. Do you still ride your bicycle?'

'Bicycle!' She gave a low chuckle which reminded Bridie of the girl she had once known. 'I haven't ridden a bike for ages, but I think it's still in the shed. I'll get it out and dust it down. I had used up most of my petrol ration coming down to visit and now I am hoarding what I have – just in case Mother feels up to going for a drive, or anything.'

'Of course. I'm sure you've done the right thing in the circumstances, Fiona. With your qualifications and experience you will easily get another job when you're ready, and I'm sure your mother will appreciate you being with her.'

'Speaking of Mother, I must be getting back. Our next-door neighbour is sitting with her for an hour or two. She's very good. I think she realized I needed a break more than I did myself. I promised I'd be back on the three o'clock bus. But we have only talked about me and my troubles. I assure you I'm not usually such a bore, or such a moan – but I do thank you for listening, Bridie.'

'That's what friends are for,' Bridie smiled. 'My car is just down the street. I could give you a lift home if you like. It's only two or three miles further.'

'That would be wonderful.' Fiona accepted gratefully. 'Then you can give me all your news as we go.' She glanced at Bridie's ringless fingers. 'I see you're not married. Well I'd have heard if you were. Mother always tried to keep me up to date with news of old friends. She told me when your brother's plane was shot down. It must have been a dreadful worry to your parents. For you too. He had a very lucky escape, I believe? Is he all right now?'

'Conan is fine. Sometimes you can detect a slight limp but he never admits to it, or lets it hold him back.'

'I can imagine. I suppose he's back at the farm, longing to take over from your father? I seem to recall he always liked to take charge and do things his own way. I remember you asked me to ride his bicycle back from our village to Lochandee the day he went away to the RAF. Wasn't that because he didn't want your parents to know, or something?'

'We-ell, he did tell them, but only at the very last minute. He didn't want Mother to drive him to the station, though, in case she got upset. Anyway he's back safe and sound which is more than can be said for a lot of the young men who went away.' Bridie sighed. 'But Conan has not returned to the Glens of Lochandee to farm. He and a-a friend have bought a few acres of land near the main road from Carlisle to Lockerbie. They are building up a garage business – mainly doing repairs but they have one lorry and do deliveries, mostly to farms. Anything to turn a penny at present, but you know Conan. He's ambitious and full of plans. They have built a workshop with a small flat above it – if you can call it that.'

'Basic is it?' Fiona raised her expressive eyebrows at Bridie's dry tone.

'You can say that again. Father built an extension on to our house at Lochandee so now we have a bathroom with hot and cold water on tap and an Aga cooker in the kitchen, so we are a bit more civilized than we used to be. Conan and Nick both come to have a bath at our house, and a good meal whenever they can.'

'I seem to remember Conan always liked to make his own decisions, but Gerry and his friends admired him. Is the man called Nick his partner? Do they get on all right?'

'Ye-es. I think so. They were at the same camp most of the time during the war. They were good friends. Nick and some of the others used to come to Lochandee whenever they had leave. Nick – Nick Jones – he's from Wales originally.'

'Mmm, I see.' Fiona eyed Bridie shrewdly, seeing the heightened colour in her cheeks. 'A bit special is he, this Welshman called Nick?' Bridie's blush deepened and Fiona chuckled. 'I can see that he is.'

'Oh, we're not engaged, or anything . . . Well not officially anyway.'

'You mean you have a private understanding,' Fiona suggested, smiling. Bridie threw her a glance and returned her attention to her driving, but after a few seconds of silence she burst into speech.

'You could say we did have an understanding.'

'Did have? Bridie?'

'Well . . . since we are exchanging confidences today,' Bridie sighed. 'Nick and I both thought we would get married as soon as he was de-mobbed. That was two years ago. Nick would like to be engaged, but I refused until we could set a date for the wedding. I do love him, I really do, but he's just about as pig-headed as Conan when it comes to wanting his own way!'

'O-oh. Poor you then, Bridie. I do recall Conan being very much his own person even when we were all just kids at school. Of course we all thought we were so grown up when the war came.' Fiona chewed on her lower lip and Bridie guessed her thoughts were on Gerry.

'Well, we are grown up now. I was twenty-two last May. Nick is six months older than Conan.'

'I'm twenty-four, nearly twenty-five. Conan was two years ahead of me and Gerry at school, so he and your Nick must be about twenty-six.'

'Nick will be twenty-seven just before Christmas. We could both live at the Glens of Lochandee. There is plenty of room for us. It's only a few miles for him to travel to the garage. But, oh no! Nick has his pride and he is so damned independent! He and Conan have put everything they have into building up their business and Nick says he will not marry until he can afford to feed and clothe his wife and provide his own roof.'

'What do your parents think?'

'They don't interfere, but they like Nick. They wouldn't mind him living at Lochandee but Father says he understands and respects Nick's point of view.'

'What about your baby brother, Bridie?'

'Baby! Ewan is seven. He'll be eight in January. All he thinks about is farming.'

'Just like his sister Bridie, then?' Fiona smiled. 'You simply lived for your animals, I remember.'

'Ye-es . . . That's another thing,' Bridie said slowly. 'I can't bear the thought of leaving the Glens of Lochandee. I was born there. It's my life . . . Aunt Alice understood how I felt. She left me her share in the farm, but since Nick knew that, he has been even more determined to prove himself a success in business before we marry. Sometimes I feel so torn in two.'

'I know how you feel, Bridie,' Fiona said seriously. 'Older folks say life will sort itself out, but sometimes I wonder how it can when I feel so . . . so rudderless. Success and money aren't everything . . .' She shuddered. 'It's an awful feeling to find you're almost completely alone in the world. I don't feel I belong anywhere now, or to anyone. So . . . so do be careful not to push your Nick too far.'

'Oh Fiona! Please don't ever feel you are alone. I shouldn't have burdened you with my problems when you've far more serious ones. It's just that Nick and I had another argument last night and it's still fresh in my mind. You must come to the Glens of Lochandee. I'll call to see you too, if I wouldn't be intruding?'

'Oh, you'd never intrude, Bridie. I'd love you to come. Mother would be pleased to see you too. Her body is frail but her mind is as lively as ever so long as we can keep the pain under control without too much medication.'

'Right, that's a date,' Bridie promised.

The Sinclairs' square, two-storey house was built of red sandstone. It was set back from the road with a curving sweep of drive leading to the front door and a stable block and outhouses to the side. Bridie thought it seemed far too big for one elderly lady. As the car drew up at the garden gate, Fiona saw Mrs Jackson, their neighbour, peering out of the window. She let the curtain fall and by the time Fiona had thanked Bridie for the lift and climbed out of the car, the front door was open and Mrs Jackson was waiting on the steps. Even at a distance Fiona sensed her agitation. There was something wrong. Her heart was pounding as she ran up the drive.

Two

B ridie saw two small figures wending their way along the street as she drove through Lochandee village on her way home. Her mind had been on Fiona dashing away, barely taking time to say goodbye, but when she saw Ewan, her young brother, she realized school must be over for the day. She was even later than she had thought. She drew the car to a halt beside them.

'Jump in quickly, you two, if you want a lift.'

'Oh, good-ee, Bridie,' Ewan whooped and pulled open the car door with alacrity. It was a long walk from school, up through the village and along the road to the Glens of Lochandee. He was hoping to get a bicycle for his eighth birthday in January. Lucy Mason hung back. 'Come on Lucy, get in quick,' Ewan urged.

'Mama said I had to stay at Carol's until she came home,' Lucy said. 'But I'd rather go with Ewan. He says there's a poorly calf.'

'Yes, I've just been to the vet's for medicine to make Moonbeam better. Hop in then. I'm late as it is, so your mum and I will be a bit later finishing the milking tonight. I expect she'll be glad to know you're with Ewan.'

Lucy scrambled eagerly into the car. The farm was like a second home to her and she needed no persuasion.

'Isn't that Carol's two girls just ahead?' Bridie asked.

'Yes, we were going to play at houses but I like being at the farm best.'

'That's good.' Bridie drew the car to a halt again beside

the two older children. 'Will you tell your mother I'm taking Lucy back to the Glens of Lochandee with me please, Joanne? Just say Beth may be a bit later getting home tonight.'

Beth Mason had worked at the Glens of Lochandee most of her life, starting as soon as she left school when she was thirteen. She had missed a few years after she married Harry Mason. They had taken over her grandfather's cycle shop in the middle of the village and Harry had added small electrical goods and repairs. They had been doing nicely until war was declared.

Harry had been one of the first to be called up for active service and Beth had been unable to carry on the little business without him. They had been forced to close the shop so Beth had scrubbed out the empty rooms and taken in a family of evacuees. At the time, Beth and Harry had been longing for children of their own but Beth had begun to despair of her wishes ever being fulfilled. Consequently she had welcomed Carol Williams and her two small girls. Carol's husband was in the navy and he had urged her to leave their home in Glasgow for the relative safety of the border village of Lochandee. Less than a year later his ship had been torpedoed and he had been lost at sea. When the war ended Carol had decided to settle in Lochandee and she now rented a house just fifty yards or so further up the street from Beth and Harry. The two families had remained friends, helping each other whenever they were needed.

There were some good things to have come out of the war and the painful separations, Bridie reflected as she listened to Ewan and Lucy chattering happily in the back of the car. They had been born within a fortnight of each other, nine months after Harry had returned to camp and Conan had left to join the RAF. Bridie had been almost fifteen at the time and she remembered the comfort Ewan had brought to her parents, and even to herself, compensating a little for Conan's absence from their close family circle.

Lucy's birth on a bleak February day in 1941 had seemed

like a miracle, bringing inestimable joy to Beth and Harry. Bridie loved both the children in spite of the mischief they often caused.

Beth had returned to work at the Glens of Lochandee as soon as she had recovered from Lucy's difficult birth. Farm workers were in short supply with most of the able-bodied men fighting for their country and all available hands were needed on the farms and in the factories. So Lucy and Ewan had grown up together and had quickly become as inseparable as twins. Their elders, with the exception of Beth, were often amused by their identical mannerisms. When comments were made about any similarity between the two children, Beth would exhibit a rare irritation.

'Och, it's just that Beth likes to think her "wee treasure" is unique,' Ross Maxwell chuckled, 'but Lucy is just a normal wee bairn and she has just the same mischievous smile and twinkle in her eye as Ewan.' In fact their eyes were quite similar – an unusual greenish-blue which often sparkled with laughter, and sometimes with temper. Harry claimed Lucy's eyes were the same colour as his mother's, and that her beauty came from Beth, but everyone knew he would have been as proud as Lucifer even if Lucy had looked like a monkey.

Beth had spent most of her life at the Glens of Lochandee and she loved the farm and the circle of kindly folks she knew so well. So she had continued working in the dairy and house and helping with the poultry, even when the war was finished. Harry had been offered a job at the electrical repair shop in Annan and he cycled eight miles to work every morning and back again each evening.

'I feel a job will be more secure than trying to start up a cycle shop in a country village again,' he explained to Bridie's parents. 'The war has made people restless for change. I reckon Conan has the right idea with his ambitions for a garage and buses to take people further afield.'

'I hope you're right,' Ross said gruffly. 'Conan has never wanted to farm so I've just had to accept his decision.'

13

'We're just thankful he came home safely, and you too, Harry.' Rachel Maxwell smiled.

'Not half as thankful as I am,' Harry grinned. 'My only ambition now is to see Lucy grow into a fine young woman and get a good job to earn her living. I'd like fine if she could be a teacher, or something like that, so I'm pleased you've still got work for Beth at the Glens of Lochandee. We try to put a wee bit by every week, ready for her future, so we appreciate the butter and milk and bacon Beth brings home, especially with the rationing still going on for so many things.'

As soon as Bridie drove into the yard that afternoon, Rachel came out to greet her.

'You've been a long time, Bridie. Your father has started the milking with Beth. We were worried about you. Did the car have a puncture?'

'No. I've brought the drench for the calf and I gave Ewan and Lucy a lift home from school, but I must change into my breeches and get on with the work.'

'Don't you want some tea first?'

'No thanks, Mum. I met Fiona Sinclair in Lockerbie. We had tea at Stevenson & Wilson's. It delayed me a bit but I'm really glad we met. I'll tell you all the news at supper. I'd better hurry, we shall be late as it is.'

'Yes, and Nick called while you were out. He's c—'

'Nick? He called? This afternoon?' Bridie froze, one foot on the stairs. 'What did he want?'

'He didn't say. To see you, I suppose. He was driving the lorry because he had been delivering a load of linseed cake to a farm on the other side of the glen.'

'Oh.' Bridie didn't know whether she felt angry or disappointed.

'Bridie?' Rachel hesitated, reluctant to pry, but she recognized the expression on her daughter's face. The set mouth, the spark in her blue eyes.

'Yes?'

'Have you quarrelled with Nick again? He . . . he seemed very tense. And so are you. Is there anything I can do?'

'No, Mum.' Bridie turned away. She was surprised to find tears stinging her eyes. She was sorry she had missed Nick. She longed to be with him – night and day. That was the trouble. They wanted to be together so much. It was getting harder and harder to say no when Nick took her in his arms and kissed her with such passion. She felt angry. Why did he have to be so stubborn? So proud? So independent?

'I invited him to supper,' Rachel called after her. 'He said he would come as soon as the garage closed. I expect Conan will come too. He's always ready for a good meal these days. I don't think they eat properly . . .' Her words tailed away as she realized Bridie was no longer there. She had hurried to her room to change. Rachel frowned and bit her lip. She had believed everything would be rosy as soon as the war ended and she had her family around her again, but life was not like that.

She turned her attention to the two children. They had brought a kitten in with them and they were rolling on the rag rug, giggling at its antics.

'Hey, you two. Change into your old clothes. You must remember there are no coupons to spare to keep buying you new school clothes. Then come and have some tea before you go out to play.'

'Yes, Mither.'

'Aye, Mrs Maxwell.'

The two youngsters answered cheerfully and went on playing with the kitten. Rachel sighed. How lovely to be so young and carefree. Her thoughts turned back to Bridie. She had a shrewd idea what was wrong between her daughter and Nick. They had waited long enough and Bridie was ready for marriage. She suspected Nick would welcome it too, but only when he could afford to keep a wife. The garage which he and Conan had started was making steady progress but it was slow. Every penny they made seemed to have a use before it was even in their hands. Conan had no ties and his only ambition was to make a success of his business. Rachel could understand Nick feeling frustrated. He wanted the business to be a success too, but he also wanted to have enough money in his hands to keep his wife, and probably a family. Life was never simple.

'That was a big sigh.'

Rachel spun around to face her husband. 'I didn't hear you come in, Ross. I thought you were at the byre, helping Beth with the milking.'

'I was but now that Bridie is back they don't need me.'

'Can we come with you to feed the calves, Dad?' Ewan asked, looking up from the kitten.

'Only when you have both changed into your old clothes and eaten your tea,' Rachel said firmly.

'Hurry up then,' Ross chuckled. 'I'll wait five minutes.' He pulled out a chair and sat down at the table. The big cream Aga kept the kitchen warm but he had liked the open fire better. The shining black lead and burnished steel, the high fender with the leather-topped stools attached at the corners – they had always made him feel warm and secure. In spite of his success Ross still felt the need to belong.

'There was a letter from the brigadier's solicitor in the post this morning,' he said casually.

Too casually, Rachel thought instantly. Over the years she had learned to recognize every little trait in Ross's nature.

'Oh,' she said and waited.

'Brigadier Jamieson died in Canada on the twelfth of October.'

'But that's a month ago! I'm glad for him though, poor soul. At least he will be at peace now and out of pain.'

'You're right, of course.' Ross nodded. It was typical of Rachel to consider the man himself rather than how his death might affect them. 'I wonder why his daughter didn't write to tell us sooner?'

'I don't suppose she felt up to it. Anyway she would know

we couldn't go to Canada to attend his funeral. I must write her a letter to express our sympathy.'

'Yes, I suppose so. I can't help wondering whether it will affect us though. The tenancy of Wester Rullion, I mean.'

'Aah.' Now she understood what was bothering Ross. 'I hadn't thought of that.' The brigadier had owned Wester Rullion, a farm a few miles from the Glens of Lochandee. Ross had started renting the land from the brigadier during the war and it had enabled them to grow more corn and keep more cattle and sheep. 'I suppose it will belong to his daughter now?'

'I expect so. Maybe we shall just go on paying the rent through the solicitor as we have done since the brigadier went to live with her in Canada. There was no mention of changes in the letter. We shall just have to wait and hope for the best.'

'Dad, Dad, is Moonbeam going to die?' Ewan called, bounding down the stairs with as much noise as a baby elephant. Lucy followed hard on his heels.

'I don't know yet, son. We're going to give her the medicine Bridie brought for her. Get your clogs on if you're going to help.'

Beth always kept some old clothes at the Glens of Lochandee for Lucy, knowing she would spend every minute with Ewan on the farm if she got the chance. The two children clattered happily after Ross, intent on helping feed the calves.

Bridie and Beth had only just finished milking and washing up when Conan and Nick drew up in the old car they used for running around.

'You're early,' Bridie called when her brother poked his head around the dairy door. 'Haven't you any work at that garage of yours?'

'More than enough.' Conan grinned. 'We're just better organized than you are, aren't we, Nick?' But Nick merely nodded vaguely, his gaze fixed intently on Bridie's tense face.

She did not meet his eye and his heart sank. He knew she was still smouldering from their disagreement, but he simply could not bring himself to accept charity from her parents. Besides, he didn't want to share their first home together with anyone, he wanted his bride to himself.

'Hey, Beth,' Conan called as Beth busied herself fixing Lucy on to the back of her bicycle for the ride home. 'That rascal of yours is getting too big for that.'

'I'm not a rascal, Uncle Conan. I've asked Dada for a bicycle for my next birthday and Ewan wants one as well.'

'Well your Dada will have to earn a lot of money then, young lady,' Conan teased. He looked at Beth. 'Tell Harry we could use an extra driver on Saturday afternoon if he's not working. We've done up the little bus we bought and we've got a few bookings already.'

'I'll tell him, but I hope it's a lot safer than it looked the last time I saw it. I expect Harry will be glad of a bit extra with this young miss and her wants.' She smiled fondly at Lucy.

Listening to this Bridie's mouth tightened.

'I suppose you're driving on Saturday too, then?' she said, looking at Nick.

'No, as a matter of fact I'm not.'

'Nick told me he had a more important job to do this Saturday afternoon,' Conan told her sharply and she could tell by his tone that her brother was not pleased. She sensed they had had a disagreement and she guessed it was over her.

During supper Rachel sensed the tension between Nick and Conan as well as between Nick and Bridie and her heart sank. Ross sensed it too and mentioned news of the brigadier's death, hoping to take their minds off their own problems.

'You never told me that,' Bridie said indignantly.

'I only heard this afternoon,' Rachel placated.

'Will it make a difference to the tenancy of Wester Rullion?' Conan asked.

'We don't know yet. I may telephone his solicitor tomorrow and enquire.'

'This may be your chance to buy the plot of land you were wanting, Nick,' Conan said and saw Nick flush angrily. 'Aah, I see you haven't discussed your plans with the lady in question yet!' Conan teased.

'No I have not, and why don't you mind your own business.'

'It is my business when my partner talks about wanting to build a house instead of putting the money back into the garage,' Conan countered. 'And it's my business when that same partner goes around all day with a face fit to turn the milk sour.'

'Conan!' Rachel remonstrated. 'For goodness sake have some tact.'

'Tact!' Bridie muttered. 'Big brother doesn't know the meaning of the word!'

'Well, there's one thing for sure, you'll never get me under any woman's thumb the way you seem to have got Nick. I hear you ran into Fiona Sinclair. Now there's another who always wants to be in control, just like you, my bossy little sister.'

'Hey, you two, that's enough!' Ross commanded sternly.

'Yes, it is,' Rachel agreed pushing her chair back. 'If you're all finished eating I'll see Ewan to bed before I wash up.'

'I'll wash up, Mother,' Bridie said.

'And I'll help,' Nick volunteered. 'There's peace we shall have to talk then. Not Conan's favourite place, the kitchen sink, I do know that.'

'You're right there,' Conan nodded. 'I'll go and sit by the fire with Father until you're ready to leave.'

As soon as they were alone Bridie turned to Nick, her eyes questioning.

'Duw! There's wanting you, I am. I can't go on like this!' he said. 'Know how much I love you, don't you, Bridie. But I can't move in here, not with all your family. Not just foolish pride, like you think. Just the two of us, I want, see. Told Conan, I did today – time we started taking money out of the business for ourselves. Need a bit of land, I do, to build a little house for us – one we could extend when we have our children. And when we can afford it,' he added half under his breath. 'A bank loan I'm wanting, and there's money I need, to repay it.'

'Lately I've had a feeling you are regretting going into partnership with Conan, Nick.'

'No, not really. Putting all of my capital into the garage just, I regret. The work, and the challenges, I do enjoy; but Conan, so ambitious he is! Not one bus – a fleet, he wants!' He lowered his voice. 'All I want is you . . .' He moved behind her and slid his arms around her waist. Bridie leaned back against him and he nuzzled her neck and his hand slid lower over her flat stomach.

'Nick . . .' she breathed, feeling the desire awakening as it always did when Nick caressed her in that certain way he had. 'You don't want soap suds around your neck, do you?'

'You know what I want, bach.' He sighed. 'Maybe Conan is right? Always he seems to know when it's time to make the next move. Maybe I should go to see the solicitor. Do you think your father will mind if I ask to buy a plot from Wester Rullion land next to the garage?'

'He only rents it anyway and a plot for a house wouldn't make much difference.' At that moment Bridie was shaking the suds from her hands and turning within the circle of Nick's arms, eager for his kisses. She did not consider the consequences of a house beside the garage, or that it would mean leaving her beloved Lochandee.

Suddenly they were both startled by a knocking at the back door.

'Who can that be at this time of night?' Bridie mused, going to open the door. 'Fiona! Come in, come in . . .' Her voice tailed away at the sight of Fiona's white strained face. 'Whatever's the matter?' she asked in concern.

'It . . . it's mother. I-I . . . She had collapsed when I got back home this afternoon, Bridie. I sent for the doctor immediately. He . . . he sent her to hospital. She . . . she died just over an hour ago . . .'

'Oh Fiona, I'm so, so sorry.' Bridie gathered her old friend in her arms and held her trembling body. Slowly Fiona pulled herself together.

'I went with her in the ambulance. She . . . she didn't regain consciousness, Bridie. I-I c-couldn't talk to her . . . couldn't ask her . . .' Silent tears began to roll down Fiona's face. 'I hope you don't mind me coming here. One of the nurses gave me a lift to the crossroads and I c-couldn't face going home yet.'

'Of course you couldn't. I'm glad you came to us.'

Fiona struggled to find her handkerchief and dry her eyes. It was then she saw Nick. He had just finished washing the last of the dishes and setting them to drain.

'I'm sorry,' Fiona gulped. 'I-I didn't realize you had company. I-I must go . . .'

'Of course you can't go home to that big empty house. This is Nick, by the way. I think he will understand how you're feeling because he's been through it himself.'

'Yes, Bridie's right.' Nick came forward, holding out his hand. 'I'm pleased to meet you, Fiona, but I'm sorry it has to be in these circumstances.' Fiona summoned a wavering smile. 'Shall I put the kettle back on for a cup of tea? I don't suppose you feel like eating but it would be better if you could.'

'Nick's right, Fiona, even if it is only tea and toast. Dad and Conan are in the room. I'll bring you a tray in front of the fire if you like?'

'Oh no!' Fiona dabbed ineffectually at her face. 'I can't imagine Conan having much time for weeping women, whatever the circumstances. D-do you mind . . . ?' Over her shoulder Bridie saw Nick raise his eyebrows in surprise.

'Come on, I'll show you the bathroom and you can wash your face while I make the toast. Then you can have it in here if that's all right?'

'Anywhere,' Fiona shivered, 'so long as it's not at home.'

'We'll make up the spare bed after you've eaten something,' Bridie suggested. 'I know Mum will want you to stay.'

'Yes, that's a good idea,' Nick agreed, pushing down his disappointment. He longed for a good long talk with Bridie. The more he thought about asking for a bank loan and building a house for them, the more optimistic he felt, but he knew there would be no opportunity to discuss it tonight. He had quite forgotten Bridie's love for Lochandee and it did not occur to him that the prospect of living anywhere else would appal her.

When Bridie returned to the kitchen alone he made the tea while she cut bread for toast.

'It sounds as though your friend knows Conan well? Don't they get on together?'

'Oh, we all travelled on the same bus to school. Fiona is younger than Conan but she could always hold her own with him in any debate. She was a real rising star at school and Conan had always been the one who was brilliant. She didn't hero worship him like the rest of the girls and I suspect my big brother may have been a little . . . well, you know!' Nick threw back his head and chuckled.

'Know, I do! His own ideas, Conan has. Trouble there is if anyone opposes them. But on Saturday we'll talk. Make our own plans, we will.' He grinned. 'Then he'll have to accept them. I'll call for you just after lunch. Go for a short drive somewhere . . .' He broke off as Fiona reappeared.

Three

The following morning Fiona looked pale and there were deep shadows beneath her eyes, but she had regained her composure, outwardly at least. Rachel, ever a keen observer, suspected she was deeply troubled beneath the calm facade but Fiona insisted she must go home. There were arrangements to make for her mother's funeral and other things needing her attention.

'I can't thank you and your family enough, Mrs Maxwell,' she said with real sincerity. 'Last night I felt I was alone in a dreadful nightmare. Perhaps it was coincidence that I ran into Bridie yesterday, b-but sometimes I wonder if these things are meant to happen? Does that sound silly?' She gave Rachel a wan smile.

'Indeed it is not silly, lassie. When you've seen as much life as I have you realize that some things are preordained, and one thing we all need is friendship. Remember you're welcome here any time.' Fiona nodded and gave a grateful smile but Rachel saw her mouth tremble and knew she was only hanging on to her self-control with a great effort. She wondered why Conan was convinced Fiona Sinclair was a girl who was always in control of every situation. Later she mentioned her concerns to Bridie.

'Fiona was certainly full of grief last night, shock too, I think. She said her mother had cancer but she hadn't expected her to die so soon. She is full of remorse because she has spent so little time with her in recent years. It must be awful to be an only child and so alone, especially now. I hope you didn't mind me asking her to stay over-night, Mum?'

'Not at all, dear. I'm pleased you thought of it. We all need friends at times like this. I was an only child too, remember, and I know what it's like to be alone in the world. I shall never forget the kindness of your Aunt Meg and Uncle Peter. Did you offer to accompany Fiona to make the funeral arrangements?'

'Yes, but she said she would be all right. She liked Nick and she said he was right about things not being quite so alarming in the daylight.'

'Of course she would like Nick, everyone does. Even your father, and I didn't believe he would consider any man good enough for his wee girl,' Rachel teased, giving Bridie a glimpse of her dimpling smile. 'How will you feel about living away from Lochandee, Bridie, if he does buy a plot of land to build a house near the garage?'

'I should hate it!' The words were out almost before Bridie knew she had uttered them and she looked at her mother, wide eyed and troubled.

'It may be a choice you'll have to make, dear,' Rachel warned with some anxiety. 'Nick and the home he provides for you, or Lochandee. I must say we should miss your help here if you have to leave but I wouldn't like to see either of you hurt. Nick is ready for marriage and he's getting impatient, I suspect.'

'Don't talk about it, Mum. I can't bear the thought of leaving Lochandee and my animals, and Bill and Sandy, they've worked at Lochandee for as long as I can remember. I couldn't bear not being here. It's my life! Auntie Alice trusted me to care for the Glens of Lochandee.'

'Have you told Nick that?'

'No. He would be hurt if I said I wouldn't go to live wherever he lives. I almost hope he doesn't get a plot of land. But then I don't know what we shall do. O-oh why does life have to be so complicated!'

'Dear Bridie, you don't know what troubles are yet. Nick is a fine man and he loves you. That's a very precious thing but don't expect him to wait forever.'

'Fiona said much the same thing!' Bridie frowned.

'Compromise is the only solution, dear. You think about it.'

Bridie remembered her mother's advice, and Fiona's, when Nick came to collect her on Saturday afternoon.

'I've got a reprieve from the milking,' she told him gaily. 'Beth said she might as well be working too, since Harry will be driving Conan's bus. So she's doing the milking with Sandy Kidd and Father.'

'A-ah, good it is then, bach. We'll make the most of it. Take you for a drive then, I will. Get away on our own for a bit, eh. Maybe we could go to the first house at the cinema afterwards?'

'That'll be lovely. I know it's a cold day but I brought a thermos and some sandwiches. Maybe we can have a picnic if we find a sheltered cove near the shore. Have you enough petrol?'

'Yes, been saving it up, I have. No time to go anywhere, see, with so much work. Making a profit, we are though.'

'Will it affect business at the garage if the government go ahead with their plans to nationalize road transport, as they've done with the railways?' Bridie asked anxiously.

'Have to wait and see, we will. But it's not work we'll think about today, eh?' He glanced at her and smiled. 'There's pretty you are in your coat, Bridie. New is it?'

'Mmn, and it's lovely and warm.'

'I hope it's me you're dressing up for.'

'Of course it is. Who else would it be?'

'Don't know, do I? Always afraid I am, i'case somebody else might come along and snatch you away,' Nick said seriously. Bridie put her gloved hand on his knee and gave it a little squeeze.

'No chance,' she grinned. Nick took his hand from the steering wheel and held hers where it was against his thigh.

'I couldn't bear it, Bridie. I can't wait much longer . . .'

'I know.'

'Went to see the brigadier's solicitor yesterday, I did . . .'

'Goodness, you haven't wasted any time, Nick!'

'Wasted enough already, we have. He doesn't see any reason why I shouldn't be able to buy three-quarters of an acre near the garage. Thinks the whole farm will be to sell soon, he does. The brigadier's daughter has no plans to return to Scotland, see. All her family are in Canada, settled there, they are.'

'He thinks she'll sell Wester Rullion!' Bridie sat up straight, the dreamy smile gone from her face. 'I'll bet Dad doesn't know that. He was supposed to be going to see the solicitor too and he never said anything – at least not to me.'

'Better not mention it then. He may not want to worry your mother.'

'No-o. You could be right. He'll be upset though. He's put so much time and effort into getting the farm back into production – we all have. We would have to cut back our dairy herd too.'

'Duw, Bridie! Wish I'd never told you, I do,' Nick said impatiently. 'Forget your precious cows for one afternoon, can't you? Prospect of getting our own home, there's thrilled you should be.'

'I-I am. But you know farming is my life,' Bridie said defensively. 'It's all I've ever done, all I know. Nick . . . times have changed since the war. Lots of women work now. I know this is not the right time to talk about it, but if we did build a house, would you mind if I kept on working at Lochandee?' She was relieved to see a slow wry smile spread over his lean face.

'Never expected anything else, did I, bach? Always knew Lochandee, and your beloved cattle, were my biggest rivals, didn't I? But surely you would not spend as much time with them as you do now though, and there's children we'll be having, I hope. They will not take second place with you?' The look in his eyes brought the colour rushing to Bridie's cheeks and Nick chuckled. 'There's looking forward, I am, to making babies with you, Bridie Maxwell.' He threw back his head this time in a great laugh of delight at the sight of her deepening blush. Then he remembered Bridie had never had any other boyfriend except himself. He had almost snatched her from the schoolroom. He sobered and his voice was tender. 'The luckiest man alive, I am, when I'm with you. You'll not forget it, bach?'

'Not so long as you keep telling me,' Bridie promised demurely. 'Where are we going?'

'Anywhere. There's good it is, just having you to myself for a day. Sandyhills, is it? A long walk along the sands, we'll have? If it's cold you are, I'll warm you, and we can eat our picnic in the car. Please you, does it, Bridie?'

'Sounds fine to me. I love your Welsh lilt, Nick. It is always more pronounced when you're happy or excited.'

'Speak my best English, I do, for your parents. But ba-ad, it is, when I'm angry,' he mocked in a throaty roar, 'so Conan tells me. Forgetting him and his old garage today, we are though. So – ' he grinned wickedly – 'there's a little kiss and cuddle I get for afters, is it . . .'

It was a sunny day for November but the clouds were scudding before a stiff breeze. The Galloway hills were purple curves against the blue-grey of the sky, while the green tufted arms of the cove stretched out into the Solway Firth. Nick and Bridie were well wrapped up as they strolled happily hand in hand with Nick stopping every now and then to skim a flat pebble along the creeping waves. Bridie knew she wanted to be married to Nick more than anything else in the world, but her heart ached at the thought of leaving Lochandee. Today she would not think about it.

'I am going to Mrs Sinclair's funeral on Monday,' she said. 'Fiona says it will be very quiet because they have so few relations. I don't suppose you would be able to come with me?'

'As a matter of fact I had thought about it. Like your friend Fiona, I do. What I saw of her anyway. Sorry, I was too. But Conan seems to feel he ought to attend the funeral so we can't both be away from the garage.'

'Conan?' Bridie stopped in surprise.

'Mmm. Surprised, I was too. Not much love lost between Fiona and Conan, I thought. But he says you have both known her a long time and he feels he ought to go with you.'

'Fiona is genuine and sincere, and she does feel things, whatever Conan says. She was engaged once but Gerry was killed during the war and she has concentrated on her career since then. Anyway that brother of mine is a fine one to talk! All he thinks about is being a successful garage proprietor.'

'Dedication is different for a man, he says. But I think it is a Maxwell family trait,' Nick said seriously, but he stopped and drew her into his arms, holding her close. 'I'm not criticising your family, my darling.' He looked more serious than Bridie had seen him being recently; more like the days when he had gone back to camp during the war. 'But sometimes I wonder whether I can live up to the standards you all set.'

'What standards?' Bridie frowned, leaning back to look into his face. 'I don't understand.'

'Your father now, he is absolutely dedicated to farming, and your mother has spent her life helping him build up the Glens of Lochandee, and now he's improving the land at Wester Rullion. If he owned it he'd be improving all those derelict buildings too, I shouldn't wonder. Whenever I am delivering to any of the farms, your parents are always regarded with respect. Everyone tells me how hard they have worked, how successful they are in spite of the shortage of labour. Conan is determined to prove he is just as big a success with the garage. Then, Bridie bach, there's you, devoted you are to your cows, ambitious to breed a champion. Or a famous bull, or both.'

'Oh Nick . . . do you think we're . . . we're . . . ?'

'You're wonderful is what I'm thinking!' He bent his head and kissed her, banishing her fears as their passion mounted, moulding her body to his on the wild deserted shore with only the wheeling gulls for company.

It was not until later that night, when she was alone in bed in the darkness, that Bridie remember the unspoken doubts which returned to shadow one of the happiest afternoons and evenings she could recall.

Rachel faced a dilemma of her own when Ross returned from seeing the brigadier's solicitor.

'When I think of all the time and work we've put into getting the land into good heart only to see it sold when our lease expires in eighteen months,' he said despondently. 'If the buildings were repaired it would be as good a farm as Lochandee.' He shook his head in disbelief. He knew the brigadier's daughter and her family were settled in Canada but it had never occurred to him that she would sever all links with the old country. 'We shall have to reduce our cattle numbers when we lose the tenancy, and we shall have a lot less land for grain and potatoes.'

Rachel understood Ross's disappointment and dismay. She knew he had hoped the tenancy would continue indefinitely. They had both hoped Ewan would farm the land one day and by then they might have been able to buy it. As always they found comfort in each other's arms. Later, lying wakeful in the darkness, Ross knew he still loved Rachel as much as he had when they were young. She could still make him feel attractive and virile. He was forty-six but he didn't feel old tonight, he felt restless and full of energy. He could hear the sound of Rachel's steady breathing and he knew she was asleep. He crept out of bed and down to the kitchen.

More than two hours later, his head still buzzing with figures and calculations, he crept back into bed. Rachel stirred but she did not waken and he resolved not to worry her until he had consulted Jacob Niven, the elderly solicitor who had advised and helped him when he bought the Glens of Lochandee in the face of every conceivable obstacle.

After Mrs Sinclair's funeral Bridie helped Fiona hand round the refreshments they had provided between them. One by one the few remaining mourners took their leave and Bridie helped Fiona clear the dining room. Only Conan remained in the large silent house, waiting to escort her home.

'I ought to be getting back to the garage,' he said. 'Are you nearly ready, Bridie?'

'I-I'd like to talk for a wee while, Bridie, if you're not in a rush?' Fiona looked up at Conan, her face pale but composed. He couldn't begin to guess the effort that control had cost her. 'I'll drive Bridie home if you want to go.'

It was clear she didn't care whether he stayed or not, Conan thought. Fiona was the only female, young or old, who could ruffle him so easily.

'You see,' she said, 'I-I've made up my mind to sell this house and buy a smaller one, and I need some advice about solicitors and things . . .'

'Then of course I'll stay.' It had been a morning funeral and it was only midday. Bridie wondered whether Conan really needed to rush away so soon. She felt irritated with him. 'For goodness sake, Conan, sit down a minute. You know as much about the local solicitors as I do. Father uses the Nivens from Lockerbie. Old Mr Niven is almost retired now but Father seems to get on all right with his son. Didn't he help you buy the land for the garage and get a licence to build your flat and the shed for repairs, Conan?'

'Yes. Yes, Niven's all right,' Conan said absently, his eyes moving around the large room. 'It's seems a lovely big house. Are you sure you should make such a decision so soon? I mean, aren't people supposed to wait . . . ?'

'Everyone says don't rush into things,' Fiona grimaced. 'I've given exactly that advice myself to clients. 'But . . .'

she shuddered. 'I hardly ever lived here. I've no childhood memories, only recent sad ones. It's far too big. Mother bought it thinking it was a good investment. I suppose it was really, but I just know I could never, never make it my home. So the sooner I can move out, the better I shall feel . . . I-I think.'

'Oh well, if it's what you want.' Conan's mouth tightened.

'If you're serious about buying a smaller house, Fiona, and if you really do mean to settle down here in the country, then there is a nice house for sale in the village of Lochandee. It's not far from Beth's,' Bridie said.

'I thought the cottage near Beth's was to rent,' Conan said.

'Oh, there is that one too. I'd forgotten about that. But if you want to buy a house, Fiona, the one that is to sell was built by the Mackenzies who live in the big house on the hill on the other side of the loch. It was built just before the war started for Mr Mackenzie's mother. She died a month ago. It has a bathroom and a lovely little kitchen, as well as two front rooms and two bedrooms. At the back the garden goes right down to the burn. It's lovely.'

'Oh, any house with a bathroom is heavenly to hear Bridie talk,' Conan teased. 'She's obsessed with bathrooms since father built one at the Glens of Lochandee.'

'Well, I notice you enjoy using it too, big brother, but you never clean the bath afterwards. Besides I was just reading the other day – only forty-six per cent of houses have bathrooms so it is a luxury you should appreciate. And Fiona's used to having one, aren't you, Fiona?'

'Yes. I don't think I would like to go back to filling and emptying the tin bath in front of the fire.'

'Oh, of course not.'

Bridie glared at her brother. Was he agreeing or was he mocking? He raised an eyebrow at her.

'You go if you want, Conan, and leave us to our talk,' she said irritably.

31

'All right, I'll do that.' He stood up, but he hesitated, looking down at Fiona and the smooth sweep of fair hair which so often hid her expression. 'If you need two strong men and a lorry to move your furniture you can rely on Nick and me . . .' he offered.

Fiona looked up startled. She stared at Conan.

'I do believe you mean that, and I would be truly grateful. I scarcely know where to begin. Mother has . . . had so much furniture. Some of it came from her grandparents and she never threw anything out. The drawers and cupboards are full of linen and china. I shall have to dispose of most of it, when I move to a smaller place.'

'Maybe the new owners would want to buy some of it?' Bridie suggested.

'Yes, it would be better not to get rid of anything until you sell the house. Besides, some of the things may be antiques,' Conan suggested. 'Nick and I used to have a friend . . . You remember Mark, don't you, Bridie? He was killed during the war.'

'Yes, but . . . ?'

'His father knows all about furniture. He restores antiques for lots of the gentry. Nick and I always get a card from Mark's parents at Christmas. I'm sure Mr Murray would give you his opinion on anything which may be valuable. He does travel up and down the country quite a bit. He told us a lot of family treasures were destroyed during the bombing and those who still have money are always on the look-out for replacements. He says some of the Americans have got a taste for English furniture too since they were over here during the war.'

'I didn't know that. What do you think, Fiona? Would you like Mr Murray to have a look?'

'Well not if he had to come specially. I doubt if there is anything of real value and there are some things I'd like to keep for sentimental reasons . . .'

'Shall I ask if he has any plans to come up to Penrith? I

know he has friends there,' Conan said. 'It wouldn't be all that much further and I'm sure Mother would put him up for a night, don't you think so, Bridie?'

'Of course she would be happy to help. It sounds worth asking anyway. What do you think, Fiona? Will you leave it to Conan to get in touch? That wouldn't stop you going ahead and seeing the solicitor and setting things in motion, if you're sure it's what you want?'

'Yes, all right, thank you, Conan.' Fiona looked at him with her wide grey eyes. 'I'd be grateful for your help, if you wouldn't mind.'

'No problem.' Conan nodded. 'I'll write tonight.' He wondered why he always felt so defensive in Fiona Sinclair's company. Even now, when she was supposed to be vulnerable and full of grief, she was cool and in control, her manners as impeccable as ever. Why should that irritate him?

Four

Another week had passed before Fiona was able to arrange an appointment with Jordon Niven. He was younger than she had expected to be in business on his own, but then she recalled his father had built up the firm and he was merely taking over. She wondered how he would have done on his own merits. The thought made her wary and on her guard.

'Is there something in the air down at Lochandee?' he asked. 'You're the third client I've had in a fortnight. But I understand you want to sell as well as to buy?'

'Yes, that's correct. The Maxwells from the Glens of Lochandee recommended you to act for me.'

'I see . . . At this rate Mr Maxwell will be asking me for commission. Now if you could give me some details first, Miss Sinclair?'

'I have a full description written out ready for you.' Fiona took an envelope from her leather bag and handed it to him. He raised his eyebrows in surprise at the neatly typed sheet of paper and the detailed descriptions and sizes.

'How very efficient. Are you sure you need a lawyer?'

'Yes, I'm an accountant not a legal expert.'

'You're an accountant!' He eyed her with sharp interest. 'Where are you working now, if you don't mind my asking?'

'I'm not. I resigned from my post because I wanted to be with my mother . . .' She bit her lip, striving for the composure she valued above all else, especially in male

34

company. 'She did not live as long as the doctors had expected so . . .'

'So now you regret your decision?'

'Not at all. I shall not return to the city – at least not for some time. I was a company accountant latterly.' She told him the name of her firm. This time his eyebrows almost disappeared into his thatch of black hair. He asked her some pertinent questions about her work and she knew he was well acquainted with the type of businesses she had dealt with.

'I have a couple of friends who are accountants. One of them is in Glasgow. We were at university together. I did think of studying accountancy myself but Father persuaded me to become a lawyer so that I could take over the family firm. I've no regrets really, though sometimes I could do with an accountant to deal with death duties and some of the estate matters. Now that the government have introduced Pay As You Earn taxes for employees I foresee it being only a thin edge of the wedge. I reckon most businesses will need an accountant to advise them before many more years have passed.'

'Yes, I am considering setting up a small accountancy business once I have bought another house and settled in.'

'Surely you will find life very tame down here? I mean after the cut and thrust of the city financiers?'

'If you mean more peaceful, then that is something I would welcome right now. If I change my mind later I may go back to the city – perhaps to Edinburgh.'

'I see . . .' Jordon Niven looked at her thoughtfully, his fingers pressed together in a peak, elbows resting on his desk. 'I wonder . . .' Then he shook his head, reminding himself that his father still had a final say in matters affecting the firm. 'Anyway, I think it will be a fairly simple matter to procure the house you have in mind,' he said more briskly. 'I will contact the solicitor concerned and obtain more details regarding the price and so forth.'

'Oh, I know what price they are asking. I have just sold

my flat so I could afford to buy it right away if necessary. I thought you might try offering a little less first? I believe their price seems reasonable though and I wouldn't like to miss it. I have friends in the village of Lochandee.'

'Very well, I will follow your instructions. Now regarding the sale of your own property. I may have a client who would be interested, a family looking for a large house in the country. They would prefer some ground with it though. I will make enquiries. Can I contact you if they wish to look quite soon? I know they would like to get fixed up. They will not quibble unduly over the price provided the property is what they are looking for.'

A little while later Fiona left the solicitor's offices feeling more satisfied and settled in her mind than she had for some time. If only she could rid herself of the feeling of guilt.

Nick had also been busy with appointments. The manager of his bank had agreed to arrange a loan, just enough to buy a plot of land and build a modest house. Privately he was impressed by Nick's caution and his plans to extend only when he could afford it, but he had insisted he must take out an insurance to cover the loan, especially as he was self-employed and his own capital was tied up in the business. Nick agreed to return when his solicitor had negotiated the purchase of enough land to build on, and when he had completed his enquiries regarding planning permission and a licence to obtain building materials.

Ross had not fared so well with his own negotiations. His need was for a much larger loan if he was to have any chance of buying Wester Rullion. One of the stumbling blocks was the small mansion house and the grounds in which Brigadier Jamieson had lived and which had been empty since he emigrated to Canada. The house was far too large for an ordinary family but the brigadier's solicitor was intent on protecting his client's interests, and his own. He knew there would be little demand for such a large house on its own, so he insisted that the farm and house must be sold together.

'The mansion house is just a white elephant to people such as us,' Ross repeated while Rachel went on ironing at the kitchen table and doing her best to console him.

'Perhaps it's for the best, Ross. It looks as though Nick is going ahead with buying a plot of land to build a house for Bridie. Even if she comes back to Lochandee to work she will not be here all the time, and if they get a family . . . We shall miss her help badly.'

'Maybe you're right,' Ross sighed. 'Anyway I shall have to see Mr Niven again and tell him we are unable to offer. I'll wait until after Christmas now though.'

'Yes, you do that, dear. Speaking of Christmas, do you think Ewan will be very disappointed when he gets a piano accordion instead of a bicycle? He really had set his heart on a bike and Lucy is getting one.'

'Well, he will just have to wait. Harry said it wouldn't be ready until his birthday if we wanted a second-hand boy's bike. That's only four weeks away.'

'Yes, I suppose so,' Rachel sighed. 'Things seem to be scarcer than ever since the war ended.'

'Everything is being exported to get the balance of payments down. War is a costly business.'

'Mmm, I suppose this is what they mean when they say "Britain can make anything, but Britains can't buy anything". Don't you think?'

'Possibly, but Ewan likes to have his own way. It will not do him any harm to see Lucy can have some things first. He's getting a bit bossy with her but she's beginning to stand up to him. I do believe she has as much fire in her as he has.'

'I know. I heard Conan telling her not to give in to him. Of course he adores both of the children really.'

Ewan was bitterly disappointed when he didn't get a bike for Christmas and he barely looked at the small piano accordion which Ross had managed to buy second-hand from a man he had met while playing the fiddle at one of the village dances. He was frequently in demand for his own musical skills and he hoped Ewan would enjoy learning to play an instrument. So far Bridie was the only one who had inherited any of his own musical talents, but they had been unable to afford an instrument and music lessons when she was younger. As it was she was often in demand to sing at the local concerts and she seemed content. Sometimes Nick and Bridie accompanied him to the dances and performed a duet.

Ross liked Nick and he was happy to welcome him as a son-in-law, but he did not relish the day when Bridie would leave Lochandee. She knew every one of the cows and calves by name and their breeding, better than he did himself these days. It was her life. Ross sighed. It didn't matter how much a man tried to plan, things didn't always go the way he wanted.

It was the end of the second week in January when Fiona telephoned to ask if Bridie could meet her that evening.

'I have three bits of news to tell you,' she said mysteriously.

'Good news, I hope?' Bridie prompted.

'One very good, one disappointing, and one I'm not sure about.'

'Och, you're a tease, Fiona,' Bridie laughed. 'I'll see you as soon as the milking is over this evening.'

It transpired that Fiona had been successful in buying the house which Bridie herself had recommended and she was delighted at the prospect of moving into Lochandee village as soon as possible.

'The disappointment is that the people who came to see this house think it's too small, and not enough ground.'

'Too small! Whatever do they want? A mansion, for goodness sake!'

'I don't know,' Fiona shrugged, 'but Mr Niven is going to

advertise it now – which brings me to my other bit of news. He has offered me work for two days a week. It'll be nothing like I was doing, and nothing like the money, but I'm thinking of accepting. He says he has various clients who ask for advice or help with their accounts and there is the death duties side of things. It would make a change for me and he says if I build it up to more clients it will be up to me whether or not I take them on. Do you know him, Bridie?'

'No, but Father does, and he has great respect for both young Mr Niven and his father. He has an appointment with them this week but I'm afraid they will not get any business this time. Wester Rullion land, plus the big house and the parkland, are too big an undertaking for us and the brigadier's solicitor refuses to sell them separately in case he gets left with the house. Besides . . . I don't know how Father would manage everything at both farms when I move away from the Glens of Lochandee.'

'Has Nick bought the land then?'

'Not yet but he can get a bank loan for it. Mr Niven advised him to wait until he knew he could get permission to build and a licence for materials. He didn't think there would be a problem but he's looking into it.'

'You don't sound exactly over the moon about it all,' Fiona said shrewdly.

'I long to be with Nick, it's just . . . I hate the thought of living away from the farm and the animals. I shall go back every day to begin with but . . .' she blushed rosily.

'But Nick wants a family?'

'We both do.'

'Of course. I'm sure you will be wonderful parents, Bridie. I saw Conan visiting Harry and Beth the other day. I was surprised to see how patient he is with Ewan and Lucy. He was teaching Lucy to ride her bicycle in the village.'

'Conan has been friendly with Harry and Beth for as long as I can remember. He first got his interest in machines from Beth's grandfather. He used to have a cycle shop. Harry and

Beth took it over but when Harry was called up he asked Conan to clear it out and wind up the business for him.'

'I see. Maybe there is more to Conan than I had realized from our school days. I think I shall enjoy living in Lochandee. Beth introduced me to Carol and her two daughters and Harry says I've to let him know if there are any little jobs I need doing. They're all so friendly.'

'When do you plan to move?'

'As soon as Nick and Conan can arrange it for me. I shall leave a lot of the furniture here until the house is sold, of course.'

'That reminds me. Conan had a letter from Mr Murray – you remember his friend's father, the one who knows about old furniture and such things.'

'Oh yes! I didn't think Conan would remember.'

'He's usually quite good at keeping his word. Anyway, Mr Murray will be visiting his friends in Penrith at the beginning of February so he is coming to stay at the Glens of Lochandee for a night. Conan will tell you the exact date when he hears properly.'

'It's very good of him.' Fiona cast an uncertain glance round the large sitting room. 'I can't see there being much of interest though. I hope he'll not think we're wasting his time.'

'Conan had the impression he was pleased to be remembered. He lost both of his own sons during the war. They were twins and both in the air force. It must have been terrible.'

'It's tragic. Has he any other family?'

'Only his wife, and Conan thinks she's never really recovered from the death of her boys. He reckons her stepsister makes her worse. He said she ranted on and on even when he was staying there with Mark and his parents. Both he and Mark were glad to get away in the end. Conan thought she was a bit . . . well a bit screwy. He said she made him feel really uncomfortable. And guilty.'

'Guilty?'

'Well . . . she raved on about them bombing innocent women and children in Germany. He said she really got under Mark's skin, and upset him. They were already aware of the cruelty of war, but what were they to do? Sit back and let the Germans bomb British women and children instead? War is such a terrible thing. But I don't need to tell you that . . .'

Ewan was delighted to get the longed for bicycle on his birthday at the end of January. He even agreed, albeit reluctantly, to go for music lessons.

'You're lucky. I wish I could go,' Lucy told him.

'I'll teach you. I'll tell you what the man teaches me,' Ewan declared gravely, unaware of his parents' amused smiles. The two did almost everything together, but music lessons were beyond Harry and Beth's budget for their young daughter. Her education was Harry's priority. He dreamed of Lucy becoming a teacher.

Fiona had been working for Jordon Niven for three weeks when he mentioned her friendship with the Maxwells of Lochandee.

'I'm afraid your friends the Maxwells will be disappointed. I've tried every argument to persuade the late brigadier's solicitor to sell the Wester Rullion farm without the Mansion House and parkland.'

'Is that what's preventing Mr Maxwell from buying the farm?' Fiona asked. 'Because it can only be sold as one lot?'

'Yes, it puts the asking price well out of his reach. Anyway he has no use for the big house or the parkland. If he had that kind of money to spare it would be a better investment to build a new house and farm buildings in the middle of the Wester Rullion land.'

'Yes . . . I see . . . Look, I know this is none of my business but the Maxwells are good friends and I'd like to help if I can. The family you sent to look at my mother's house . . . are they fixed up yet?'

'No, not a hope! There's nothing on my books that would suit them.'

'Well, if the sale of my mother's house goes through to Mr and Mrs Woods – as you seem to be expecting . . . ?'

'Oh I am. We're almost ready to sign if you can give an entry date. They have three teenage sons and a married daughter with twins. They think it's ideal.'

'Good. When I get the money for it I could loan Mr Maxwell the extra he needs to clinch the deal for Wester Rullion, including the big house but . . .' She held up her hand to silence Jordon Niven's objections. 'Please let me finish. I'm not silly about these matters. It would have to be a legal arrangement, and only if – a very big if – you can sell the Mansion House for Mr Maxwell to the clients you sent to me.' Jordon Niven stared at her while the words registered, his eyes widening as understanding dawned.

'Jesu, woman! You're a genius! I never thought of that. I wonder . . . Do you think they would be interested?'

'I don't know. I've never seen the Mansion House, but your clients wanted more rooms and more ground than I had. We would need to be pretty sure they would buy before we encouraged Mr Maxwell to buy the whole lot. I'd hate him to be left with a white elephant and a debt he can't afford.'

'Mmm . . . Your training in big business has given you a different outlook on things. Not many farmers would have thought of taking out a loan to buy the Glens of Lochandee when Mr Maxwell did it. He's done well, but any business we discuss in this office is confidential, remember.'

'Of course. You do not need to tell me that, Mr Niven,' Fiona said stiffly.

'No, no, I can see you're a professional. I think I will ask Mr Maxwell to procure the keys to the Mansion House. We'll arrange to take a look and show my clients as well. I don't want the brigadier's solicitor to get wind of our plans though or he would probably do the deal himself and still charge the Maxwells more than necessary. There's always been a bit of rivalry between our two firms so I wouldn't mind getting one up.' He grinned disarmingly and winked at Fiona.

'Never trust a lawyer, eh!' she smiled wryly.

'You know, Fiona Sinclair, you're a very attractive young woman when you smile so beguilingly. I was a little bit afraid of the serious Miss Sinclair who first came to my office a few weeks ago . . .'

'Afraid! A-ha, you can tell that to the marines!'

Later that evening when Fiona had time to mull over their discussion, she was filled with anxiety. Suppose Bridie's family were let down at the last minute if the sale of the Mansion House fell through? It would be all her fault. She was so worried she telephoned Bridie and arranged to meet the following evening.

'Don't worry,' Bridie told her. 'Father is old enough to weigh up the risks and he would never think you were interfering if you help him get what he wants. Why don't you come to supper tomorrow evening and you can explain your idea to him, but don't mention that the temporary loan would be coming from you. Just tell him Mr Niven can arrange it. My father and Nick are so proud and independent they need their heads banged together.'

But Rachel could see how eager Ross was to go ahead with the purchase of Wester Rullion and it worried her.

'Don't hold me back, Rachel,' he pleaded. 'We've always done things together and we may never get another chance to buy a farm for Ewan. We shall certainly never get the opportunity to buy as sitting tenants again.'

'That's true.'

'We managed to pay off the loan for the Glens of Lochandee and there were no guaranteed prices, or markets then.'

'But we were younger. We worked so hard.'

'I'm only forty-six! I don't feel old. Besides Ewan is keen to farm and it will not be long before he's ready to work. Anyway I don't think it's the brigadier's daughter who is pushing us to the limit, I reckon it's her solicitor. The better the price the more he gets himself.'

'It's not just the money and another bank loan which worries me. How will you manage to run both farms without Bridie?'

'Oh, I'm sure she'll come back as often as she can.'

'In the beginning maybe, but not if they get children, Ross. It wouldn't be possible, or fair to Nick.'

'No-o.' Ross frowned. 'Do you think she will be happy, even with Nick? She's never been away from her cows and calves, the farm . . . '

'I don't know. I think it has to be her own decision though. Much as I love the farm and our animals, I'd have gone to the end of the world for you when we were young.' She dimpled up at him and Ross hugged her close.

'Only when we were young?' he chuckled. 'Not any more?'

'Go on with you!' Rachel laughed. 'You're just fishing.'

Jordon Niven had got his teeth into the deals over Wester Rullion and the Mansion House. He felt a need to prove himself both to Miss Fiona Sinclair and to the rival firm of solicitors. He was ninety per cent certain now that he could sell the mansion and parkland to his clients. That in itself would be a good bit of business. If he could knock a few hundred off the land for Maxwell while they were doing the deal, that would please him even more.

Even so he was astonished when the other solicitor readily accepted his offer for the whole property. Almost before the deeds were drawn up and signed he began negotiating the sale of the mansion house. He dare not take any chances with this sale falling through.

Five

R achel tried to be happy for Ross over the purchase of Wester Rullion, but in her heart she was filled with anxiety. The debts and risks seemed far greater now than when they had staked everything they had to buy, and to keep, the Glens of Lochandee. There was so much more to lose now, and a grown family to consider. She sensed Bridie was not happy with the changes taking place in her own life either, and Rachel longed for all those she loved to be happy and content.

'It's not just moving away to live beside the garage,' Bridie confided when her mother brought up the subject. 'I'm proud of Father and all the improvements he makes, but now that he's the owner of Wester Rullion he'll never stop until he gets everything the way he thinks it should be. The buildings must have been neglected for years before he even heard of the farm but he thinks they should be improved instantly now they belong to him. All his time and money will be spent at Wester Rullion now.'

'But that's what has earned him so much respect from neighbouring farmers, dear,' Rachel defended, while secretly admitting Bridie was right.

'I know, and I'm proud of him too, Mum, but have you considered who will see to the dairy herd when I move to the garage with Nick? Sandy Kidd and Bill Carr are both good men but they're general workers and they're getting older. So is Father.' Suddenly she couldn't repress a shudder. She couldn't imagine life without her beloved father.

'We all miss Alfie too,' Rachel sighed. 'He may have had half the wits of a normal man but he possessed twice the strength and he was so willing.'

'Poor Alfie, he was so loyal to the Glens of Lochandee, and all of us who belonged here. There's one consolation though, he would have hated to die anywhere else. Aunt Alice said he was born at the Glens of Lochandee and she hoped he would stay here until he died, and he did.'

'Yes, and I believe he was happy in his own way,' Rachel agreed, nodding.

'Do you think Father will try to hire another man now that he has two farms to run?'

'I don't know,' Rachel said doubtfully. 'He did buy a second tractor to help with the work.'

'Machines are splendid for some things but they can't attend to the animals,' Bridie responded crisply, indicating her own tension and anxiety far more clearly than any arguments.

Nick was growing more and more impatient and he often misinterpreted Bridie's silence when he tried to discuss their future.

'Changed your mind about marrying me, have you Bridie? Now it is I would like to know, not when I've bought the plot of land. Any day now I shall be hearing if I am allowed to build there.'

'You know I want to marry you, Nick . . .'

'I know do I? But . . . ?' His voice was cool. 'Your doubts and reservations I'm hearing in your voice, Bridie.' He watched her chewing worriedly at her lower lip and he longed to seize her and kiss away all her doubts and fears.

Bridie couldn't bring herself to tell him she hated the thought of leaving Lochandee and her beloved animals but Nick had already guessed and it angered him. He wanted to be the centre of her universe. He wanted them to work together as her parents had done.

Recently he and Conan had installed a petrol pump and sales were good. They often needed an extra pair of hands to attend to customers when he and Conan were busy or called out to a breakdown. Then there were accounts to send out and bills to pay and neither of them liked the paperwork. Conan did not like the repairs to farm machinery either but he had to admit they were making a useful contribution to their profit and Nick refused to turn away trade. They had bought a reconditioned army lorry and he made deliveries of feed, lime, fencing posts, logs and anything else which came their way. He enjoyed exploring the local countryside and getting to know the farms.

Conan still hankered after buses and he or Harry Mason now spent most weekends ferrying small parties of people to the shore in the summer, or to dances, concerts and occasionally to the theatre or pantomime in the winter.

Even Jordon Niven was surprised at how quickly and smoothly the dealings over Wester Rullion had gone through. The re-sale of Mansion House followed on without a hitch and both he and Fiona breathed a sigh of relief when only the delivery of the deeds remained.

Ross Maxwell had trusted them to make the best deal possible on his behalf, but he was surprised and delighted with the final settlement. He found himself seven hundred and fifty pounds better off than he had expected, and the new owners of Rullion Mansion seemed highly satisfied with their acquisition. They had even asked his advice on the management of the parkland for their ponies.

It was the beginning of March when Mr Matthew Murray arrived to advise Fiona on the disposal of her parents' furniture. Conan had arranged for him to stay the night at the Glens of Lochandee and Rachel liked him at once. He was slightly built and his face was kind and sensitive.

'I think he is a very genuine person,' she whispered to

Ross as they lay side by side in the darkness. 'I feel so sorry for him losing both of his sons during the war. He says his wife scarcely leaves the house now, but he feels her sister encourages her to stay in instead of getting out and meeting people.'

'Aye,' Ross agreed softly, drawing her closer, 'we've a lot to be thankful for. Is Bridie taking Mr Murray down to Fiona's tomorrow?'

'Yes, but I've asked him if he would like to stay an extra night now that he is here. He has agreed, so either Conan or Nick will show him around the district after he has finished at Fiona's, then they are all coming back here for supper. He thanked me so nicely for making Mark welcome when he used to come on leave with Conan and Nick.'

Later the following evening as they all sat around the large dining table, Matthew Murray told them it had been an enjoyable and worthwhile visit. He beamed at Fiona.

'You hang on to some of those smaller pieces, young lady, especially the jade and your father's chess set. By the time you're as old as I am, I guarantee they'll be worth four times as much as they are now. I agree it would be easier if you can dispose of some of the large items locally, but I will send you a reliable dealer to see the rest. I promise you he'll offer a fair price. Mind you – ' he turned to smile at Rachel – 'it's a long time since I saw anything as rare, or as valuable, as the vase you have sitting on your mantelshelf there.' He nodded towards the high dining-room fireplace. I was having a good look at it while you were bringing in the meal.'

'My old vase?' Rachel blinked in surprise.

'Old vase – well yes, it's that all right. I trust you have it insured?'

'Insured?' Rachel laughed. 'Of course not. It was a gift from an old lady of ninety I knew when I – when I was a girl . . .' She looked to Ross at the other end of the table. Those far off days seemed like another lifetime. 'It . . . it was her greatest treasure.'

'Yes, I can believe that. How did it come into her possession?'

'The vase had been a wedding gift to her grandmother, I think, from the laird – her employer. She loved the unusual shape and the blue blossom. She knew I liked it too.'

'Yes, it is unusual and I believe the initials S above the J and F are those of the potter. If I'm right it would be made about 1750 . . .'

'As old as that!' Rachel gasped incredulously.

'If I'm right,' Mr Murray repeated cautiously. 'During the war part of the Liverpool city museum was bombed and amongst the treasures which were destroyed was a mug with the name Thomas Fazakerley on it. The bright colours used on the mug often appear on Liverpool delft, but there are only photographs now to remind us of what became known as the "Fazackerley palette" you see.'

'I-I had no idea . . .'

'It is fortunate then that the vase is still in such excellent condition. If ever you want to sell it I suggest you take it, in person, to one of the London auction houses. There is great interest in work attributable to specific potters. Even though money is not so plentiful since the war, there are at the moment two wealthy collectors who will go to enormous lengths to secure a desirable piece such as yours. At a guess I'd say you would get at least a thousand pounds for it, maybe even twice that if there are two collectors bidding against each other.'

'What?' Rachel's eyes and mouth were round with shock. 'I-I don't believe it . . .' Her face had gone quite pale and the young folk were all staring from her to Mr Murray.

'A lot of "ifs", of course.' He smiled ruefully and broke the tension. They all began to talk at once but Rachel's mind was travelling back through the years. Minnie Ferguson had taken her under her wing when she was eight years old, after the death of her mother. She had passed on many of her skills until Rachel's father had died when she was almost

sixteen. It was then she had gone to live with the Maxwells. She shuddered, recalling Gertrude Maxwell's bitter
resentment at being forced to take her in. She remembered
the day she had received the black-edged letter informing
her of Minnie's death, and the news that she had left her
the vase.

'Much good an old thing like that will do you!' Mistress
Maxwell had sneered. 'A few sovereigns would have been
more use.' Rachel raised her eyes and met Ross's down the
length of the dining table. She knew he was recalling the
bitter woman who had resented both of them and done her
best to keep them apart. She came out of her reverie to hear
Fiona speaking.

'It is time I was going home,' she said, feeling the
family might want to discuss the discovery of the vase
without her.

'I'll give you a lift home, Fiona,' Nick offered. Conan
frowned at him.

'I'll take her. It's time I was going anyway, and I expect
you and Bridie have plenty to talk about – as usual.' He
pushed back his chair and as he passed Bridie he gave her
a brotherly thump. 'For goodness sake send him home a bit
more cheerful tonight. If that's what being in love does to a
man I thank God I'm immune.'

'Don't you be so sure you are,' Ross warned. 'And give
Nick and Bridie time to work out their own problems.
Everybody gets them sometime or other.

'They do indeed,' Mr Murray agreed with a sigh. 'But the
love of a good woman is one of the greatest gifts a man
can have.'

'Aye,' Ross winked at Rachel, 'I'll agree to that any time.'
Conan looked from his father to his mother, saw her pink
cheeks and snorted. Surely his parents were too old to be
flirting, and in public too.

'If you're ready, Fiona?' His voice was more abrupt than
he realized.

'I'm sure Bridie will take me home if it's a trouble to you,' she said stiffly.

'It's not a trouble or I wouldn't have offered. You said you were ready to leave, and so am I.'

'Very well.'

'He hasn't changed since he was the bossy head boy on the school bus, has he?' Bridie grinned.

'No, not that I've noticed anyway.' Fiona stood up with a wry grimace for Bridie.

'Are you sure you want a lift, Miss Sinclair?'

'I shall be with you just as soon as I have thanked your parents and Mr Murray,' Fiona told him calmly. 'I'm sure even you wouldn't wish me to forget my good manners, Conan?'

'Of course not,' he muttered, aware of the amused glance which had passed between his parents, not to mention Nick's knowing grin. Even young Ewan, who had been half asleep, was regarding him curiously with his head on one side. He scowled and bid them all a general good night. But as he passed Mr Murray he stopped and shook the older man's hand, thanked him for coming and wished him a safe journey home. There was genuine respect and sympathy in his gaze as their eyes met. There was no need for words. They were both remembering Mark, full of regrets that he was not with them tonight.

When he had left the room Mr Murray turned to Rachel.

'Your son is a fine young man. You will be proud of his success one day, because that is what he means to be – a success in his own chosen field. Right now he seems to have a need to prove himself . . .'

'Like father like son,' Rachel agreed.

'Yes, maybe it is inherited, the yearning to do well. I know Mark had a great respect for Conan, as did the rest of the crew. They knew they could depend on him . . .'

Nick sat up straight, suddenly alert. Did Mr Murray think Conan was in some way responsible for Mark's death? They might have their differences over the garage business but Nick knew he would defend Conan to the last over anything to do with their time together in the RAF.

But Mr Murray sighed and went on again: 'I knew after Bobby was killed that Mark cared less for his own life. They were identical twins you know. They did everything together . . .'

'Yes,' Rachel said gently. She laid a comforting hand on his arm. 'It would have been dreadful to lose one son, but to lose them both . . .' She trembled at the thought. Mr Murray patted her hand.

'We were not alone. War is a cruel thing and there were whole families wiped out. We must be thankful that we are alive and can live in a free country.'

Quietly Bridie pushed back her chair and gently took Ewan's arm. He was almost asleep.

'I'll see him to bed,' she nodded at her mother.

'And I'll read him a bedtime story,' Nick volunteered, seizing the opportunity to spend a little of the evening alone with Bridie while their elders talked of times past.

Ewan no longer needed bedtime stories. He could read his own, but he was asleep almost before he tumbled into bed. Nick seized Bridie around her waist and drew her close as soon as they were alone together in the warm kitchen.

'I can't wait for us to be married, Bridie,' he whispered into the soft hollow of her throat. 'Soft as silk your skin is . . .' He felt her trembling response. He knew she loved him almost as much as he loved her, but he was still afraid he might lose her. 'Expect to get permission to build our house, I do, in a couple of weeks. Your father's land it is now. I shall have to buy the ground from him.' He felt Bridie stiffen slightly in his arms. 'All this – ' he waved a hand towards the window and the farmyard beyond – 'means so much to you, I know, bach. But us, together, alone . . . There's all I want, see.' His voice was tense, his dark eyes penetrating. 'Not to share you with your family, not all the time. Can you understand that?'

'Yes, oh yes, I do understand,' Bridie whispered as his mouth claimed hers. Nick's Welsh accent was always more pronounced when his emotions were involved. She could feel the passion in him, his desire as he moulded her body to his own. She leaned away from him, still in the circle of his arms.

'We will set the date for our wedding, I promise, just as soon as you get all the approvals through, Nick . . .'

'A date! You agree? Really mean it, do you Bridie? My love . . .' His kisses were gentler now. He knew the sacrifice she was making, giving up her home and the farm to live in a little house beside the garage. 'Some day, somehow . . . I'll make it up to you, my darling girl.'

Rachel did not sleep well that night. She was restless and her thoughts were on Mr Murray, the vase, and on Minnie Ferguson who had left it to her as a last treasured gift. She did not need the vase, or anything else to remind her of the old lady who had treated her with all the love and kindness of an adopted granddaughter. Minnie had taught her the skills of the house and the dairy until she was as competent at sixteen as any woman. Inevitably her thoughts turned to Gertrude Maxwell, the woman who had treated both herself and Ross with such malice. She shuddered in the darkness, but eventually she drifted into sleep.

She was still tired when it was time to rise but her mind was clearer and as she washed and dressed in the bathroom she reached a decision, but she would tell no one except Mr Murray.

Six

It was Bridie who drove Mr Murray to the station to catch the train south the following morning. When she returned she told her mother she and Nick had decided to set a date for their wedding.

'Nick is just waiting for all the agreements before he instructs Mr Niven to buy the plot of land. He will have to negotiate with Father now he is the owner, I suppose? Unless the solicitor withheld the plot? Nick was supposed to have an option on it, I think.'

'I don't know,' Rachel said absently.

'Are you all right, Mum? You look very pale, tired too . . .' Bridie frowned.

'I'm fine. I slept badly last night. I-I think I might go into town this afternoon if you will be around for Ewan getting home from school?'

'Yes, of course. It would do you good to have a look around the shops. There's a few of the new fashions coming in with the swirling skirts. They'll be lovely for dancing.'

'I think my days for swirling skirts and dancing are past,' Rachel said, summoning a smile at Bridie's enthusiasm. 'We shall have to think about a wedding gown though, and bridesmaids, but we'll wait for all that until you have fixed the date. I expect it will take at least six months to build a house.'

'Nick was hoping they would do it in three months. We are just having a small house to begin with. We thought a September wedding, after the harvest is in.'

'I see . . .' Rachel's anxiety returned, but she turned away and for once Bridie was preoccupied with her own thoughts.

Bridie seemed to alternate between excitement and desire, and a dreadful coldness in the pit of her stomach at the prospect of leaving the Glens of Lochandee. Apart from her own love of the farm where she had been born, she had an uneasy feeling that she was letting down Alice Beattie, the woman who had been her benefactor and entrusted her with the care of her beloved land and animals.

Rachel had not told anyone she was going to see Mr Niven, the solicitor, but she had forgotten Fiona was working there two or three days every week now. They greeted each other in surprise.

After Rachel and Jordon Niven had talked for a little while and Rachel had laid her tentative plans before the young solicitor, she sighed.

'There are so many "ifs" and time is short. I suppose you think I'm silly to try to interfere?'

'Not at all, Mrs Maxwell. Your motives are beyond reproach – the health of your husband and the happiness of your daughter. But as you say, much depends on the successful sale of the vase. I presume this Mr Murray is entirely trustworthy if it does turn out to be as valuable as he suspects?'

'Oh, I'm sure he is.'

'Then I shall do my best to co-operate if you let me have your instructions.'

'Would you mind if I had a word with Miss Sinclair before I leave? You see I don't want my family to know about this visit until I'm sure the vase can raise enough money to carry out my plan, and I had forgotten Fiona would be here.'

'That's all right. I'll ask her to come through. You will find her most discreet – in fact I believe she may prove a great asset to our business. She sees problems – and their possible solutions – very clearly, and she is an extremely intelligent young woman. Any time you wish to convey a message to me you may entrust it to Miss Sinclair if that is easier than coming into town.'

'Thank you, I'll remember that.' Rachel smiled with relief. It was all so much easier than she had thought. If only . . .

Rachel was on the road for home but her mind was on Fiona Sinclair's parting remark. She was not only an accountant, she had a fine understanding of human nature. If she was right in her opinion of Nick, and in her heart Rachel knew she was, then her comment was worth some thought. She decided to make a detour by the garage, though she knew it was unlikely she would find Nick alone there, or that he would have time to talk with her. The more she pondered, the more she felt Fiona was right. It was imperative to have Nick's opinion, and to have him on her side.

Nick was lying full length beneath a small truck when Rachel drew the car to a halt. She knew by the disappointment on his face that he had expected it would be Bridie when he recognized the Lochandee car, but he hid it quickly and smiled a welcome.

'I'm sorry, Mrs Maxwell, you have just missed Conan. He was called out to a breakdown so I don't think he'll be back for at least an hour.'

'That's all right, Nick. As a matter of fact it was you I wanted, but I can see you're busy.'

'Nothing I can't put off for half an hour. The owner of the truck doesn't need it until Saturday. I . . . er . . . I'd invite you into the flat . . .' He flushed. 'A bit of a mess it is . . .'

Rachel laughed aloud, a young, pretty laugh Nick thought, and his arms ached for Bridie. She was like her mother in many ways.

'I can imagine the state of it with two young bachelors. This will do very well and you can keep an eye on the petrol pumps at the same time.'

Nick nodded and swept aside a pile of papers and dusters to make a seat for her. Rachel regarded him seriously.

'I want to talk to you about the future, Nick. If, and I mean if, it can be arranged, how would you feel about moving into the house at the Glens of Lochandee and paying a rent for it, instead of taking out a bank loan to build a house here?' Nick's face darkened instantly, his mouth tightened and his dark eyes sparked with anger. Rachel felt her heart sink.

'Bridie has put you up to this!' He straightened as though he would walk out again. 'Too good to be true, it was! She would live here with me, she said, and set a wedding date. I knew . . .'

'No! Wait, Nick, let me explain . . .'

'You don't need to.' He spoke slowly and carefully now but his words were clipped with anger. 'I know exactly how Bridie feels about leaving the Glens of Lochandee, especially now she believes her father will spend his time at Wester Rullion. She did not need to be sending you. The whole affair we'll be calling off now!' Nick turned on his heel to walk away.

'No, Nick!' Rachel grabbed his arm in panic. 'Bridie doesn't know anything about this. I don't want her to know. Nor her father, not yet. Please wait until you've heard what I have to say. What I would like to do . . . Please?'

'If Bridie doesn't want me on my terms then she doesn't love me enough to be my wife.' Nick's face was set and stubborn and Rachel knew Fiona had been right about him. He was vulnerable but he was proud and fiercely independent.

'Listen to me, Nick, please. If you love Bridie at all, the least you can do is hear what I have to say. I've just been to see Mr Niven myself – not for your sake, or for Bridie's. You two are young, you have all your lives before you. Of course you will have problems, but you will solve them because I know you do love each other. It is my own husband I'm worrying about. If you marry Bridie and take her away there will be far too much for Ross to manage alone, especially now he has bought Wester Rullion. He will not rest until he has paid back the bank loan and I know how frustrated he was as a tenant with an absentee landlord and no repairs done to drains or fences, not even a shed to store tools, even less house cattle or store grain. He will want to do everything at once now that it is his own property.'

'So you want me to move in with you all?' Nick said tightly, already shaking his head.

'No. You heard what Mr Murray said about my vase? I thought about little else all night. This morning I made up my mind and I asked him to take it with him to get another opinion, and to sell it if he's right. He seems convinced he is. The money from the sale would help to build a small house, but not for you and Bridie. It would be for Ross and me, Ewan too, of course. I would build it right in the middle of Wester Rullion, instead of here beside the garage . . .'

'It's serious you are?' Nick stared at her incredulously. 'Since yesterday evening? You have given it consideration . . .?'

'I have. A great deal, believe me, Nick. It kept me awake most of the night. I loved Minnie's old vase, but I loved it for sentimental reasons. If it really is so valuable I should be almost afraid to dust it. I packed it up carefully in one of the wooden boxes which the animal drenches come in. Mr Murray took it with him this morning. Bridie thought he was taking home a box of eggs.' She laughed excitedly, but still a little nervous. 'Think about it, Nick. Some day Ewan will farm Wester Rullion. It would need a house then, as well as buildings for animals. It makes sense to build a house there now, instead of you buying a site to build one here.'

'I suppose it does from Bridie's point of view,' Nick said consideringly.

'Not just Bridie,' Rachel insisted. 'Ross would be living on the spot at Wester Rullion, and I should be at his side, where I belong. That's what I want, to be able to watch over him, have him come in for a rest and a cup of tea when he needs one, a change of clothes when he gets caught in the rain . . . Giving a hand when he's moving cattle. You know how he is . . .'

'I do. A good wife you are, Mrs Maxwell.' Nick's face lightened in a reluctant smile. 'A good mother you are too. Bridie—'

'Yes, Bridie's place would be at the Glens of Lochandee, but the two of you would be alone together there. Alice Beattie left her share to Bridie and we know the dairy herd is safe in her hands. That is what she does best. She enjoys her animals.'

'I know that very well . . .'

'But you will be there to help her, Nick. The government insists we must carry on ploughing land and growing crops until Britain can feed her own people again. We can't feed the present day population on yesterday's farming methods. Bridie doesn't like that side of things but she understands and accepts it, as we all do. I know you would help her with the tractors and machinery and maintaining them. Conan tells me you're good at that sort of thing, and more patient with repairs than he is. But . . .' Rachel sighed. 'We shall have a huge burden of debt until we can pay off Wester Rullion. We can't afford to let you and Bridie have Lochandee rent free . . .'

'Charity I would not accept! A rent we shall pay for Lochandee if you do build the house at Wester Rullion.'

'You're a good laddie, Nick. If we have any money to spare after the house is built I would like a hen house and a pigsty, and maybe a shed to rear a few calves. I've never been without animals around me. I'd be lost without anything. We'd need the eggs and a house cow for milk and a bit of butter . . .'

A slow smile creased Nick's tanned face. Rachel saw his teeth, white and even, catch his lower lip, but his attractive grin would not be denied, and he shook his head.

'If Bridie is like her mother I shall find myself doing her bidding without even noticing.'

'Oh Nick! Am I so bad?' Rachel said anxiously.

'Of course not.' Nick sobered. 'In fact it sounds to me

as though you are the one who will be making the sacrifices, selling your treasured vase and leaving the Glens of Lochandee.'

'Yes, it will be a wrench, I admit it. But the only place I've ever wanted to be is beside my husband. Some day I think you and Bridie will understand that. But Nick . . . everything depends on Mr Murray being right about the value of my vase, and getting someone to buy it. Can I have your promise that you will not breathe a word of this to anyone, especially to Bridie?'

'I promise, but I think I should go ahead and take the bank loan as arranged, at least for the present. The plans will probably go through quicker if the house is being built beside the farmstead. In fact I don't know why we didn't think of it before. Even if the vase isn't worth much it makes sense to build the house there. Some day I will sell it to Ewan for a huge profit,' he grinned.

'You mean you would go ahead even if I can't sell the vase, or if Mr Murray is wrong about its value?' Rachel demurred anxiously.

'Yes, the arrangements would be just the same as before except the house would be further from the garage.' He gave a wry smile. 'And I shall save the money instead of buying a plot.'

'Yes. Of course. I hadn't thought of that, Nick.'

'More importantly, Bridie would prefer living at Wester Rullion to a house right here, beside the garage. It's not so far for me to walk over a couple of fields to work. If things don't work out as you hope, this would be a sort of compromise for Bridie – not as good as staying at Lochandee I know, but . . .'

'You would do that, Nick?'

'Well yes, anything, we-ell almost anything, I'd do to marry Bridie. I want to start building as soon as we get permission.'

'But it will be our secret?'

'I think we need to consult Mr Maxwell about the exact site. I suggest it ought to be the opposite side of the farmstead from the old house where Mrs Forster lives. I feel quite sorry for her living there all on her own since Mr Forster died. I should think she'll be glad to have people living nearby.'

'Yes, you may be right about that. She never goes out anywhere. It's as though she is waiting to die too, poor woman.'

'It may be possible to repair some of the old buildings for pigs and hens.'

'Oh Nick, you're very considerate of everyone.' Rachel got to her feet again and reached up to kiss his cheek, chuckling when she saw him blush. 'I've always thought you would make a lovely husband for Bridie and now I know you're going to be a wonderful son for Ross and me as well. I really do appreciate your co-operation, and your ideas are so sensible.'

'But you think we shouldn't breathe a word to Bridie?'

'No. Fiona Sinclair knows because she was at the solicitor's when I called, but she promised to keep my secret. I can scarcely believe the vase can be worth enough to build a house and I'd hate to build up Bridie's hopes of staying at Lochandee and then disappoint her.'

'Very well, a secret we'll keep it until after the wedding. A real surprise it will be for Bridie if everything goes well. I'll enquire about permission for a change of site without delay.'

'And I'll let you know what Ross thinks. Thank you, Nick, for listening, and for being so understanding.'

Seven

Ross had played the fiddle since he was big enough to hold one and playing came as naturally to him as singing did to Bridie, so he was bitterly disappointed when Ewan showed no inclination to learn the piano accordion, or any other musical instrument. Ross did his best to persuade his younger son to practise but Ewan considered every moment spent indoors as time wasted.

'Look, it goes like this.' Ross played a few notes to illustrate the tune and then a few more. 'Remember, you have to play with the proper fingers as Mr Urquhart teaches you.'

Lucy was watching them intently. She longed to take the accordion from Ewan and have a go herself. She couldn't read the music as he was learning to do, but she was sure she could imitate the tune which Mr Maxwell had just played.

When the telephone rang Ross sighed and went to answer it.

'Let me have a go, Ewan?' Lucy pleaded. Ewan needed no persuading and quickly wriggled out of the straps, placing them over Lucy's slender shoulders. Slowly she began to finger the keys, experimenting, playing a bit of the tune, and then a bit more, listening intently to each note.

'That's a lot better . . .' Ross began when he returned to the kitchen. He stopped and stared. 'Surely that wasn't you playing, Lucy?' Her small face went red and she looked near to tears.

'I-I'm s-sorry, Mr Maxwell. I only wanted a wee go . . .'

'Och, don't be sorry, lassie.' Ross smiled with delight. 'You can play the notes better than Ewan and you haven't had a single lesson, have you?'

'N-no. Daddy says he can't afford to buy me an accordion or pay for lessons.'

'Let me hear you play the tune again?'

Lucy struggled with the notes, then a few more, then a few more still.

'Do you know the tune, Lucy?'

'Aye, it's called "Roamin' in the Gloamin". Daddy's always humming it to Mum when he's in a good mood.' She tried again and this time the tune was almost complete. Ross was astonished.

'Do you know any more tunes Lucy?'

'Daddy hums "I Love a Lassie" as well.' Stumbling slightly she picked out the notes, slowly, then more confidently as she got the hang of it. 'What are the wee buttons for, Mr Maxwell? And why has one got a dimple in it?'

'They're the chords, like playing two or three notes at once to fill in the background. You'd need lessons for them, I think.'

'Yes.' Lucy sighed resignedly, knowing that was impossible. She wriggled out of the straps, turning to hand the accordion back to Ewan, but he had seized his chance and disappeared outside.

When Ross met Beth crossing the yard to the dairy with a bucket of milk, he stopped to tell her how good Lucy was with the accordion.

'She has a natural ear for music. It's a pity she can't go for lessons with Ewan.' He was surprised when Beth seemed more alarmed than pleased by Lucy's musical talents.

'Harry has put his foot down,' she said sharply. 'He has set his heart on saving up for Lucy to go to college. He wants her to be a teacher and earn a decent living. He hasn't been himself lately so I'm not going to pester him about music lessons.'

'Is Harry ill, Beth?' Ross had known her since she had

come to the Glens of Lochandee as a little maid of fourteen, even before he and Rachel were married.

'No, I don't think so, but he never snaps at Lucy and he had her in tears the other night because she kept on about music lessons. He has a bit of indigestion sometimes but he must be as fit a fiddle the way he rides that bike o' his to work in all weathers. He's just been a bit tired and irritable lately.'

'Maybe he's doing too much extra work for Conan at weekends?'

'Och, he likes working at the garage. Anyway he never turns down a chance to make an extra half-crown. He says when Conan buys another bus he'll give up his job and work at the garage all the time. Sometimes he takes Lucy with him on a Saturday. Conan has been showing her how to work the petrol pumps. He told her he would give her a job in the school holidays when she's twelve. Now she can't wait!' she sighed. 'It's going to be a long three years!'

'I'm tired of finding excuses for Ewan,' Rachel announced crossly the following evening. 'He doesn't bother to practise. If you want him to keep going with his music you'll have to take him yourself, Ross.'

'All right. I'll ask Mr Urquhart how he's progressing while I'm there. I expect that's why we had to pay the money for a term in advance. He'll just have to stick at it.' Ewan groaned aloud at that and pulled a long face.

'I never asked for an accordion,' he pouted. 'And I never wanted to go for lessons either.'

'It's a wonderful opportunity,' Rachel coaxed. 'When you get good at it you could go to entertain at the concerts with your father, like Bridie and Nick do sometimes.'

'I don't want to entertain at concerts. I don't like music. I want to be a farmer.'

Rachel shrugged. It was true, Ewan had shown not the slightest inclination towards music but Ross had longed for one of his sons to take after himself, and Conan had never been interested in music either.

Mr Urquhart hesitated when Ross asked his opinion. The old man needed the money he earned from teaching pupils, but he had known almost immediately that Ewan was never going to be a good accordion player.

'If you want my honest opinion, Mr Maxwell, Ewan hasna much natural inclination and he doesna want music enough to work at it.' Ewan turned red. He thought his father would be furious. He didn't know his mother had already guessed what the verdict would be and she had reasoned with Ross over it.

'Well, I can't say I'm not disappointed,' Ross admitted now, 'but I can understand it must be hard work teaching a reluctant pupil. I don't suppose you would consider giving a few lessons to a little girl we know for the rest of the term, in Ewan's place? I think you'd find her much keener to learn, and unless I'm a bad judge, she has a natural ear for music. Goodness knows where she gets it from as neither of her parents are musical.'

'I'm sure I can take your word for the child, Mr Maxwell. It's a bit unusual but I suppose I could take her for the next few weeks. Who is she?'

'Her name is Lucy Mason. She's the same age as Ewan . . .'

'She's three weeks younger than me,' Ewan interrupted indignantly.

'Don't interrupt,' Ross said sharply. 'Her mother was old Mr Turner's granddaughter. You may remember he had the bicycle shop in Lochandee village before the war. Beth has worked at the Glens of Lochandee since she left school.'

'Aye, I remember Mr Turner,' Mr Urquhuart smiled. 'He made me a good bike from his parts. It's still in the shed round the back. All right then, I'll try the wee lassie.'

When Ewan triumphantly announced that he was finished with the music lessons and that Lucy was to go in his place for the rest of the term she danced with joy, but Beth stared at Ewan in dismay. Her face went bright pink and then so white that even Ewan noticed and asked if she was going to be sick. Beth shook her head mutely, but she felt sick in the pit of her stomach. Most of the time she lived a happy and contented life with a husband she loved dearly and a small daughter who was their pride and joy. But sometimes she had a nightmare feeling that someone would guess her secret. She knew it was impossible really but that did not stop the cold fingers which could clutch at her heart at an unexpected word or a smile, bringing memories flooding into her mind.

'We don't want charity,' she said to Rachel as soon as she saw her.

'It's nothing to do with me, Beth, but I assure you it's not charity because the lessons are paid for anyway and the accordion would just be a constant reminder of Ewan's failure and Ross's disappointment. I hope Lucy gets enough lessons to teach her the basics. If she does, she can keep the accordion, if she wants it. Let her have a go and you will please all three of them. You know how much I hate tension between the men in my family. We had enough of that when Conan wanted to join the RAF against his father's will.'

'Aye, I-I remember,' Beth stammered, her cheeks burning again, then paling.

'Are you all right, Beth?' Rachel frowned in concern.

'Aye, I'm fine. 'Spect it's my age,' she mumbled, 'making me hot . . .'

Rachel nodded, accepting her explanation. 'At least Ewan is desperate to farm, so that pleases Ross.'

'Aye, he reminds me of Bridie when she was that age. Have they set a date for the wedding yet?'

'Not exactly but they thought it would be the end of September. The new house should be nearly finished by then and the hay and harvest will be over. Nick is planning to take Bridie away for a honeymoon – somewhere right away from Lochandee he says but it's to be a surprise. I hope Bridie agrees. She's never been away to stay.'

'Och, she should take the chance while she can. Once they

settle down with a family and the farm they'll be tied here for years.'

'You're right, and things have changed since the war finished. The days are gone when people got married in the morning and came home to milk the cows and carry on as usual.'

Rachel had had no word from Mr Murray and with a sinking heart she was beginning to accept that Ross had been right. Eventually she had told him she had asked the furniture restorer to take away her treasured vase, to have it properly valued, and to sell it if his own opinion was verified. Ross didn't believe that a bit of an ornament could be worth nearly enough money to build a house; and his heart swelled with love for Rachel. He feared she would be bitterly disappointed and he loved her with all his old gentleness and passion by way of comfort. Her cheeks flushed as she remembered how gentle and loving he had been with her. Ross could still fill her with an all-consuming passion, just as he had when they were young, but now there was a deeper, gentler love, a slower more pleasurable pathway to the pinnacle of joy they shared together.

'Dearest Rachel, I know how much that vase meant to you,' he had whispered against her throat. 'I never thought you would part with it. I'm sorry your dreams for keeping all of us happy have been shattered.'

'But it may just take longer than he thought . . .' She clung to her hopes and dreams. 'If Mr Murray does get a good price for it, Ross, will you agree to us buying the house at Wester Rullion instead of Nick?'

'It's a big "if", but of course I would. I don't know why we never thought of suggesting Nick should build it there before, especially now he doesn't need to waste good money buying a separate plot of land.'

'No, but he is planning to use the extra cash to make the house a little bit bigger than he originally planned for himself and Bridie. So you will agree to live there? You and me and Ewan, if I do get the money for the vase, I mean.'

'Leave the Glens of Lochandee!' Ross had never really considered the prospect seriously and Rachel knew he had just been humouring her. In spite of all their nights of tender loving she was not sure whether he would move if she really did get the desired fortune for the vase, but that possibility seemed more and more remote as time passed and there was not even a postcard from Mr Murray.

As it was Nick had got the licence for the building materials and he had applied for the variation in the site and size. He expected to get permission to start building any day now.

Bridie had cheered a little at the prospect of living at Wester Rullion instead of at the garage.

'But nothing will ever be the same as living here, at the Glens of Lochandee,' she confided to Rachel. 'I promised Aunt Alice I would never leave here. I don't think she would have left her share of the farm and the land and the animals to me if she had thought I would desert them.'

'You're not deserting them, Bridie. Anyway I'm sure Alice would have wanted you to marry the man you love, and Wester Rullion is only a few miles away.'

'I suppose so,' Bridie acknowledged uncertainly. 'Did Conan tell you he's not very pleased with Nick for building a house away from the garage?'

'I gathered there was some tension between them over it, but Conan does like things his own way. I'm sure he will make a success of his business, but he will have to learn to consider other people. After all, Nick has just as much at stake as Conan, and they are partners. I hate to admit it, but I think Nick has his feet more firmly on the ground.'

'Less ambition, Conan calls it,' Bridie said glumly, recalling Nick's account of the argument. 'I think he hoped Nick would always be there, on the spot, to deal with the repairs and orders and petrol, and all the little things that keep the business ticking over. Conan wants to concentrate on this dream of his to have buses driving up and down the country, full of grateful holidaymakers.'

'Well that will not happen until petrol comes off ration, and even then I expect the prices will rise.'

A week later Nick drove into the yard in the old lorry they used for deliveries. He peeped the horn to alert Bridie, then he jumped from the cab and ran to greet her, scooping her up in his arms and swinging her round in his excitement.

'We've got it! Permission to start building our very own house!' Like Ross he had little hope of Bridie's mother selling her vase for more than a few pounds, but so long as he and Bridie had a home of their own somewhere, anywhere, he would be happy. He set her on her feet and looked down into her face, seeing her soft, smiling mouth only inches away. He found her irresistible and he kissed her long and hard. Bill Carr and Sandy Kidd were crossing the yard at that precise moment and both gave a whistle and wide grins. Bridie flushed to the roots of her hair. Underneath her capable exterior she was incredibly shy. Nick chuckled at the sight of her pink cheeks.

'I can hardly wait to discover if you blush all over, Bridie,' he whispered, his dark eyes dancing. Bridie's colour deepened even more. 'Now there's a celebration tonight we'll be having. Do you want to go to the pictures, Bridie bach? Or shall we be really extravagant and go out for dinner?'

'Can we afford it?'

'Deserve it, we do. I'll tell Conan I want the car. There's your glad rags you'll be needing. I'll book a table at the new restaurant that's opened in Dumfries. Fiona's boss took her there. Excellent, she said it was.'

'You've seen Fiona? When?'

'O-oh the other day,' Nick said vaguely, but Bridie noticed his heightened colour and wondered.

Eight

B ridie and Nick spent a blissful evening making plans. Their meal was delicious in spite of the continued rationing of many staple foods and the atmosphere seemed made for lovers. A three-piece orchestra was playing softly in the background, making it easy to believe dreams really could come true, at least for tonight. Bridie felt relaxed and happy, her blue eyes soft and full of dreams as she met Nick's smiling dark gaze. The tables were partially screened by plants and trellises and every now and then a few couples took to the floor beneath the shaded lights, moving slowly to the music on the polished area nearer the musicians.

Nick and Bridie ate at leisure, enjoying being together with nothing in the world to interrupt their easy chat, their pleasure in each other's company.

'I can't wait for us to be married and have time together like this every day,' Nick said, caressing the back of Bridie's hand with his forefinger. 'And even better every night,' he added softly and the intensity in his dark eyes sent tingles down Bridie's spine.

'I know . . . Surely it will not be long now you have permission to start building?'

'You'll not regret it, Bridie, I promise. I know how much it means to you leaving Lochandee, but some day, somehow, I'll make it up to you.' He rose and drew her on to the dance floor. They were perfectly in tune with each other and with the romantic atmosphere. Bridie was pleased she had worn her yellow cotton dress with its swirling skirt, in spite of

70

her mother's warning that she would catch cold. The style accentuated her narrow waist and firm young breasts and the smouldering look in Nick's eyes made her heart beat faster.

They had enjoyed a lovely meal and several dances. 'One more drink we'll have with our coffee, then head for home.' Nick sighed. 'There's a thousand times a night I'm wishing we were living in the same home, sharing the same bed.' He chuckled softly at the pink in Bridie's cheeks. 'There's pretty you are when you're blushing and still so shy I can scarce believe it, Bridget Mhairi Maxwell.'

Nick had drunk more wine than was his habit and he drove slowly and carefully on the way back to Lochandee, but the roads were almost deserted. Petrol was still rationed and few people drove purely for pleasure. Just before they reached the village, he drew into the shelter of a stretch of woodland and stopped the car. He turned and drew Bridie into his arms, kissing her with an urgency which took her by surprise after the dreamy pace of the evening. She guessed it was the wine, as well as the news that they could start building their own home, which was adding fire to his blood. He undid the buttons of her coat and slipped his arms around her, feeling her quiver in response as his hand explored the softness of her body beneath the thin material of her dress. Bridie's breath came faster as Nick slipped one hand beneath her skirt, feeling the tops of her best silk stockings and the thin satin suspenders. She was a little shocked at his dexterity in opening one singled-handedly. She clung to him as he stroked the bare skin of her thigh, still gently, but Bridie felt the passion growing in him, and in herself, too.

'Soon it is we'll be getting married, my love . . . soon . . .' His voice was husky. 'Couldn't we . . . just this once . . . Bridie . . . ?' Bridie's lips were clinging to his, her heart racing. Desire flared to match his own as his hands aroused so many sensations. She had never felt quite so wanton . . . but always her mother's voice came into her mind – gentle and clear, and so very insistent. She could almost see the anxiety in her eyes, looking down into her own. She had been twelve or maybe thirteen at the time. One of the girls at school, only two years older than herself had had a baby.

'You're almost a young woman now, Bridie. I had no one to explain to me about being a woman and all that it means – like making babies. You must never let any man try to make a baby with you, Bridie, not until you're married.' Her mother had been so earnest, her face full of loving concern. Bridie remembered staring back, bewildered and anxious.

'I-I don't understand, Mama . . . ?'

'You will one day. It is so easy to make a baby, especially if you think you love someone or want to please them.'

'But how can I make a baby?'

'When we want the cows to have a calf, you know we put them beside the bull?'

'Of course, but . . . ?'

'And months later the cow has her calf. Men and women are just the same, except we are not animals and we should be married first, make our vows before God in church.' Her mother had shuddered. Bridie still puzzled over that conversation, but she had never forgotten. There were still many things she didn't really understand about men and women and right now she yearned passionately for Nick to hold her tighter and tighter . . . For him to . . .

'No, Nick! Please, we must not make any babies – not yet . . .' There was panic in her voice. She wanted whatever it was Nick wanted, but she could not forget her mother's warning, even now.

Nick caught his breath, paused, then with an impatient sigh he drew away from her. He leaned back in his own seat, head thrown back, drawing in great gulps of air as he strove for control. He rested his elbow on the window, his head in his hand. Bridie glanced at him miserably, feeling cold, bereft.

'I-I'm s-sorry, Nick,' she said in a small, wistful voice. 'I'm sorry if I'm a disappointment to you . . .'

'No.' He drew another deep breath. 'No, you won't be a

disappointment when we're married. There's shy you are, underneath, that's all. I should have known better and a car isn't the right place for our first time. There's carried away, I was.' He sighed heavily. 'But Bridie . . . we'd be safe, you know. We don't need to take any chances about making babies if that's all that worries you. I could send away for some French letters if . . . well if you'd let me then . . . ?'

'French letters?' Bridie was totally confused. 'Why are you changing the subject? Are you drunk, Nick?'

'No, I . . . You've never heard of French letters? Duw, I was thinking there's not a single girl left in this country who hasn't heard of them, not since the war.'

'Well I haven't. What . . . ?'

'Don't you girls talk about anything except recipes and clothing coupons! Fiona hasn't lived all her life in a little village. What does she talk about, I wonder.' It was not a question. Bridie heard exasperation in his voice. Their glorious evening was beginning to turn into a miserable fiasco. She had failed Nick and she didn't know what to do about it.

'Oh forget it!' He opened the car door and grabbed the starting handle.

After Nick had dropped Bridie off at the farm he drove back to the flat but he sat for a long time in the car, pondering the events of the evening. He did love her. He'd been attracted to her since she was no more than fifteen, the first time he came to Lochandee with Conan. He had heard her sing at the village concert – 'A Nightingale Sang in Berkeley Square' – and he knew he would never forget her. Like most of the young men who had known they could die tomorrow, he had taken his pleasures if it suited him, but ever since he had known Bridie returned his feelings, he had remained faithful to her. Surely it was only her sheltered upbringing that was holding her back? He had rarely smoked since he was demobbed but he wished he had a cigarette now. He'd heard some of the men in the forces talking about frigid wives. He'd often thought they were making excuses for their infidelities, but now he wondered. Surely Bridie wouldn't turn out to be cold and unresponsive? Nick knew his Celtic breeding could never stand such a punishment. Everything about Bridie was soft and warm and caring. He shook himself. He'd drunk too much wine and it had depressed him. He dragged himself out of the car and went inside.

Back at Lochandee, Bridie did not sleep well. She felt young and gauche and ignorant of the world beyond Lochandee. She knew Nick had been disappointed tonight. Moreover, alone in the darkness of the night reality returned and she couldn't dispel her misgivings at the prospect of moving to the new house which so excited him. It would go ahead quickly now. She ought to be overjoyed. Nick had even changed the site to try and make her happy, or so she believed, but she could not share his enthusiasm when it meant leaving the Glens of Lochandee.

Two evenings later she cycled down to see Fiona who seemed to have settled quickly into her new home. She was surprised to see Beth there too, quite at home sitting on one side of the fire.

'Harry is listening to Lucy playing her accordion pieces,' she said. 'She just loves that noisy old thing, and Harry dotes on every tune she plays for him. Then they're going to have a game of drafts so I thought I'd just leave them to it and pop across here.'

'Beth brought me one of her apple pies,' Fiona said with a smile at Bridie. 'I'm going to get fat at this rate. She knows all my weaknesses already.'

'Fat!'

'That'll be the day!' Beth and Bridie said in unison.

'Beth spoils me anyway. Apart from her cooking I'm glad of a friendly chat. I feel I belong here already.'

'I'm glad,' Bridie said warmly.

'I can't thank you enough for telling me this place was for sale, and for recommending Mr Niven as a solicitor. I'm working three days a week for him now. Oh by the way, did you enjoy your meal with Nick the other night, Bridie? He asked me if there was anywhere you would specially like for a celebratory meal. It's lovely, isn't it?'

'Yes, it was. Er . . . Fiona, have you ever heard of French letters?' Bridie asked innocently. Beth gasped and put a hand over her mouth. Fiona's eyes widened and for a moment Bridie thought she saw a flash of amusement in their clear grey depths but it was swiftly hidden as she lowered her lashes.

'Well? Have you heard of them or not?'

'You'd do better to ask Beth than me,' Fiona said.

'Oh no. We never used them.' Beth's face flushed and then went pale. How could she admit that she and Harry had never needed them. They had both longed for children, at least four they had planned, but as they'd discovered, life didn't go according to plan. In fact, sometimes it went terrifyingly wrong when you least expected it.

'Well, what are they?' Bridie demanded, feeling foolish and wishing she'd never mentioned them.

'I've never had occasion to use them either, Bridie,' Fiona said gently, 'but I can tell you it's just a slang expression for condoms – you know things that men wear to . . . to prevent their wives getting pregnant.'

'O-oh!' Bridie's face flamed and now she was the one who clapped her hand to her mouth. 'I-I see . . .'

'I expect you and Nick have lots to discuss before the wedding,' Fiona said calmly. 'I'm sure it must be better to talk about things beforehand.'

'Y-yes. We . . . I wondered whether you would be my bridesmaid, Fiona?'

'Why, yes! I'd be honoured. Thank you for thinking of me, Bridie.'

'And Lucy,' Bridie turned to Beth, glad to talk about other things to hide her mortification. 'Do you think Lucy would like to be a bridesmaid, Beth?'

'She'd love it, I know she would. Are you sure you want her, Bridie? I-I mean has Nick any relations you ought to ask first?'

'No. He has no close family. It will not be a big wedding but I think some of his friends from the RAF will come. We haven't fixed a date but we hope it will be at the end of September.' Bridie stood up. 'I'd better leave you two to chat.'

'Oh, don't go yet!' Fiona said. 'I'll make a cup of coffee.'

'Not for me, thanks,' Beth said. 'I'd better pop back over the road and get that bairn o' mine to bed. Harry would never think of telling her to go.' She had half intended asking Fiona's opinion about a niggling worry concerning her health, but now she was glad Bridie's arrival had prevented her mentioning it and making a mountain out of a molehill. She grinned to herself at the comparison.

When Beth had gone, Bridie looked at Fiona miserably.

'I made a real fool of myself, didn't I?' She bit her lip.

'Not at all, Bridie,' Fiona reassured her kindly. 'When you live in the city and mix with lots of different people they talk about things our parents would never have discussed, even between themselves. Er . . . I know there is a book if you want to know about birth control though. I'll find out the proper name for you. I'm sure you and Nick will be really happy once you're married. He seems very caring and considerate.'

'Mmm . . . if we don't fall out before then,' Bridie muttered glumly.

'You won't – not seriously. Nick loves you and he'll wait, if you ask him – and Bridie . . .' Fiona's pale face flushed bright pink, but she bit her lip and went on: 'Gerry and I didn't wait. I wish we had now. It w-was so . . . so fumbling and hurried and . . . and sordid. It . . . it was awful. I wanted to g-give him something to remember me by. Deep down I-I think I knew I might never see him again.

76

I really thought I l-loved him. We were both so dreadfully young, so inexperienced.'

'I'm sorry, Fiona.' Bridie's eyes were round with surprise. She had always believed Fiona would be in control of every situation she ever came across.

'Promise me you won't tell anybody, Bridie.'

'Of course I promise. I wouldn't dream—'

'No, no, I know you wouldn't really. I only told you because I can see something's troubling you, and I can guess Nick thinks he's waited long enough. Let him wait just a bit longer, Bridie, and I'm sure you'll not regret it, and neither will he.'

'You're a good friend, Fiona. I-I was feeling really wretched – and stupid. You make me feel much better.'

'That's what friends are for and you've helped me more than you'll ever know. I feel as though you've drawn me into your own circle of family and friends. Beth is becoming a good friend now we're getting to know each other. I didn't think we'd have anything in common but it's amazing the things we find to talk about. Just one thing we don't agree about – ' she gave Bridie a wry smile – 'and that's your brother.'

'Conan?'

'Yes. Beth and Lucy believe he can do no wrong, but he always brings out the worst in me. He makes me want to argue with him whatever we discuss.'

'Oh oh, that's Conan all right, but I don't suppose Beth expresses any opinions to oppose his own. That would get a bit boring for you and me, I think. Anyway Beth's known him nearly all his life. Her grandfather first got him interested in mending and making bicycles. When he died Harry and Beth got married and took over the shop so Conan spent his spare time with Harry after that.'

'Harry really dotes on Lucy, doesn't he? I hope she never lets him down. I mean she may not want to be a teacher, or she may not get good enough grades – though I must say she seems a bright child, as well as very lovable. It's just such a big responsibility being an only child. You may inherit all your parents' worldly goods, but you are the only one they have to pin their hopes on.'

'I never thought of that, Fiona. Even Beth is a bit anxious in case Lucy doesn't live up to Harry's expectations.'

'Few people realize what a responsibility it is.' Fiona sighed. 'At night, when I'm on my own, I feel so guilty about leaving my own mother. I can't get her out of my mind.'

'I don't think you've anything to feel guilty about. You gave up a promising career because you felt she needed you. You weren't to blame that she had less time than everyone expected.'

'No? I wish I could be sure about that,' Fiona mumbled and turned away, but not before Bridie had seen a glint of tears in her eyes. 'I'll make some coffee.' She disappeared into the kitchen. Bridie sensed she needed to leave the room in order to gather the control which Fiona prized so much.

Rachel felt Bridie was more subdued than she ought to be for a girl looking forward to her wedding in a few months' time and she guessed it was the thought of leaving the Glens of Lochandee and her beloved cattle. She felt sick at heart when she thought about the high hopes she had had when she packed up her vase and put it into the care of Mr Murray. Her only wish had been to make all her family happy, and keep Ross from being overworked. She had judged Mr Murray to be a man of integrity and he had let her down. She wished she had never let him take away her cherished vase, never allowed herself to be won over by his tale of riches beyond her dreams. She had wanted nothing for herself, but the vase had reminded her of her childhood and the love and kindness old Minnie Ferguson had shown her after the death of her own mother.

At last she admitted her doubts and suspicions to Ross.

'I never did believe a vase could be worth anything like Mr Murray told you, Rachel my love, but I know it had great sentimental value for you, and for that alone it makes me angry that he tricked you into parting with it. I believed him to be a genuine man myself but it seems he deceived both of us.'

'That's the hardest thing to accept. If he'd written to say the vase was worthless I wouldn't have minded so much, except that I might have got it back, but we've heard nothing from him since he left.'

'Fiona seems to have benefited from his advice,' Ross mused. 'According to Bridie, the collector he recommended paid good prices for her father's jade and ivory figurines, and a chess set.'

'I know, and the local antiques dealer gave her a decent price for her furniture once he realized she understood the proper value, and she said that was only due to Mr Murray's advice. I just hate to think we were so wrong about him.'

'Well, at least some good came out of it. Your idea of building the house at Wester Rullion instead of at the garage. Nick seems happy with the new site, in fact I believe he's looking forward to living there.'

'Nick's looking forward to getting married and I don't think it would matter where he lived so long as he has Bridie to himself. He's a good lad. I just hope they will be happy together.'

'Dear Rachel, you worry too much about all of us. Bridie will be fine.'

'I hope you're right, but I'm not so sure . . .'

An unexpectedly bitter wind at the beginning of May sent the young lambs scurrying for shelter and Bridie was extra diligent in her shepherding in case any were starving from lack of their mother's milk.

'Mother has taken the car to get Ewan and Lucy home from school,' she said to Beth when she joined her in the byre at milking time. 'I wouldn't be surprised if we don't get some trees blown down, it's so wild. If it hasn't calmed down by the time we're finished milking I'll give you and Lucy a lift back to the village. We'll tie your bicycle on the back of the car. It's almost impossible to walk against the wind when it takes away your breath.'

'Thanks, Bridie. It's more like midwinter, and it was such a lovely weekend. I just hope Harry remembered to put his waterproof cape back in his bicycle bag. He and Lucy had it spread on the grass in the garden on Sunday to have a picnic tea.' Beth grinned. 'He's just a big bairn at heart, my Harry. He enjoyed it as much as Lucy.'

'It's lovely that he takes time to play with her, though,' Bridie said with a smile.

'Oh he does that, whenever he's not out earning money to educate his "wee princess", as he calls her. I don't know what he'll do if she ever lets him down. She's coming on really well with the accordion so he hadn't the heart to refuse to keep on with the lessons. Mr Urquhart has great hopes for her and he's convinced Harry that music would be an advantage if she does become a teacher.'

It was still bitterly cold when the milking was finished so Bridie kept her promise and drove Beth and Lucy back to the village.

'Harry is usually home before us but I don't see any smoke coming out of the chimney. Maybe he'll be later tonight if the wind's against him,' Beth remarked as she climbed out of the car and unloaded her bicycle. 'I shall need my trusty old steed to get to work in the morning. Run in, Lucy. Dinna stand there with your teeth chattering, lassie.'

Bridie had only just washed and changed and sat down at the table when Ewan shouted, 'Fiona Sinclair wants you on the phone, Bridie. She sounds all funny.'

'Are you all funny . . . ?' Bridie grinned as she aimed a pretend fist at her young brother's head.

'Not "funny" funny. Queer like,' Ewan insisted just as Bridie took the phone from him.

'Fiona?'

'Oh Bridie! C-can you come? It's Beth. She's hysterical. I-I don't know what to do . . . It's the shock, I think.'

Nine

'I don't understand, Fiona? Why is Beth hysterical? What's happened?'

'It's Harry. He's d-dead, Bridie! Two men found him by the roadside. With his bicycle. On the brae leading up to Lochandee.'

'Harry! Dead? Fiona, are you certain?'

'Yes. I heard Beth screaming. I was just getting out of the car. I-I've called Doctor McEwan. I-I didn't know who else to contact.'

'Beth's like family to us. I'll come right away.' Bridie's face was white.

'I'll come with you,' Rachel said immediately.

'Oh my God! Harry? I can't believe it.' Ross stared at his wife and daughter. 'I can't believe it!'

'Somebody will have to stay with Ewan, Ross. You'll get him to bed if we're not back?'

'Of course, but if there's anything Beth wants me to do . . . I'll start the car for you. Wrap up, Rachel.'

'Yes. Phone Conan and Nick. Tell them what's happened.'

Doctor MacEwan had already confirmed Harry's death by the time Rachel and Bridie arrived at Beth's cottage.

'I warned him a few months ago. He had a heart condition known as angina. The exertion of cycling up hill against such a bitter wind has proved too much. I'm so sorry, Mrs Mason.' Beth was quiet now but she stared at the doctor, white-faced, disbelieving. She was shivering. He looked at

Rachel standing beside her, a comforting arm around her.
'I'll leave something to help her sleep,' he said quietly, 'but
she ought not to be left alone.'

'I-I could stay,' Fiona volunteered, her face even whiter
than Beth's.

'That's all right, lassie,' Rachel said. 'Beth and I have
seen each other through troubles before. I'll stay with her
tonight.' She turned to look at Bridie who was cuddling
Lucy on her knee and trying to comfort her. 'It might be
better if you took the bairn back to the Glens of Lochandee
with you, Bridie. Ewan's company will help her as much
as we can. Ask your father, or Conan, to come down here
in the morning. There'll be . . . be things to do . . .'

Every family in the village, and many beyond it, were
represented at Harry Mason's funeral. Fiona was astonished. She had not known Harry for long but she knew
he had always been cheerful and willing to help. Even so
he had seemed such an ordinary unassuming family man
in every way. Five of his ex-army comrades had travelled
many miles to pay their last respects, and the shop in
Annan, where he had worked, was closed for the afternoon. Customers and colleagues attended his funeral. Beth
was quietly overwhelmed and thankful for the generous
funeral tea which Rachel and Bridie had provided on her
behalf.

Doctor MacEwan had advised that she should return to the
routine of her work at the Glens of Lochandee without delay.
He felt it might help her come to terms with the shock and
the awful loss, and he knew how vital it would be to earn
whatever money she could with a child to feed and clothe.
He'd heard Lucy was a bright wee thing at school and old
Mr Urquhuart said she was the best music pupil he had had
for years.

So a few evenings later Beth and Bridie talked quietly
together as they put the first milking machines on the cows

with the rhythmic pulsing a familiar soothing sound in the background.

'Your friend Fiona is proving a wonderful help,' Beth confided. 'She understands everything. She's done it all so recently for her own mother and she's promised to deal with Harry's insurance policy for me. I dinna understand all the wee writing they put on the bottom o' the pages. She's only young but she's that calm and capable, and easy to talk to, spite o' her fine education.'

'Fiona will be pleased to help you, Beth, as we all are. She told me what a good friend you'd been, helping her settle into her new house, and introducing her to folk in the village.'

'Aye, I never knew how much we all need friends 'til now. Carol and the two lassies have been champion . . . But Bridie, I dinna ken how I'd manage without you and your mother and father. I'll need my work . . .' Her voice broke on a choking sob as Bill Carr came into the byre to see whether the first milk was ready to take to the dairy for cooling.

'You know there will always be a place for you with this family, Beth,' Bridie tried to reassure her when Bill had trundled the milk churn away. 'In fact we shall need you more than ever when Nick and I move to Wester Rullion.'

'Aye, that's what your mother said. It's really worrying her, you moving away, I mean. She's afraid your father might do too much . . .'

'Harry's death has given us all a shock. He was too young to die.'

'The minister said it was the Lord's will,' Beth said flatly. 'But that's not much comfort when you're on your own at the fireside of a night. Your father asked if Lucy and me would like to move into the farmhouse, to save paying rent on my cottage, but . . .' She shook her head from side to side in a bewildered fashion.

'I know, Beth. We don't blame you for wanting to keep your own wee house, and Fiona agrees it would be better if you can. She looks at situations differently to the rest of us, almost as though she anticipates things we never dream of.'

'Aye, she has an old head on her young shoulders – that's what my grandfather would have said.'

Building the house at Wester Rullion was not progressing as fast as Nick had hoped. He knew some materials were scarce and his home was not considered a priority when there was a greater need to house the thousands who had been rendered homeless during the bombing. Even so he was growing impatient with the builders' progress.

'Nothing will persuade me to postpone the wedding,' Nick whispered urgently as he held Bridie in his arms after taking her to the cinema. 'I've waited too long already. I shall have to share your bed at Lochandee after all.' He chuckled at Bridie's blush.

'I hardly like to mention the wedding when Beth is still grieving for Harry, but I know she was pleased when I first asked Lucy to be a bridesmaid.'

As it happened it was Beth herself who mentioned the wedding.

'I'm glad my poor bairn has something to look forward to,' she said wearily. 'She's been ever so good and I know how much she misses Harry. The other day when she came in frae school she said "Dinna worry, Mam. I'll look after you. I've told Mr Urquhart I'll be stopping accordion lessons". I'd been fair worried about telling her I couldna afford them after the term finished.'

'Lucy seems to have grown up all of a sudden,' Bridie said slowly. 'She was doing so well with her music too.'

'Aye, but Mr Urquhart says she'll get on fine if she keeps at it now, and if she gets stuck she's to go and ask him. He said he wouldna charge because she's a lassie with real talent and he'll be proud to help her.'

'I'm glad. It's strange how these things crop up in families. Harry said there was no music in his family and I know your

85

family are not musical either, Beth,' Bridie mused. 'It's a gift.' She was surprised to see the colour rush into Beth's pale face, then recede as swiftly, leaving her whiter than before. She would have been shocked if she had known Mr Urquhart's thoughts in that direction. He had noticed how many of her mannerisms were identical with those of Ewan Maxwell. The old man had lived long enough to know there were skeletons in the cupboard of most families and he was convinced Ross Maxwell must have sired both the bairns.

'Your mother seems to be worrying about the wedding,' Beth said, deliberately changing the subject. 'She's always liked Nick so it can't be that, and nobody can say the two o' ye have rushed into it. In fact I'm surprised Nick has been sae patient.' She gave a wistful smile at Bridie's blush. She missed Harry dreadfully and she didn't think she would ever get used to being without him, whatever folk said about time healing.

Rachel was not worried so much as sick at heart over her failure to pay for the house at Wester Rullion. All her plans had come to nothing. Mr Murray had let her down badly and left her with neither her vase nor the money.

'Don't worry,' Nick consoled, 'I never really expected you would be able to buy the house and I intend to keep it well within my bank loan. This is a lot better site than I should have had beside the garage so some good has come out of your idea,' he said cheerfully, 'and it will be a good investment for me. I shall sell it to Ewan at double the price!' He gave a teasing grin, but then he sobered. 'I'm really pleased we never raised Bridie's hopes of staying at Lochandee though.'

'Yes. I feel so let down by Mr Murray,' Rachel muttered. 'And I know Ross ought to be here, at Wester Rullion, carrying out his improvements. He spends most of his time here already and I don't think he realizes how much responsibility Bridie takes for the dairy herd and the day-to-day running at Lochandee.'

'No, I suppose not,' Nick said slowly. His own dreams for Bridie's future, and his own, were more concerned with rearing a family than rearing calves. He loved children and he knew Bridie did too.

A week after her chat with Nick, Rachel had a far worse cause for concern. They were only beginning to come to terms with the consequences of Harry's death when another blow befell them all.

Bill Carr was a conscientious stockman and he had never ceased to be grateful to Ross and Rachel for giving him a job when none of the other farmers dared risk arousing the factor's anger and spite. Bill and his young daughter, Emmie, with her frail infant, had made their home in the little cottage at the back of the farmstead and he had been there ever since. When the war finished, Emmie had married Sandy Kidd's son and the pair had moved to a farm on the other side of the glen.

Whenever Ross had an engagement to play the fiddle at one of the concerts, Bill always volunteered to make the nightly check of the cattle and the two remaining Clydesdales before he went to bed.

He had traversed the farmyard hundreds of times during his time at Lochandee but on this particular night his heel slipped on a smooth granite cobble as he was closing the upper half of the stable door. It was such a simple thing but Bill fell awkwardly and his temple hit the sharp corner of a brick protruding from a wall at the side of the stable door. He was a strong man but the blow on the side of his head knocked him out. The wound at his temple bled freely.

The night wind stirred the dust of the farmyard in little flurries. A farm cat padded softly on his nightly prowl. Later an owl called eerily as he hunted in the darkness. His victim squealed in pain and terror. Bill Carr was oblivious to the night sounds, and to the increasing chill of the cold stones where he lay, and to the rain which began to fall just before dawn. His life's blood ebbed steadily away.

It was Bridie, first out to the byre and the milking as usual, who came across Bill's inert body. She ran at once for warm blankets and Doctor McEwan lost no time in coming. One glance at his face told Bridie and her parents that Bill's condition was serious.

'He has lost a lot of blood. I'll phone for an ambulance. We need to get him to hospital immediately.' He turned to Rachel. 'He has a daughter, I remember. Can you contact her?'

'He is so bad?' Rachel's low voice reflected her shocked dismay.

'I'm afraid so,' Doctor MacEwan said nodding. 'If you can give me the number of the farm where his daughter works I'll telephone myself and explain to the farmer. It's imperative she should get to the hospital without delay.'

Bill clung to life for nearly twenty-four hours before finally succumbing to death's clutches. He did not regain consciousness and Emmie was distraught. Strangely it was Beth who found the strength and the words to comfort her. Rachel remembered how Beth had taken Emmie under her teenage wing when Emmie had first come to the Glens of Lochandee, a frightened, bewildered girl, far too young to have been forced into motherhood, and later stricken with grief when her baby died during the diphtheria epidemic.

Bill's death was a sad blow to them all. He had been a hard worker all his life and a gentle and caring man with people and animals. The summer season was rapidly advancing to harvest time and each long day was busier than the one before, or so it seemed to Ross and Bridie. Sandy Kidd was no longer young and his pace was slower. His wife had once helped with the milking but that was in the days before the war and before the milking machine had been installed. She had helped with turnip hoeing too but she was no longer fit for such tasks.

Ross was worried. The traditional farm workers still moved on term days at the end of May and November, and the end of November seemed a long time away. Moreover there were fewer people wanting agricultural work since the war. Men no longer wanted to toil from dawn to dusk and longer, every day of the week and in all kinds of weather. They had been awakened to other ways of earning a living, shorter hours and easier tasks, often with better pay. Ross could scarcely blame them when his own son had refused to return to work on the farm. Conan wanted the best of both worlds, Ross reflected with a flash of the old bitter disappointment in his firstborn son. He wanted to live amidst the peace and beauty of countryside but he took the changing scenes and seasons as his God-given right. He never considered the labours needed to plough and sow before a harvest could follow, the sweat and toil of fencing, ditching and laying hedges. Year after year as spring followed winter and a new flock of lambs adorned the grassy knolls, the rigours of winter were forgotten, except by those who had rescued starving animals from snow storms or waded through muddy fields to give them food. Ross sighed and did his best to ignore the gnawing discomfort in his stomach. He knew it was aggravated by his present anxiety, yet even when farming was at its hardest he had never wanted any other way of life himself and he knew he would never understand how any son of his could be so different.

Nick on the other hand seemed happy just to be alive, and to have put the hell of war behind him. Although his work was at the garage, he took a lively interest in everything that went on at the Glens of Lochandee and all the other farms round about.

Conan and Nick realized the pressure of work at Lochandee was serious since Bill Carr's death but they had two buses and a lorry now, as well as the petrol pumps, and they had little time to spare themselves. Conan had taken several bookings for weekend trips with the buses and he was missing Harry as his spare driver. Nick felt it was his duty, as a partner, to help but it meant that he and Bridie had less and less time to spend alone together. Conan had roped Beth in to help with the petrol pumps on Saturdays. He knew she needed all the extra money she could earn and he valued her help. She was honest and helpful with the customers. Lucy usually accompanied her and she seemed content to watch Nick or Conan repairing machines or working on cars, and if they were both away driving she stayed in the small kiosk and practised her lessons or read her books. There was no doubt she was intelligent and likely to do well at school and it saddened Beth that Harry's dream of his daughter becoming a school teacher was now impossible. He had believed that was the pinnacle of achievement for a young woman.

Ewan missed Lucy's company and often pleaded with her to stay at the Glens of Lochandee. Lucy would have preferred to be at the farm with Ewan but she had grown very protective of her mother since her father's death and she accompanied her whenever she could. Both Nick and Conan brought her bags of sweets since they had come off ration, but in the middle of July the sugar ration was reduced to eight ounces again and sweets were put back on ration at four ounces a week.

'I hope they don't put clothes back on coupons,' Bridie fretted. 'Do you think we should buy the material for my wedding dress, Mother? And Fiona said she had seen some lovely yellow crêpe de Chine in Binns for her dress and Lucy's. It will suit Lucy beautifully with her green eyes and dark curls, and Fiona likes yellow.'

'Yes, it's time we bought the material. I saw Miss Mackintosh in the village and she said she would like to start on the bridesmaid's dresses soon. We seem to have been so busy since Bill died.' Rachel sighed heavily. She was tired herself. She helped with the milking in the evenings while Bridie was working at the hay with Sandy and Ross. Nick came to help them whenever he could get away from the garage but he and Conan seemed to have little spare time either. There was more machinery on farms than there had been before the war and many of the farmers were unused to maintaining and repairing it. Consequently many of them turned up at the garage asking for Nick. He was clever at mending and adapting and he was patient too. Ross was pleased his future son-in-law was becoming so popular in the district.

They had all accepted that the new house would barely be finished by the time of the wedding but they were too busy struggling to get the last of the meadow hay gathered in and make a start on the harvest to worry about houses.

Rachel decided to write one more time to Mr Murray but she felt angry and thoroughly sickened when there was no reply.

'I have no proof that I ever gave him my vase,' she lamented to Ross.

'And there's no proof that it had any value anyway, my love,' he comforted.

'It was valuable to *me*. It doesn't matter about the money, it's the principal. It was Minnie Ferguson's most treasured possession and she left it to me. I suppose it serves me right for parting with it but I only wanted the money so that we could go to live at Wester Rullion and start building it up for Ewan, and I still think Bridie should stay here. I don't want you overworking and killing yourself, like Harry.'

'Ha, but Harry had something wrong with his heart. There's nothing wrong with me, except I'm not as young as I was when we came to Lochandee. We shall have to hire another man at the November term to replace Bill, but I've been asking around for some casual workers to help with the harvest. They will expect to be fed and they'll be more likely to stay if we feed them well. I think I should arrange to get another pig killed.'

Rachel groaned inwardly. That would mean brawn and sausages to make and the lard to render. Even with the extra hours Beth was working there never seemed to be enough time for all that needed to be done.

Aloud she said, 'I'll see that the cellar is scrubbed ready to cure the bacon and hams.'

Ross manage to hire three casual workers to help with the

harvest. He rode on the binder in place of Bill, with Bridie driving the tractor. Sandy Kidd did not like any of 'the monster machines' and was happier with a brush and shovel and wheelbarrow, cleaning out the byres and calf houses and caring for the two remaining horses, or stooking corn.

The three casual workers were named Tom, Edgar and Peter and Ross showed them how to set the sheaves of corn into stooks so that the grain would dry out ready for carting into the stacks. All went well so long as Ross was in the field himself, but for the brief spells when Sandy Kidd relieved her father on the binder Bridie noticed the men slackened their pace and fell behind.

She soon realized it was the older of the three, the man named Edgar, who was the ring leader. She had taken an instinctive dislike to the way he leered at her from the moment he had appeared in the farmyard and she had caught him snarling at the other two more than once, presumably ordering them to go slower. She hated the sly look in his eyes.

Peter was Polish and had been a prisoner of war. He had adopted the anglicised name and, left to himself, Bridie felt he would have been the best worker of the three. He was pleasant-faced, with a boyish smile and wistful dark eyes. They learned later that he and his father had worked on a farm in Poland but both his parents had been killed and he had no wish to return to his homeland now.

Tom was quiet and he had a bad squint in one eye and seemed a bit slow in his wits, but he was strong and willing so long as Edgar was not around.

Most of the harvest was at Wester Rullion because the Lochandee fields were needed to graze the cows and calves and provide the hay for their winter feed. Bridie did not look forward to working with the three men so far away from home. It was bad enough when her father was there, riding the binder, but later he would be needed to build the stacks and she would be left to organize the loading of the carts in the field.

Her fears proved correct the very first day they were loading sheaves on to the carts. Edgar caught her round her waist as she was climbing on to the cart. His breath smelled of tobacco and the stink of stale sweat from his dirty clothes and unwashed body made her gag.

'Let me go!' she flared angrily.

'I'm just giving ye a helpin' hand.' His grip on her waist tightened and he tried to draw her closer. Bridie gave his shins a hard kick.

'Ouch! Yer stupid bitch! What yer dae that for?'

'I don't need a helping hand from any of you, so keep your hands to yourself in future.'

'Oh aye? Well, we'll see about that afore this lot's gathered in.' His shifty eyes travelled over the fields of stooks. 'Ye'll not be sae prim an' proper when ye're flat on yer back beneath a cart. Women! Ye're all the same. All ye need is mastering . . .'

'Here's the boss coming!' Tom hissed through the gap in his front teeth.

'Weel that's all right, Tommy boy. There's plenty o' room for him.' Edgar turned to greet Ross with an obsequious smile. It made Bridie seethe with scorn. 'Mornin', Mr Maxwell, and a fine harvest day it is tae be sure.'

Ross returned his greeting apparently oblivious to the tension in the air.

Ten

Bridie felt her tension increasing with every hour she spent in the company of Edgar Ritter. The way he eyed her every movement made her flesh creep and she felt he was seeing right through the clothes she wore. She despised his lazy ways and snide remarks and his determination to influence the other two workers annoyed her.

During harvest, with the eternal battle to beat the weather, it was customary to eat picnic meals in the field to save time. Bridie had worked with other men ever since she left school and all of them had behaved like gentlemen, never commenting when she disappeared behind a hedge after lunch. But she was convinced she could not trust Edgar Ritter. Her breeches were a necessity for working, especially since she was the one who built the loads of corn on the carts, but they made a quick dash behind the hedge almost impossible and the prospect made her edgy and uneasy.

'For goodness sake, Bridie, what was that for? And why are you so jumpy?' Nick asked when he received a sharp blow in the ribs from Bridie's elbow. It was Sunday and her father insisted only essential work should be done. They could work at the harvest by the light of the moon until midnight every day of the week, but the Sabbath was sacrosanct. So Nick and Bridie welcomed a few hours to themselves, but she shook her head at the suggestion they should go to inspect the new house which would soon be their home.

'I've seen enough of Wester Rullion to last me for a long time,' she said abruptly.

'Oh?' Nick's brows shot up. 'I thought you usually enjoyed working at the harvest? What's wrong, Bridie?'

'O-oh, I expect it's just me, but I can't stand Edgar Ritter. I hate working with him. He's the oldest of the three casual men Father has hired for the harvest.'

'How old is he?'

'I don't know but according to Tom his wife divorced him and he wishes he was still in the army. He was living with another woman at Carlisle but she's put him out and now he's in lodgings.'

'So . . . ? Is that all you have against him?'

'No-o . . . it's the way he leers at me. And he never misses a chance to try and maul me if he's anywhere near.' She shuddered. 'Then there's the inconvenience of spending all day in a field without any toilets.' Nick began to grin. 'It's all right for you men! It's never been any bother to me either how men behave but I wouldn't trust Ritter not to . . . not to . . .'

'I see . . .' Nick was serious now, frowning. 'A peeping Tom, is it?'

'I'm sure he'd be that and more if I gave him any opportunity. Honestly, I hardly dare to drink in case I need to go to the toilet during the day.'

'Not drink and the weather so hot? There's not good for you, Bridie. Can't you be for asking your father to do something?'

'There's not much he can do. We're short of labour as it is. The odious little man is oh-so charming whenever he sees my father, but the minute his back is turned he's making nasty comments and telling the others not to work so fast. Anyway, my father is needed in the yard to build the stacks and the men know that's where he'll be most of the time. Peter would be a really good worker if Ritter would leave him alone.'

'So then, and which field will you be harvesting tomorrow?' Nick asked thoughtfully.

'The second top. When we reach the top field I shall

probably run down to the garage and join you and Conan at lunch time, but it will be another three days before we get to that field. And that's another thing, we lost a lovely little heifer calf yesterday. The mother had calved it without help but I expect Sandy forgot about her. The calf still had the skin over its nose and it suffocated. She is one of our very best cows too. I can't bear the thought of them being neglected when I'm away from Lochandee every day.'

'Oh, Bridie, surely your father will keep an eye on them once the harvest is finished? His cattle they are too, and he did build up the herd himself, and the farm, before you were old enough to help him.'

'I know he did, and he loves the cattle as much as I do, but you should hear the plans he has for Wester Rullion now that he's bought it. He can't wait for Ewan to leave school and help him make changes.'

'Regretting you've agreed to marry me, is it, and live in our new home? Right am I, Bridie?'

'No, of course I'm not. I-I want us to be married more than anything else in the world, but I just hate the thought of leaving Lochandee and my cows.' She turned in the circle of Nick's arms and raised her face to his. He bent his head in a lingering kiss, unable to resist her.

'I'm glad, because there's not much longer I can be waiting, Bridie Maxwell,' he whispered huskily. His mouth moved to the soft hollow at her throat, and his hands, strong and capable, moulded her closer and closer until she felt the desire in him.

'Oh Nick, I do love you . . . I'm sure everything will be wonderful for us.'

The next day a lone figure came loping over the field from the opposite direction to the farmstead. As he drew nearer Bridie realized it was Nick and she began to smile.

'Hi, Miss Maxwell, I thought I might join you for a picnic

lunch today if you've no objections?' he called in his best English accent.

'None at all, Mr Jones. It will be a pleasure,' Bridie responded with a widening grin, her heart beating with delight and tenderness. How typical and how thoughtful of Nick to come and give her his moral support.

'Well! That'll be a bloody first!' Edgar Ritter muttered scathingly. 'We've not seen much sign o' pleasure in the stuck-up little bitch.' The smile died from Nick's face and his eyes were cold and hard as he stared back at the man's insolent face. 'There's no need tae look at me like that, man! I'm telling ye she's—'

'My fiancée?' Nick finished softly. He bared his teeth in a travesty of a smile and stepped closer to Ritter. 'There's more you were wanting to say, eh?' His voice hardened.

'Your wh-what?' Edgar Ritter spluttered. 'Fiancée is't? Well I dinna envy ye, mate. She's like a bloody iceberg.'

'Duw! There's a civil tongue in your head you're needing. And if—'

'And if I dinna,' Edgar mocked. 'What could a fancy bit boyo like you do, Taffy? Taffy was a Welshman, Taffy was a thief, Taffy—'

Nick took two swift strides and grabbed the man by his shirt collar, twisting it tightly until he spluttered for breath.

'There's a good lamping you'll be getting if you can't stop your mouth.'

Bridie glanced uneasily at Tom and Peter but she was amazed to see them turn away to hide their smiles. They were enjoying seeing Ritter meet his match, she realized with relief. Nick gave one more twist and then shoved Ritter away from him with enough force to send him sprawling on his back amidst the sheaves. They heard him swear profusely as Nick took Bridie's hand and led her away to a more secluded spot to eat their picnic in peace.

Before he left Nick produced a whistle, like those used by policemen.

'Keep this handy. If he bothers you give a good blow. We may not hear it down at the garage if we're working on an engine, but he's not to know that.' He grinned. 'The noise will probably give him the fright of his life. Now, Bridie, I'll keep an eye on him while you make yourself comfortable behind that big stook. Then a really passionate kiss I'll be needing from my girl. That will be giving him something to think about. Iceberg indeed!' Nick chuckled at the sight of Bridie's pink cheeks. He often had to remind himself that she was still a shy young country girl. His heart raced at the thought of making her his wife.

'I'm glad I came today,' he whispered against her mouth before he kissed her long and hard.

'Mmm, so am I.'

'Tomorrow I'll come again, if I can get away.' He chuckled softly. 'Don't look now, but scowling fit to bring the rain on, he is. And the stupid oaf will not be forgetting you belong to me. There's no more bother you'll be having from him.'

The following day Conan arrived over the fields. He drew Bridie aside to eat their lunch.

'Nick was needed to repair a binder so he asked me to come in his place. He said you'd been having bother with one of the men?'

'He's not been so bad today. He scowls and mutters unpleasantly, but I can cope with that. It was good of you to come though, big brother. I've had a feeling lately that things weren't going so well between you and Nick?'

'Have you? Has Nick been complaining?'

'No, he's very loyal to you as a matter of fact, but when I mention the garage he isn't as enthusiastic as he used to be, and he doesn't talk about it so much now.'

'He's a good sort, old Nick, but maybe we shouldn't have rushed into business together after the war. We shall always be good friends, I'm sure of that, but sometimes I think we both want different things from life. I want to be as great a success with my business as Father is with his farming.'

'You mean you feel you have to prove yourself to him?' Bridie asked, biting hungrily into a bacon sandwich.

'Not just that. I really want to grow bigger, to have more than one garage and a couple of buses. All Nick thinks about is getting enough money to pay off the loan he's taken to build you a house. I'm beginning to think it would have been better if he'd moved into the Glens of Lochandee. At least that way he wouldn't have needed to take so much money out of our business and we might have expanded a bit quicker.'

'You mean that would have suited you and no one else matters! Anyway, Nick put more money into setting up the garage than you did!' Bridie reminded him indignantly. 'And how would you like to move in with your in-laws if you were newly married?'

'I've no intention of getting any in-laws. Anyway I thought you always wanted to stay at the Glens of Lochandee and go on breeding your precious pedigree Ayrshires?'

'It is, well it was. But I understand how Nick feels and I want us to have some time to ourselves, especially when we are newly married.' Bridie's cheeks flushed at the look in Conan's eyes. He shook his head in mock sorrow.

'This thing called love!' he teased. 'It sure makes a fool of a man.'

'You just wait until it happens to you, big brother!'

'I'll make jolly sure it never does happen.'

'Don't you want a wife? And children? You're so good with Ewan and Lucy, Conan, surely you want a family of your own?'

'It's not something I've thought about. Anyway I've no time or money to spare for such things.'

'Och you!' Bridie pushed him sideways. 'You'll just end up a crusty old bachelor. Now just keep an eye on that awful man while I pop behind the hedge over there.'

The harvest was almost over and people were already calling at Lochandee with wedding gifts. Emmie and her husband

Frank called to bring a set of towels, beautifully wrapped and with a large satin bow. They stayed to chat over tea and shortbread.

'I miss not having my father here to visit,' Emmie sighed as she followed Rachel into the house.

'We've missed your father too, lassie. And Frank's father is not as fit as he was.'

'No, we were just saying the same, Mistress Maxwell,' Frank Kidd said earnestly. 'I remember when I was here as a laddie he could have forked a load of corn to the stack in half the time it took that new man ye've got.'

'You saw the men working then, Frank?'

'Aye, we went round by the stack yard before we came inside. I just wanted a word with Father. You see, whenever I ask Mither how she's keeping she just says "fine", but I can see she's . . . she got something seriously wrong. She's as skinny as a wee sparrow and I never remember her being thin.'

'Aye, laddie, we've been anxious about Dolly too,' Ross nodded. 'Are you thinking it's . . . it might be cancer?'

'It's what we fear, Emmie and me.' He turned the conversation to other things as Beth and Bridie came in from the milking.

'My, it's a fine time you two are having working on a farm without cows to milk!' Beth teased them with the familiarity of old friends.

'Not so fine when it comes to pay day though,' Frank sighed. 'Twenty-three bob a week doesna go far. No weekend work or overtime when there's no cows, ye see, and tractors dinna need fed and groomed like the horses do. We've only one pair o' Clydesdales left now. I'd swap ye your place at Lochandee any day, Beth.'

'Are you serious, Frank?' Ross asked swiftly. 'We shall be looking for another man at the term. It'll not be easy getting a man as good as your father, lass.' He looked at Emmie. 'Bill was a grand stockman.'

'Aye,' Emmie nodded, swallowing the lump in her throat. 'But he always said how good you and Mistress Maxwell were to us when we first came to Lochandee. He never forgot.'

'Well he certainly repaid us.'

'Mr Maxwell . . . are ye meaning? I mean would ye consider taking me on again?'

'If you wanted to come back to work at the Glens of Lochandee I would certainly consider you, Frank, but we only have Bill's wee cottage to offer remember.'

'Can I discuss it with Emmie and let you know?' Frank asked eagerly.

'Yes, you do that, laddie.'

'There's no need to discuss it, Frank, not as far as I'm concerned,' Emmie said, her eyes shining. 'I'd love to come back to the Glens of Lochandee. It'd be nearly like old times.'

'Well then!' Frank looked at Ross. Ross looked at Rachel.

'Were you listening, Rachel? These two young folk canna think we're so bad. They're both wanting to come back to work for us.'

'That's good news then,' Rachel said. 'And I'm sure it will be a great relief to your father to have you near, Frank.'

'Aye, there's that tae.' Frank frowned. 'We dinna think Mither will be here much longer. If Emmie had been willing I'd have moved back in with them and helped father take care o' her . . .'

'I'll do that, so long as they want us, Frank,' Emmie said gently. 'Your folks were aye good to me and my father.'

When they were in bed later that evening Rachel turned to Ross.

'I'm pleased Frank and Emmie are coming back to work here. We know both their families and they are reliable. I've wondered how Sandy would manage without Dolly but now I'm sure Emmie will take good care of him. Beth says Emmie told her she can't have any more children of her own. Something to do with the trouble she had giving birth

101

to the factor's bairn. She was little more than a bairn herself then, if you remember.'

'I remember Bill Carr and Emmie arriving here very well, and the frail babe in her arms. Not one of them looked fit to survive, even less to work as Bill did. It will be a relief to know we shall soon have Frank back. I had been considering taking on young Peter to work at Wester Rullion. You know the Polish lad who has been helping with the harvest? He's been used to farm life. He'll make a good man with the right guidance. He would need lodgings though. I asked Nick if he wanted a lodger but he said definitely not. He wants his bride to himself.'

'You can't blame him,' Rachel smiled in the darkness and cuddled closer.

'No, I don't.' Ross's arms tightened. 'We've been lucky, Rachel. I still love you as much as ever.'

'I do hope Nick and Bridie will be happy too . . .'

'Bridie will be fine. She'll soon forget about cows when she gets children of her own. Are you still worrying about that vase and not being able to pay for the house at Wester Rullion?'

'And you, Ross. I worry most of all about you, especially after Harry dying so suddenly. But it's not just the money and spoiling all my plans for everyone. I shall always feel let down by Mr Murray. I still can't believe he turned out to be such a cheat, especially after we made his son so welcome when he came with Conan and Nick during the war.'

In true Scottish tradition people came to the house with wedding gifts large and small for Nick and Bridie. They were greeted with a glass of sherry or a cup of tea and shortbread, although most of them would still return to the traditional show of presents which was held a few nights before the wedding. Rachel and Beth had cleaned the house from top to bottom in readiness. Most people came with genuine good wishes and admiration, but there were always one or two who were curious to see what a neighbour had given, or to view the house if they were not in the habit of visiting.

Rationing or no, Rachel was determined that Lochandee's reputation for hospitality must be upheld. Sandwiches and savouries were prepared, apple tarts, shortbread and fruit cakes were baked.

'I don't think we have all this fuss in Wales,' Nick complained when Bridie told him she was busy helping her mother prepare. 'Like having all the parish it is, before the wedding even begins. Back home the guests see the presents after the wedding.'

'We-ell it will not be long now and it will all be over,' Bridie soothed.

'There's hard it is to wait for you, bach!' Nick growled softly and pulled her into his arms, refusing to release her.

It had been a great relief to Bridie to see the last of Edgar Ritter and the end of the harvest. She had lost weight and Miss Mackintosh insisted she must attend for a final fitting to have her wedding dress taken in at the seams.

'Fiona's and Lucy's are finished,' Bridie told Beth, 'and I thought they looked wonderful. Lucy is like a wee fairy.'

'Aye, she's so excited I can hardly get her to sleep at night,' Beth said wryly.

She was genuinely pleased for Bridie and Nick, but inwardly she was dreading the wedding and prayed she would not burst into tears. She was determined to hide her own wistful longing and secret apprehensions. She would miss Harry for as long as she lived but they had had their happiness. All she asked of life now was to be allowed to see her only child grow up to be a woman. Dolly Kidd's illness had reminded her of her own mortality. How long had Dolly been ill? None of them knew. She had never been a woman who worried about her family's health, or her own. Dolly had never complained. Beth suppressed a shudder. Her own fears were just imaginary, she told herself with determination. She must stop worrying and keep well and strong for Lucy.

Three days before the wedding Fiona was busy at her work in Jordon Niven's offices when she glanced idly at a newspaper which one of the clients had left behind. It was a London broadsheet and the pages were folded back where the previous owner had been reading. Fiona moved closer to look at the picture of a vase and read the caption beneath. It was in black and white but as she read she drew in her breath and her eyes widened.

'Whatever are you reading to make you look so furious?' Jordon Niven asked with a smile on his way through the room he had allocated her as an office.

'It's this vase! They are going to sell it at Sotheby's and they are expecting it to fetch a record price. It's difficult to be sure from a newspaper photograph but it looks like the same shape as Mrs Maxwell's vase to me, and Mr Murray said it was unusual.'

'So what does that signify?'

'Don't you remember? Mr Murray valued my mother's furniture. He told Mrs Maxwell he believed her vase was quite valuable. She let him take it away with him, to try and sell it. She dreamed of paying for the house which is to be built at Wester Rullion. She planned to move in there with her husband and young son. But she has heard absolutely nothing since Mr Murray left, taking her vase with him.'

'Er . . . yes, I believe I do recall hearing about that. But I never did believe anyone could sell a vase and get enough money to build a house.'

'Well listen to this then!' Fiona's grey eyes were bright with anger and anticipation and Jordon Niven thought what a waste it was for such an attractive young woman to be so bent on a career. Behind that calm cool exterior he was convinced there was a woman capable of great passion. Distracted as he was by his thoughts he paid little attention to the passage Fiona was reading aloud until he heard her demand.

'Surely you could do that? The Maxwells have been good clients for you.'

'What? Do what?'

'Don't look so startled. I'm only asking you to write to Sotheby's and query the ownership of the vase in question and its recent history. I don't want to worry Mrs Maxwell so near the wedding, nor do I want to raise her hopes if I'm wrong.'

Eleven

The day of Bridie's wedding dawned crisp and clear. She made her way to the byre for the last milking she would be doing for a whole week and for a moment she stood gazing across the glen to the distant hills of Galloway beyond the gleam of the Solway Firth. Looking to the south she saw the peak of Skiddaw outlined clearly against the sky while on the opposite side of the glen the woods were changing to the bronze and gold of autumn. There was mist in the hollows like a mystic sea, a sure sign of a good day ahead. Bridie loved autumn with its vivid colours and the satisfaction which came with the culmination of the year's labours. She stretched her arms high above her head and breathed deeply in the fresh morning air, feeling exhilarated and happy.

Beth came peddling up the road on her bicycle.

'It's going to be a lovely day,' she called. 'Happy is the bride that the sun shines on and all that!' Bridie grinned at her and waited for her to park her cycle. Together they carried the heavy milking-machine buckets to the byre, with their dangling teat clusters clanking against the sides. Sandy Kidd joined them with the churns.

'Well lassie, it's going to be a good day for your wedding, eh?'

'Aye, and she doesna look a bit nervous, does she?' Beth declared.

'Nothing to be nervous about. Nick's a fine fellow. They'll make a grand couple. Frank and Emmie have promised to come over and help me get the milking done tonight so you can all enjoy yourselves at the dancing. And dinna be fretting about the cows while ye're away.'

'But Frank and Emmie are coming back down to the village for the dancing afterwards, aren't they?'

'Aye, I reckon so.'

When Rachel entered the church she felt a knot of emotion gather in her chest. The doctor's wife and the minister's wife had decorated the pews and windows of the church and the old building looked warm and beautiful with the glow of autumn fruits and flowers and the sun streaming through the leaded windows. The golden yellow of the bridesmaids' dresses seemed an ideal choice and both Fiona and Lucy looked lovely with their posies of yellow rosebuds and carnations. She felt so proud of Conan and Nick, standing together, tall and erect in their dark suits, both so lucky to be alive after surviving the ordeals of war. Several of their fellow airmen had come to the wedding, and Nick had been delighted to welcome a distant relative and her husband who had travelled all the way from Wales on the train. There were gaps in their own family but she was truly glad Meg and Peter had managed to come, as well as Polly, Peter's eldest daughter and the twins, Rory and Max, both now grown into fine young men, exactly a year younger than Conan. She shuddered, remembering how near to death Meg and her baby boys had come all those years ago back in Ayrshire.

The tone of the organ changed and the congregation rose to the strains of Wagner's bridal march. Rachel heard Beth sniff loudly behind her and she had a struggle to hold back her own tears as Bridie came slowly down the aisle on Ross's arm. She had always thought her daughter cheerful and pretty and lovable, but today she looked incredibly beautiful in her white lace gown with its silk taffeta underskirt. Miss Mackintosh had made an excellent job of fitting the neat bodice and long tapering sleeves, and the oval neckline showed Bridie's creamy skin to perfection. The lace veil covered her shining curls adding an air of elegant mystery. How tall and slim she seemed with her high-heeled satin shoes. Rachel heard Nick draw in his breath as she reached his side. She saw them smile at each other.

Please God, let them be happy all their lives through, Rachel prayed silently.

The grounds of the little church were full of well-wishers and children waiting excitedly for a glimpse of the bride and groom, followed by the usual scramble for pennies which Conan, as best man, would scatter for them.

There had been no shortage of volunteers to help at the reception which was being held in the village hall and people had been generous with gifts of coupons for extra sugar and flour for the baking. Doctor MacEwan's wife and a few of her helpers had brought even more decorations for the hall, and the flowers and greenery and balloons gave the little building a truly festive look.

'It's the proudest man on earth I am today,' Nick whispered to Bridie as they stood together for photographs in front of the church. He was rewarded with a radiant smile which the photographer managed to capture.

As they made their way to the hall, Ross walked beside Bridie and Nick.

'I'm glad your Aunt Meg managed to come, Bridie, but I think there will be little else done but gossiping until she goes away again,' he chuckled, nodding to where Rachel and Meg were walking, heads close together as they caught up on the family news.

'Yes, and I see Conan and Fiona are managing to be civil to each other for today,' Nick grinned. Bridie followed his gaze to her brother and bridesmaid.

'They make a handsome couple when they're together. It's a pity they always seem to argue,' Bridie agreed.

'A few toasts later on will be making them more friendly with each other, I think,' Nick suggested wickedly. 'Conan was a sociable boyo after a whisky or two when we were in the RAF, and there's a few old friends of ours here to join him.'

'I don't think Fiona drinks much alcohol,' Bridie said.

'A toast to our happiness she'll be drinking, surely?'

'Probably, but I'm not sure. But it doesn't matter, we shall be happy anyway,' Bridie smiled and received a warm squeeze of her fingers as agreement.

It seemed no time at all before the tables were being cleared and folded away for the dancing to begin.

'It wouldna be a Maxwell wedding without a dance,' the leader of the little band announced, 'although we shall be missing our star player tonight with Ross taking to the floor with all the pretty women I see around the hall. Lucky man!' Everyone cheered. 'Now, make way for the bride and groom.'

Bridie felt she had never been so happy as she circled the hall, secure in Nick's arms.

'Duw, but it's beautiful you look tonight, Mrs Jones. Have I told you so already then?' Nick whispered in her ear, and chuckled at her startled glance. 'You were forgetting you're Bridget Mhairi Jones now then?'

'Yes, I had. Now that I'm your wife then, don't you think you ought to tell me where we're spending the next week of our life together?'

'A surprise it is. But we're not going far for tonight, that's for sure.' He watched in delight as Bridie blushed. 'I've been saving up my petrol though. Tomorrow we shall be getting away from everyone for a few days. It's my old haunts in Wales I would like to have been showing to you, but I couldn't quite manage that distance. Travelling by train now, I didn't fancy that for our honeymoon.' He glanced around the hall. 'Is it Fiona I should be asking to dance next, or should it be your mother?'

A couple of hours later Fiona unfastened the long row of tiny buttons and helped Bridie change into a pale blue dress and matching coat with a frivolous little hat perched on top of her dark curls. They were in the small side room off the main hall and Fiona carefully hung Bridie's wedding gown on a high hanger.

'I'll take your dress and Nick's clothes across to my house after the dancing and you can collect them when you return from your honeymoon. What skill and patience Miss Mackintosh must have. I shall have to ask Beth to help me unfasten the wee buttons down the back of my dress or I shall never be able to get out of it tonight.' She smiled dreamily and started to hum a tune which the band had been playing earlier.

'Fiona, I've never seen you so relaxed and . . . and . . . happy.'

'I thought you were going to say merry? I think I am, a little maybe. I'm sure Nick kept topping up my glass whenever I wasn't looking. I noticed he had an extra bottle beside him and I didn't see him drinking much himself, but somebody certainly emptied it.'

'Mmm,' Bridie smiled noncommittally. 'I think Conan has had his fair share the way he was chattering when he danced with me.'

'Oh, so that's what's making him such charming company tonight.'

'Is he? Charming, I mean?'

'Oh very, quite irresistible in fact. I don't know when I've enjoyed myself so much, Bridie. I'm so glad you asked me to be your bridesmaid. Did you see Ewan and Lucy dancing together? They looked so sweet. I heard your Aunt Meg saying they looked just like brother and sister.'

'Mother will really enjoy having Aunt Meg to stay for a few days. They don't see each other much but they write regularly and Aunt Meg has been a good friend since Mother was orphaned when she was sixteen.'

'Yes, I gather Conan is quite fond of her, and of Polly too. But Polly is her step-daughter, isn't she, so she's not really related to your family?'

'No. Uncle Peter's first wife died when Polly's twin sisters were born. Polly is a teacher in Glasgow. She's staying at Beth's tonight and travelling back tomorrow.'

'I see.' Fiona would have liked to ask more about Polly but her natural reserve reasserted itself and she accompanied Bridie back to the hall to have one last dance with her new husband before they made their escape. She had heard some of Nick's friends planning to decorate his car with tin cans and balloons and Lucy was desperate to throw confetti.

Escape was probably the right description for their departure, Fiona thought with a happy smile. Her smooth hair gleamed more gold than brown in the overhead lights. She caught Conan watching her and moved across to join him. She felt relaxed, liberated from her usual inhibitions. The desire to hold her own in any argument with him had temporarily evaporated. She felt at peace with the world in general.

Bridie was surprised at the warm hug she received from her father when they went to bid her parents goodbye. Over her head Ross murmured gruffly, 'You'll take good care of my lassie, Nick?'

'I shall try my best.'

'You can't do more than that, Nick,' Rachel smiled and kissed his cheek. 'We're so happy to welcome you as another member of our family at last.' Nick smiled back at her. He liked Bridie's mother, always had, ever since he had first visited the Glens of Lochandee with Conan on leave from the RAF. He was really sorry she had been so disappointed over the sale of her vase. Not that he minded where he lived so long as he could repay his bank loan and he and Bridie could make a home together on their own.

The moon was full and round as only a harvest moon can be. As soon as they had driven a safe distance from the village, Nick stopped the car and removed the tin cans and balloons, but it was impossible to get rid of all the confetti. When he climbed back in again he drew Bridie into his arms and kissed her gently.

'My wife,' he said softly. 'My own at last.' He felt Bridie smile against his lips. 'Come on, we'll get to our hotel. I've booked the best room they have at the King's Arms in Dumfries. Bonnie Prince Charlie is supposed to have stayed there. Tomorrow we will drive up to Ayrshire and have a little cottage all to ourselves. It looks on to the sea with a view of Ailsa Craig. A man from that area came into the garage to have his car repaired. We got talking while I was working on it and he recommended the cottage. It had belonged to his mother and his wife has just started letting it to holidaymakers. He was very grateful to me for fixing his car to get him home so he promised to have everything laid on in the way of linen and food, and logs for a fire if we need it.'

'It sounds lovely,' Bridie agreed.

'I'm looking forward to being just the two of us, and I think my shy little bride will prefer some privacy too . . .'

The evening was drawing to a close when Fiona remembered she had promised to take Bridie and Nick's wedding finery across to her house. Beth had already left with a very tired Lucy.

'I'll help you carry everything,' Conan volunteered. 'Mother and Father have already gone home with the Sedgemans, and Polly has gone to Beth's.'

'All right, that would save me coming back,' Fiona agreed gratefully. Conan followed her into the house and up the stairs to the spare bedroom where she wanted to hang Bridie's dress. Conan stumbled on the stairs behind her.

'You know, Conan Maxwell, I think you are too inebriated to think of driving back to your crummy little flat,' she giggled.

'And for once, Fiona Sinclair, I believe I agree with you,' Conan grinned. 'I would have gone back to the Glens but they have a full house already.'

'You can sleep in this spare bed if you want.' Fiona patted the plump feather mattress with its blue satin eiderdown and matching bedspread.

'I can? It looks v-very inviting, but what would it do to your reputation if anyone finds out?'

'Och, my character is unblemished as far as the Lochandee folks are concerned. Anyway, I'll shoo you out at the crack of dawn. Your car is parked across at the village hall so no one will know where you are. Do you fancy a cup of cocoa before we turn in?'

'Mmm . . . I could fancy more than that.'

'Well, if you're good I'll lace it well with some good French cognac.' She led the way back to the living room and switched on an electric heater. 'My father must have had a whole crate of brandy hidden away. There's about six bottles still here.'

Conan was amazed to see the generous measure which Fiona poured into each cup. He guessed she was not in the habit of measuring out spirits. She kicked off her high-heeled shoes and sank into a chair beside his, cradling the cup in her hand.

'Haven't we done well? Not a single argument all day!' He draped his jacket around a spare chair and removed his tie, then he raised his cup a little unsteadily in a toast.

'I'd drink it up if I were you. Whoever does your washing wouldn't thank you for chocolate stains down your lovely white shirt.' She grinned at him.

'You know I rather like the new you, Fiona Sinclair.'

'Well, I'm afraid I can't go around every day with flowers in my hair and wearing a long yellow dress. Oh gosh!' she clapped a hand to her mouth. 'I quite forgot I needed to ask Beth to unbutton all the tiny loops down the back. I can't get out of it myself!'

'Och, that's no problem. I'll unhook you when you're ready to go to bed.'

'Mmm, maybe you'll come in useful after all then,' she

113

waved a hand airily in his direction. 'I think I'm ready now but at the moment I don't feel all that sleepy even though it's been such a long day.' She uncurled herself from the big chair and took their cups to fill with water in the kitchen.

Tidy and methodical to the last, Conan reflected and grimaced at the thought of the cheerless and untidy flat he would return to. He would miss Nick more than he had realized.

'I think I'll take you up on your offer of a spare bed if you're sure, Fiona.'

'Even when I'm a b-bit in-inebriated I don't say things I d-don't mean. At l-leasht I don't think I d-do.' She blinked at him. 'Th-that brandy must have been stronger th-than I shought. Let's get upshtairs be-before my legs give w-way.'

She led the way, stumbling slightly as she hauled herself up by the banister to her bedroom. Conan followed her in as she turned her back towards him for him to help with the unbuttoning.

'Th-there's an awful lot of wee buttons . . .'

'I'll soon manage them, if you'll stand still . . .' The long row of buttons reached almost down to the bottom of her slender back. The warmth of her skin, the fragrance rising from her hair made his fingers tremble, but Fiona waited patiently in a hazy glow. It didn't seem strange when Conan released the last button and slipped the dress slowly from her shoulders until it fell in a cascade of golden yellow around her feet. She didn't resist when he bent his head and kissed the knobbly little bone at the back of her neck, rather she leaned back against him lifting her head obligingly when his lips trailed a path of fire, nibbling softly at her ear and forward to the hollow of her throat. She turned meekly in the circle of his arms and lifted her mouth to meet his, vaguely aware that the yearning for him had been there throughout the long day they had spent together.

Conan was not a man of steel and he had drunk more than usual. Fiona was one of the most attractive, and most challenging women he had ever met. Her lips were soft and yielding but their first real kiss was like adding a match to a box of fire crackers.

Fiona offered no resistance when he pushed the narrow straps from her shoulders and allowed his mouth to trace the path of the rustling silk as it slipped slowly to her waist. She felt deliciously free and unfettered as she raised her arms and clasped them round his neck. She felt his heartbeats thundering against her own, but nothing seemed to matter. Conan was strong and young and as fit as a man could be. He raised his head and tried to look into her face but her cheek was resting against his chest and she made no protest when his trembling fingers released the long lacy suspenders and gently eased the remaining bits of underwear to the floor.

He lifted her as effortlessly as he would a child. She looked up at him dreamily. His blue eyes held her clear grey ones as he laid her on the bed. She curled up as her eyelids closed as innocently and as trusting as a child's. For a moment Conan stared in disbelief. He shook his head. Disappointment washed over him. Then with a wry grimace he drew the bedclothes over her. It was the first time a woman had simply ignored his advances, even less gone to sleep on him. He had always been the one who decided how far he would go. Of course his rejection had to come from Fiona Sinclair, who else? She had always been a challenge to him, but never this way. Beneath the bedclothes her long slender limbs made him quiver with desire. Damn Fiona! Damn all women! Even so, he bent and picked up her gown and draped it over a chair, then as an afterthought he lifted her underwear and placed the flimsy items on top. Would she remember? What would she think when she awakened and found herself undressed? His anger evaporated and he grinned drunkenly.

When Conan wakened he could barely see his wristwatch but he gasped when he realized it was already five o'clock. He felt groggy and deflated and he was tempted to turn over and go back to sleep. Most of the villagers had no reason to rise so early on the Sabbath, but there were always odd ones who were up and about. He pulled on his clothes and on impulse he peeped into Fiona's room. Her soft even breathing told him she was still sound asleep. He sighed and crept downstairs and out of the front door. He did not see Beth as he walked swiftly across the quiet village street to his car. She was dressed for the milking and about to mount her bicycle. Her eyes and mouth rounded in surprise at the sight of Conan. She watched him start up his car and drive away, her mind full of speculations.

Twelve

Fiona felt her head was filled with sawdust. Or was it bricks? she wondered as she moved it on the pillow. Her eyes fell on her clothes draped over a nearby chair and she realized she was completely naked beneath the bedclothes, yet she had no recollection of getting undressed. She frowned as hazy memories began to stir: Conan opening the buttons down the back of her dress, Conan . . . ? She struggled to remember. What had she said? More importantly, what had she done . . . ? She clasped her hands to her burning cheeks in horror, but that did not prevent the wanton sensations haunting her subconscious. Sensations she had never experienced before, nor ever expected to feel. How could she ever face Conan Maxwell again?

It was early afternoon when Beth saw Fiona wandering aimlessly in her front garden. 'Hi, Fiona, how are you feeling after all the excitement?'

Was Beth regarding her more shrewdly than usual? Or was that just her imagination? She shook her head, and immediately wished she hadn't.

'Terrible! I'm not used to alcohol and I'm sure Nick filled up my glass at least twice for the toasts.'

'Aah, is that the way of it?' Beth chuckled. 'Well, Lucy is feeling flat and tired, and it's making her very cross. Polly Sedgeman left just after lunch and she's missing the company and excitement. I don't suppose you feel like taking her for a good long walk around the loch side? The fresh air and exercise would do you both good by the looks of it.'

117

'Yes, well, why not, if Lucy wants to go?'

'Can she stay with you until I get back from the afternoon milking when you return, or is that asking too much? I'd take her with me but the rest of the Sedgemans are staying at the farm and there's plenty without Lucy.'

Even to herself Beth didn't want to admit she preferred to keep her daughter away from Conan's Aunt Meg after her shrewd observations at the wedding. Then this morning Polly Sedgeman had been telling Lucy about her work as a teacher and answering her eager questions. She had smiled at her enthusiasm, then remarked how much Lucy reminded her of Conan when he was a boy. Strangers often saw things more clearly than those closest, Beth decided.

'Don't look so worried, Beth,' Fiona said gently, mistaking the cause of the older woman's anxiety. 'Lucy is never any bother. She's such a bright wee girl and I enjoy her company. We'll have tea together when we've been for a walk.' In fact she would welcome Lucy's company to distract her from her own thoughts, but she couldn't tell Beth that. Most of the folk in the village would be horrified if they knew Conan had stayed the night with her, albeit in separate rooms. She was not even certain if he had spent the whole night in a separate room. She suddenly felt hot all over.

It was the middle of the following week when Jordon Niven came into Fiona's office waving a letter and smiling broadly.

'Your letter, and my signature, have brought some results from the London auctioneers,' he grinned.

Fiona flushed warily. He had told her, rather irritably, to write the letter herself since she had insisted something ought to be done about Mrs Maxwell's missing vase. She suspected he thought it was a waste of time because they had no proof that the vase in the paper, or any other vase, had ever belonged to Mrs Rachel Maxwell. When he had read her letter he had raised his eyebrows and added his illegible signature without a quibble.

'You should have been a lawyer instead of an accountant. Succinct but diplomatic,' he had declared. 'You've just stopped short of accusation but there's enough facts presented to make them look into things, I'd say.'

She took the auctioneer's letter from him and read it twice.

'No wonder we never heard! In a way I'm so glad – not that Mr Murray is dead, I mean, but that he didn't let us down. Poor man. I really liked him and in my heart I couldn't believe he was a rogue dealer. Mrs Maxwell felt disillusioned too so I'm sure she'll be glad to know it's not his fault she hasn't had any replies to her letters.'

'It's a pity she didn't keep a copy of her letters. The dates might have helped.'

'I could always ask her if she did. She may have written them roughly first and then copied them off.'

'Yes, you do that then. Before you do so though, you might make a few enquiries about Mr Murray's family. Conan Maxwell and Mr Jones must have known his son quite well. They may have visited his family too. It is difficult to know whether Mr Murray's sister-in-law, what's her name?'

'Miss Pierce?'

'Yes, whether she is a cheat and a liar, or whether she genuinely believed Mr Murray owned the vase, but it does sound as though it could be the one Mrs Maxwell entrusted to him, and that it is the item which is up for sale. The problem will be proving that Mr Murray didn't buy it, of course.'

'Yes, I suppose so . . . There was nothing written down as far as I know. Mr Murray just mentioned it as part of the conversation. I was there. Apparently, the next morning Mrs Maxwell asked him to take it away but she didn't tell the family because she wanted it to be a surprise if the vase did prove valuable. As you know she planned to pay for the house at Wester Rullion herself. She did tell me she had packed the vase in a wooden box. She reckoned if it was strong enough to transport bottles of animal medicine

119

all the way from Lancashire it should keep her vase secure and protected too. She smiled when she told me because the box was stamped in black with the name of the veterinary manufacturers – Marginson's, I think, or was it Bell's . . . ? Anyway I wonder whether the auctioneers would keep the packaging?'

'I don't know. Do you want to phone London and see what you can find out? You're getting me quite interested in this little case, Fiona.'

'It's not a "little" case to the Maxwells. It could make such a huge difference to them if it is worth as much as Mr Murray predicted. Poor man, imagine breaking his hip and then dying of pneumonia.'

'He was very unfortunate. Doesn't he have a wife, or is she dead too?'

'I understood his wife is frail and often indisposed, though I got the impression Mr Murray felt his sister-in-law made her more of an invalid than she really was. They lost both of their sons during the war and he said his wife had never really got over it. Miss Pierce is her half-sister. She moved in with them, supposedly to care and comfort her, but I had a feeling there was not much love lost between her and Mr Murray. Of course I was only in his company for a day, but he was so knowledgeable and sometimes whilst reminiscing he gave things away.'

'And you are a good listener, Fiona, so he probably enjoyed your company. So, it is really Miss Pierce's word against Mrs Maxwell's.'

'Mmm, I suppose it is. Hey! Wait a minute! Surely Mr Murray must have kept some sort of accounts for his business. I mean a ledger or something? If Miss Pierce says he bought the vase there must be an entry to say how much he paid for it and the date?'

'There speaks the accountant!' Jordon smiled. 'I doubt if many small businessmen keep much in the way of accounts, although the government are beginning to tighten up on them since the war. I suppose it would be worth enquiring, especially if this should turn nasty.'

'Nasty?'

'It is surprising how far some people will go where money is concerned.'

'Mrs Maxwell is not like that! Not at all like that!'

'I was thinking more of Miss Pierce . . .'

'Oh.' Fiona's indignation subsided. 'I'm sorry. I suppose you mean Miss Pierce will claim Mr Murray bought the vase, so it is part of his estate for her sister, and herself, to enjoy? Which means we are back to examining his ledgers. I'd guess he was very methodical about such things. He knew exactly what items were worth and what it would cost for renovations and materials.'

'Well, don't get your hopes up too high. He may have kept the figures in his head, or on the back of a cigarette packet.'

'He didn't smoke.'

'You know what I mean.'

'Yes,' she sighed, 'and I can see you think it's a lost cause. Don't humour me, Jordon. I'm not a child . . .'

'Far from it! All right, all right, but I suggest you find out all you can about the family, and without delay. Ask Conan Maxwell about any conversations with Mr Murray's son which might give us a clue about them. Were they wealthy? Did they live beyond their means? Did they own their house?'

'They did. It sounded quite a large house too.'

'Well, you know the sort of things to ask. Now I'd better get on with some work to pay the rent,' he said dryly.

When he had gone Fiona considered his suggestions. She had to face Conan sometime and it would be better if she chose the time and place to suit herself. She had always confronted trouble head on, at least until her mother's illness and her death. She didn't think she would ever rid herself of the feelings of guilt her death had caused her. Facing up to

Conan was different and the sooner she made herself see him the better she would feel, or so she hoped.

Later that afternoon Fiona turned her car in the direction of the garage which now had an imposing sign: *Maxwell & Jones.*

She saw Conan as soon as she pulled into the forecourt. A lorry was just driving away and as far as she could see there was no one else around. She breathed a sigh of relief and lifted her head high. She willed herself not to blush at the sight of Conan. Her mouth was set and her grey eyes cool. She had dealt with unpleasant encounters during her work in Glasgow, but this was different. If only her heart would stop beating so fast. There was nothing to be afraid of. She had to keep calm, control her emotions.

At the sight of her car Conan's first reaction was surprise, but in the next instant his greeny-blue eyes sparkled. He wondered how much Miss Fiona Sinclair remembered of the night of the wedding and how far he would dare go with teasing her.

Fiona slid gracefully out of the car and smoothed down the skirt of her neat navy suit. She had taken particular care to present the image of the capable, aloof businesswoman. Clothes and grooming gave a woman confidence; she had learned that a long time ago. She willed Conan not to mention the night of the wedding. She lifted her chin, squared her slim shoulders and walked towards him, carrying a leather folder under her arm. Her hair was a smooth curtain on each side of her oval face, expertly cut to curve into her slender neck. She held herself erect and walked gracefully towards Conan.

'Mr Niven and I hope you may be able to help us with some business concerning Mr Murray,' she said briskly. 'It won't take long. Do you have time to answer a few questions now?' She met his eyes defiantly. She saw the sparkle of amusement and watched it turn to surprise, and then to anger.

'All the . . . ?' Bloody hell! Was this the same sexy, desirable woman he had almost gone to bed with? He looked back at the cool grey stare, the firm mouth. She could have been a stranger meeting him for the first time. He almost wished she was. His expression grew grim. Well if that's how she wanted it, he could be cold and distant too. But deep down he felt shaken, and . . . and what? Disappointed? Cheated? He gave his head a swift shake.

'Come into the office,' he said curtly. He wished he'd tidied up a bit. There was scarcely a place for her to sit, especially in her immaculate business suit.

'I suppose you know your mother entrusted Mr Murray with her vase, after he advised her of its possible value?'

'Vase?' Conan blinked, trying to concentrate on what she was saying.

'Yes, the vase she kept on the mantelshelf in the dining room. Did she tell you she had entrusted Mr Murray to take it to the London auctioneers to get an expert valuation, and possibly to sell it?' Fiona knew her tone was impatient but Conan was staring at her instead of concentrating on what she was saying, and he unnerved her.

'I didn't know, or if I knew I've forgotten. Does it matter?'

'Of course it matters, especially to your mother.' Fiona explained about Mr Murray's silence, his failure to answer her letters. 'Your mother was terribly hurt. We had begun to think he was trying to cheat her.'

'I'm sure he'd never do that! Mark's family were really decent people! All except his aunt anyway.'

'Aah!' Fiona said with satisfaction. 'Can you tell us anything about Miss Pierce?'

'Us? Who wants to know?' Conan demanded warily.

'Well,' Fiona sighed, then she spoke defiantly. 'You may think I'm interfering but I only wanted to help your mother to carry out her . . . her plans.'

'Plans? What plans?'

'Er, well if she didn't tell you what she intended to do, then I can't tell you either, but she did come to Mr Niven for advice and I was assisting him. So—'

'I see, so my mother trusted you before her own son? Her own flesh and blood! And you've made a mess of it! Now you're asking me to get you out of it! Well, you can—'

'No! You've got it all wrong. It's not like that!'

But Conan was glad to give vent to the anger boiling within him and he didn't care that he was jumping to wrong conclusions. He just wanted to shatter the cool composure of the young woman who could get under his skin as no other ever had.

'Not like what?' he sneered. 'The clever Miss Sinclair giving my mother bad advice and then coming whining to me to help find an excuse! Well I'm—'

'Shut up and listen!' Fiona snapped rudely. Conan's eyes widened. He opened his mouth but before he could speak Fiona said quietly, 'Mr Murray is dead.'

'Dead? Mark's father is dead?' Conan slumped against a cupboard.

'Yes, that must be the reason your mother received no replies to her letters. I'm going over to tell her when I leave you, but first we wanted to know about Mr Murray's family.' She drew out the newspaper cutting reporting the forthcoming sale of the vase in London. 'I saw this by chance. It looks like the same vase to me. Do you think it is? If so – and it seems it may be worth a lot of money, just as he said – would Mr Murray's family try to pretend he had bought it from your mother?'

'He had no family. Mark and Bobby were both killed during the war. His wife . . . Well, I'm not sure. I think she has been in and out of a mental hospital since Bobby's death.'

'Think back, please. For your mother's sake, not mine,' Fiona urged. 'Tell me anything you can remember. Were they likely to be in debt?'

'Oh no, I shouldn't think so. At least, not the Murrays, not then. Of course, I know it cost a lot of money each time Mrs Murray had to go into hospital because the government hadn't started this new free health policy then. Even so I got

124

the impression they were quite well off when I visited with Mark. They had a lovely big house in Derbyshire . . .' Conan had forgotten Fiona now. He frowned in concentration.

'Mark didn't have many relations but his mother had an older sister – half-sister anyway. Aunt Cynthia, but he used to call her Aunt Sinister. He spoke quite bitterly about her whenever he had been home on leave. He felt she didn't want his mother to come to terms with Bobby's death. She kept raking up everything about him and going on and on. I remember clearly after one leave Mark looked exhausted when he came back to camp. His mother was having treatment for her nerves. "My aunt would drive me up the bloody wall and over the top of it, if I had to put up with her every day," he said. The next time we had leave he came up to Lochandee instead of going home. He came several times after that. He couldn't understand why his father didn't tell his aunt to go home and leave his mother in peace. He said his mother felt sorry for her. His father felt she'd brought on her own troubles with her jealousy and spite.' Conan looked at Fiona. 'If Mr Murray is dead, then I suppose that means his wife is at the mercy of her sister now?'

'I don't know. We only know that Mr Murray was having the vase valued and now the auctioneers have received instructions to sell it. According to the newspaper report it is expected to fetch a record price, but the instructions to sell didn't come from your mother. Mr Niven . . .' Fiona faltered, her face colouring. 'Well he asked me to draft a letter asking for more details and querying the sale. He signed it,' she added defensively. 'I-I just hoped I could get some good news for your mother. It was her own decision to entrust the vase to Mr Murray. She only came to the office for advice afterwards . . .'

'I see . . .' Conan's mouth tightened. 'It seems you are more in my mother's confidence than I am anyway.'

Fiona bit her lip. She guessed he was hurt that his mother had not confided in him. She could only hope he would understand when Mrs Maxwell told him what she had hoped to achieve. Somehow she got the feeling he still held her responsible in some way. There was nothing she could do about that.

Conan watched moodily as she walked back to her car and drove away.

Thirteen

It was almost the end of their honeymoon and Nick and Bridie couldn't believe a whole week had flown so quickly. They lay in the big feather bed in the cottage by the sea. The curtains were open and the morning sun glinted on the white tipped waves which seemed to be dancing almost into the room as they watched, entranced by the continual movement of the ocean. The island of Ailsa Craig was visible in the clear morning light but at night it was hidden from sight and only the silver path of the moon stretched mysteriously to a realm of pure delight.

'There's pleased I am, managing to make you forget your animals for once,' Nick grinned as he looked down into his wife's dreamy eyes.

'I have barely given them a thought,' Bridie confessed. 'I'm so glad you arranged for us to have this time on our own, Nick. It's been absolute bliss.'

'No regrets is it then, bach, having to cook on your honeymoon? Wanted you to myself I did. Pampered in a posh hotel, you should have been.'

'No-o, I'm glad we came here. We've hardly done any cooking anyway with Mrs Bonnie leaving us a meal ready every evening. The hotel was a delightful experience but I felt so . . . so . . .'

'Newly married and shy, was it?' Nick chuckled. 'I guessed you might. Mind you, there's a wanton woman I'm having for a wife now, and only a week on our own together. No idea I had . . .'

'Och you!' Bridie aimed a fist at him. He caught it and opened her fingers one by one to place a kiss in her palm before he drew her into his arms. 'Are you regretting marrying me then?' she whispered against his lips. 'I could always go back to being the shy Miss Maxwell if you would prefer?' She looked up at him under her thick lashes and her eyes were bright with laughter.

'I wouldn't – and you couldn't. It's the love of my life you are now, Bridie.' Nick's voice was husky as he kicked the bedclothes to the side.

'Aren't you hungry?' she asked softly, knowing full well what his answer would be by now.

'Passionately. Eat you all up, shall I . . .' He grinned, pretending to nibble her smooth, warm skin, moving his lips until the rosy pink nipples hardened and he felt her quiver with a desire to match his own.

'Dear God, it's the luckiest man alive, I am,' he said hoarsely a while later. 'So shy you were, Bridie. Wondered, I did, whether I could be patient enough. There's feared I was of alarming you. So much I wanted you, so long . . . Life is more wonderful than I ever dared to dream.'

'I wanted you too, Nick,' Bridie said softly, 'but I was always a little . . . afraid. Mother was so emphatic about not making love before marriage. Even before I knew you, when I was quite young in fact, she warned me. It was as though . . . as though, oh I don't know. She seemed to believe it could only lead to unhappiness. Now I feel free, with nothing to fear, and I do love you so much . . .'

Nick kissed her gently.

'I wish we didn't have to return to the real world quite so soon,' he sighed. 'Will you mind very much if I've given you a baby, Bridie?'

'I'd love a baby, Nick. Well, your baby anyway,' she grinned provocatively.

'It had better not be anyone else's, Bridget Mhairi Jones! Seriously, Bridie, I wish our house had been ready for us to move into but it looks as though it may take a few weeks yet. The builder is way over the time he said.'

'It will soon pass, and at least I have a big bed to share with you at the Glens of Lochandee,' she teased.

'A-ah and there's the most important thing, eh?'

'When mother and father were first married they had to share the house with Aunt Alice Beattie, and Beth was a live-in maid then.'

'Yes, well I expect we shall survive for a little while, so long as that young brother of yours doesn't come barging in on us unannounced,' he said grinning.

'Gosh, I hadn't thought about Ewan.' Bridie blushed at such a prospect.

When they arrived back at the Glens of Lochandee Bridie was dismayed to see her father looking pale and haggard and she noticed he barely ate anything when Conan joined them for supper.

'Is Father unwell?' she asked her mother as they stood side by side washing and drying the dishes.

'He's complained of feeling sickly recently, even before the wedding. I couldn't persuade him to see Doctor MacEwan until yesterday. He has prescribed some stomach powders. He thinks it may be an ulcer.'

'Oh surely not! I've never known Father be ill before, I mean really ill.'

'No, he's always had a healthy constitution but he's not as young as he was when we bought the Glens of Lochandee, and—'

'But forty-seven isn't old, Mum, and Dad has always seemed so young and fit.'

'Yes, he has, hasn't he?' Rachel smiled. 'But I think he's worrying a bit. In a way the war helped us pay our debt to the bank when we bought the Glens. Prices held steady and there was a demand for everything we could produce. He's afraid there may be changes now the war is over, as there were after the First World War. There was no market for anything then, however hard people worked on the farms. That would be the end for all of us if we can't repay the money to the bank. Bill Carr's death was a blow too, and Harry Mason's death was a terrible shock. He was only the same age as your father. I expect it's the combined effect of everything that has upset his stomach.' She patted Bridie's shoulder. 'He's missed you too. He's realized how much responsibility you take for the dairy and the cows and he's not looking forward to you being away at Wester Rullion.'

'Oh, but I shall come back every day for the milking. Nick says he'll check over my bicycle and get a new tyre for it.' She grinned. 'Nothing will keep me away.'

'Maybe not,' Rachel murmured doubtfully. Looking into her daughter's radiant face she wondered how long it would be before she became a grandmother. She was not sure whether the idea appealed to her or not, but she did know that a baby would prevent Bridie cycling all the way from Wester Rullion every morning.

'Don't look so worried, Mother,' Bridie chided gently. 'As far as prices are concerned I can't see how the government can change their present policy while there is such a shortage of all the main foods we eat. There was so much devastation in other countries too, or so Conan and Nick say. I'm sure Dad will soon see things are going to be all right, especially when Frank and Emmie move back here at the end of November.'

'Yes, I expect you're right, dear,' Rachel said smiling back. 'It's so much easier to be optimistic when you're young and strong though.' She frowned. 'I hadn't meant to tell you this, Bridie, but I gave my vase to Mr Murray and asked him to sell it. I wanted to build the house at Wester Rullion so that your father and I could live there, with Ewan of course. I knew how much happier you would be if you could stay here, especially when you already own half of the land and the dairy herd. Besides, I thought it would be easier for your father, and better for Ewan too. He will inherit Wester Rullion one day, unless he changes his mind about wanting to be a farmer.'

'I don't think he'll ever do that! But Mum, what a pity you've sacrificed your vase. You didn't really believe it was worth enough to pay for a house, did you?'

'Mr Murray seemed fairly sure it was because it was an unusual shape and he said it bore the initials of the potter. He promised to get an expert's opinion, but I never heard from him again.'

'But even so . . .'

'Fiona has seen an article in one of the London newspapers about a vase. She said it looked like mine as far as she could tell. She believes Mr Murray was right. Someone else is claiming ownership of the vase in the sale though, and Fiona thinks they may be trying to cheat me out of it.'

'Oh surely not! It's not like Fiona to let her imagination run riot.'

'No, she's intelligent and shrewd and I trust her judgement implicitly but it seems Mr Murray has died. Fiona came to see me yesterday and she thinks that's the reason I've never heard from him. She suspects his sister-in-law may be claiming the vase, either as her own or as part of his estate. Her sister would be the beneficiary then, but she would benefit herself indirectly too.'

'How awful – I mean for Mr Murray to die so soon. Surely his sister-in-law would not be so mean and dishonest?'

'Well, we don't know for certain, and it will not be easy to prove it is my vase. I've no receipt or anything. I acted foolishly, I realize that now, but I thought I was doing the best thing for everyone and I did want to give you a surprise. Nick knew. That's why he agreed to build the house at Wester Rullion. Now I feel I have let him down too.'

'Nick knew? He never said!'

'It was to be a surprise for you.'

'And he agreed to live here at the Glens of Lochandee?'

'Yes, if I could afford to build the house at Wester Rullion.

131

I don't think he minds where he lives, just so long as he can be independent and have you to himself in his own home. He loves you very much.'

'Ye-es,' Bridie said softly. 'Yes, but I didn't realize just how much. I'm sorry you parted with your vase, Mum. I know how you treasured it, whether it was worth a lot of money or not.' She gave Rachel an impulsive hug. 'I shall do my best to see Father is not overworked or worried.'

Jordon Niven had discussed the story of the vase with his father and been astonished to find Jacob Niven was just as indignant as his attractive assistant, and just as keen to see Mrs Rachel Maxwell receive justice. Consequently he had applied to the auctioneers to have the proceeds from the sale withheld until the true owner could be established beyond doubt. The auctioneers had written to say this was not possible unless they were furnished with more proof.

Fiona decided to travel down to Derbyshire to see Miss Pierce and find out whether the woman was intentionally claiming the vase, or whether she had genuinely believed it was Mr Murray's. She felt partially responsible because it was on her account that Mr Murray had visited the Maxwells and she had benefited greatly from his advice. More galling, she knew Conan blamed her. She insisted on making the journey in her own time and at her own expense. Jordon Niven had just agreed, albeit with some doubts, when Nick came into the office in a rare state of anger.

Looking at him, Fiona realized for the first time that Nicholas Jones was not the placid, easy-going man she had first thought, in fact he was something of a sleeping tiger. Tall, slim hips, long-legged and with his dark wavy hair, she could see exactly how Bridie had been attracted to him, but as he stood towering over her desk, shoulders erect, his square jaw jutting, she knew he would make a formidable opponent. In his anger his Welsh accent was accentuated and the words tumbled forth in a torrent.

'You've had a quarrel with the builder? But why? What's happened?'

'Didn't expect me to turn up so near the end of the day, did he? There's loading cement and bricks on to a lorry they were, taking them away to another site! Another site,' he repeated through gritted teeth. 'My materials, for my house! Driving our own truck, I was. Thought I'd call at the farm on my way back to the garage. One of the labourers thought I'd come to collect some wood. "I'll load your boards in a minute, mate," he calls. Didn't know what he meant, did I? Asked a few questions, I did. There's Brady, the bast . . .' Nick bit his lip, his mouth white and tight with anger. Jordon Niven appeared at the communicating door but he did not interrupt Nick's tirade. 'Siphoning off the materials allocated for my house, he was. There's a thief and a cheat he is, and getting backhanders no doubt. Know now, don't I, why he kept telling me the bricks, or the wood, or the sand had never been delivered. Unsuitable! Or any old excuse to explain the delay. Told him to clear out, I have! Blustered and swore, he did, demanded money too, immediately! Compensation for breaking the contract, is it? Not from me. Needing some legal advice, I am. He—'

'Perhaps a warning from the police for reselling materials wouldn't be such a bad idea,' Jordon Niven said quietly, having listened to Nick's account. 'If they steal from your allocation they will do it with other people. As far as payment is concerned, you can make him wait a while. You did have an estimate?'

'Of course. On a strict budget, aren't I? Knew that, he did.'

'Get another builder then and deduct the cost of finishing the house from the original estimate. Then pay Brady the balance. He'll quibble of course, but if he's had a police warning he'll know you mean business and he'll not be keen to sue in case anything else comes to light. If there's any real trouble come back and see me. I'll handle Brady and his gang.'

'And where will I be finding another builder to take over? A joiner, too. Longer than ever it will be before Bridie and I can move into our own home now,' he groaned despairingly.

'Oh, I don't know,' Jordon reflected thoughtfully. 'I had a good young chap to repair my garage and a few other jobs. He works on his own but his brother is a joiner and I expect he could hire a labourer to speed things up. Shall I ask him to come and see you?'

'Thank you, if you would? Nothing to lose, have I? What is his name?'

'Billy Young,' Jordon answered, then he turned to Fiona. 'So you'll be away from tomorrow? You'll telephone and let me know how you get on?'

'Yes.'

'Going away, are you, Fiona?' Nick asked as Jordon left the office.

'Yes.' Fiona coloured faintly. 'I'm going down to Derby-shire to see what I can make of Miss Pierce. I-I've only just decided. The auctioneers will not withhold the proceeds from the sale of the vase without some sort of proof that Mrs Maxwell may be the owner. I haven't mentioned it to her yet because I don't want her to worry about the cost of pursuing it. I'm doing this in my own time. I feel a bit responsible, and I'm so angry. Mr Niven, Jordon's father, agrees with me. He thinks we must see Mrs Maxwell gets justice.'

'Yes,' Nick nodded slowly. 'I see how it is you feel. I don't suppose there's much hope when there's no written proof?'

He said much the same to Conan when he arrived back at the garage half an hour later and recounted the events of the day.

'You mean to tell me Fiona Sinclair is going all that way on her own, on behalf of my mother?'

'Well, yes . . .' Nick looked uncertainly at Conan, noting the pulse pounding in his square jaw, the eyes flashing green; sure signs of his displeasure. 'No need to be getting steamed up about it, boyo. Not charging your mother for her time, is she, or anything else. Truth is, Fiona doesn't want to worry her. Just wants to see justice done, doesn't she now. There's a rare female she is – attractive, intelligent, genuinely kind as well . . .'

'Aren't you a bit newly married to be admiring other women?' Conan asked irritably.

'There's all of those things, Bridie is, and more besides.' Nick grinned, relaxing a bit after his earlier fury. 'Just wishing I could be having her to myself, I am. I like your family very much old boy, but I'm wishing they were anywhere but in the same house as us. Bridie . . . well she gets so inhibited. Cramps my style a bit, I confess, when there's young Ewan eyeing my every move.'

'Aye, I can imagine,' Conan said nodding his agreement, but his expression told Nick his mind was still on Fiona Sinclair and her proposed trip.

As soon as Nick had left, Conan went into the flat and grabbed himself a sandwich and had a quick wash and change of clothes. Smoothing down his damp hair he set off to see Fiona Sinclair.

He had reckoned without Fiona's stubborn determination to do things her way. She was surprised to see him standing on her front-door step and she could not suppress a faint colour rising into her cheeks. It was the first time he had called at her house since the night of the wedding. He came straight to the point, unwilling to admit that the memory of that evening had come flooding back when he saw her in her own surroundings once more. It made him more grim than ever.

'Nick tells me you're setting yourself up as a private investigator . . .'

'I am not doing any such thing!' Fiona's cheeks coloured hotly now, but with anger rather than embarrassment. 'We need proof that the vase belongs to your mother, or at the very least we need to prove there is some doubt as to the rightful owner. I can't just sit back and let someone else claim it and I know your mother is worried about running up legal fees, or seeking publicity. I understand that, so just let me do things my way.'

'And what if this woman turns out to be really nasty? Or worse. Mark was always on edge and uneasy about her.'

'Och, don't be silly. She may be acting in good faith, or at worst she may prove to be a greedy and malicious person, but that will not harm me.'

'You can't be certain about that. I'm coming with you. Nick says you were planning to travel down by train tomorrow. Well you can forget about that. We'll go by car but I can't pick you up before eleven. There's a few arrangements I have to make before I go.' He did not wait for Fiona to agree or disagree with his plans. He simply turned on his heel and left her staring after him.

'Well!' she gasped as the door shut firmly behind him. 'Well!' She sagged against the door. Seconds later she stood erect, her small chin raised defiantly. No one told her what to do, least of all Conan Maxwell. She would go on an earlier train. In fact she would go tonight if she could get a connection. She could go part of the way at least and be gone from Lochandee long before Conan came back.

Fourteen

C onan arrived at Fiona's house an hour earlier than he had stated, so he was surprised to find the door locked. Further up the street he saw Carol weeding in her immaculate little garden and further down the street there were several of the villagers chatting at the door of the grocery store, as well as three men at the smiddy. He frowned, feeling conspicuous in his best suit. He turned the car and drove slowly up to Carol's garden gate.

'Have you seen Fiona this morning, Carol?'

'No, sorry. Oh! Come to think of it she called in at Beth's when I was there last night. She was on her way to catch a train, I think. Beth said she wouldn't be back for a few days. Shall I give her a message when I see her again?' She eyed Conan's smart figure, his long legs and narrow hips. His dark suit made him seem taller, his shoulders broader, and he stood so erect. Carol had never looked at another man since her husband died, but just for a moment Conan's handsome figure stirred emotions she had believed quite dead. But when her gaze travelled upwards she saw the cold anger in his eyes.

'I-I . . . Was Fiona expecting you?' she faltered.

'Apparently not!' He drove away furious with himself and with Fiona Sinclair. If she left last night there was certainly no point in his driving all the way to Derbyshire on his own. He would not admit to his feelings of frustration and when he returned to the garage he found it difficult to be civil to Nick's grinning banter.

'And if you give one more of those smug . . . satisfied nods, I'll . . . I'll . . .'

'Give me a black eye, boyo?' Nick's grin widened. 'And you think I'll stand here and let you. Come on, Conan, admit it! The first time in your life, it is, you've met your match with Miss Fiona Sinclair. A mind of her own she has. Capable too, and every bit as intelligent as you are. What's more, she's all woman!'

'She's a bossy, interfering, stubborn female!'

'My, my, got under your skin, she has,' Nick chuckled gleefully and ducked back under the lorry he was working on, leaving Conan to mumble angrily on his way to the flat to change into his working clothes.

Fiona had arrived late in the evening at Sheffield and stayed there overnight, but by ten o' clock the following morning she had made her way to the little Derbyshire town and Mr Murray's address. She realized at once it was not a house belonging to an impoverished family. It was an imposing detached villa built in the local grey stone of the Derbyshire peaks. It had a wide drive and a well-kept garden. She glimpsed out houses to one side and guessed there must be a garden to the back of the house as well. She waited until the door was opened by a cherubic-looking little woman, then she dismissed the taxi driver, telling him she would welcome the short walk back into town after she had concluded her business.

On closer scrutiny Fiona wondered whether the woman's red eyes were due to a bout of weeping or whether she had a very bad cold. She explained that Mr Murray had undertaken some business while in Scotland. Letters to him had remained unanswered and she had travelled down after learning of his death.

'It'll be Miss Pierce you'll need to see, Miss . . . She . . . she's taken charge now.' The woman gave a hiccuping sniff and Fiona realized she was indeed distressed.

'Perhaps I've come at a bad time?' she said gently. 'It's just that my business is rather urgent. Can you tell me where I could find Miss Pierce, please?'

'Her lives here now. Her taken over . . . ev-everything.' There was more of a muffled sob this time. Fiona wondered why she was so upset. 'She's gone sh-shopping.'

'I see.' Fiona bit her lip. Under normal circumstances she would never have come all this way without making an appointment but her intuition had told her that an element of surprise might be beneficial if someone was trying to cheat Mrs Maxwell out of her vase. 'You can come in and wait if you like, Miss. Mr Murray . . . He n-never turned anybody away without a glass of sherry or a cup of tea . . .' She wiped the back of her hand across her eyes.

'Well, if you're sure it will be all right, I'd prefer to wait. And a cup of tea would be really welcome, but only if you'll join me. If you don't mind me saying so, you seem rather upset and my mother always believed a cup of tea soothed a troubled spirit.'

The woman's expression lightened for a moment, and she indicated Fiona should step into the sunny porch with its Italian mosaic floor. A large green plant stood on a porcelain pedestal in one corner. She opened a heavy door with two beautiful stained glass panes and Fiona followed her into a wide hall. She glanced around with interest. There were three polished oak doors on either side and a short flight of stairs at the far end. A beautiful brass-faced grandfather clock ticked away the minutes and beside it was an elaborately carved oak settle which even Fiona recognized as extremely old, and probably valuable.

The woman would have shown her into a large sitting room but she said quickly, 'I wouldn't feel I was being such a nuisance if I could join you in your kitchen? I don't want to keep you back if you have work to do.'

'Work . . .' The woman's voice broke on the word and she busied herself with boiling the kettle on a large anthracite stove which seemed to take up almost one wall of the large sunny kitchen. 'We'll have no work soon, no h-home either, if . . . if she has her way.'

'Have you worked for Mr Murray a long time?'

'Aye. I started here when I was thirteen, working to old Mistress Murray.' Her eyes took on a sad, far away look. 'There were three maids then, well two and Cook, but we didn't have 'lectric things like the washer. It's marvellous.'

'And you stayed on after you were married?' Fiona prompted, noting the plain gold band on the work-roughened hand.

'Aye. My George was gardener's boy, then second gardener. Now there's only the two of us . . .' She bit back a sob. 'And we'll soon be gone. We would have understood if Mr Murray had sold the house, after his lads were k-killed in the war, and Mrs Murray being taken poorly and everything. "No, no," says he. "We shall never leave this house. It has been in my family for three generations. Besides, Bunty . . ." He always called George by his surname because he liked it better. "Besides, Bunty," he says, "you and Martha have been here all your lives and I promise you will have your home in the cottage as long as you live." There it is, Miss, down at the bottom, through the trees.' She drew Fiona to look through one of the heavy sash windows, while she poured their tea and set out home-made scones and a fruit cake.

'Goodness! The garden is huge.' Fiona was surprised. Almost screened by trees and shrubs at the far end, she could just see the roof and chimney of a small stone cottage.

'Aye, it's big, but George doesn't grow as much as he used to do when the lads were here, and the other maids lived in. Our little patch opens on to the back lane . . .' Suddenly, as though overcome, she sank on to a kitchen chair and began to weep, striving for control, but unable to stifle the sobs.

'Oh, Mrs Bunty! Whatever is the matter? Have I . . . I mean would you like me to leave . . . ?'

'Oh no, Miss, no! I'm that s-sorry, an' and I shouldn't be bothering you with my troubles.'

'Sometimes it helps to talk about your worries,' Fiona said uncertainly.

'She . . . she only told me j-just before you c-came. She says she's going to sell everything. This house, and our cottage, and all Mr Murray's lovely things . . .' She tried to stem the tears and fished frantically in her apron pocket for her handkerchief.

'Do you mean Miss Pierce?' Fiona asked, her grey eyes widening.

'Aye.'

'But surely she can't do that? I mean, doesn't it all belong to Mrs Murray now?'

'Aye, it should do, but she's always been jealous o' the mistress, and her such a kindly soul. Whenever Miss Pierce came to stay she made Mrs Murray ill. It was bad enough when the lads first went to war but she's been terrible since they were killed. She never let any of us forget. On and on she went. Mr Murray was glad to go away on his business when she came. Ranted on something awful she did. She kept telling Mrs Murray that Bobby and Mark had murdered innocent children with their bombs. Never a minute's peace from her. She said that's why they had to die. It was only what they deserved. There's no wonder my poor mistress has nearly gone off her head.'

'Surely no one would be so cruel! I thought Mrs Murray and Miss Pierce were related?'

''Tis true, Miss. Same mother, different fathers. I tried to tell her she was upsetting her own sister. She said I was nothing but an ignorant servant and I should keep my mouth shut. "Martha is more than a servant, Cynthia," Mrs Murray told her. "She's been my friend here since I married. She loved my boys like her own." I did that, Miss. George and me, we were never blessed with children. We loved Bobby and Mark . . .' Her voice trembled.

'I'm so sorry, Mrs Bunty.' Fiona leaned forward and patted her arm. 'Mark stayed several times with friends of mine in Scotland.'

'With Master Conan? You know Conan?' Martha Bunty's eyes brightened and Fiona felt a pang of regret. Perhaps she should have allowed Conan to accompany her after all. 'He stayed here once or twice with Mark, and another friend called Nicholas.'

'Nick! You knew Nick too? He's married to Conan's sister now. Bridie is a very good friend to me.'

'Aah! I'm ever so glad to hear that. I'm pleased some of our brave young men came home safely.' She trembled visibly, indeed it was more of a shudder. 'I shouldn't be talking so much, and you a stranger, Miss, b-but you just arrived when I was upset, and now I don't feel you're a stranger no more . . .'

'I know what you mean,' Fiona said softly. 'It was through Conan Maxwell that I met Mr Murray. My mother died some months ago and Mr Murray advised me about her furniture and other items. He was very kind and understanding. He . . . er, he was going to sell a vase for Conan's mother. Do you know anything about a vase, or Mr Murray's work . . . ?' Fiona felt like a traitor taking advantage to pry.

'Mr Murray kept most of his work in the old stables. They're next to the garage at the side of the house. He always kept it locked up. She has the keys now.' She frowned thoughtfully. 'I remember Mr Murray had something in a wooden box when he came back from his journey up north though. He invited a man to see it. I know that because they came into the house afterwards and I took them a tray of coffee. They were laughing because it said "cattle drenches" in black letters on the sides of the box and he said he'd never imagined such a box of cattle drenches could contain anything so valuable. Mr Murray said he was pleased to have his opinion because he was an expert on such things. The man said it would be well worth the trouble of taking it to London.

When I'd set out the cups and poured the coffee I left them. Miss Pierce was standing right outside the door and I nearly bumped into her. She glared at me and told me to get back to the kitchen, but she didn't go in to join them. She just stood there, listening I expect. Mr and Mrs Murray never spoke to me like she does,' she said with another hiccuping sob.

'They were probably discussing Mrs Maxwell's vase then,' Fiona said slowly. 'It was packed in a wooden box like that to keep it safe. Do you know who he was – this man?'

'No, Miss. I'd never seen him before. I know he worked for auctioneers in London and he was going to America to see a . . . a client.'

'I see. Then I must speak to Miss Pierce. You see the vase belongs to Mrs Maxwell and it is quite valuable. Mr Murray was only taking advice on her behalf, as a favour. He offered because she had been kind to Mark, I think. But somehow there has been a mistake. It is in the hands of auctioneers in London now and they are going to sell it but they don't believe Mrs Maxwell is the rightful owner.'

'Can't you just tell them they've made a mistake, Miss?'

'I'm afraid not,' Fiona gave the little woman a rueful smile. 'Apparently it could be worth hundreds of pounds so they want proof of ownership. They probably think Mrs Maxwell sold it to the person who sent it to them. I believe that must have been Miss Pierce. If Mr Murray had sent it himself he would have made sure it was in Mrs Maxwell's name, I'm sure he would. I'm hoping Miss Pierce will tell them the truth when I explain. Do you know whether she is an executor – the person who has taken charge of Mr Murray's affairs since his death?'

'I don't know about 'secutors, Miss, but she says everything is in her hands now and that's why we've to leave.' Mrs Bunty's eyes filled with tears again. 'I know the solicitor told Mrs Murray everything belonged to her now and he would help her make any decisions. When Miss Pierce heard him she screamed at him and said he hadn't carried out the instructions her brother-in-law had sent from the hospital and she was going to . . . to sue him.'

'Did he know Mr and Mrs Murray?'

'Oh yes. They were friends. He often came to dinner when Mrs Murray was well.'

'So what did he do? I mean when Miss Pierce shouted at him?'

'He walked out. She kept shouting that her sister was insane and couldn't make decisions. He said she was the one who was . . . was un . . . balanced? When he'd gone she kept muttering, "I'll show you, I'll show you, you pompous oaf. Nobody will ignore me in future." She had a sort of wild gleam in her eyes. The very next day she got the police here. She said Mrs Murray had attacked her with a knife – here, in this very kitchen. I know she didn't. She wouldn't. She couldn't. She's as gentle as a lamb. She was sitting at the table, at that end. She was chopping vegetables for some soup. She liked to do little jobs in the kitchen. Sometimes she asked what Bunty and me were doing. Sometimes we talked about the lads and the happy times . . .' Her chin wobbled and she wiped away a tear with the corner of her apron. 'You know, Miss, about when they were young and the house was full of laughter . . . Then, Miss Pierce came in. I turned my back to them and got on with peeling the potatoes at the sink there. The next thing I knows she's screaming like a stuck pig and there's blood running down her hand. She grabbed a towel and phoned for the police. They took away my poor mistress.'

'But surely Mrs Murray denied it?'

'She fainted. She never did like the sight of blood. Miss Pierce shoved me out of the kitchen into the garden. She ordered me to go home and stay there until she sent for me. George saw the policemen bundling Mrs Murray into a sort of black van and she was crying. He tried to talk to her but the policemen barred his way.'

'That's terrible!' Fiona said, her eyes wide and incredulous.

Mrs Bunty looked at her, then lowered her eyes. She began to speak, then stopped. Her hands were twisting knots in her neatly pressed apron but she seemed unaware of what she was doing. As though making up her mind she leaned forward and lowered her voice.

'She's wicked. We, Bunty and me, we think it was her fault Mr Murray took pneumonia. That's what killed him. Shock, and lying all night on the cold floor, the doctor said. He had fallen on a big patch of grease outside his workshop. He often worked in the evenings. He was on his way back into the house for the night. We . . . we went to see him in hospital – George and me. She doesn't know. She told us we weren't allowed to visit. We . . . we just wanted to see him, Miss . . .'

'I understand. It was natural. You've known him a long time.'

'Yes, we have that. He could scarce get breath though, but his eyes lit up when we went in, Miss. He was pleased, I know he was . . .'

'I'm sure he would be pleased to see you both,' Fiona said gently.

'Aye, that's when he . . . he told us how she – Miss Pierce – found him after he called out for help. She dragged him along the path. Then she left him. All night!'

'Oh surely not. He must have been confused . . .'

Mrs Bunty shook her head vigorously. 'He said the grease was right outside his workroom door, just like a skating rink. He didn't know how it came to be there. He knew he had broken a bone. He said he heard a crack and felt an awful pain. Miss Pierce heard him shouting for help, he said. He pleaded with her to get George, and phone the doctor. He said she never spoke . . . just kept on dragging him along the path. Then she left him. Outside the door, Miss! All night on the hard cold pathway.'

'Surely he must have got confused . . .'

'Well, I found him there next morning when I came up to

do the fires and cook breakfast. He . . . he was in terrible pain. He kept going unconscious.'

'But where was Miss Pierce then?'

'Upstairs in her room. So was Mrs Murray, but she'd had a sleeping pill. She'd been keeping ever so well until Miss Pierce came back and said she was moving in permanently. To take care of her poor sister, she said.' Martha Bunty gave a contemptuous snort. 'Mr Murray said he would see about that. Anyway, Miss Pierce said neither of them had heard Mr Murray if he did shout for help. That was her story.'

'Who did you believe?'

'Oh, Mr Murray, of course. He knew he was very ill, but his mind was clear. The nurse wanted to send us away but he said we must stay until he'd finished, even if it took him all night. L-looking back I-I th-think he knew he was going to d-die and we'd never see him no more.' Tears filled her eyes again, but Fiona could only pat her shoulder in silent sympathy, as she remembered the sprightly gentleman that Mr Murray had been.

'He . . . he made us promise to look after Mrs Murray – my Hannah, he called her. I-we didn't tell him that Miss Pierce had shut her in the little room halfway up the stairs and wouldn't let us see her. She wouldn't let anybody see her, not even the vicar when he came to call. All smiles and sympathy she was, with him, but she gave my poor mistress nothing but bread and a drop of milk. She made her use one of them chamber pots fixed under a chair.'

'A commode,' Fiona said automatically

'I think that's what she called it.'

'Didn't Mr Murray wonder why his wife had not been to see him?'

'Miss Pierce told the nurses the shock had upset her and she wouldn't come out of her room. I-I didn't like to tell him the truth, poor man. What could he have done?'

If even half of Mrs Bunty's tales were true Fiona decided Miss Pierce was not a pleasant person to know, and certainly not someone to trust.

'Can you tell me where Mrs Murray is? Do you think she would see me?'

'Oh Miss! You can't go there! She's in the asylum!' Mrs Bunty's voice was hushed with shock.

'Do you have the address? Could you write it down for me?' Fiona took a notebook from her bag and handed her a pencil. The old woman wrote slowly and carefully and passed the notebook back to Fiona.

'Do you know the name of Mrs Murray's solicitor? Does he know she is in the asylum?'

'I don't think Miss Pierce would tell him. She doesn't like Mr Wainwright. Will you tell him, Miss? Will he bring her home?' she asked hopefully.

'He may do. But first I must speak to Miss Pierce. Do you think she will be much longer?'

'It's hard to tell, Miss. I've made some soup. There's plenty but she's not one to offer hospitality, not like Mr and Mrs Murray. Would you like a bowl now and a slice of new bread?'

Fiona accepted gratefully, suddenly realizing how hungry she was and how the time had flown.

'Does your husband come in for lunch?'

'He used to do. We had all our meals here, in this very kitchen. Now he has to have it at home – on his own.' Mrs Bunty frowned. 'Mrs Murray wouldn't like that. Once, when the doctor had given her some new medicine, she talked and talked. She told me her mother belonged to a wealthy family and they sent her to a school in Switzerland to finish her education. While she was there one of the German masters he . . . he . . . well, you know, Miss . . . against her will . . . She was only seventeen when Cynthia, that's Miss Pierce, was born. It was a terrible disgrace to the family. They'd sent her to a little cottage in the hills with an old servant.

When the servant died she stayed there on her own with the child. One day a gentleman came walking by and stopped to ask for refreshment because it was so hot and he had lost his way. He began to visit regularly. They married and they had a little girl. That was my mistress. She said Cynthia was ten years old by then but she was always jealous. She shook her head and said it was sad and Miss Pierce was to be pitied rather than blamed. She was such a gentle soul herself. She said Cynthia must have taken after her father because their mother was a sweet, kind person. Then, I remember ever so clearly, she grabbed my hand. She said . . .' Mrs Bunty stifled a sob. 'She said she hoped I'd always be there to help her against her sister's jealousy. She said it was like a poison . . . I think it was the medicine made her talk, Miss, but I'm sure it was what was in her heart.'

'I see . . .' Fiona felt she should not have listened to Mrs Bunty's tales but she needed to find out all she could about Miss Pierce. She shivered and wished she had waited for Conan Maxwell to accompany her after all. The woman sounded either unscrupulous or, as the solicitor had said, unbalanced. Even so, she was glad she had come in person. She understood why there had been no reply to their letters now.

'That was delicious, Mrs Bunty,' she said laying aside her soup spoon. The old woman smiled and was just about to warm the teapot for a cup of tea when they heard a cab drawing up at the front door. Swift as lightening Mrs Bunty grabbed the empty soup plate and stuffed it in a cupboard, whisking away the side plate and bread-crumbs an instant later. She smoothed her apron nervously and moved out into the hall to greet Miss Pierce.

'Y-you have a visitor, Ma'am.'

'I do not wish to see anyone. Get rid of—'

Fiona had moved to the door behind Mrs Bunty and now she stepped forward, holding out her hand. The woman was even taller than herself, erect and with iron-grey hair drawn back in a tight bun which emphasized her angular features. She was intimidating to say the least.

'My name is Miss Sinclair,' Fiona said politely. 'I was a client of Mr—'

'What are you doing in my house? How dare you . . . ?' She turned on Mrs Bunty and for a moment Fiona thought she was going to strike the old woman. Mrs Bunty clearly thought so too, judging by the way she cowered back against the wall.

'I asked your housekeeper for a glass of water,' Fiona said quickly. 'I have come a long distance and—'

'You have no business in my house.' She moved as though to open the door but Fiona stepped in front of her.

'I came to see Mrs Murray. I am from Scotland and I am here on behalf of Messrs Jacob Niven & Son, the solicitors representing a client of the late Mr Murray.' Fiona's voice was cool now, her manner formal as she drew herself to her full height, head high, her slim shoulders erect. She felt an instinctive distrust of the woman who was staring at her with pale hard eyes. She had to summon all her will-power not to shiver visibly. She could well imagine how overwhelming Miss Pierce would be to a person as gentle and nervous as Mrs Murray was reputed to be.

'Your client sold the vase. It is too late to claim it back now it has proved valuable. Good day to you.' Again she made a move towards the door.

'A-ah . . . Did I mention I was here about a vase?'

The pale grey eyes glittered with fury as Cynthia Pierce stared back at her. Her thin lips opened and shut twice before any sound came. The narrow features turned an ugly shade of purple, then paled alarmingly.

'You had better come with me. We shall discuss your business in private.'

She began to lead the way towards the wide staircase. Fiona caught the look of alarm in Mrs Bunty's eyes. She remembered the small room halfway up the stairs where

Mrs Murray was supposed to have been held a prisoner in her own home.

'I can listen to your explanation perfectly well here, thank you,' Fiona said firmly. 'All I require is—'

'I don't discuss business in front of servants.' Her icy stare sent Mrs Bunty scurrying back to the kitchen. Miss Pierce's thin mouth tightened even further as her eyes rested on Fiona. She willed herself not to flinch at the sight of such cold hatred.

Fifteen

Fiona remembered she had promised to telephone Jordon Niven to tell him whether she was travelling on to London to oversee the sale of the vase on Mrs Maxwell's behalf, and also to give him an update on her meeting with Miss Pierce. He had suspected the woman would be obstinate, even angry, but neither of them had expected she would be quite so brazen, and certainly not so formidable.

The next afternoon the vase would be sold in London but the proceeds would not be paid to Mrs Maxwell unless she could furnish proof to the auctioneers that she was the true owner. There was no time to waste, but she felt she had Miss Pierce's measure now. Again she wished Conan had been with her, though she knew her pride would never allow her to admit it to his face.

Suddenly she remembered what Mrs Bunty had told her about Mr Murray's death and her belief that Miss Pierce was the cause of it. Now that she had met Miss Pierce she had no reason to doubt anything the distressed little housekeeper had told her, and if she could use her knowledge to persuade Miss Pierce into telling the truth . . . ? One way or another she must – not only for Mrs Maxwell's sake, but also for Mr Murray's. She owed him that. He might still be alive if he had not come to Scotland to value her own inheritance.

Her eyes hardened and she squared her shoulders as she recalled the polite gentle man Mr Murray had been. He had not deserved to die. Had Miss Pierce stooped so far as to spread the grease outside the door of his workroom? Had she

151

intended him to fall? Fiona bit her lip, unable to comprehend such a vile motive. And yet . . .

'Miss Pierce,' she began, enunciating each word clearly and with precision. 'We both know Mr Murray brought Mrs Maxwell's vase here to get an expert valuation for her, and to arrange the sale. He was doing it for a friend. He appreciated the way she had welcomed his son—'

'His son!' Miss Pierce spat. 'Young murderer! That's what he was.'

'No! He gave his life for his country. Many fine young men gave their lives, on both sides. They did what they were asked to do.'

'They were murderers, I say. Spoiled brats, just like their mother. She had everything she wanted, everything, do you hear me! Her father doted on her. *My* mother doted on her. And what of me, her firstborn child? Forgotten, set aside! The elder sister, the ugly one, the unwanted one. What did they care about me!' She snapped her fingers in a loud click. 'Nothing! Well, we shall see who is best in the end. I'm in control now. I shall make the decisions. Do you hear me?' She stepped alarmingly close to Fiona and it was only with a supreme effort that she stood her ground and stared back into the contorted features of the bitter twisted woman.

'All this has nothing to do with my client's vase. You leave me no option but to go to Mr Murray's solicitor and tell him you have made false claims on property which had been entrusted to his client.'

'Wainwright knows nothing about the vase. I heard Murray and his colleague discussing it. Rare and valuable, they said. Now he's dead and the dead can't speak. Who was to tell whether he bought it or borrowed it or who it belonged to? It's mine, I tell you. I mean to have the money from the sale of it. Something of my own. I'm sick of depending on charity. Sick of it, do you hear?' Her voice rose in a frightening frenzy. 'Now get out of my house!'

Her eyes glittered insanely and Fiona shuddered. Everything told her the woman was unbalanced, obsessed by past wrongs – real or imaginary. She was the one who needed help, probably more than her sister.

Outwardly Fiona assumed a calm she did not feel. Her voice cool and clipped.

'You are being dishonest about the ownership of the vase, Miss Pierce. It makes me suspect you may have been deceitful in other ways. Perhaps you have many secrets to hide? You leave me no option but to ask Mr Murray's solicitor, Mr Wainwright, to look into the ownership of the vase, and if necessary have the police investigate the circumstances surrounding Mr Murray's death.'

Immediately she knew she had found the chink in Miss Pierce's armour. The tall woman stared at her like a mesmerized rabbit, then slowly she seemed to shrink before her eyes. She sank down on to a hard hall chair. Her angular features crumpled and she bowed her head in a gesture of defeat.

'He had so many beautiful things,' she muttered hoarsely. 'But the vase . . . I knew it was not part of his estate. They said it was rare. They s-said . . .' She looked up at Fiona and gave a wave of her hand. 'Don't you see? All I wanted was a little money of my own – some independence at last . . .' The erect figure sagged and her head drooped again.

Fiona felt a stir of compassion. Then she remembered the distress of Mrs Bunty, and her account of Mrs Murray, supposedly banished to an asylum. No doubt that had been easily accomplished given the poor woman's record of depression since the death of her sons. Miss Pierce had been ruthless.

'Your sister did not harm you, did she? You harmed yourself and then had her sent to an asylum, didn't you? You wanted control of her and everything that was here.' Fiona gestured at the house.

'How do you know that?' The grey head shot up, the pale eyes were wide and fearful now. It had been no more than a wild guess but Fiona knew she was right.

'Your sister does not deserve to be locked away. She is no danger to anyone, is she?'

'She does, she does!' Miss Pierce almost screamed and Fiona recognized the rising hysteria and shivered. 'She's always needing the doctor. Hundreds of pounds he paid to get her the best treatment. Nerves they said – since she lost her sons. He said I made her worse. I made her suffer. Suffer?' Her voice rose higher. Her pale eyes were wild and glaring. 'She's never known what it is to suffer. She deserves to be locked up. Out of my sight. She took my place. She stole my mother, I tell you. She had everything! E-everything . . .' Suddenly the large boned frame began to shake and harsh gasps were torn from her. Fiona bit her lip, half afraid to touch her, yet unable to stand aside. Out of the corner of her eye she saw Mrs Bunty peering fearfully round the kitchen door.

'Telephone the doctor, please,' she said quietly. She was thankful Miss Pierce didn't seem to hear. It was painful to see the breakdown of such a strong and forceful character, yet underneath the hard exterior Fiona sensed there was a lost and vulnerable child, who had grown into a bitter, unwanted woman.

As Fiona alighted from the train at Lockerbie she resolved to keep the details of her experience to herself. She knew Conan would be more convinced than ever that she should have waited for him, and in her heart she knew he was right. She had reckoned without Mrs Bunty's gratitude, volubly expressed to Mr Wainwright, the Murrays' solicitor. He in turn relayed the housekeeper's account to Jordon Niven, along with his own appreciation of the way she had handled Miss Pierce so successfully when both he and Mr Murray had failed to accept her unbalanced state, even less to do anything about it. He assured them that Mrs Maxwell would receive the proceeds from the sale of her vase in due course, but it would take a little time for the correct details to be sorted out.

Fiona found she was regarded as something of a heroine by Mrs Maxwell after Jordon Niven had paid her a visit in person.

'You seem to know such a lot, and how to do so many things,' Beth told her admiringly. 'Mrs Maxwell is ever so grateful to you. Now I would like to ask you a really big favour, Fiona, but I promise we'll still be friends if you refuse.'

'Ask away.' Fiona smiled, but she was surprised and a little shocked when Beth finally voiced her request.

'It would be such a relief if I knew someone like you would be Lucy's guardian if anything happened to me,' Beth said earnestly. 'I'm so afraid of her being left all alone in the world now that Harry's gone. You're so wise about things, Fiona. I haven't much money but I know Lucy would listen to your advice, especially about education and work.'

'Oh Beth, Lucy will always have you to guide her,' Fiona said warmly. 'You'll probably see Lucy's children grown up and going to college.' She had meant to be reassuring but to her dismay Beth looked ready to burst into tears.

'Every night I pray I shall be spared to see Lucy grow to be a woman and independent. That's all I ask,' she said fervently. 'I can't afford to send her to college to be a teacher as Harry hoped, but surely . . .'

'Don't worry about it, Beth. Lucy is a bright child and there are scholarships, you know. I promise when the time comes I will help you find out all I can about what is available and between us we'll find a way for Lucy to do whatever she decides.'

'Aah, Fiona . . . you dinna ken what a relief it is to hear you say that. S-sometimes I feel so alone without Harry.' Her voice broke and this time the tears would not be denied.

'Oh Beth, I know how much you miss him, but please don't worry. You're not alone.' Fiona put a comforting arm around her shoulders and drew her into the kitchen. 'I'll make us a cup of tea. And just remember, I'm honoured that you have such faith in me. I hope I can live up to your expectations.'

'Even if you couldn't, I know you'd do your best. Mrs Maxwell says you are both clever and kind, and totally unspoiled. Were you very lonely being an only child, Fiona? I'd have loved Lucy to have brothers and sisters.' She sighed. 'It just never happened for Harry and me.'

A little while later as she sipped her tea, she said, 'Aren't there things you've got to do to make sure you are Lucy's guardian? Papers, I mean?'

'You want to make it official, Beth?'

'Yes, if you're willing. Not that I think my half-sister or brother would want anything to do with her, especially when there's no money in it for them,' she added bitterly. 'Anyway, we never see them. But I'd feel happier if it was all legal like. Could you – would you see to it?' she asked anxiously.

'Of course I will, if you're sure that's what you want. And you can always change your mind later. I'll ask Mr Niven about it.'

'Will it cost much?'

'It will not cost you anything, Beth, so don't worry, and don't even think of anything happening to you either.'

She was rewarded with a wan smile and as Fiona lay in bed that night she pondered on Beth's request. It was not like her to worry about her own health. She was as strong as a horse and she had worked hard all her life. Yet Fiona had an uneasy feeling that Beth had her own reasons for providing a guardian for Lucy. It was a wise precaution she supposed, and wondered whether her parents had worried about her being an only child. Again she felt the pangs of guilt as she remembered the time she had spent away from home. Yet her mother had never complained, never criticized. Fiona fell asleep vowing to do her best to help Lucy and Beth in any way she could.

Sixteen

Rachel was overwhelmed by the trouble Fiona had taken over her vase, but when she heard she was to receive a cheque for nineteen hundred pounds she sank on to a chair in disbelief.

Never in her life had Rachel expected to own such a sum of money. It gave her the utmost pleasure to know Nick would be able to repay his loan to the bank now that she could buy the Wester Rullion house from him. She had enough to finish the building of it and furnish it to her heart's desire for herself and Ross and Ewan. Her only sadness had been the news of Mr Murray's death but she was glad her trust in him had not been misplaced after all.

Ross was pleased on that score too. He knew how much Rachael's judgement of people meant to her, but now that a move from the Glens of Lochandee was a real possibility he was not so sure he wanted to leave the farm which represented so many of his dreams and had claimed so much of his youth. At forty-seven he still had dreams and ambitions, but he was less sure he could achieve them.

'But Ross, you are full of plans for improving Wester Rullion,' Rachel said when he voiced his doubts. 'You can't be in two places, and you can't do everything. Besides, half of Lochandee already belongs to Bridie. Alice Beattie knew how much she loved the life here, how deeply she cared about the animals. Surely it makes sense for us to move to Wester Rullion instead of Nick and Bridie?'

'I don't see why any of us need to move. Why can't we all stay as we are?'

Rachel smiled gently. He sounded like a wistful small boy.

'Nick wants to be independent and have a home of his own. He was an only child, remember. I don't suppose he's used to being surrounded by people all the time. Anyway I'm sure you must remember how much you longed to have me to yourself. You didn't even want Conan around,' she teased, and gave him the old dimpling smile which never failed to charm Ross.

'I still like having you to myself,' he said softly. 'I'm not that old yet.' The look in his eyes still brought the colour to Rachel's cheeks.

'Och, go on with you! Anyway there's Ewan to consider too. He's set his heart on farming at Wester Rullion as soon as he's old enough to leave school. He thinks he'll marry Lucy and they'll live happily ever after.' She chuckled. 'But seriously, Ross, surely it would be better for Ewan to learn about the vagaries of the different fields, the wet hollows, the parched knolls, the crops and seasons. He needs the chance to absorb all the knowledge you can give him, as young boys do. It will be good for him to watch the farm develop from the beginning, and to know we are doing it for him, and later with him.'

'I suppose you're right,' Ross sighed. 'It doesn't look as though the house will be ready before Christmas now though. The builders let Nick down badly. No wonder he sacked them.'

'Yes, Nick can use his authority and stand his own corner when necessary,' Rachel said slowly. 'I feel Bridie will be safe in his care, but sometimes I wonder what will happen if he and Conan have a serious disagreement. I'm not at all sure they both see the garage business developing in the same direction.'

'Well that's their concern, my love. They're both grown

men and we can't go on protecting our children for ever. Besides, I sometimes think Conan only thrives when there's a challenge. It makes him more determined.'

'Mmm, just like his father,' Rachel murmured, her green-blue eyes sparkling.

Bridie was overjoyed at the prospect of staying at the Glens of Lochandee, especially when Nick declared he didn't mind where he lived so long as he was master in his own house.

'If my memory is right,' he grinned, 'I don't think we shall have the place to ourselves for much longer anyway. Am I right, Bridie?'

'A-ah, you've guessed?' Bridie blushed. 'I think you may be right but I don't want to tell anyone until I'm certain. It will be lovely having a baby of our very own. You are pleased, Nick?'

'Of course it's pleased I am, my darling girl.' He hugged Bridie tightly. 'It's three little girls I would like, all just like you.'

'And I would like three little boys, just like their daddy.'

'I hope that's me then!'

'Of course it's you! Who else could it be?'

'Lamp him on the spot, I would, if it was anybody else!'

'Lamp him?'

'Knock him flat . . .'

'Oh, Nick, you're crazy!' Bridie chuckled and hugged him back. 'And I do enjoy it when you go back to your Welsh twang. Much as I love Mother and Father I must say it will be wonderful being on our own. Besides, I've all sorts of plans for the cows as well. Father seems to forget I'm not a little girl any more. I have ideas of my own.'

'What sort of plans?' Nick asked idly.

'There's artificial insemination for one thing. Father thinks it's unnatural and a waste of money but it's becoming quite reliable I hear, and it was started near here, you know. If we must keep Friesians as well as Ayrshire cattle at least we could buy semen from really well bred bulls for some of our best animals – bulls we could never afford to buy in the flesh. Some of the semen is imported from good Dutch bulls to improve the confirmation of our own British Friesians.'

'And you think your father will agree to that once he's at Wester Rullion?' Nick asked doubtfully.

'Well I'm hoping he will get so engrossed in his plans there, that he will let me get on with things in my own way.'

Nick said nothing but he raised his brows sceptically. He did not envisage his father-in-law leaving many decisions to his only daughter, capable though she was. Secretly he hoped Bridie would be content once she had a baby to care for. She loved children, as he did himself, and she was a born mother. He loved her with all his heart and his own happiness would be complete when they had a family of their own.

Christmas came and went and still Bridie and Nick kept their secret to themselves although Bridie was now almost three months' pregnant. She was blooming with good health and happiness and she did not want her parents to postpone their move on her account.

Rachel was excited about the move to Wester Rullion and the new house. Although she had been truly happy at the Glens of Lochandee she had inherited much of the furniture from Alice Beattie. She had been grateful, but this house would be her very own to furnish and decorate as she pleased. Ross found her enthusiasm infectious. There would be little spare money for immediate changes to the farmstead but the markets were holding up better than he had dared to hope, mainly because the politicians were still desperate for homegrown food. This state seemed likely to continue while there was rationing. Everything that would help the balance of payments was exported so there was little money to spare to bring in vast quantities of imported food as had happened before the war. The prices were still controlled by the government so that people could afford to eat without striking for increased wages. In an effort to compensate for this, and for the continuing regulatory controls, subsidies

160

for ploughing and liming the land were being continued. Ross longed to improve, and go on improving all the land he owned. Lime was one of the essential elements and he intended to make good use of the government aid to make Wester Rullion as productive as the Glens of Lochandee.

'The better crops I grow the more straw we have to make manure and there's nothing like it for improving the texture of the soil and increasing the yields, whether it be grass, cereals or turnips,' he lectured Nick. 'It all goes round in a cycle. If only I had a good big bullock shed at Wester Rullion. Bullocks make plenty of good manure.' He sighed heavily.

Bridie glanced anxiously at Nick but he was always tolerant with her father's farming conversations. Now he looked at her and smiled, knowing how much she wanted Ross to turn his attention to Wester Rullion.

'How about building a big shed with sheets of corrugated tin?' he suggested. 'We've been asked to transport several loads of the stuff from one of the camps that's being demolished. I should think you could buy them fairly cheaply. You would need some good strong poles though.'

'My word, Nick, that's a splendid idea. I'm glad you're part of my family. Can you find out the price for me? I suppose you wouldn't like to go over to Wester Rullion tomorrow and help me measure up to see how many sheets we should need?'

'Oh, Father! Sunday is Nick's only free day,' Bridie protested. 'Anyway you've always told us we shouldn't work on the Sabbath.'

'Och, a bit of measuring isna work. Besides, I expect your mother would come too and do some measuring for the house.' He grinned at Rachel. 'Her measuring is endless. If it's not curtains, it's carpet squares, and then its linoleum and—'

'Well, you wouldn't like to live in a barn,' Rachel said firmly. 'So yes, I'll come with you tomorrow. We should be moved in by next week, I think.' Nick gave Bridie a wicked wink but Rachel saw it. 'And I can see you two will be glad about that,' she quipped.

As it happened no one went to Wester Rullion the following day. Frank Kidd came up to say that his mother had died during the night. Although Dolly's death was expected and a welcome release from the pain she had suffered in the past weeks, it was clear that Frank was having a struggle to control his grief.

'Well, Frank, you and Emmie did the best thing when you moved into the cottage with your parents in November,' Rachel said. 'She has told me several times what a comfort it is to her knowing your father will not be alone.'

'Aye, Mistress Maxwell, and I know it's for the best. I couldn't bear to see her suffer and I dinna think Emmie could have gone on much longer staying up at nights to care for her. She's been a real angel.'

'Yes, you've both looked after her well and it will bring you great consolation later.'

They had all known Dolly Kidd for many years and her funeral was a sad occasion but Rachel was dismayed that Beth seemed so inconsolable. She supposed it was because the funeral had brought back memories of Harry's death. She knew nothing of Beth's secret fears, or that Dolly's death had increased them.

'Don't be sad for Dolly, Beth,' she said gently the following day when Beth could not stop talking about her, and kept bursting into tears. 'She was glad to go in the end, you know, no more pain. She told me she was thankful she had lived to see her boys grow up and come home safely.' Beth's sobbing increased, interspersed with apologies, but she could tell no one what was really troubling her.

Rachel decided it might be good for Beth to have a change from the routine of milking and she could certainly use her help to get the new house ready and everything moved into place.

'How about coming to stay at Wester Rullion until we get

everything in order, Beth. I'm sure Lucy could stay with Carol for a few days, or Bridie would keep her.'

'No! No, no, I don't ever want to leave Lucy,' Beth sobbed, 'and she doesn't want to leave me.' This was true. Rachel had noticed how the little girl accompanied her mother everywhere since Harry Mason's death, almost as though Lucy was afraid she might suddenly disappear too.

'Well, bring Lucy with you then. She could sleep with you and I'm sure it wouldn't harm her to stay away from school for a couple of days. I really think the change would do you good, Beth, even if it is only a different kind of work. And I'd appreciate your help.'

At last Rachel and Ross moved, with Ewan, to the new house. Sandy and Frank, with Emmie's help, were to shepherd the sheep over to Wester Rullion. It would take them most of the day but Bridie welcomed the peace and quiet. Nick was at work but she planned to make him a lovely meal when he returned for their first evening alone together. As usual she went to check up on the cows before going in for her own midday meal. She was surprised see Lochandee Star had started to calve. She wondered why Sandy hadn't mentioned it before he left.

The Star family was one of their best. As a small girl Bridie could still remember the devastating effects of a foot and mouth epidemic. All the Lochandee cattle and sheep had been slaughtered, including her own pet calf, Silky Socks. In an effort to compensate and console her, her father had given her the very first black and white calf to be born at the Glens of Lochandee. She had called the little calf Star and she had matured and borne several calves herself. The elderly cow which Bridie was now observing with concern had been Star's first heifer calf. The whole family were sweet-tempered, placid animals and had proved themselves valuable for their breeding and production.

Swiftly Bridie unfastened the chain around Star II's neck

and guided the cow from the byre into a nearby pen, kept specially for sick or calving animals. The two tiny ivory coloured feet were already showing and Bridie wondered how long the cow had been struggling to give birth.

'There old girl,' she patted the cow. 'I'll give you a few minutes to settle into your pen and lie down, then I'll come back and see whether you need a little help.' Most of the older cows gave birth without assistance so long as there were no complications like a twisted foot or hind feet first, so Bridie did not anticipate any trouble. In any case she had been helping with births of cows and sheep since she left school.

When Bridie went back some time later the birth was no further forward and Star II was lying flat out, groaning, panting, pressing, and groaning again, but without the slightest effect. Bridie grimaced. There was nothing for it but to take off her jacket and roll her sleeves as high as they would go so that she could check what was keeping the calf from being born. Everything seemed straightforward except that the calf seemed big and Star II was already getting tired. She collected two clean ropes and slipped one over each small hoof, struggling to tighten them on the wet slippery legs. Then she fastened a short bar to the ends of the rope as she had helped her father do scores of times. There had usually been two people to pull on the bar each time the cow pushed. Today, for the first time Bridie could remember, there was not a single soul at the Glens of Lochandee except herself.

She knew there was no time to send for help if the calf was to survive. The calf's head seemed far too big to push its way through the narrow passages and out into the world, but inch by inch Bridie alternately eased and pulled with infinite patience, ignoring the pain in her arms and abdomen as she wedged her feet and took the strain. At last, with a stupendous combined effort, the head emerged. Star II had had enough. She rolled to her feet, almost winding Bridie as she knocked her against the wall, but the calf was long bodied and it was still hanging with its hind quarters hooked inside the cow. It was crucial now that the calf should be born swiftly and breathe of its own accord, but the cow was exhausted.

'Please lie down or keep still,' Bridie muttered under her breath, almost in tears with weariness and frustration. Eventually the calf was born, but even before she bent to massage it and try to stimulate it into breathing, Bridie knew it was a lost cause. She persevered but there was no sign of life. Carefully she collected the ropes and bar and took them outside to be washed. She felt utterly drained and every muscle in her body had been strained to the limit.

Bridie made her way to the silent house and stripped off her wet and bloody clothes. She washed carefully then sank on to the hearth rug in front of the Aga.

She had no idea how long she had lain there but she knew she must have fallen asleep. In dawning horror she realized what had wakened her. The pain was excruciating.

'My baby!' she gasped on a sobbing breath. 'Oh please, oh please, dear God, don't let me lose our baby.'

Seventeen

Rachel was almost as upset as Bridie and Nick over the loss of the baby. Irrationally she blamed herself for leaving Lochandee, and insisted on returning to nurse Bridie back to health.

'You're young, lassie, there'll be other babies soon,' she said brokenly, in an effort to comfort Bridie. She didn't notice Doctor MacEwan's grave expression, nor the imperceptible shake of his head. He could not say with certainty that Bridie would never bear another child but he had grave doubts, so he maintained a troubled silence.

Nick was more distressed than he would have believed possible. He felt deprived. He was angry that Bridie had put the cow's welfare before that of their unborn child, but the sight of her white tear-stained face had stilled the words of recrimination. She was suffering enough remorse for the two of them without him adding to her misery. Later Doctor MacEwan drew him aside.

'Your wife will need all the love and understanding you can give her. Be patient if she is low in spirits. It is a sad and traumatic event in a woman's life and they all react differently.'

'Do my best, I do,' Nick said abruptly.

'I'm sure you will. Bridie told me how much you both wanted this baby and I have every sympathy with your loss too, but a woman's whole system needs time to adjust, in addition to her own mental distress.'

A couple of weeks passed and Bridie remained listless and

depressed but eventually Nick and Ross, between them, persuaded Rachel she should return to her own home and allow Bridie to pick up the threads of her life again. Reluctantly, Rachel agreed but her heart ached for her only daughter, knowing there was little more she could do to comfort her. Moreover Nick had grown quiet and withdrawn and she felt it was better that they should be alone together.

Bridie sensed Nick held her responsible for the loss of their child, but he could never blame her more than she blamed herself.

Back at Wester Rullion, as Rachel had predicted, Ross was eager to make alterations. He had almost completed the new bullock shed and had already asked Nick to procure more corrugated tin to add a lean-to for storage of fodder. Rachel herself had bought hens to bring in cash for the household expenses. They had two milk cows which she milked by hand, and the six pigsties, which were part of the original farmstead, had been repaired and were occupied by one elderly sow and five fine young gilts. These were to be Ewan's responsibility every day after school.

Mrs Forster, the widow of the original Wester Rullion tenant, had sunk into a decline since the death of her husband. Now her life in the old farmhouse at the other end of the yard had been livened up by all the activity. The occupation of the new house by Mr and Mrs Maxwell and their adventurous young son had given her a new interest and Rachel was kind to her elderly neighbour. It had been too much effort to keep the hens and pig on her own. Her cow had long since gone dry and been sold, so Rachel kept her supplied with milk and butter and eggs. Consequently her health and energy had begun to improve with the added nourishment.

Most days Ross employed Peter, the young Polish man from the camp who had helped with the harvest. He was becoming almost a permanent part of life at Wester Rullion and Mrs Forster got used to seeing him passing by with the horse and cart. Recently Ross had taught him to drive the Ferguson tractor and he always gave her his shy smile and a little wave if he saw her in the garden. She had no idea how homesick the sight of her and her low stone house made him feel, but he had no plans to return to Poland. He knew his mother and sister had been killed and he had received no answer to the many letters he had written to his father and elder brother. He could only assume they were dead too and he resolved to make a new life in a new country. He was grateful to the Maxwells for giving him employment and to Mrs Maxwell for a good midday meal, far better than anything he got at the camp. Gradually his English was improving too.

One day when Ross had stopped to pass the time of day with Mrs Forster, she mentioned his young worker.

'Aye, he's a grand laddie, but then he was used to farming back home in Poland before the war. If we'd had a bothy I would have taken him on permanently if the authorities would permit it.'

Neither of them thought any more of this conversation until one wild windy day at the end of March. Peter was passing Mrs Forster's garden when a powerful gust lifted her newly washed blankets like huge balloons. They billowed and danced in wild abandon but the weight was too much for the ancient clothes line and it snapped. Swiftly Peter jumped from the tractor and over the wall, catching the blankets in his strong arms before they became stained with grass and mud. Only one of them would need to be washed again and Mrs Forster was truly grateful. He fixed up a new rope and helped her hang out the blankets once more, answering her questions about his homeland and his family in his broken English.

Later that evening Mrs Forster went over to the Maxwell's new house for the first time and Rachel welcomed her warmly, wondering what had persuaded her to come after she had refused so many times before.

'I've been thinking,' she began diffidently, 'perhaps I could give the boy, Peter, board and lodgings in my house? I'd like to think somebody would have treated my own laddie kindly if he'd been taken a prisoner over there. And . . . and it would be company. It never seems worth cooking just for me, but if I'd a laddie to feed again . . . ?'

'What a splendid idea, Mrs Forster! Are you sure?'

'Aye, aye . . .' She gave a trembling sigh. 'It's time I cleared out my ain laddie's room and let him rest in peace. It'll take me a week or two though. I'll give it a coat o' fresh distemper.'

'I'm sure Peter would be happy to help you do that,' Ross suggested. 'He's a willing laddie and good with his hands. I'll get on to the authorities tomorrow and see whether there are regulations we have to follow. If they approve I'll pay his board and lodging directly to you and he will get the rest of his wages.'

Bridie was also relieved to hear of the new arrangement to make Peter a permanent worker because her father had kept taking Frank and Sandy over to Wester Rullion to help him, instead of leaving them to get on with the work at the Glens of Lochandee. She had become increasingly irritated.

'I'll still need them sometimes, lassie,' Ross told her. 'But you can borrow Peter in exchange when you're busy with the harvest and things like that.'

'It's just as well there'll not be so much travelling,' Rachel said. 'They expect petrol rationing will end soon but did you hear the Chancellor has just put on eight pence a gallon in tax in the budget? That will make it three shillings a gallon!'

'Speaking of travelling, Mother, have you noticed how tired Beth is these days by the time she's cycled here? She must be worse on the days she works at Wester Rullion. And as for helping at the garage on Saturdays, I think she must be exhausted before she gets there.'

'Yes, I had noticed. Beth doesn't seem to have been herself since Dolly's death. Conan usually collects her and Lucy on

Saturdays to save them the cycle ride over to the garage. I think it is good for Beth to serve at the petrol pumps, apart from the extra money she earns. She always liked company. Ewan is not so pleased though. He thinks Lucy is his friend to the exclusion of everyone else.'

'Yes, I know.' Bridie summoned a wan smile. The very mention of children made her heart sink and the news about Princess Elizabeth expecting her second child in August only made her feel more of a failure than ever.

'And you, lassie?' Rachel asked gently. 'Are you feeling more like yourself?'

Bridie didn't answer. She knew she was abrupt and short-tempered with everyone these days, and most of all with Nick, and she couldn't seem to help herself. Usually she had snapped out the words before she knew they had even formed in her mind. She couldn't even make love with Nick. The prospect of it filled her with apprehension. She knew Nick's patience was wearing thin and that made her more tense than ever. Worst of all she felt Nick was watching her every time she went near the cows. He blamed her work for the loss of their baby, but the cows were her life, all she had left, and her resentment was growing. He could not control her daily routine. And anyway it was too late now – all much too late. She had lost the baby. Nothing could alter that.

Things came to a head at the end of May. After ten years of rationing, petrol could suddenly be bought without coupons. Trade at the garage was hectic. Everyone seemed to be taking to the road and there had been several minor breakdowns, all demanding Nick's attention. Conan had taken a bus load of holiday makers off for the Whitsuntide holiday and Nick returned home late, hungry, tired and frustrated. Bridie had long since made his evening meal and eaten hers alone. When he finally arrived it was to find Bridie in one of the fields rubbing down a newly born calf.

'There's more you're thinking about your bloody cattle

than about me!' he accused. 'Alike you are, you and Conan, obsessed you are with your own lives, your ambitions.'

'I can't help it if you choose to come in at all hours for your meal!' Bridie flared back. 'I waited an hour for you and if yours is wasted it's your own fault.' She did not try to soothe him. She turned her back and marched up to the house. Nick followed grimly. As soon as they were inside he slammed the door and seized her from behind. He was sweaty and his clothes were stained with grease and oil. Bridie resisted with all her strength, but she was small and Nick was strong, and he was determined to be master.

'There's a wife I'm wanting when I do come home,' he panted, 'not a bloody dairymaid.' It was not in Nick's nature to be cruel. Although he was ruthless as he removed Bridie's clothes, and then his own, his natural gentleness returned as he felt her soft silken skin beneath his hands, his lips. He knew he was being unreasonable in forcing Bridie but he had waited long enough. Bridie strove to repress the unexpected surge of desire at his touch but it was impossible and afterwards she lay weeping silently on the rug where he had left her, confused and scarcely knowing whether she was glad or sorry. She heard Nick in the bathroom, washing off the day's grime, but it was the slamming of the back door, the sound of his truck's engine starting up which brought her to her senses. He had not eaten the meal she had prepared. He had not said where he was going.

When Nick did not return, Bridie listlessly cleared away the remains of the meal. She paced the floor as the shadows lengthened but it was almost midsummer and it was still light outside. The birds were gathering together in evensong before they settled to their nests. Several times Bridie went outside to stare down the farm road but there was no sign of Nick's return. Eventually she slumped dejectedly on to a chair and put her head on her arms on the kitchen table, and wept. The hot tears flowed freely as though intent on washing away all the trauma and emotion of the past months. At length she dried her eyes and washed her face. It was dark outside now but there was still no sign of Nick. Had she driven him away for ever? Had he returned to the flat he had shared with Conan? She went to the telephone. She could hear the distant shrilling and visualized the untidy, cheerless flat, but there was no reply.

Bridie wakened stiff and cold and realized her own phone was ringing. Blearily she fumbled her way into the hall and lifted the receiver.

'I was just about to put it down. Sorry if I wakened you, Bridie. It's me, Fiona.'

''S all right. I wasn't in bed. What time is it?'

'After midnight. Er . . . I thought you might be worried about Nick, Bridie?'

'Why should I be worried?' Bridie snapped. Then: 'I'm sorry, Fiona. We . . . we . . .'

'Had a row, I suppose?' Fiona said dryly. 'Well, Nick's here, at my house. I thought you'd want to know.'

'Wh-what is he . . . ? Why is he . . . ?'

'I don't think he knows where he is, and anyway he's asleep now on my settee. Carol helped me get him inside. He's as drunk as a lord and certainly not fit to drive his truck home.'

'Carol . . . ?' Bridie echoed sharply.

'She came over to talk to me about Beth. She's concerned about her. We got chatting about Glasgow and other things. Her children are away at a holiday camp and it was later than we realized. She saw Nick rolling about the village street on her way to her house so she came back to tell me and helped me get him inside. I reckon he'll sleep until morning and he'll probably think he has three heads when he does waken, but he'll be all right for now.'

'I see. Thanks.'

'Bridie? Are . . . are you all right?'

'I'm fine. Good night.' Bridie put the receiver down and slowly climbed the stairs, wishing she had not been so short

172

when Fiona was only trying to help, but Nick liked Fiona very much and the fierce stab of jealousy she had felt had been unexpected. She got into the big bed, only to toss and turn and wet her pillow with yet more tears. Would she ever get out of this deep despair, she wondered dismally. Would Nick come back?

Eighteen

B ridie was emptying the last pail of milk over the cooler the following morning when Nick drove up in his truck. She half expected him to make some bitter comment about her work but she was dismayed at the pallor of his face, accentuated by the dark stubble and shadows beneath his eyes. He did not even see her in the dairy door as he made straight for the house, head down. Bridie left Emmie and Frank to finish up in the byre and followed him. She kicked off her wellington boots and padded silently into the kitchen. He was sitting at the table, his tousled head bowed over his hands. He did not look at all like the proud young airman Bridie had fallen in love with, or the handsome groom who had awaited her at the altar less than a year ago, but a wave of infinite tenderness filled her breast until it was almost a physical pain. She wanted to cradle him to her like a child.

'Nick . . . ?' She moved towards him and put a tentative hand on his shoulder. He looked up briefly, then bowed his head in silence.

'Wanting me out, I suppose, after last night,' he said flatly. 'It's back to the flat I'll go, to Conan.'

'Oh, Nick.' Bridie was almost in tears. 'That's the last thing I want.'

'Is it?' he said dully. Then he raised his head. 'Is it? Is it, Bridie?' His dark eyes scanned her face. 'Even . . . even after last night . . . ? Even after . . .' He bowed his head in his hands again. 'I don't know what came over me,' he said gruffly.

'Nick . . .' Bridie pulled out a chair and sat beside him at the table. 'Nick, it was probably the best thing you ever did. I-I've been so selfish. I should have known you were hurting too . . .' Her voice shook. 'I-I promise I'll be careful if only we can have another baby. I-I didn't meant to . . . I-I just never thought I could lose our baby.' Her voice broke. 'And I feel so . . . so wretched, almost like I murdered it,' she added in a whisper.

'Oh no, Bridie! There's my girl now. You mustn't feel like that.'

'But I do, and I know you think it was my fault. I'm so unhappy, Nick, so short with everyone – even Fiona, last night.' She couldn't tell him how jealous she had felt. Nick reached out and clasped her hands where they lay on the table.

'Listen, Bridie, so long as we have each other . . . Well, I know now, that's all that really matters as far as I'm concerned. I seem to have waited for you for half a lifetime, and then . . . then . . .'

'And then I shut you out,' Bridie said huskily. 'I didn't mean to, honestly. I-I just feel so . . .' She shook her head from side to side. 'It's as though I'm in a black cave and can't find my way out. But I do love you, Nick. I need you so much.'

'And I love you too,' Nick said huskily. 'So long as we have each other we'll get through this somehow.'

Nick was patient with Bridie in the months which followed, but there were days when she seemed unable to shake off the melancholy moods. They were triggered by any mention of babies and the rejoicing over Princess Elizabeth's new baby girl brought on a particularly black depression. Nick was brooding anxiously when Doctor MacEwan called at the garage to ask him to check his car engine. He told him of Bridie's despondency.

'The best thing you can do is try to distract her attention. How about buying her one of these new television sets?'

'A television? That's a luxury I can't afford.'

'Regard it as an investment in your wife's health.'

'I can't imagine Bridie sitting down and watching pictures,' Nick said slowly. 'But she does listen to the new radio programme. *The Archers* it's called, and it's about farming. Makes a difference that, I suppose.'

'A-ah yes. It's surprising how many of my patients are listening to it. Isn't it supposed to bridge the gap between the townspeople and country folk?'

'Probably. My father-in-law says they put topical farming news on it – and the main characters read out notices from the Ministry. He thinks the government are encouraging the BBC to influence the farmers by letting them know what's needed for the good of the country.'

'Like a sugar-coated pill, eh?' Doctor MacEwan chuckled. 'Well, Ross Maxwell is no fool so I suppose he's probably right. But you take my advice and think about buying your wife a television set. She can always knit or do the mending while she's watching it in the evenings. It will take her mind off her own problems. And by the way, my wife is hoping you and Bridie will sing a duet at the concert she's organizing at the end of September. I think she has already asked Ross to play the fiddle and I believe young Lucy Mason is going to play the accordion if she's not too nervous.'

'Beth it is more likely to be nervous, I'm thinking,' Nick declared ruefully.

'You could be right. Mr Urquhart tells me Lucy has real talent. I believe he gives her a few free lessons now and again. But he says she's a natural and your father-in-law gives her all the encouragement she needs. Apparently he plays along with her whenever she's staying at Wester Rullion.'

'Yes, so I do believe,' Nick agreed nodding. 'And young Ewan gets very irritated with them for "wasting time indoors"!'

'Och, it wouldn't do if we all had the same talents, would it? Who should I get to keep my motor car running, if you were like me, Nick?'

'Somebody would be coming along, I expect. I reckon you should consider changing it though. A reliable car it is, you're needing in your job. You'd find the modern ones far easier to drive and to start.'

'Are you trying to sell me one?'

'No, not really. Haven't gone into car sales yet, have we now. Get one for you, we could, if you would like one. The Morris Oxford is a nice little car.'

'Mmm, I'll think about it. It's taken me long enough to get used to this one and I don't like changes.'

When the doctor had departed Nick thought over what he had said about a television set. Maybe he would enquire about prices next time he went into Annan. The garage was doing well enough but Conan seemed to begrudge every penny that was taken out for personal use. But Bridie's peace of mind came a long way ahead of the garage or pleasing Conan. According to the government the average wage was now seven pounds and eleven shillings a week, yet they allowed themselves only three pounds a week. He couldn't afford to buy a television on that and he didn't like the idea of this new hire purchase system that some of the shops were offering, tempting people into buying things they couldn't afford. The prospect of a mortgage had been bad enough and he would certainly have needed to take more money out of the business if Mrs Maxwell had not relieved him of that burden. There was nothing for it but to have a serious word with Conan. They were equal partners, but so far Conan had made most of the decisions about business. Bridie was his sister so surely he would agree the that doctor's advice ought to be followed if it would help her spirits.

Conan was aghast when Nick told him of his plan to buy a television for Bridie, especially when he mentioned taking the money out of his share of the garage profits to pay for it.

'A television! That'll cost a fortune!'

'A hundred and fifteen guineas, if you want to know.'

'A hundred and fifteen! That's—'

'Purchase tax there'll be on top of that. Twenty-seven pounds, nine shillings and five pence . . .'

'You're mad! You'd be cheaper going to the pictures every night! Even at one and nine a time! We'll never build up a fleet of buses if you throw money away so frivolously,' Conan argued fiercely. 'Tell Bridie to pull herself together. Why don't you have another bairn if that's what she wants?'

Nick's eyes narrowed and his mouth tightened. 'You do know about these things then, do you? Duw man! There's a bell you do have on every bloody tooth . . .'

'Hey, steady on, Nick!' Conan looked at him sharply. He knew that tone, the Welsh accent, the anger. 'I didn't mean to—'

'Canting on you were! Never consider Mother Nature do have a hand in things, do you? If that is all you care for your sister's happiness and health, then time it is we parted company.' Conan gazed helplessly at the white line around Nick's mouth, the fury in his eyes. 'You buy as many buses as you want – but you do pay out my share first.'

'Oh, Nick! Come on old man! I didna realize things were as bad as that for Bridie. After all she still has her cows and her calves and chickens.'

'You do think they can be picked up and cuddled!' Nick said sarcastically. 'It's a heartless baa . . . devil you are, Conan Maxwell. Anyway, Bridie is frustrated with the farm. You Maxwells, a challenge it is you want in your lives, always, isn't it? Bridie works hard and what is she? A glorified milkmaid! Your father is still the boss. I ask you . . .'

'A-ah, now that, I can believe.' Conan nodded thoughtfully. 'I'm glad I made my break for independence when I did.' He grinned, but the grin faded in the face of Nick's cold stare. 'Well Bridie does get half the profit for the Glens of Lochandee,' he said defensively.

'If there is any she hasn't seen it. Your father is like you, Conan, he knows which way he wants to go. Right now he wants to improve Wester Rullion. Nothing else matters.'

Nick took a deep breath and strove for calm. 'But it's not the money that matters to Bridie, or to me. She needs something to stimulate her interest. Your father makes all the decisions about the farm and the breeding of the herd – not that I blame him. It's his life too, and he built up the herd. It was Doctor MacEwan who suggested getting a television and I mean to take his advice. I'd do anything to help Bridie get over losing the baby and regaining her usual spirits.'

'Oh well, I suppose you know best.' Conan shrugged, but Nick knew he was thinking of the other bus he was planning to buy.

'Anyway,' Nick said, 'while we're discussing things, we never did agree about buying another bus. We should do better with a cattle lorry, I'm thinking. Always the farmers are asking me why we haven't got one yet. A lot of business there is, transporting their cattle to and from the markets.'

'Och, a cattle lorry! Who wants one of them – certainly not me!'

'Well, I think it would be a good proposition,' Nick said stubbornly and he turned on his heel and left Conan staring after him thoughtfully.

The television proved a serious distraction for them all. Even Fiona often stayed to watch in the evenings and sometimes Meg came too, collecting Lucy after school and bringing her too if it was a Friday night. Nick felt the company was good for Bridie, especially when he was working late at the garage.

Beth thoroughly enjoyed the films and the panel game with the gruff old man in it. It helped her forget her own worries, at least for a while. The horror she had felt watching Dolly Kidd's suffering and her subsequent death began to recede and her own spirits improved.

The year ended, winter progressed slowly. One bitterly cold day in February Ross drove over to the Glens of Lochandee. He wanted to talk about the farm. He was as full of enthusiasm as ever and Bridie wondered where her parents got all their energy.

'The government are going to pay five pounds an acre if we will plough up more grassland for cereals,' he announced. 'I wondered if Nick would bring the Lochandee plough over and help us at Wester Rullion, if he has any spare time from the garage? I'm thinking of ploughing up the parkland adjoining the mansion house ground and—'

'Oh Father, you're surely not going to do that! It's lovely there with the massive oak trees.'

'You're as bad as your mother.' Ross frowned. 'She doesn't approve either but—'

'Anyway, the cereals wouldn't ripen so evenly in the shade of the trees.'

'I hadn't thought of that. You could be right, lassie.'

'I suppose you heard about the death of the King this morning? Is Mother very upset? Princess Elizabeth has only just set out on her tour of Kenya.'

'The King's dead? I didn't hear that, but then I didn't listen to the radio this morning.'

'It's true. I heard it myself.'

'Ah well, the poor man. He wasna in good health, and he has to take his turn, just like the rest of us. We're all just mortals, whatever our state. Anyway, what about Nick and this ploughing? Even if I don't plough the parkland I could plough some of the other fields and get them reseeded with a better grass mixture when I get them into a rotation. I think we ought to plough Buttercup Field here as well.'

'Oh no, Father. We have enough land ploughed at Lochandee as it is,' Bridie protested. 'I don't know why the government want so much land for cereals when the cows and sheep need grass. They are even talking of cutting the cheese ration back to one ounce a week again and it's nearly seven years since the war ended, for goodness sake.'

'Well the politicians know what's best for the country – or at least they think they do,' Ross added thoughtfully.

'I can't understand, Father, why you are so modern about farming in some ways and yet you won't even consider using artificial insemination to improve the dairy herd.'

'Oh, lassie, you're not still going on about that, are you? Forget about it and put the cows with the bull as we've always done. You've got to be sure of getting them in calf regularly – no calves, then no milk. You know that well enough by now, Bridie. It's a question of economics.'

'I know that, Father. That's why—'

'Don't forget to ask Nick if he'll come and help me with the ploughing. He's a better hand with the tractor than I am.'

'That may be so but he scarcely has time to breathe. Conan leaves him to do all the repairs while he's off driving his buses.'

'Aye, the business seems to be going well for them. Conan was telling me he's employed another man full time, mainly to drive one of the buses. He's already getting bookings for day trips for the summer, and some for a whole week each.'

'Is that so?' Bridie asked tightly. 'And I suppose Conan will expect Nick to do all the other work while he's away.' She often sensed that Nick was not happy about the garage business and the way they were expanding but he rarely discussed it with her. She suspected he did not want to criticize Conan because he was her brother and on the whole they were a close family, even if they did have their different opinions on business.

But even Bridie did not realize just how frustrated Nick was becoming with his working life at the garage, and consequently at home. He sometimes felt like a seething cauldron, reaching the point of explosion. He and Conan had been such good friends during their time together in the RAF but these days they rarely seemed to be on the same wavelength at all.

The days lengthened as spring arrived but Bridie's frustration and unhappiness grew. All around them new life burgeoned but for her there was no sign of a baby. Nick had begun to wonder whether she would ever conceive again. He was bitterly disappointed but he refrained from commenting.

He knew Bridie shared his disappointments and he sensed she was also beginning to share his doubts, but she kept her own council, until one fine morning in May when her heart yearned for a child. She mentioned the possibility of adopting a baby. He was so shocked he vetoed the idea before he had even thought about it, then he hurried off to work without giving her the chance to discuss it.

All thoughts of babies and adoption were temporarily banished from Bridie's mind as she listened in horror to the radio announcement later that day.

'Oh no! Did you hear that, Beth? There's an outbreak of foot and mouth disease.'

'Wh-what did ye say? Foot and mouth . . . ?' Beth's face paled. She would never forget the terrible slaughter she had witnessed when she was young, long before she had met Harry. 'It's for certain?' she asked in a whisper, staring at Bridie's white face as she listened intently to the rest of the report.

'Yes, it's been confirmed. All cattle movements have been banned in this area. I must phone Wester Rullion. I must find out if they've heard the announcement. Father will have to stay at home. He can't come over here . . . He can't . . .'

'He'll ken that, Bridie,' Beth assured her solemnly, remembering how strict and grim Ross Maxwell had been with everyone when the last outbreak had occurred in Dumfriesshire. 'We shall have to get baths ready for disinfectant and put them at the road end.'

'Yes, and we must make a notice,' Bridie said anxiously. 'We don't want anyone coming in or out. I'll phone Mother first though. And Nick. He'll have to stop going to other farms with deliveries. He might bring it back here. I can still remember how awful it was the last time . . . Dear God, please keep it away from us this time . . .' Bridie blinked back her tears and turned away from Beth's sympathetic gaze. She couldn't bear the thought of losing all their precious cattle. Nick would have to stay at home. So would her father. They must not take any chances.

182

Nineteen

The dreaded disease spread in pockets throughout the county, cancelling shows and markets and bringing movements to and from farms to a halt. At first Nick welcomed the excuse to stay at the Glens of Lochandee with Bridie but he soon began to realize that there was very little farming business at the garage anyway. He could only guess what attempts some were making with their own repairs but almost without exception the farmers kept themselves to their own premises.

Each morning Ross telephoned the Glens of Lochandee, issuing instructions to Bridie and asking the same questions about the stock.

'We're taking every precaution we can,' she insisted tensely.

'But Nick has gone back to work, I hear. Does he . . . ?'

'Yes, Father, he understands how serious it is, and yes he does disinfect his boots, in fact he leaves a spare pair in the box at the road end and he never comes up the road in the ones he wears for the garage.'

'Well you can't be too careful and—'

'Nick offered to strip naked at the road end if it would stop us worrying,' Bridie said more sharply than she realized.

'There's no need to be sarcastic, Bridie, it's a serious thing and I've struggled for years to build up a herd that's a bit better than average. It'll break your heart if you lose all the cows you've reared from wee calves—'

'I wasn't being sarcastic,' Bridie interrupted, near to tears.

'But Conan was nagging at Nick to get back to work. He said the buses still needed maintaining and there were other people with cars besides farmers and they needed repairs. In the end Nick felt he had to go. He stayed at the garage for a few nights but he hated it – and so did I. He really is careful, Dad, I promise you, and he never goes to any of the farms with deliveries.'

'All right, all right, lassie,' Ross said, hearing the tension in Bridie's voice. 'It's just such a worry and I hate being cooped up here.'

'We're managing fine, Dad, really we are. Frank and Sandy never leave their cottage and Emmie gets my groceries and butcher meat from the vans to prevent them coming near the farm.'

Nevertheless there was no joining forces with Wester Rullion to get the turnip hoeing done, nor to help with the hay, as outbreaks of the disease continued as the summer progressed. It was four and a half months after the first outbreak and time to cut and harvest the corn before the foot and mouth outbreak was finally ended.

'In the beginning I really believed you and your father were making an awful lot of unnecessary fuss,' Nick admitted ruefully. 'No idea, had I, that it would last so long. Dreadful it is,' he declared, shaking his head as he listed some of the farms where he had previously made deliveries. 'Many more there must be too. According to this paper it reports they've slaughtered 21,400, including pigs and sheep.'

'Yes, I was just a child when it happened before in this area,' Bridie nodded, 'but I can still remember the horror of it.' She shuddered involuntarily. 'I'm truly thankful we escaped this time.'

All thoughts of the previous year's foot and mouth outbreak were forgotten the following summer as the whole country prepared to celebrate the coronation of Queen Elizabeth II. Nick thought half the Lochandee villagers must be coming to watch it on the television at the Glens of Lochandee, judging by the amount of food Bridie and Beth had prepared.

'We don't want to be making food and miss any of the excitement,' she told him as eagerly as a child, 'and it goes on all day so everyone will need to eat.'

'Perhaps it's just as well Conan and I are working then,' he said grinning. 'We'd be sadly outnumbered by women-folk.'

'Yes, Father felt the same but he's coming over in the evening so maybe Conan will come back with you? Ewan's coming with Mother but I hope he doesn't fidget and keep wanting to go outside.'

'Well, I can't imagine the laddie being all that interested.'

'Neither can I, but Lucy will be here and it's still a case of where one goes the other goes too. I thought they might have grown apart now they are both at Dumfries Academy but Beth says they often help each other with their homework.'

'Yes, Lucy comes over to the garage every Saturday to help Beth at the petrol pumps. Bright little thing, she is, and Conan now, he has so much time and patience, makes young Ewan quite cross, it does.'

'Well, he's a bit young to be jealous.' Bridie chuckled.

'I'm not so sure about that,' Nick said seriously. 'Possess-ive young pup he is, especially where Lucy is concerned, and of course she's impressed with Conan because he can drive a car and a bus. Pestering your father to let him drive the tractor, Ewan was, I heard.'

'Yes, I believe you're right, but it worries Mother. She's sure he'll have an accident.'

It was an exceptionally cold day for June but everyone enjoyed watching the coronation, marvelling that it was actually taking place as they watched, even if it was in black and white. They could only imagine how beautiful the golden coach must look, not to mention the young Queen in her robes and crown.

At the end of the day everyone thanked Bridie for allowing

them to come and for feeding them so well. Carol had brought two of her neighbours, and her daughters. Lucy went home with them, leaving Beth to help Bridie and Emmie with the milking.

'I'd better be going home too,' Fiona said, feeling flat at the thought of her own empty house.

'Oh, don't go yet,' Bridie said. 'There'll be lots more pictures on the newsreels tonight. Stay and have supper with us. I've made a huge shepherd's pie and it's apple pie and cream. I know that's your favourite pudding. I don't know how you stay so slim, Fiona.'

'Aye, you stay, lassie,' Rachel said. 'You can help me with the washing up and putting the room back into order before Nick comes home, or he'll think we've had a real old party.'

'All right,' Fiona nodded. 'Just so long as I can be useful. I'm certainly no use at milking cows,' she smiled ruefully.

'There's plenty of us tonight. We'll be as quick as we can,' Bridie promised.

'It gives me a chance to tell you again how grateful I am for all you did to get the business of the vase sorted out,' Rachel said as they washed and dried the dishes. 'It's wonderful. I'm sure I should never have received a penny if it hadn't been for you, Fiona.'

'Glad to help,' Fiona said simply. 'I received a short letter from Mrs Murray's housekeeper, Mrs Bunty. She says Mrs Murray is progressing wonderfully now that she's safely home again and she's got a lovely young nurse companion who can drive the car. They go for short trips into the country when the weather is fine.'

'I'm so pleased to hear that,' Rachel said warmly. 'I've thought about her often, although we never met. It must have been awful to lose both her sons and then her husband.'

'Yes,' Fiona agreed softly. There were times when she herself felt very alone, in spite of her work with Jordon Niven and the good friends she had made since moving to

Lochandee. She couldn't account for her restlessness and recently she had pondered the possibility of returning to the city and a more challenging job again. She felt her present life was lacking purpose. Sometimes Lucy came to ask for help with her homework and Fiona enjoyed her company and her bright intelligent young mind. At such times she wondered whether she should enquire about retraining to become a teacher herself, but so far she had done nothing to change her routine.

Much later that evening, when the men had seen all that interested them about the coronation, the conversation drifted back to work as it usually did. Ross suddenly turned to Bridie.

'I nearly forgot to tell you, lassie. I've bought a young Ayrshire bull for you from Mr Drummond. They're going to deliver him after the Castle Douglas sale and—'

'Oh, Father!' For a moment Nick thought his wife was going to burst into tears, then he saw the twin patches of colour stain her cheeks and he realized she was extremely annoyed with her father. 'You know I wanted to try some new blood lines. You knew I wanted to try the artificial insemination for some of the cows, but even if you couldn't agree to that you could at least have consulted me about buying a bull.'

'Och, this is a well bred young bull,' Ross said.

'I thought we'd agreed you would choose the bulls for the Friesian cows and I should select my own breeding for the Ayrshires.'

'But you're just a lassie . . .'

Bridie jumped to her feet, grabbed a tray of teacups and hurried away into the kitchen. She knew if she didn't get out of the room she would either quarrel with her father or burst into tears, or both. Nick half rose to follow but Fiona had already risen and she gave him a sympathetic glance as she lifted the other tray and followed Bridie.

'I'll just help Bridie with the cups then I'll give you a lift home, Beth.' There was no reply from Beth. She was sound asleep in her corner of the large settee and she looked pale and exhausted. For the first time Rachel was shocked to notice how gaunt Beth's face was in repose. She had always had such round cheeks and a healthy colour.

In the kitchen Bridie clattered the cups into the sink in angry frustration, but Fiona knew she was near to tears.

'Father thinks I'm still a child!' she muttered, 'yet he leaves me to manage the dairy and milk the cows and all the work there is to do. Then he doesn't believe I can use my brain enough to study the pedigrees to select a bull. I know the strengths and weaknesses of our own cows better than anyone. I feel so . . . so . . .' Her voice shook and she bit her lip. 'If only I hadn't lost my baby it wouldn't have been so bad! Now there seems to be no satisfaction in anything I do. Nick's right, I'm just a glorified milkmaid.'

'Oh, Bridie, I'm sure your father means well,' Fiona comforted her.

'Maybe he means well.' She turned to look at Fiona. 'Yes, I know he does really, but if only he could see, I want to make my own decisions. Even if I make mistakes, I want to try out my own ideas! He just doesn't understand that.'

'Well, I suppose it is still his farm . . .' Fiona said gently.

'Half of it is mine. Aunt Alice Beattie left it to me. She knew how much I loved the Glens of Lochandee and the animals. It's my life, Fiona. Especially . . . especially if I can't even have any children to bring up and love and . . .'

'I'm sure you will, one day, Bridie. You're not that old yet.'

'I'm twenty-seven! We've been married nearly four years now. I'm sure Nick's given up hope. I don't think he's all that happy with the garage either. Father and Conan are alike, they want to make all the decisions themselves. Sometimes I wish . . . I wish . . .' she shrugged. 'What's the good of wishing!'

'No good at all unless you do something to make your

wishes come true,' Fiona said wryly. 'Why don't you ask your father if you can buy his share of the Glens of Lochandee, then he can use the money to carry out his plans to Wester Rullion. He might even build a byre and have a dairy herd there, or . . .'

Bridie had turned to stare at Fiona, her mouth in a small 'O' of surprise.

'If only I could,' she breathed softly, 'but where would I get the money?'

'Well, Nick was going to get a bank loan to build the house, why not ask him to get one to buy half a farm?'

'Do you think it might be possible?' Bridie asked wide eyed.

'I don't know. You'd need to ask the bank manager, but at least you would have the land as security and land doesn't disappear. In fact it seems to be more in demand now than it has been for years, according to old Mr Niven. Seriously, Bridie, I'm not the one to advise you but you could ask the bank manager's opinion. You'd probably need to take out a life insurance too. The thing is, would your father agree to sell his share even if you and Nick can raise the money?'

'Oh, I couldn't ask Nick to help. He has enough worries and problems with the garage business. Conan is wanting to buy another bus. That will be four they've got, but he does seem to get plenty of bookings for them and he loves arranging the journeys and routes and where to stay. I think that's what makes Nick so frustrated. He's not interested in the bus trips and holidays, but Conan says it's the way things are going since the war. People want new sights and experiences because they're still restless. Do you think we are all restless, Fiona? I must admit I feel that way but I thought it was just me.'

'O-oh, it's not just you, Bridie, not by any means.'

'Well, don't breathe a word of this to anyone will you, Fiona? I'm really going to look into it, but I want to do it myself.'

'If you did manage to get a bank loan, Bridie, do you think you could manage to repay it on your own?' Fiona asked anxiously.

'I think so, over a long time, but I'd need to discuss the costs. I've been keeping a set of accounts and records, just so I could see how economical things are, and what we might need to cut back, or increase. I will take them in to the bank manager when I get an appointment.'

'Good for you!' Fiona said admiringly. 'But you always were intelligent and practical. I don't suppose your father realizes how much he underestimates that side of you.'

'Then I shall have to show him,' Bridie said with a gleam in her eye.

As she drove home with a weary Beth beside her, Fiona wondered how it was she could solve other people's problems, yet she could find no solution to her own restlessness.

Nick had expected Bridie to be in low spirits when they went to bed later that night but he was surprised to find her strangely elated. He did a swift calculation but no, he thought sadly, it couldn't be the start of another baby making her that way. Whatever it was he enjoyed her passionate responses to his loving. He wouldn't mind if there was a coronation every day if it had this effect on her.

It was some weeks before Bridie found time and courage to make an appointment with the bank manager. There was the turnip hoeing and sheep shearing and her father asked her to send Frank and his father over to Wester Rullion to help. Haytime followed. Meanwhile Bridie was marshalling her thoughts and her arguments to deal with the bank. If that interview was successful she would need even more arguments to convince her father. Nick suspected there was something on her mind but he was far from happy with his own business or he would certainly have paid more attention.

Conan had mentioned the possibility of employing a

woman full time to supervize the petrol pumps and take telephone bookings for bus trips. Two days later the woman had started work. Nick seethed inwardly. It was clear to him that Conan had already made the decision and acted upon it before they had even discussed it. Moreover Nick disliked Daphne Higgs instinctively. She had long fingernails painted scarlet and it was soon clear she had little intention of serving the customers with their petrol if she could avoid it. Some of the local farmers had accounts which they paid monthly and most of them paid promptly, but Mrs Higgs did her best to put obstacles in their way and said she preferred to work with cash on the spot. One of the customers approached Nick and complained about her attitude.

'It's not as though I've ever owed anybody money in my life, Mr Jones, and that woman makes me feel like a criminal.'

'There's new she is,' Nick apologized, 'but a word I'll be having with her. You go on as you've always done.'

'I'll be going somewhere else unless she changes her tune, I can tell you that. Sam Mackie had the same trouble with her yesterday over his account.'

After three similar complaints in one afternoon Nick stormed up to the little kiosk in a temper.

'Mrs Higgs! Duw, but there's trouble you're causing here. You'll have to go if you cannot run things the way we tell you, woman!' His dark eyes flashed at the sight of her insolent stance. 'No time I have to be getting out from under vehicles, soothing ruffled feathers and you not bothering to be pleasing the customers and writing up their accounts now.'

'Have to go, will I?' Daphne Higgs put her hands on her well-rounded hips and thrust out her ample bosom, which Nick thought seemed likely to pop out of her blouse like giant peas from a pod. 'And who do you think you are, Taffy, trying to tell me what to do? If you've any complaints you'd better tell the boss.'

'There's strange now,' Nick said softly, but his mouth was tight. 'Just let me be telling you, I am the boss.'

'I'll just bet you wish you were!' the woman jeered. She eyed Nick's greasy overalls and dirty hands with disdain. Nick's eyes narrowed dangerously.

'Conan omitted to give you *all* the facts now, did he, Mrs Higgs! Well there's promising you I am, one more complaint and you're fired.'

It was the following Saturday when Beth and Mrs Higgs quarrelled and Nick was glad he was not in the garage that afternoon. If he had not felt so sorry for Beth he would have laughed at Conan's predicament with the two women almost coming to blows. It was Fiona who reported the quarrel to Bridie.

'But Beth blames herself,' she said slowly. 'I'm a bit worried about her. She said she felt so tired it was almost a relief to give up the work at the petrol pumps on a Saturday.'

'But I thought Beth needed the money.'

'She thought she did. I think she manages quite well on what she earns between Wester Rullion and Lochandee. She just had it in her head that the more she could earn the better chance Lucy would have of becoming a teacher, but I think she knows now she couldn't pay for Lucy to go to college unless she won some kind of grant, and of course there is a possibility of that, I think.'

'I expect Beth will tell me all about it when I see her on Monday,' Bridie said, 'but I wonder what Nick will say. I get the feeling he doesn't like this Mrs Higgs, or trust her for that matter.'

'He doesn't? Maybe Beth was right then, after all. You see she began to suspect that Mrs Higgs sent her out to serve all those who pay on account, and any strangers. Beth and Lucy were eating their sandwiches for lunch and it was Mrs Higgs' turn to serve the next customer. It was Doctor MacEwan and Mrs Higgs insisted Beth should leave her lunch and attend to him. He pays on account. Beth realized then that she always served the ones likely to pay cash. She thought she had seen Mrs Higgs pocketing the money for one of the sales but she wasn't certain so she didn't mention that to Conan.'

'Even so it's a wonder Conan let Beth leave,' Bridie reflected thoughtfully. 'They've always been the best of friends.'

'I know, but I think Beth persuaded him it was better this way because she can only work Saturdays and Mrs Higgs is there six days a week. Anyway, he's promised Lucy a Saturday job at the pumps after her next birthday. She'll be fourteen then.'

'So she will,' Bridie marvelled. 'Is there a Mr Higgs by the way?'

'I've no idea. Doesn't Nick know?'

'No. He and Conan barely mention her. I believe her appointment was a sore point.'

'Well, never mind Mrs Higgs. I came to see how you got on with the bank manager. I feel quite anxious, Bridie, in case my ideas are all bad ones.'

'Don't worry, Fiona. I'm glad you suggested the idea and I'd seek your advice if I needed it, but I know these decisions have to be my own. To tell the truth my interview with the bank manager was a bit of a let-down after I'd got myself so keyed up for it. He was so non-committal. He kept my accounts though, the ones I do for myself. He said he wanted to study them further, then he would get in touch. He might even want to see the farm, he said. That really alarmed me. I'm proud of Lochandee and the way we keep it, and the stock, but suppose he arrives on a day when Father is here, or when Nick's at home? Now I'm living in a state of anxiety.'

'Would it be so bad if Nick knew, Bridie? Aren't wives supposed to confide in their husbands?'

'Yes, and I would, but Nick would probably feel he ought to be able to help me with the money. He thinks it's bad enough me owning half the farm. That almost came between us before we were married. Anyway, I want to prove that I can do it, and then I'll tell him when the time is right and he's not all worked up and unhappy about his own affairs.'

'I suppose you know best, but I think he may be a bit hurt if he ever finds out from someone else before you confide in him yourself. Your Nicholas always gives me the impression of being really proud and independent, with all the fire of his Celtic ancestors.'

Twenty

When the bank manager telephoned to make an appointment to see the Glens of Lochandee, Bridie was in a state of apprehension. She hadn't really thought he would pay a visit to the farm and she was petrified her father or Nick would turn up at the same time. His name was Mr Craig and he had only been at his present branch for eight months. Bridie was not sure whether it was good or bad that he was not so well acquainted with her father as the last manager had been. She worried and fussed and the tension of keeping it all to herself made her want to scream. Surely he would not bother coming if he didn't think there was a possibility of lending her the money to buy her father's share?

He arrived promptly at two o'clock. He was silent as he walked at Bridie's side and her tension mounted. Occasionally he stopped to look at something she had thought would be of no interest to him. He asked several searching questions from time to time and Bridie felt it was worse than sitting exams when she was at school. Afterwards she realized what a thorough check he had made of the facts she had already given him. At last he turned to face her, looking her steadily in the eye.

'Do you really believe your father will be willing to sell his share to you, Mrs Jones?'

'There seemed little point in asking him unless I could get the money.'

'And if I say I will consider you for a loan – subject to all the usual conditions of course,' he added hastily, 'you think your father will agree?'

'No. But I intend to do my best to persuade him if . . . if . . .' She looked at him, hope dawning. 'Are you saying I have a chance of getting a long loan then?'

'Possibly, but your father . . . ?'

'I hope to carry on myself one day and I would rather try now, while he is alive and well and can offer me advice if I want it.'

For the first time there was a hint of a smile on his stern face and he nodded.

'I think that would be wise. My grandfather was a farmer but times were hard and he refused to allow my father to make any decisions. My mother felt there was little but hard work and poverty in farming and she influenced my choice of career, but I shall always retain an interest in the countryside. I'm pleased to see things are changing gradually but it is a pity it took a world war to bring better prospects for those who produce our daily bread. Anyway, perhaps you would make an appointment to see me again, let me know how you have progressed with your father? We'll take it from there. Meanwhile I am impressed with the Glens of Lochandee. It was fortunate indeed that you did not lose such fine stock to the foot and mouth disease last year.'

'We were very lucky,' Bridie said fervently. 'And I did keep the farm running without Father actually being here then,' she added eagerly.

'Will you be selling any of your pedigree stock at the sales?'

'Oh yes,' Bridie's eyes sparkled. 'I'd just love to top the market or win one of the big shows – just to prove that a woman can do it.' Mr Craig chuckled at that.

'I wish you luck, Mrs Jones.'

The following morning Bridie telephoned Wester Rullion to speak to her mother. She had not slept well, with her mind busy marshalling the arguments she would put before her father. If her mother was there too she might hope for a little support. At least she would listen. If only she could persuade her father to listen too.

'Hello, Mum. I'd like to come over to Wester Rullion to talk to you and Dad this afternoon. Will you both be in, straight after lunch?'

'That'll be nice. I've just been digging some of my new potatoes from the garden. Would you like some? Is Nick coming with you?'

'No, just me. I want to talk to you both.'

As soon as she put the phone down Rachel did a little dance down the hall. Was Bridie coming to tell them she was expecting another baby at last? The prospect made Rachel happy and she hummed as she worked for the rest of the morning.

Neither Ross nor Rachel could miss the determined gleam in Bridie's eyes. It was a look that reminded Rachel of Conan, and, of course, of Ross, but Bridie had always been the happy, easygoing one in the family.

'I want you to listen to what I have to say, Dad,' she began, and swallowed her nervousness with an effort. 'Please, please listen first, before you say anything.'

'That sounds ominous,' Ross frowned. 'Have you blown up the tractor?'

'No! Nothing like that. I want to buy your share of the Glens of Lochandee. I want to farm on my own . . .' She had not meant to say it so bluntly but her carefully prepared sentences had flown out of her mind.

'You want to what!'

'Please listen to me? If I paid you for your share in the Glens of Lochandee you would have money to carry out all the improvements you want to make here, at Wester Rullion. You might even decide to build a byre and have a dairy here, if you really want a Friesian herd. It would be good for Ewan too, if he's going to farm. You could take the Friesian cows from Lochandee. That would make less stock for me to take over, and I prefer the Ayrshires anyway and—'

197

'I can't believe this, Bridie.' Her father sounded hurt and she bit her lip. 'And where do you think you're going to get the money to buy my share? Nick hasn't any to spare unless he's drawing out of . . .'

'I've already spoken to the bank manager,' Bridie inter- rupted swiftly. 'He has been out to see Lochandee. He said he was very impressed,' she added proudly. 'This has nothing to do with Nick and I don't want you to mention it. He has enough to worry him with the garage, and Conan's ambitious schemes. Mr Craig has agreed to arrange a long-term loan so that I would pay back the same amount each month when the milk cheque comes. If you will only agree to let me buy out your share?' She looked from her father to her mother, and back again. She had never seen either of them so speechless before.

'You must be crazy,' Ross said coldly, his blue eyes darkening with anger now. Her mother looked at her, her face pale and full of disappointment.

'I'll n-not stay for tea,' Bridie said in a choked voice. Turning away, she almost ran from the house in case they should see her own tears and bitter disappointment.

Nick had had another disagreement with Conan at the garage and he returned home feeling depressed and unhappy with the way his life was turning out. He couldn't visualize the years stretching ahead of him, buying one coach after another and planning tours for other people to enjoy while he sweated his life away on their maintenance.

He looked forward to getting home to Bridie, even con- fiding in her about his disillusion, but he sensed at once she was withdrawn and unhappy. He watched her brew the tea and place it on the table, then she forgot to pour any. She toyed with her food, which was unlike her. When he looked closer he was almost certain she had been crying. He pushed his chair back and drew her to her feet, wrapping his arms around her.

'There's a hell of a day, I've had. Another quarrel with

Conan – ' he laid his cheek against her soft curly hair – 'and I'm thinking your day has been just as bad, bach. Is it another disappointment over a baby, my love?' His tone was gentle and loving and Bridie struggled to keep back her tears. She was tempted to tell him of her plans and her father's angry reaction, but he had enough trouble in his own business, and working with Conan. So she stayed silent and snuggled against him. His arms tightened.

'Anything I'd be giving to get away for a day or two,' he muttered without hope.

'You would? Do you mean it, Nick?' Bridie drew her head back and stared up into his face. 'Could you? Could we go away? Now? Just the two of us?'

'You would leave the cows, Bridie? The rest of the hay?' His eyes were wide with astonishment.

'Right now I'd like to be anywhere but here, so long as I'm with you. Can you get away from the garage just now, Nick?' She watched as his mouth hardened and a determined light glinted in his dark eyes.

'Wanting to go, you are, then we go. Yes, Bridie, yes, there's a holiday we'll be having, bach. It will be doing Conan good to be left on his own. We'll see how he copes. But what about the farm?'

'We've almost finished the hay. Frank and Emmie will manage the milking with Beth there to help, and Sandy will see that everything is all right for a day or two. I'll ask Emmie to attend to the poultry and feed the calves. She would welcome the extra money, I think. Beth gets tired easily these days without any extras. Emmie is sewing new curtains for the cottage and I know she has other plans when she can afford the money.'

'There's proper homemaker she's getting,' Nick nodded his understanding. 'All right, my love,' he grinned. 'Pouring me a cup of cold tea is it now?'

'Och, my goodness!' Bridie clapped a hand to her head. 'My mind is wandering.'

'When we've finished I'll telephone the garage and tell Conan I shall be away for a few days. Going down to explain to the Kidds, are you? Then in the morning we could be getting early away, before anyone has a chance to hold us back. Where would you like to go?'

'Anywhere!' Bridie answered fervently. Nick was surprised but it was exactly what he needed himself and he knew how hard Bridie worked.

'Spoil ourselves, we will,' he decided. 'A really decent hotel we'll have for a couple of days. Maybe Edinburgh? London if you like. We could go to the theatre, see all the places you saw on the television during the coronation . . . ?'

'I'd love that, but it's such a long way to go for such a short time.'

'There's right you are. Settling for Edinburgh then is it, for this time?'

A little later Bridie heard Nick's voice raised in anger as he talked to Conan on the telephone. Big brother does like his own way, she thought. Perhaps it's time Nick stood up to him. But she knew Nick hated quarrels as much as she did herself, especially when he and Conan had been such good friends before they became business partners.

She often felt Conan would benefit from having a wife and learning to share, but he showed little sign of wanting a permanent relationship. Nick had told her that Daphne Higgs flirted with him outrageously but none of them knew what had happened to the elusive Mr Higgs and Bridie hoped her brother had enough sense not to get involved with her. According to Beth, Lucy hated Mrs Higgs but then Bridie was beginning to think Lucy was developing a schoolgirl crush on Conan. He was obviously unaware of it but he had always had more time and patience for Lucy than anyone else, except perhaps their mother.

'I'll wait until morning to tell Mother we shall be away,' Bridie said when Nick returned. She summoned a wan smile for Nick's benefit. 'We don't want Father coming rushing over, asking questions.' She looked closely at Nick, seeing the tight line of his mouth, the bleak look in his eyes. 'Is Conan being difficult?'

'Damned awkward, he is.'

'But we're still going?'

'Definitely. Right now, if Conan was not your brother, Bridie, there's leaving the garage for good, I'd be!'

'Oh dear. Are things so bad? Sometimes I wish . . .'

'What do you wish?' Nick demanded, but Bridie shook her head.

'What's the good of wishing for the impossible? What would you have done, Nick, if you and Conan had not gone into partnership?'

'I don't know – a small garage, a lorry or two perhaps – certainly not buses and more buses as Conan wants. The devil of it is, he's good at it. Enjoys people, he does, and arranging tours. He's making it pay and he can't see why I'm not as pleased as he is. He doesn't understand that I want to be at home at nights and spend my time with my wife.' He looked into Bridie's eyes with an intensity which brought the colour to her cheeks and set her heart fluttering. She went to him and hugged him tightly.

'I do love you, Nick.'

'And you know how much I love you, but just in case you need reminding . . .' He bent his head and kissed her, taking her breath away as desire flared like a fire, consuming them both.

Rachel was too surprised by Bridie's brief telephone call to ask questions, or to comment on the discussions and arguments she and Ross had had after Bridie dropped her bombshell the previous afternoon. She understood how frustrated Bridie must feel. She understood her own daughter and knew she was too intelligent to be content with taking orders and never making her own decisions. Her disappointment over her continuing childless state could only add to Bridie's restlessness in Rachel's opinion and her heart ached for her.

On the other hand she knew the Glens of Lochandee held a large part of Ross's heart, and his youth, as it did her own. She felt torn between the love and understanding she felt for Ross and love and anxiety for Bridie. One day she would go on farming the Glens of Lochandee without either of them.

Ross was still hurt and furious. Privately he had resolved to see the new bank manager himself and ask him what he was thinking about, agreeing to such a substantial loan for a mere lassie.

When Rachel told him Nick and Bridie had gone away for a few days he was even more dismayed.

'What kind of way is that to carry on a business? Demanding to take over the whole farm one minute and running away the next! It's—'

'Bridie didn't demand,' Rachel reminded him gently. 'At least she was willing to pay for what she wants. I think she must feel very frustrated, and perhaps it is not just the farm. Nick must have wanted to go away too, after all. Perhaps they both want us to realize how much work she does, and how much responsibility she has already.'

'Are you taking her part?'

'You know I'm not taking anybody's part. I'm trying to see things from her point of view, and consider what will be best for the future – for all of us, especially Ewan. After all, you can't leave Bridie without anything from us. Her share of Lochandee was a gift from Alice, possibly because she could foresee exactly how you would regard a daughter who wanted to farm the Glens of Lochandee, but surely you will expect her to carry on one day. Then there is Conan. Most of the money we gave him towards the garage business was a repayment of the legacy left to him by Sam Dewar. I do want Ewan to be a farmer and he loves the life here already, but we can't leave everything we possess ourselves to one son and forget about Conan and Bridie. Think about it, dear . . . ?' Rachel gave him her dimpling smile.

'You witch! You know very well I can't be angry when you

give me one of those beguiling looks of yours.' He pinched her cheek gently. 'You're still as bonny, Rachel, and I don't know what I'd have done without you. But I still think it's irresponsible of Bridie to take off like this.'

'You know as well as I do, Bridie would never go away and neglect her animals.'

'I didn't think she would, but I can't rest until I've been over there to see everything is all right.'

Ross almost hoped he would find something needing his attention at the Glens of Lochandee, but he had to admit everything was neat and clean and the animals were in excellent condition. Sandy Kidd and Frank seemed more than happy to work for Bridie and there was no doubting Emmie's contentment at being back at the Glens of Lochandee.

Rachel was right, he thought. What Bridie lacked in physical strength she made up for with her organization, and she did love the animals and life at Lochandee. One day she would carry on there without him. His anger had cooled somewhat by the time he was ready to keep his appointment with Mr Craig, the bank manager.

He missed the cows and the routine of milking, but more importantly it was the dairy and Lochandee which was bringing in most of the profit, and it was doing just as well under Bridie's management as it had under his own. Wester Rullion would be more profitable if it had a dairy. She was right about that too. He had considered sending Ewan back to Lochandee when he was older, to learn to milk and manage a dairy herd, but maybe that was not such a good idea after all. All in all, Ross was feeling calmer by the time he entered the bank, though still far from convinced that he was ready to let Bridie take out a large loan to buy his share of Lochandee. He could scarcely bear the thought of it belonging to someone else, even his own daughter.

Mr Craig was younger than he had expected for a bank manager and Ross was taken aback. Maybe he was getting old himself, he thought, but that idea did not please him.

He didn't feel old and there were a lot of things he wanted to do yet.

'Good morning, Mr Maxwell. I thought you might want to see me, but I'm pleased to make your acquaintance anyway.' Mr Craig was affable enough but Ross saw his eyes were shrewd. He indicated a chair. 'I expect you are surprised that we are considering a loan for your daughter?'

'Yes, I am,' Ross spoke abruptly.

'She has considerable collateral with her own share of the Glens of Lochandee.' Ross reddened slightly. He never really considered that half of Lochandee belonged to Bridie. It was all in the family and he was the head of the family, or so he had believed, until he heard Rachel's point of view. Mr Craig eyed him carefully and then went on. 'As a matter of fact I gave the matter extremely careful consideration, not least because it is unusual for a woman to want so large a sum. You should be proud of your daughter, Mr Maxwell. Too many sons wait for their parents to die so they can step into their shoes. Your daughter is quite prepared to make sacrifices to gain her independence. She told me she would prefer to have some time farming on her own while you are still alive and able to advise her.'

'Well I suppose if you put it that way,' Ross mumbled.

'As you probably know, I have been to the farm, and I was impressed, but I was even more impressed by the set of accounts your daughter presented to me.'

'Accounts? Bridie doesn't have the farm accounts . . .'

'These were management figures, costs, income, overheads and so on. Very methodical. Your daughter knows exactly how much money is coming in and whether it is from the milk, the eggs, or the few pigs and sheep. More importantly she knows what her expenses are.'

'I didn't know Bridie kept figures of her own. We run it all together as one business.'

'Yes, so I gathered when I looked at your account. I came to the conclusion that your daughter and the Glens of Lochandee could finance a loan quite well if the markets continue as they are, but I am not so sure what that leaves for your own income from Wester Rullion.' He eyed Ross expectantly.

'Mmm, well that's because we don't have a dairy there, at least not yet. It needed a lot of improvements and I have been putting money into it for draining and ploughing and reseeding. Soon I shall have the whole farm into rotation.'

'And do you think Wester Rullion will be able to stand alone and make a profit from the crops and sheep, that is if you sell your share of the Glens of Lochandee to your daughter?'

Ross stared across at Mr Craig and frowned. His colour deepened.

'Are you suggesting my daughter makes a more profitable job of farming than I do? Let me tell you, Mr Craig, I have spent most of my life so far building up the Glens of Lochandee, and the pedigree dairy herd. Bridie is a good manager, and I'm proud of her, but she has taken over a first-class farm. One day I expect Wester Rullion to be in the same class. Meanwhile I need to use the profit from the Glens of Lochandee to get it there.'

'I understand,' Mr Craig nodded. 'I am relatively new to the area so I have made several enquiries, not least from my predecessor, Mr Harrison. He knows you well, I believe? He tells me you made an excellent job at the Glens of Lochandee. He expects you will make Wester Rullion just as good in due course. So. Am I to understand you would like me to refuse the loan to your daughter until you feel your own farm will generate sufficient profit without her contribution?'

'I hadn't thought about it like that,' Ross said, disconcerted. 'As a matter of fact Bridie has suggested I should build a byre and take the Friesian cattle from the Glens of Lochandee to Wester Rullion. Maybe that's what I ought to do now, but I need to think it through. I should need at least one extra man if we had a dairy, but I think it would make Wester Rullion more profitable to stand alone.'

'In that case I hope you and your daughter can reach an amicable agreement. In the meantime, I noted the loan you took out to buy the Wester Rullion land has been reduced considerably. You have a better record than most of my farming clients. It will be a good recommendation if you require additional capital to set up your new dairy herd. I understand some farmers are building milking parlours and loose yards instead of byres now?'

'That's mostly in the east of the country,' Ross said, surprised at a bank manager taking an interest in such things. 'The loose sheds require more straw for bedding than we have in this area, though we do have more than most between Wester Rullion and Lochandee. It might be worth considering.'

'I believe there are some trials going on for pumping milk into tanks instead of milk churns too, but they have to be emptied by a special tanker. Some of the farms are too small to allow access. I fear it may put a lot of small farms out of business if it takes off.'

'I suppose you're right,' Ross frowned. 'Access to the dairy is something to bear in mind then, if I do build a new dairy. Everything seems to be changing fast since the war finished.'

Ross was deep in thought as he made his way home.

Twenty-One

N ick was determined that he and Bridie should enjoy every minute of their brief escape from daily routine and he booked them into a comfortable hotel not far from Princes Street. Although it was still only mid-morning when they reached Edinburgh, it was August and the city was alive with holidaymakers.

'I'm afraid we have only one room left, sir,' the smiling receptionist told Nick. 'It is one of the best. It has its own bathroom,' she added proudly.

'We'll take it,' Nick said promptly, 'for two nights, please.' Bridie was thrilled with the unexpected luxury of the wall-to-wall carpet and the pretty floral curtains which matched the bedspread and eiderdown cover, as well as the cushions on two small chairs.

'Do you think they had all this before the war? It looks new. They must have got it the minute materials came off coupons.' She sat on the big bed and bounced like an excited child. Nick grinned and immediately pushed her back against the soft covers, smothering her face with kisses, until she laughingly pushed him away and struggled to her feet.

'Time enough for that, Mr Jones, when I've explored all this luxury.' She did a little pirouette in front of the triple mirror on the dressing table, then went to investigate the white painted doors with their shiny brass handles. 'O-oh look, Nick. This one isn't a wardrobe. It's a bathroom – just for us. It has a shower too. I've never had a shower. Isn't it marvellous?' She turned to look at him. 'Can we afford all this?'

207

'For you, bach, anything.' Nick chuckled and caught her around the waist, swinging her off her feet, delighted with Bridie's childlike appreciation.

Afterwards they went out to explore the city, walking miles as they marvelled at monuments and buildings, the gardens and the castle keeping watch over the city.

'There's beautiful it is, the building, the architecture . . .' Nick said in his Welsh sing-song voice and Bridie knew his admiration was genuine. He had a finer side to him which appreciated the talent of the men who had made building design into an art.

Much later they bought food and wandered hand in hand in the sunshine, down into the gardens to enjoy it at their leisure. Neither of them wanted to spoil this precious interlude with talk of problems and frustrations. They had left all that behind.

Although the continued rationing and scarcity of some foods did not permit a lavish menu, the food at the hotel was beautifully cooked and looked almost too good to eat in Bridie's opinion. They were both too tired to go to the theatre and the receptionist told them the best seats would be booked anyway. She offered to telephone to book seats for the following evening if they wished to go.

The following morning Bridie gazed in the shop windows as they wandered along Princes Street once more, wending a leisurely path in the general direction of the Royal Mile and the castle, which Nick longed to explore in detail.

'Isn't that lovely,' Bridie said dreamily, gazing at a scarlet coat in one of the plate-glass windows. 'The style is just like Princess Margaret wore to the coronation Thanksgiving service. It's called the princess line because of the long seams and narrow waist and full skirt.'

'Is that right?' Nick teased. 'Come on then.' He took her arm and led her into the shop. 'If it fits you we'll buy it.'

'Oh no, Nick! I-I didn't mean that. Anyway, where would I ever wear a coat like that?'

'To go to the kirk, or into town. Come on, Bridie, I want to buy it for you as a present, call it a belated birthday gift if you like.'

'You saved up your coupons and bought me a box of chocolates for my birthday.'

'Well this can be for your next one then. Come on, Bridie, try it on while I'm feeling extravagant. Anyway, I like it with the black velvet collar and black buttons.'

It fitted Bridie beautifully and Nick beamed at her and nodded to the assistant.

'We'll take it. I'll pay now but if you'll parcel it up we'll call in on our way back to the hotel.'

Outside Bridie felt like skipping with happiness. 'You're so generous, Nick.'

'A-ah,' Nick grinned, 'there's payment I'll be having in return.'

'What would you like me to buy for you then?'

'Tonight I will be telling you, Mrs Jones.' Bridie blushed at the sight of his wicked grin and flashing eyes, but she returned the squeeze of his fingers.

'All right, Mr Jones,' she chuckled. 'I'll do my best.'

After lunch they climbed up to the castle and spent several hours browsing and exploring.

By the time they were ready to return to the hotel the sky had darkened ominously and long before they were halfway back the heavens opened and the rain fell in sheets, or so it seemed to Bridie. Hand in hand they ran until they were both too short of breath to run any further so they lifted their faces to the rain and made the best of it. They were soaked by the time they reached the hotel. They removed their shoes and scurried to their room.

'A good hot shower it is we're needing, bach. Off with all those wet clothes, girl.' Nick helped her open her buttons and peel off her dress. He couldn't resist running his hands down her bare arms, and seconds later Bridie found herself standing naked before him, sure she must be blushing all over. 'Duw, but there's pretty you are,' he said softly. She felt as shy as she had on their wedding night but Nick turned her towards the shower with a gentle slap on her rear.

'Be getting the water hot will you, bach? In beside you I'll be before you know it.'

'Both together?'

'Of course,' Nick grinned. 'Can't think of anything better, can I?'

A little while later Nick gently brushed the wet curly hair from Bridie's forehead.

'First time it is I've made love in a shower,' he said gruffly, pressing Bridie's wet body close to his one more time, delighting in her silken skin and her trembling response.

Several times during their brief holiday Bridie was tempted to tell Nick about the bank loan and how she had planned to buy her father's share of the Glens of Lochandee, but there seemed little point after her father's angry refusal. There was no hope now of her dreams ever coming to fruition. She had never wanted to burden Nick with her frustrations, even less the worry of a loan. So she said nothing. Later, she excused her silence because she had had no wish to spoil their precious idyll, but she learned the bitter lesson that silence was not always golden when it came between man and wife, and was interpreted as deceit and lack of trust, or worse.

Twenty-Two

Nick and Bridie arrived back at the Glens of Lochandee just as the milking was finishing.

'Aye, aye,' Frank teased. 'I reckon you timed that nicely.' Bridie grinned in return, pleased to be home again after all. Everything had gone well but she was dismayed to see Beth looking so exhausted.

'I hope you haven't been doing extra work because I've been away, have you, Beth? You look so tired.' To her consternation she thought Beth was going to burst into tears, but she seemed to gain control of herself and moments later she was summoning a smile and telling them she had discovered a broody hen with ten chicks which had been hiding herself in the stack yard. Bridie guessed she was deliberately changing the subject.

'She was lucky the fox didn't get her and her chicks then,' she responded cheerfully, but she was still worried by Beth's pallor. She didn't look at all well. 'How is Lucy? Has she got her exam results yet?'

'Oh yes!' Beth's eyes shone with pride. 'She was first in her year again for both English and French.' Her face suddenly crumpled and she turned hastily away from Bridie, mumbling something about forgetting to turn off a tap in the dairy. Bridie watched her hurry away and wondered what could be causing her so much distress when Lucy was doing so well. She was the light of her mother's life.

After they had eaten Nick took the dogs and went for a walk around the fields while Bridie telephoned Wester Rullion.

'Hello, Mum, I'm just letting you know we're safely home and everything is all right here,' she announced cheerfully.

'I knew everything would be all right, but your father has been over each morning just to check.'

'I'm sure there was no need for that!' Bridie said indignantly.

'I know dear, but you know your father so don't be too hard on him. Remember he has spent the best part of his life at the Glens of Lochandee and it was not always the prosperous farm it is now.'

'I know. I'm sorry,' Bridie said sighing. 'We had a lovely time though and Nick bought me one of those princess-style coats with a narrow waist and flared skirt.'

'That's good then. So are you feeling more like yourself? More cheerful again?'

'Yes, I suppose so.'

'Don't be impatient, Bridie. You'll have too much responsibility one day. Make the most of your life while you can, you and Nick. If you give your father time, I think he may come round to some of your proposals when he's mulled them over in his mind. He certainly doesn't like the idea of you having a big bank loan though, nor does he approve of you taking one out without telling Nick.'

'But Lochandee is my responsibility. Nick has his own business and his own problems with it!'

'Yes, so I gather. Conan called in briefly yesterday evening. He is very annoyed with Nick for going off on holiday at short notice and leaving him with everything to do. One of the buses broke down on the way back from a trip to Ayr. He had to hire a bus from another firm to bring the passengers home because Nick was not here to go and fix it.'

'Well, poor Conan!' Bridie said sarcastically. 'It will do him good to see how much work Nick does, and what it feels like not to be consulted about his partner's plans.'

'But Conan does appreciate Nick, Bridie. He says he is a first-class mechanic, far better than he is himself. He had another problem too. He discovered Mrs Higgs has been stealing cash. He saw her putting it into her pocket after a petrol sale. He made a note of the time and the amount. It was missing from her sales book and from the cash box. She said it was just an accident but I think someone must have alerted him already. Of course there was an awful row and he dismissed her immediately but it meant he had no one to serve at the pump and take the money, except himself. He phoned to ask Beth to go to—'

'So that's it! I thought Beth looked exhausted this afternoon when we got back. If Conan—'

'But Beth didn't go to the petrol pumps, Bridie. She's been bothered with backache recently and it seems to make her very tired. Lucy told Conan she was not well and had taken aspirins and was lying down. Conan fetched Lucy instead. Apparently she manages very well, and Conan or Nick are usually around in case there are any customers who try to be awkward, with her being so young. After all, Beth was working all the time at the Glens of Lochandee when she was not much older than Lucy.'

'So everything is all right again? At the garage?'

'Well, Fiona has been helping out too. I suppose they will need to get someone else when Lucy goes back to school after the holidays. Ewan was furious with Conan because he and Lucy had arranged to go to the cinema. He accused Conan of trying to monopolize her and take her away from him.'

'Poor Ewan,' Bridie sympathized. 'I suppose it's only calf love, but he is a bit possessive where Lucy is concerned.'

'I'm afraid he is and he doesn't understand how important it is for Lucy to be able to earn a bit of extra money.'

'Mmm . . .' Bridie frowned at the telephone. 'Mum, do you think Beth's worried about something? She looked so exhausted when we came back. She almost burst into tears. I've never seen her look so ill, not even when Lucy was born, or after Harry died.'

'I've noticed she's not been herself for some time, but

213

when I asked her if there was anything wrong, or if we could do anything to make things easier for her she almost snapped my head off – and that is certainly not like the Beth I've known all these years.'

'Do you think she's short of money?'

'I don't think so. At least we asked if she wanted to work more hours but she said she couldn't and Beth's certainly never been lazy. I don't think it can be lack of money that's worrying her.'

'Maybe she doesn't feel well enough to work longer hours. She certainly looked awful tonight after the milking.'

'Perhaps it's her age. Some women do have problems but she'll only be about forty-three or forty-four. If she doesn't want to confide in me, I don't know how I can help.'

'I suppose you can't,' Bridie agreed but long after she had put the phone down the picture of Beth's stricken face stuck in her mind.

The onset of harvest claimed everyone's time and energy and Bridie put her own aspirations aside, but she was as observant and caring of her fellow workers as she was of her animals and every instinct told her there was something wrong with Beth. They were working together more often too because Frank Kidd and Sandy were needed at Wester Rullion to help with the harvest there. She resolved to call on Fiona as soon as the bustle was over. Fiona often had a chat with Beth and Lucy and she must surely have noticed if there was something seriously wrong.

Nick spent his evenings driving one of the tractors to binder the corn, and later to cart it. He enjoyed the hay and harvest times, working with the other men, sharing their satisfaction when the crops were safely gathered in, and in good condition for the winter.

'I think you'd have made a farmer, Nick, if I'd had you here when you were a laddie,' Ross said late one evening. 'You certainly show more interest in it than Conan, but I don't know who would repair the tractors if we didna have you. There's so much more machinery since the war.'

'Enjoy it, I do,' Nick grinned. He got on well with his father-in-law and their respect for each other was growing as time went by. 'I'm afraid Conan is content to spend his evenings at the garage studying route maps for his tours,' he said ruefully. He didn't mention the disagreement he and Conan had had that evening before he left on his holiday. Their disputes were becoming more frequent and Nick felt he would explode one day and tell Conan what to do with the garage and the buses. The more he worked with the tractors and machines at the Glens of Lochandee and Wester Rullion the more he understood them and he had acquired a regular list of farmers who came to him for repairs, or asked him to convert some of their machines from horse power to tractors. Sometimes the garage looked more like an agricultural machinery store than a garage and this infuriated Conan, even though the income from repairs helped to spread their overheads.

As soon as the Wester Rullion harvest was gathered in everyone moved to the Glens of Lochandee and it all began again. Peter the Pole came to help as well. They all called him that because none of them could pronounce his surname, but it always made Bridie smile.

'He's thinking of changing it by deed poll or whatever they call it,' Rachel told her. 'Mrs Forster suggested he should adopt her name. It's amazing how much more lively and energetic she is since he went to live with her. I believe she is mothering him and the two of them seem to get on very well. Peter is quite clever with his hands and he has done all sorts of small repairs for her, and he painted the windows and doors outside. He has made himself some bookshelves for his room and she is helping him to speak more English.'

'He must be quite settled then.'

'Yes, I think he is. Your father told him he was thinking of getting some cows to milk and he said he milked the cows at home, but he obviously meant by hand. What he can't say he demonstrates and I think he meant his mother churned milk into butter.'

'And is Father really thinking of getting some cows then?' Bridie asked eagerly, though recently she had had other things on her mind which had pushed her own ambitions into second place. Rachel smiled as she helped Bridie peel vegetables for a large pot of soup to feed the men.

'Yes, I think he's seriously considering it. He has been reading all about milking parlours though instead of byres. You know, that's where the cows all gather in a yard ready to file into a small building where the milking machines are installed ready for the cows to be milked in small groups.'

'I see . . .' Bridie was astonished. She hadn't dared to hope her father would take her suggestion seriously, but she couldn't believe he would do so with such radical ideas. 'I don't know anyone who has a milking parlour in this area, do you?'

'There is one. Ross went to see it but it is not the kind he fancies for Wester Rullion.'

'Trust Dad,' Bridie smiled. 'He never does things by halves, does he? He'll be wanting one of those big milk tanks instead of putting it into churns next.'

'Oh yes, he's thinking about that too. More labour saving, he says, but there isn't a scheme in this area yet. Anyway, he would need to build a shed for the cows to sleep in first when we haven't a byre. He calls it a cubicle house. Apparently the cows have a single stall each and they are never tied by the neck as they are in the byre. He thinks it may be better for them to be able to wander about as they please and lie down more easily. If nothing else, Bridie, your ideas have given him a lot to think about and to be honest he has seemed more settled. He has really missed the cows since we went to Wester Rullion, and so have I. We had such a routine of milking twice a day for so many years, I think I'd be pleased to get back to it now that we've settled in. I'm not so sure about milking in one of those parlours though because I've never seen one. I expect your father will tell you all about it. But Bridie, how would you manage to make a living if he took the Friesian cows away from the Glens of Lochandee?'

'I worked it all out. We could build up the Ayrshire herd to the original numbers in about four years or five years if we keep all the heifer calves, and with a bit of luck. We would have less income during that time, of course. The only problem is, I don't think I'd be able to afford both Emmie and Beth to help in the byre.' She bit her lip thoughtfully.

'Well, we can cross that bridge if your father reaches a decision. After all, we would probably need Beth every day at Wester Rullion if we had a dairy again.'

'Yes, of course! I hadn't thought of that. I'd hate to hurt Beth or have her think we didn't want her after all these years.'

The last sheaf of corn was built into the stack and everyone breathed a satisfied sigh. It was still only mid-afternoon and Bridie was in the house alone when Ross came to find her. She was not as surprised as she might have been had she not already spoken with her mother, but she still didn't know whether he would ever consider allowing her to farm Lochandee on her own.

'I've been thinking things over, Bridie,' he began, and she didn't care for his thoughtful frown. Her heart sank. 'I can't see my way to doing things your way, lassie. It doesn't seem right to burden you with a bank overdraft, but I can't afford to hand over my share of the Glens of Lochandee either.'

'Oh no, Father! That's not what I want either. In fact I wouldn't accept it that way.'

'No, but some day my share of this place will be divided between you and Conan. Ewan hasn't been as lucky as you two,' he chuckled. 'He hasn't met a generous benefactor. I'm still surprised at Alice Beattie leaving her share to you when you were still just a wee bit of a lassie.'

'But she knew how much I loved it, and – ' Bridie gave her father a mischievous smile – 'I expect she guessed your opinion of women in business, especially farmers.'

'You may be right,' Ross nodded dryly. 'She often seemed to know what was in my mind better than I knew myself. Anyway I shall leave Wester Rullion to Ewan and I don't want to leave him a pile of debts with it. According to Mr Niven, and your friend Fiona, he will have a big enough debt to pay to the government in death duties, just for inheriting the place your mother and I have worked so hard for. Whereas you and Conan should have nothing to pay if I could get my affairs in order now.'

'What do you mean? Have you been to consult Mr Niven about it then?' Bridie frowned.

'Of course. You should know by now I don't rush into things like that. Anyway, I would like to put a dairy herd on at Wester Rullion. You were right about that, and it will make the farm more profitable, especially now it seems the milk marketing boards are here to stay and we can all be more sure of getting paid for our milk. It will take me a wee while to get the sheds ready though, but as soon as I can milk them I'd like to take the Friesians from the Glens of Lochandee. As you said, there'd be less money for you to pay out then, but you'd have less income,' he warned sternly.

'I've considered that.'

'I don't like the idea of you having a bank loan, lassie, and I'd feel a lot happier if you discussed it with Nick and see whether he agrees with your plans.'

'I would discuss it with him but he's not happy in his own business. If he thought I had a bank loan he might feel he had to stay in partnership with Conan just to support me. Don't you see?'

'I suppose so. Your mother is convinced Nick and Conan will split up and she hopes they do it before they fall out and force a sale of the business. They were good friends.

Friendship isn't always the best basis for a business partnership though.'

'I think they both see that now, but neither of them can afford to buy the share of the other and still stay in business, even on a smaller scale.'

'So you will not consult Nick before you arrange the bank loan then?'

'You mean . . . ? You really will let me buy your share, Father?' Bridie's eyes were shining.

'Aye, I think so . . .' Ross was frowning. 'Mr Niven thought it was not such a bad idea. As for your friend,' he smiled and his blue eyes crinkled, 'she said I didn't appreciate what a capable and intelligent daughter I had. She also reminded me that you left school to work at home when we most needed you, and Conan didn't want to farm. She obviously believes I owe you something, lassie, and she's right. I'll take the cows as part of my share and that leaves you to take out a long-term loan to buy my half of the land.'

'But there's the two tractors and the horses, as well as the poultry and pigs and all the equipment.'

'We already have enough pigs and poultry at Wester Rullion. Anyway, you've built them up yourself here. We don't need the horses either. As far as the tractors and the men are concerned, I hope we can still join up and help each other at times like this, hay and harvest and so on?'

'Of course we can!'

'In that case you may as well keep the two tractors that are here. They're older than the ones at Wester Rullion but you've got a good mechanic to keep them going for you,' Ross chuckled. 'Nick really understands machines like I understand cows. You've got a good husband, lassie.'

'I know,' Bridie smiled a small secret smile. If her suspicions proved correct her father would soon think even more of his son-in-law.

'So you can pay a visit to Mr Craig at the bank and tell him you need a loan for my half of the Lochandee land, but nothing more. That will be more of a burden than I approve of as it is. I'll make an appointment for us to see Mr Niven and he'll get the deeds changed into your name.'

'Oh Father . . .' Bridie didn't know whether to laugh or cry and she hugged him tightly instead.

'There, there, lassie,' Ross said gruffly, stroking her soft shining curls as though she was still his little girl. In his own heart he knew she always would be and he hated the thought of her being burdened with a huge debt, yet Rachel felt Bridie wanted, even needed, the challenge. 'I think it might work out for the best all round if your mother is right, and she usually is. Don't tell her I said so, mind!'

'I won't.' Bridie chuckled. Her mother and father still liked to tease each other. 'I'll go and see Mr Craig tomorrow, if I can get an appointment. Maybe I'll call in to see Fiona on the way home. I'm worried about Beth and I thought Fiona might know what's bothering her.'

Twenty-Three

B ridie was jubilant when she came out of the bank. Mr Craig had promised to get an agreement drawn up without delay and as soon as she had signed it he would transfer the agreed sum to her father's account. She frowned, wondering if she had been right to agree that the bank should keep the deeds for the land as security, after they had been changed into her name. Perhaps there was no choice. She might ask Fiona about that and she would consult Mr Niven if she wasn't sure herself.

Her face sobered as she drove into Lochandee village and turned down towards Fiona's house. It really was one of the nicest houses in the village and Fiona kept it beautifully. As Bridie drew up she found her working in the garden, tying up some giant dahlias.

'I never knew you liked gardening,' Bridie greeted her. 'These are magnificent, and such rich colours.'

'I'll pick you a bunch if you like, Bridie. It's such a shame they will die overnight if we get a sharp frost. Mrs Simms, the minister's wife, asked if I would cut some tonight, just to make sure she has them for decorating the church for the harvest thanksgiving.'

'Goodness me, yes, I'd forgotten it's on Sunday. So, when did you take up gardening?'

'Only since I got this house. I'm learning as I go along, but I'm getting really interested, and I'm finding it a wonderful relaxation from all the things I usually think about or read.'

'Mmm, I can believe that. What's that quotation again?' Bridie wrinkled her brow in thought.

> 'The kiss of the sun for pardon,
> The song of the birds for mirth, –
> One is nearer God's heart in a garden
> Than anywhere else on earth.

I think that's right, isn't it?'

'I don't know, but they're lovely lines,' Fiona agreed. 'You always were the one who wrote excellent essays and read such a lot when we were at school. Who wrote it, do you know?'

'It was a lady called Dorothy Frances Gurney, I think.'

'I was telling your father the other day that he under-estimates your ability,' Fiona said thoughtfully. 'I'm not sure whether I offended him.'

'Oh, you didn't. He was telling me. In fact he probably paid more attention to you. He's being very generous, I—'

'Come on in and tell me all about it then, if you've time?'

Bridie followed Fiona round to the back door and into the kitchen.

'I really came to talk to you about Beth. I'm worried about her and I thought you might know what's wrong?'

'Ah, so you've noticed too. I wondered if it was just me imagining things, but recently Lucy has told me several times her mum is exhausted and lying down, or "she's just sitting in the chair staring into space". I tried to talk to Beth about three weeks ago but she burst into tears and said there was nothing wrong with her, nothing at all. She picked up her things and rushed out. I thought I'd offended her but she came round the following evening and just carried on as though everything was normal, so I followed her example and I haven't dared mention anything since.'

'Oh dear,' Bridie sighed. 'I don't know how we can help

until she confides in us. Mother has tried to talk to her. After all they've known each other since Beth went to the Glens of Lochandee as a maid when she was thirteen or fourteen.'

'We must just be patient then and hope things come right for her,' Fiona said, 'but we all need friends sometime and I've been glad of Beth popping across to see me. As for Lucy, she's such a bright, happy girl. I really enjoy her company.' Fiona frowned, evidently considering her thoughts. 'There is just one thing . . . but really Beth asked me in confidence. At the time I didn't think much about it and it's ages ago anyway, after I came back from the business about your mother's vase.'

'You mean advice in your professional capacity?'

'Yes, well sort of.'

'Then it's better you don't tell me, Fiona. I understand, and I don't suppose it can have anything to do with Beth's present state.'

'Perhaps not.'

Later when Bridie had gone, Fiona's thoughts returned to Beth. She recalled the night she had asked her to be Lucy's guardian. Perhaps she should mention it? Maybe she wanted to change her mind. I'll make an opportunity for Beth to talk about it again sometime, she resolved, and went back to her gardening, her thoughts on Lucy.

It was the beginning of November by the time the bank loan had finally been granted and Bridie began to feel that the Glens of Lochandee really belonged to her. Two weeks later her euphoria was shattered. She heard Nick slam the door of the little truck he always used for his work at the garage. The days were short now and it was nearly dark already. Bridie hummed as she put the finishing touches to the evening meal. She wanted it to be special tonight. A little smile lifted the corners of her mouth as she turned to greet Nick.

She knew something had upset him as soon as he entered the kitchen and she saw his face, white and stern, his dark eyes glittering with anger. He stared at her and stabbed a finger at his chest.

'This is me! Nicholas Jones, your husband. My own man, I am, Bridget. Capable of supporting my own wife, I am! Some bloody waif you picked up off the street, you think? Is it then? Have you . . . ?'

'Nick? Wh-what's wrong?' Bridie stepped away from him. She had never seen him so angry, so cold.

'Wrong? Wrong is it?' He gave a bitter snort. 'Telling you I am. Your husband is it? So I am the last to be knowing? Why . . . ?'

'B-but I only knew myself – for sure – today . . .' Bridie stammered.

'Today? Duw! Stupid is it you think I am? Not going to tell me, was it? You do want to shut me out of your life! Fine then it is. Now I will go . . .'

'Nick! Wait! I-I d-don't understand . . .' But he had turned on his heel and rushed out of the door again, slamming it behind him. Bridie slumped on to a chair. She felt as though she had been punched in the stomach. How could Nick have heard? Had he seen Doctor MacEwan at the garage? No one else knew. Her face paled. Did Nick think she was deliberately keeping her news to herself again? Even from him? Surely he didn't think she would risk losing another baby? He couldn't think that, could he? A baby – it was the one thing she longed for more than anything else in the world, and she knew it was his dearest wish too.

The carefully prepared meal dried up in the oven, but Nick did not return. She went to the door and looked out but the night was dark and a chill wind was springing up. The farmyard was deserted now except for Shep, the collie dog, sleeping with his head on his paws in his kennel. Only the clink of a cow's chain in the byre disturbed the silence. Bridie felt as though there was only her in the vast dark universe. She shivered and closed the door. In the small sitting room the fire was dying down and she put more logs on. She turned on the television and turned it off again. She couldn't settle. Her stomach churned, but she couldn't eat.

The clock in the kitchen ticked away the minutes and then the hours and still Nick did not return. Bridie paced between the room and the kitchen. She put more logs on the fire until the huge basket was empty. She looked at the clock for the umpteenth time. It was after midnight, her back ached, she was tired and utterly miserable and bewildered. Surely if Nick had gone down to the village he would have been home by now? Where else could he have gone, without his supper, without even a coat? She was exhausted but unwilling to undress and go to bed alone.

Nick walked fast but without direction. He just knew he needed to get outside, to walk and walk, and not think, not allow the hurt and anger to boil and erupt like a sleeping volcano. He had no idea how far he had walked in the darkness and he didn't care, but his thoughts were in his head and he couldn't leave them behind. How could Bridie treat him as though he was no more than a lodger in her house? Conan had looked so jubilant, but he had assumed Bridie had already told Nick of her own plans, and what she had achieved. He was the only one who didn't know. Her parents had known, of course, and the bank manager, and the lawyer. Even Fiona Sinclair must have known Bridie had taken out a huge bank loan to buy the land. What sort of a husband did the bank manager think he was? Bridie had always known he wanted to provide for his wife himself. He had refused to marry her until he could take care of her. His muddled thoughts went round and round and his head ached but still he walked on, never feeling the rising wind through his thick sweater.

What was it Conan had said? 'Now you can be master in your own house and make your own decisions.' How could he be master in his own house when it was owned by his wife and the bank? Had Conan been mocking him? No, he had truly believed he knew what was going on at the Glens of Lochandee. Conan was not the type to jeer at a friend and they had been friends for a long time, in spite of their differing ambitions as business partners. Now that their partnership at the garage was being dissolved, their friendship would be more likely to continue. Nick's pace slowed as his thoughts began to see the more positive aspects of his new situation. It was not as though he had received an ignominious dismissal from a job. He and Conan had done well in the short time they had been in business together and Conan had been generous in his praise and fair in his valuation of their accumulated assets. No, he would not be a pauper once his own share of the capital was returned to him.

On one side of the narrow road a steep hill rose out of the darkness. Nick could see the eyes of a few sheep glowing yellow through the gloom and he vaulted the roadside fence and went to join them, panting as he reached the top of the hill. He stood looking down, his eyes accustomed to the darkness now. Below him he could see a few twinkling lights in farms and cottages, but the lights of the village were hidden from view. He took out his pocket watch and tried to see the time. He held it to his ear. He had forgotten to wind it again and it had stopped. He shrugged and put it back in his pocket and sank on to his haunches, and eventually more comfortably on to the grass with his back against a rocky outcrop. A quarter moon had appeared in the dark November sky and the world was silent all around him. Nick rested his head in his hands. It was up to him what he did with his life. Always he had felt his parents were everything to each other. He had not allowed himself to think of his mother since her death. In his heart he was convinced she had not fallen into the river, her drowning had not been accidental. Would it have made any difference if he had been at home with her, if he had even been free to go home to her for a while after his father's death? The memory of her sing-song lilt came clearly to him now: 'Life is what you make of it, boyo, or so I always believed, but war . . .'

She had shaken her head in bewilderment. 'War now, there's cruel it is, taking away you all. Boyos still, all of you barely from out the schoolroom.'

It was true he had never really lived any of his adult life in his native Wales, but he had retained his Welsh accent along with the passions of his Celtic ancestors. But since the war he had taken the Glens of Lochandee to his heart, along with Bridie. Did he want to live without her now? Without her and the land she loved? Could he? No, no, no! His heart cried out. Well then, you foolish boyo . . . Go to it. Make of life what you will. He could almost hear his mother's voice as though she was standing at his elbow.

Nick stood up and stretched, aware now of the chill seeping into him through the seat of his trousers, the increasing dampness in the air, settling like dew drops on his woollen jersey and his tweed cap. He looked around him, trying to get his bearings. He must have walked miles and it was impossible to see far in the darkness. He turned around on top of the hill. He and Bridie had often stood together at the northern boundary of the Lochandee land and she had pointed out the various landmarks. Was this the hill to the north of Lochandee then? Had he walked round the twisting narrow roads in a half circle? If he had, then Lochandee lay somewhere to the south west of where he stood. He looked up at the sky but the stars were hidden by the lowering clouds. What had he to lose? He wasn't even sure of finding his way back along the twisting lanes in the darkness. He would follow his instincts and cut across country. He did a few exercises to loosen up his stiff limbs and warm himself, then he set off at a jogging pace down the hill.

There were several hedges and fences to bar his way but the further he went the more certain he felt he was heading towards Lochandee and home. Home! What was it Bridie had said when he had greeted her? He had been too angry and tense to listen to her.

'I only knew for sure myself today.' His footsteps slowed

and stopped. Bridie didn't lie. She might have deceived him by keeping silent, but she wouldn't lie. He stopped dead, his heart pounding. Had she been trying to tell him she was expecting another baby? Was it possible? Usually he had a fair idea about her monthly cycles, but he had been away with one of the buses for five days, as well as two three-day trips, and had lost track. There would be no more sudden departures at two hours' notice. Conan would have to find another stand-in for emergencies now. So could it be? His heart leapt at the possibility. Was that the reason Bridie had been reluctant to commit them to two singing engagements next March?

Nick tried to control his mounting excitement but the more he thought of it the more signs he seemed to remember. He had heard that women often went off drinking tea and he couldn't remember when Bridie had last drunk tea at breakfast time. Supposing he was right, that didn't alter the fact that Bridie had gone behind his back to buy her father's share of the Glens of Lochandee.

When Nick crept into the house the warmth from the big Aga cooker came to meet him and he realized how wet and chilled he was. He glanced at the clock and whistled softly. Two in the morning! He must have walked for twenty miles or more. No wonder he felt so stiff and weary, not to mention hungry and cold. He pushed the kettle on to the hot plate and foraged in the larder for some bread and cheese. He ate it standing up and swallowed the hot tea in great gulps, feeling it warming his whole body. He stripped off his wet clothes and crept naked up the stairs to find the warm wool dressing gown which Bridie had insisted on buying for him when she knew he would be staying away with the tourists.

'What if somebody needs you during the night?' she had said. 'You can't go around naked in a hotel with all those ladies around.'

He reached behind the bedroom door and pulled it on, glad

of its comforting warmth now. He looked towards the bed, expecting to see Bridie curled up and sound asleep, but the bed was empty, undisturbed. His heart plummeted. Where was Bridie? He turned and ran swiftly down the stairs. He pushed open the door of the little sitting room and there she was, curled up like a child, her cheek cradled in her hand. He opened the door wider and even in the dim light he could see the signs of tears where they had trickled down her cheek and on to the cushion.

'Bridie . . . ?' He called her name softly, afraid of startling her. He moved and knelt beside her, laying his hand on her arm. She was so cold. He glanced at the fire but the grate held nothing now but cold grey ash. 'Bridie! Wake up. There's frozen you are . . .' Slowly she opened her eyes and blinked like a sleepy child. Then she sat up and stared at him. He saw the dawning awareness in her eyes and she drew back from him, hard back against the settee.

'Nick . . . ?' She said his name uncertainly.

'So cold you are, Bridie. Let me help you through to the kitchen and I will make you a cup of cocoa.' He lifted her effortlessly in his arms. 'You shouldn't have waited up for me.'

'You were s-so angry. I was afraid you m-might . . .'

'I know, I know. Pride it was, I suppose, and I'm sorry. There's a silly bugger I am for minding so much. But never mind that for now. What were you going to tell me when I bawled you out, Bridie?'

'About the baby? How did you know so soon? I was going to tell you over supper.'

'Baby?' he breathed softly, his dark eyes shining. He set her on her feet close to the cooker but he kept his arms around her, trying to warm her with the heat of his own body. 'Sure you are then?'

'Yes. I went to see Doctor MacEwan this afternoon.' She glanced at the clock and gave a wan smile. 'Yesterday afternoon. He thinks I'm nearly three months and I think that's about right too. Oh, Nick . . .' She snuggled against him and his arms tightened.

'Thank God,' he murmured against the crown of her head, burying his face in the soft curls. 'It's sorry I am, Bridie. I should never have lost my temper like that. Just so hurt, I was, when everyone but me seemed to know what you were up to, and Conan was so triumphant.'

'I-I don't understand what you're talking about?' She frowned and leaned away from him, staring up into his face. 'No one else knows about the baby except Doctor MacEwan, but I will tell Mother soon and I promise I shall take the greatest of care this time.'

'I know, I know you will, bach. But it was the loan I was talking about. The loan you've arranged with the bank, and never mentioned it to me. There's your husband I am, Bridie.'

'O-oh . . .' Bridie's eyes widened. She heard the hurt still in his voice although the anger seemed to have drained from him. 'Who told you about that? It couldn't have been Father because he and Mother understood why I didn't want to worry you, and—'

'Worry me, is it!' Nick almost exploded again but he bit his lip striving to keep his emotions under control. 'Why should I be worried?'

'Well, maybe not worried exactly, but I didn't want you to be under . . . I didn't want to be a burden to you. I didn't want you feeling you had to stay in the garage business with Conan because I had a debt to repay. I'm sure I can repay it in the time Mr Craig has arranged. Nick, please believe all I want is for you to be happy too and do the work you really want to do, whether it is in partnership with Conan or a wee workshop in some poky corner of the farmyard. I know you're unhappy with the way things are at the garage and I hate to see you like this . . . Nick? Wh-why are you looking at me so strangely?'

Twenty-Four

B ridie trembled in Nick's arms and hoped he was not going to explode in anger again. Both her parents and Fiona had advised her to confide in him and now she wished she had. She imagined she could see the cogs of his brain working rapidly behind his narrowed dark eyes.

'There's brilliant you are, bach. I don't know why I didn't think of it myself,' he mused and hugged her tightly. 'That cup of hot cocoa I'll be making you now, and I'll fill one of the stone pigs then we can both get properly warmed up in bed. There's freezing my feet are, and you're shivering.'

'I'm all right. Tell me what you're thinking, Nick? I didn't mean to hurt you . . .'

'I'm thinking my wife is a genius!' He looked down at her and his expression sobered. 'Conan is buying my share of the garage business and I can do exactly as I like. And you have just given me the best idea yet.'

'Conan is what? Have you agreed to split up? When did this happen?'

'You didn't know?'

'How could I know? When did you decide, and how will he manage to pay you your share?'

'You really didn't know . . . ?' Nick stared down at her and frowned. 'Drink up. We'll talk in bed.'

A little while later Bridie snuggled into his arms and he ran his hand over her stomach where the muscles were still taut. As always, he delighted in her trembling response. 'This is the most important thing in our world now, or at least in mine, Bridie.'

'You must know I want our baby more than anything else. But I still want to know about Conan and what you are both going to do if he is paying back your share in the garage.'

'There's surprised I am if you don't know. He has got the money from you, even if it is indirectly.'

'From me? No, I . . .'

'Indirectly he has and I'm still aggrieved you didn't confide in me,' Nick insisted.

'I'm sorry, Nick. I would never willingly hurt you, you must know that. I wanted to tell you several times, but then Father refused even to think about my proposals and I thought there was no point in bothering you with my frustrations when you had enough problems of your own. I wouldn't have taken a loan if I didn't think the Glens of Lochandee could pay it back. I don't think Mr Craig would have agreed anyway.'

'There's faith I have in your judgement, Bridie, but I didn't like hearing about it from someone else. Promise me you will always discuss things with me in future?'

'I promise. Now do tell me about the garage. Did you and Conan have a blazing row?'

'No, all very amicable it was, as a matter of fact. I may need to help him out for a while until he gets another mechanic and a relief bus driver. Your parents gave him half of the money you paid to your father when you bought his share of the Lochandee land. That's to be his inheritance from your parents. Over the moon, he is. Didn't expect anything more from them, see. Certainly he never expected to have it now.'

'I wonder why they've given it to him already?'

'I think they knew our partnership at the garage was not working out very well,' Nick said gravely. 'They probably wanted to help. Apparently your father is going to use the rest of the money to build a milking parlour and shed for a dairy herd at Wester Rullion. When it begins to pay he hopes to leave you a little money too, or so your parents told Conan.'

'Father has been more than generous to me already. I'm not jealous of Conan. I'm just surprised at them giving him the money now when Father has so many plans of his own to carry out.'

'I'm beginning to suspect your mother may have had a hand in things. Conan has paid me most of my share of the capital. Now we shall both be happier and your mother will be pleased about that. But more importantly I shall be able to help you pay off some of your loan, even after I've set myself up with a little repair shop. So, my dearest Bridie . . . Hush, hush now . . .' He placed a gentle finger over her lips. 'Please don't shut me out again, Bridie. Too tired are you, to hear what I would like to do?'

'No, I'm not too tired. Tell me your plans, please, Nick? I couldn't sleep until I've heard everything.'

'All right. There's you, just put the idea into my head. Mentioned a workshop in a corner of the farmyard, you did.'

'Oh but I didn't mean to . . .'

'Listen to me, girl,' Nick said softly. 'An empty shed there is, up at the little farm your father added to the Glens of Lochandee, and beside it the small barn. Ideal they will be for my workshop. Access there is, on to the side road from Lochandee village. Easy for the farmers, see, bach. Come with their tractors and implements for repairs they can. There's undercover I'd be, with the barn an' all. Wouldn't even need to lay out money for premises, see. There's happy I am getting my hands on things, adapting, finding out how they work, even improving some of the machines,' Nick said with enthusiasm. 'More mechanized farming is since the war, see.'

'Oh it is, and my Father thinks you're an excellent mechanic.' She felt Nick smile against her cheek.

'Glad I am, he approves of your husband then. Lot of regular customers I have already. Feel sure they'll keep coming if I am local. And there's Conan now, pleased he'll be to get rid of them from the garage. I plan to buy a cattle lorry too. I'd like to be around to help you when you go to market, Bridie, or to your shows with the cows. I reckon there's plenty of business to be had transporting other cattle. Most of the farmers are too busy, or too short of labour, to walk them to market now. Easier it is, taking them by lorry, and quicker. Then there's the tractor driving to do here, the ploughing and cultivations, the mowing and rowing, harvesting the corn. I know Sandy Kidd and Frank understand cattle better than I ever shall but neither of them are much good with the tractors.' He chuckled in the darkness.

'They would both agree with you there. In fact they will be relieved if you take over some of the cultivation, but Nick, I don't know how you'll ever fit in everything you plan to do.'

'When I get established I can always train an apprentice, or employ a driver for the cattle lorry, maybe even two or three if there's a demand. Who knows? It's not that I've no ambition as Conan thinks, I just don't share his ideas any more. Most important of all, I intend to spend more of my time looking after my wife – ' his hand moved back to Bridie's stomach – 'and my family,' he said softly as he sought her lips in a kiss which promised everything Bridie had dreamed of.

Fiona had not seen Beth for more than a week but Lucy had been over twice after school and both times she had remarked on how tired her mother seemed to be. Even though she was young and had her own school work and its attendant problems, Fiona sensed she was more than usually concerned by Beth's constant need to rest whenever she was at home. She hardly ever cycled now and both Bridie and Mrs Maxwell collected her in the car on the days she worked for them. Conan would have liked her to help him at the garage but Beth said she simply hadn't the energy for anything more. So Fiona made a point of going across to the cottage later that evening.

'I've just lit the fire, and I'm ready for a seat and a chat.' Beth greeted her with evident pleasure. 'Take that chair, Fiona. It's so early dark now and it's getting colder.' She shivered. 'Or is it just me?'

'The days are certainly short but I haven't felt the cold too badly yet. In fact I love crisp mornings and bright clear days.'

'Aye, each season has its charm, I suppose . . .' Beth said slowly and stared into the fire. When the silence lengthened between them Fiona looked at Beth uneasily.

'I-I just thought I should ask you, Beth . . . Well, I wondered whether you had changed your mind about wanting me to be Lucy's guardian, I mean now that she's getting older and—'

'No! Oh no. You haven't changed your mind have you, Fiona?' There was no doubting the desperation in Beth's face, the leap of fear in her eyes.

'Of course I haven't,' Fiona said softly and drew her chair closer to Beth's. She patted her hands where they lay turning and twisting in her lap. 'I'm growing very fond of Lucy and she works so hard. You must be very proud of her getting both piano and violin lessons through the school.'

'Aye.' Beth sighed heavily. 'Her music would have been a great benefit to her if she'd been able to go in for teaching.'

'Well, don't give up hope of that. I'll make enquiries about grants and scholarships if you like when Lucy gets nearer to deciding what she wants to do. Is she doing her homework just now?'

'Yes, she's in her room. She spends hours with her books. Very likely I'll not see her until bedtime.'

'I'm sure she enjoys it,' Fiona smiled. 'Don't worry about her, Beth.'

'I can't help it,' Beth whispered despondently. Her thin fingers were clenching and twisting restlessly. Fiona reached forward and clasped them in her own hands.

'What is it, Beth?' she asked softly. 'It's more than Lucy, I'm sure.'

'Lucy's my chief concern . . .' Her voice sank so low Fiona could barely hear. 'I've got a lump. Here.' She released one hand and put it to her breast, but her eyes were wide with fear as they met Fiona's startled gaze. 'I-I've had it ages. It just stayed the same and I thought it was nothing to worry about. B-but it-it's changed lately . . . Oh, Fiona, I'm so afraid – not just of dying . . . it's leaving Lucy. I c-can't bear it.' She shuddered and a hard dry sob shook her thin frame.

'Dear Beth.' Fiona heard the tremble in her own voice. 'Have you talked to Doctor MacEwan?'

'No! No, I-I hoped it would go away. I don't want an operation. My grandfather always said when they cut it with the knife it just grew faster and folks die quicker.'

'But Beth, it may be a cyst. You may be worrying unnecessarily . . .'

'No.' Beth shook her head. 'I know . . .' she said hoarsely.

'Is that why you've been so tired recently? If it is painful . . .'

'It isn't, not the lump. It's just backache makes me tired. It never seems to go away. I keep taking aspirins but they make me feel so sick . . . I hardly know what to do any more . . .'

'Then let me come with you to see Doctor MacEwan, Beth. It may not be as bad as you fear and he could give you something for the pain in your back. I promise he would never send you to hospital or make you have an operation if you didn't want to have one.'

Beth clutched Fiona's hand like a lifeline. 'You'd come with me? You'd tell him I don't want an operation?'

'I would. I'll give you all the support I can, Beth, I promise.'

'You're hardly more than a lassie, Fiona, but you're a good friend to Lucy and me. Th-there's something else I-I ought to tell you,' she whispered hoarsely and her eyes moved to the fire. She stared into the leaping flames for a long time. Fiona waited patiently, in silence. 'I've never told a soul. But you're her guardian.' Beth began to speak in short nervous sentences now. 'Not even Harry. Couldn't. W-would've broken his heart. I always meant to write a letter. I'm no g-good at writing . . .'

'Don't distress yourself, Beth. You know I'll always do what's best for Lucy whatever happens. You don't have to tell me anything.' Neither of them heard the creak of old wood as Lucy came down the dark narrow stairs from her attic bedroom.

'I-I must. Y-you see Harry wasna Lucy's father . . .' Fiona heard herself give an involuntary gasp, but she did not hear the echoing gasp from the tiny hall. It would never have occurred to Lucy to eavesdrop but now she was frozen to the spot with utter shock. She heard her mother's low faltering voice continuing. 'I loved Harry with all my heart, Fiona. I never loved anyone else. Never. It-it was . . . He had been on leave. He went away again – so soon. I missed him terribly. I-I didn't love Lucy's father. He didn't love me. He doesn't know either. No one knew!' Her voice shook and Fiona could only imagine the anguish Beth must have borne for so long, and on her own. 'He was so young. So unsure then. Just a bit of an innocent laddie going to fight for his country.' Her voice broke, but she sniffed and went on. 'He was hurting . . . needed reassurance. I-I thought he might never come back. It never happened again. J-just that once. It was a comfort – to both of us. N-nothing else. I dinna expect you can understand, a fine lassie like you, Fiona, but . . .'

'You'd be surprised how well I understand, Beth,' Fiona said in a low, sad voice, and clasped the nervously twitching fingers tightly in her own. 'Your secret is safe with me, never fear.'

'Y-you d-don't blame me then? You'll not hold it against Lucy? My poor wee bairn . . .'

'I would never hold it against Lucy. She's a lovely girl and

I'm very proud you have asked me to be her guardian, and that you have trusted me tonight.' Fiona wondered whether she should ask who Lucy's father was. Why was it so important for Beth to unburden herself after all these years? Beth remained quiet and Fiona felt she had talked enough for one night.

'We'll go together and see Doctor MacEwan,' she said more cheerfully than she felt. 'Shall we, Beth?'

'All right,' Beth said wearily.

'Just you sit still then and I'll make us a cup of tea, then I'll get off home.'

'All right. Bring a cup for Lucy please, Fiona. I'll shout her down in a minute.' She lay back in her chair and closed her eyes. 'I feel calmer now, at peace inside.' She yawned tiredly.

A few minutes later Fiona carried in the tea tray and called Lucy to join them. There was no reply.

'Maybe she's gone to sleep? Shall I peep into her room, Beth?'

'All right. She never goes to bed without saying goodnight though.'

There was no sign of Lucy in her room, nor anywhere else in the little cottage.

'She must be in somewhere,' Beth said.

'Maybe she's called on Carol?'

'She never came through here. She'd have no coat and it's a cold night.'

'Drink your tea, Beth. I'll just pop up to Carol's and see if Lucy is there.'

Lucy was not at Carol's but the girls thought they had seen her when they were on their way back from the badminton.

'She was on her bike and seemed in a hurry. She'd no coat on so she couldn't have been going far.

'Oh no!' Fiona clasped both hands to her face. Could Lucy have overheard her mother's confidences? What other explanation could there be for her to take off like that, without a word and on a cold November night?

Twenty-Five

Fiona hurried back to Beth's in a state of panic. Where was Lucy most likely to go if she had overheard their conversation? How much could she have heard? Everything? Beth's fear of dying? The truth about her father? Fiona hurried into the cottage but she stopped short. Beth still sat in the chair, the half drunk tea on the floor beside her. She was sound asleep. Fiona's first thought was to waken her, to question her about Lucy's friends, but in sleep Beth's face looked gaunt, her skin drawn and sallow. Fiona shivered. She remembered her mother in similar repose, with the same haunting spectre of death hovering over her, the dreaded cancer sapping away her life.

She stared around the cosy room. There was a mug on the mantelshelf containing odds and ends, including a pencil. She reached for it and the old envelope propped against the figure of a pottery dog. 'Back soon. Don't worry. Fiona.'

'Don't worry,' she muttered as she sped across to her own house. How could anyone help but worry when Lucy was cycling around the countryside in the darkness at this time of night. She glanced at the grandfather clock in the hall as she entered. It was just after nine and there was more than a hint of frost glinting on the cobbles and Lucy had no coat. She bit back a sob. Would she go to Ewan? He was her oldest, probably her closest friend. Fingers trembling she dialled the operator and asked to be put through to Wester Rullion. It was Mrs Maxwell and Fiona breathed a sigh of relief.

'I-it's Fiona Sinclair here, and I wondered whether you had seen Lucy tonight?'

'Lucy? Why no, she hasn't been over for a while, Fiona. Isn't she at home then?'

'No . . . er, we think she was . . . was a bit upset about something. She went off on her bike and she hasn't returned.'

'I see . . . Do you know what had upset her? Who she was likely to confide in? Carol, or the girls perhaps?'

'She's not there. I already asked. I'll telephone Bridie. She might know.'

'Bridie?' Rachel was puzzled. 'Was it something serious that upset Lucy, Fiona?'

'I-I don't know exactly, but she is worried about her mother.' This much was true, Fiona thought. She wished she did know exactly how much Lucy had overheard. Poor child. Her mother's illness was bad enough, but if she had overheard Beth's confession . . .

Lucy was not at the Glens of Lochandee either. 'You sound terribly upset, Fiona,' Bridie said with concern.

'Well I blame myself. Beth and I were talking. We forgot Lucy was supposed to be upstairs. I think she may have overheard . . . things.'

'What about Beth? Is she hysterical or anything? Do you want me to come?'

'She fell asleep in the chair, but I must go back to her. She'll panic when she realizes I can't find Lucy. Maybe she will have returned,' she said without much hope.

'I could stay with Beth, or phone around. Have you tried Ewan? Just a minute, Fiona. Nick's calling. He wants to know if he can help? He says Lucy and Conan are great friends these days. Have you tried the garage?'

'Surely she would never cycle all the way over there in the dark? She didn't even have her coat . . .' Fiona's voice was almost a sob. 'But I'll phone and see.'

'Let us know if she's there and we'll go over and drive her back while you stay with Beth. And don't worry, Fiona. Lucy

240

is a hardy wee thing. She's been a great support to Beth since Harry died.'

'I know, but this is . . . is different. I'll phone if she's at the garage.'

The telephone rang and rang at the garage but there was no reply. In despair Fiona replaced the hand piece on its cradle and went back across to Beth's cottage. She was just stirring and seemed disorientated, until her eyes focused on Fiona and memory came flooding back. She sat up abruptly.

'Have you found Lucy?'

'No.' Fiona slumped on to a chair and bowed her head. She was shivering but it was more nerves than cold. She told Beth where she had telephoned. 'No one seems to have seen her. Can you think of any other friends near enough for her to cycle?' Beth shook her head.

'What about the minister? Would she go to Mr Simms, or to Mrs Simms if she needed someone to . . . to confide in?'

'I don't think so, b-but would you phone the manse, Fiona? Please? Anything is worth trying. Mr Simms might have seen her.'

Fiona ran back to her own house to phone but there was no news of Lucy there, only grave concern and plenty of well-meaning advice. Slowly she returned to Beth's cottage, shoulders bowed in dejection, pondering whether they should alert the police to set up a search as the Reverend Simms suggested. Lucy was more mature for her age than most girls but the fact remained she was not quite thirteen years old and to find you were not the person you thought you were, or that your mother was ill and likely to die and leave you an orphan . . . Fiona shuddered. Either of those things would be enough to upset most girls older than Lucy. If she had overheard both parts of Beth's confession . . . It didn't bear thinking about.

Conan had been out for the evening and he was well pleased with himself as he drew his car into the garage forecourt. He had almost clinched a deal with a small local bus company which he was determined to take over. All that remained now were the final details to be discussed with their respective lawyers.

He was surprised to see the door of the garage kiosk slightly ajar. The catch did not shut very securely but he was sure he had locked the door before he left. He went round the corner to search for the key which he always left for whoever was on duty at the pumps. The key was missing. Frowning he pushed the door ajar and went inside. It was dark and silent and he almost closed the door and went up to his room and bed. Some instinct made him switch on the light. He was dismayed to see Lucy, her head on her arms on the grubby counter. She had obviously fallen into an exhausted doze and the light had wakened her. She looked dishevelled and it was clear that she had been crying and there was a streak of black oil down her cheek, probably off the counter.

'Lucy! My God! You gave me a fright. What on earth are you doing? How did you get here?' Conan hadn't realized how sharply he had spoken until he saw her small white face crumple in distress.

'D-don't be angry with me. I-I had to . . . to get away. I was going to Ewan, b-but he wouldn't understand. I d-didn't know where else to go. Then . . .'

'I'm sorry, lassie. I'm not angry and I didn't mean to shout, but you startled me.' He went round the counter and put an arm around her trembling shoulders. His hand brushed her cheek. 'You're frozen, Lucy! How did you get here?'

'On my bike?'

'In the dark? You cycled all this way!' Conan stared at her incredulously for a moment then common sense told him Lucy would not have done such a thing unless she was desperate. 'I'll bring a blanket from upstairs to warm you up, then I'll make us both a hot drink and you can tell me all about it.' He wondered if Beth had collapsed. He had known for some time there was something seriously wrong with her, and he knew how worried his mother and Bridie were – but why had Lucy not gone to one of them? They were both nearer than the garage.

Lucy huddled gratefully into the warmth of the grey utility blanket but she couldn't stop her teeth chattering and Conan guessed it was from nerves as much as cold.

'What time did you get here, Lucy?' he asked gently as he waited for the kettle to boil and slopped milk into two mugs.

'About half past n-nine, I think. The phone was ringing but everything was dark and I thought you must have gone to bed. I was too tired to cycle anywhere else so I was going to w-wait h-here until m-morning.' Her eyes filled with tears and they rolled silently down her pale young face.

'Is it your mother, lassie?' he asked softly. 'Have they taken her to hospital, or . . . ?'

'No! No, mother is at home, with Fiona. They . . . they were t-talking . . .' She stifled a hiccuping sob and Conan waited patiently but nothing had prepared him for the shock of Lucy's revelations. 'Ages ago Mum told me she had asked Fiona to be my guardian after D-Dad died – only he wasn't my dad!' she blurted and the sobs were uncontrollable now. 'I don't know who my father is. I d-don't know who I am. And he doesn't know about me . . . and . . . and . . .' The sobs racked her thin shoulders. Conan put his mug down carefully. He moved round the counter. He lifted Lucy from the chair and sat her on his knee, hugging her in the blanket as though she was a baby, rocking her trembling body to and fro.

'Y-you can't have heard right, Lucy. You must have made a mistake . . .'

'No.' She shook her head vigorously. 'I heard Mum say to Fiona, "I've never told a soul. But you're her guardian." She said she didn't tell D-dad because it would have broken his heart. Then she said, "Y-you see Harry was not Lucy's father . . ." I didn't mean to listen, but I couldn't move . . .' Lucy began to sob again, unaware of Conan's rigid body, his face draining of colour. 'She said "I loved Harry with all my heart, Fiona. I never loved anyone else." S-so how c-could she d-do it? How c-could she hurt my D-Dad? He loved me, I know he did . . .' The tears rained down Lucy's face now and she buried her head against Conan's chest. Gently, absently he stroked her hair.

'Of course he loved you, Lucy. We all love you very much. You must remember that. Promise me you'll remember that,' he said urgently, 'whatever happens. My mother and Bridie and me and Ewan – we all love you . . .' Even as he spoke his brain was reeling. His memory taking him back to the night he had helped Beth clear out the old cycle shop at Harry's request. It was hard to remember how young and innocent and confused he had been then, before the harsh experiences of war had hardened him. He shuddered, but he didn't doubt for a second that Lucy was his child. It explained so many things. Her green-blue eyes so like his own, so like his mother's. God! His mother was her grandmother! Ewan – his jealous possessive young brother was her uncle! What a tangle. No wonder Beth was worried. Probably things would change but what if Ewan did want to marry Lucy when they were older . . . They had always been so close. Then there was Lucy's musical talent, no doubt inherited from his own father. Her grandfather . . . Whatever would he have to say about this mess? He shuddered at the prospect of telling him. He would be furious. A thought occurred to him.

'Did your mother tell Fiona who . . . who your father is, Lucy?'

'I don't think so.' She was calmer now the storm of weeping had passed, leaving her drained and exhausted both physically and mentally. 'I didn't wait. I climbed out of Mum's bedroom window and got on my bike. I-I had to escape, to think and . . . and I just peddled as fast as I could . . .'

'So your mother has no idea where you are?'

'No . . .'

'Then I must take you back. She'll be worried sick and we

can't phone to tell her you're safe. Drink up your tea, lassie, and don't you worry, everything will be all right for you, I promise.'

Lucy obeyed and allowed him to carry her to the car, still cocooned in the blanket.

Fiona couldn't sit still. Every five minutes she went to the door and looked up and down the street, but always in vain. Beth had sat in a dazed trance for a full half hour and Fiona had no means of knowing where her thoughts had taken her, but she was grateful she had remained calm, even though it was an unnatural calm. The next time she glanced at her she looked too weary to stay awake. Now she was sleeping and Fiona didn't know what to do for the best. She wished she had asked Bridie to come down.

For the umpteenth time she went to the door and looked up and down the deserted village street. Then to her amazement the lights of a car came slowly down the road and drew to a halt beside her. It was Conan.

'Have you seen . . . ?' Her words faltered as she glimpsed Lucy's white face as she huddled in the passenger seat. Even in the dim light Fiona could tell Lucy had been crying and her eyes were dark with exhaustion. 'Where did you . . . ?'

'Let's get her inside,' Conan said grimly. In the dim light from the street lamp his face looked a ghastly white but Fiona mistook his abrupt tone and his obvious tension for anger.

'It was not Beth's fault,' she said urgently. 'If you must blame anyone then blame me for allowing her to talk.' When he didn't answer she grasped his arm. 'She's ill, Conan, seriously ill . . .' she whispered.

'I know, but I need to talk to her.' His eyes met hers, searching her face. Suddenly her own eyes widened as the truth dawned.

'You?' she mouthed silently. His mouth tightened but whether in pain or anger she couldn't tell. He gave a brief nod then opened the passenger door.

'I'll carry Lucy inside, then perhaps you'll see her into bed. She's exhausted.'

Fiona nodded and followed him up the narrow path, her mind in a turmoil. Beth looked at Lucy and held out her arms. For a moment Lucy hesitated while Fiona held her breath, then she went into her mother's arms and the racking sobs shook her. Beth wept too, but silently.

'It never made any difference, Lucy. We both wanted you so much. You were the greatest gift Harry could ever have had. You brought us so much happiness. Remember that, Lucy. Always remember that.' Listening to Beth's soft, tired voice Fiona swallowed hard and her eyes were luminous with tears when she looked up, only to find Conan's troubled gaze watching her. Eventually, with a final hug, Beth gently put Lucy away from her. 'Away to bed now, lassie. You'll need a good sleep.'

'I'll make you a drink of hot cocoa, Lucy, and bring it up for you,' Fiona offered, summoning a reassuring smile. Lucy nodded and said good night, a mixture of child and woman, in spite of her tender years.

Fiona made the drink and carried it up to Lucy's little attic room, where her books and a small desk took up more space than her clothes. Lucy was already in bed but she did not seem so exhausted now and Fiona stayed to talk, reluctant to interrupt Conan's talk with Beth and glad of the opportunity to reassure Lucy.

'I shall always be there for you, Lucy. I shall be proud to help you achieve your ambition to go to college, if that's what you decide to do when the time comes. Remember I have no family of my own so I need you too.'

'I never thought of that,' Lucy said. Suddenly she smiled diffidently and held up her arms. For the first time she gave Fiona a warm, spontaneous hug, then settled down beneath the blankets. 'Good night, Fiona. I'm glad you're our friend.'

Downstairs Conan and Beth were talking, their voices low but intense.

'I'll go now, Beth. Lucy seems settled for tonight. I'll see you in the morning.'

'No. No, please don't go, Fiona. Conan says you've guessed he's Lucy's father, and he knows I have made you her guardian. He . . . he wants me to make him her legal guardian as well . . .' Fiona looked Conan straight in the eye.

'You really didn't know? You didn't even suspect you were Lucy's father?'

'No. But now that I do know – ' he shrugged – 'well it seems so obvious. I liked Lucy anyway, and now I have a duty towards her and it is a duty I have promised Beth I will carry out to the very best of my ability.' Conan spoke with more humility and sincerity than Fiona had ever heard from him before tonight.

'I see, so I suppose you want me to – well to refuse to be her guardian?'

'Oh no, Fiona, not unless that's what you prefer?' Beth looked up at her, her eyes pleading, and Fiona smiled gently, reassuringly.

'I don't see why we can't both be guardians,' Conan said. 'It's obvious to me that both Beth and Lucy have a great deal of respect and affection for you. Anyway I expect there will be times when Lucy will need a woman's point of view.' Fiona looked at Beth.

'You've told him what you fear, Beth?'

'Yes,' she said wearily. 'No more secrets. I'm sorry you feel so hurt, Conan, but you do see I could never have hurt Harry? I hoped and prayed we should have another baby. I didn't realize until much later that he couldn't father children of his own.' She sighed, tired now. 'I don't know if he ever suspected but he never said anything. The problem is whether I should tell Lucy now or not. I can't bear for Mr and Mrs Maxwell to condemn me after all the years I have known them and had their help and kindness.' Fiona bit her lip, thoughtfully.

'I think if you tell Lucy she is sure to tell Ewan,' she said.

'Wouldn't it be better to let Conan tell his mother and father? After all, they are Lucy's grandparents and Mr Maxwell is already proud of Lucy's musical talent.'

'You make it all sound so easy!' Conan snapped.

'I'm not suggesting it will be easy. But we all have to do things we find difficult and in my opinion it is what is best for Lucy which counts. If your parents are the people I think they are they will never hold your indulgences against Lucy. They may take a little while to get over the shock, of course. As for Bridie, I've never known her to be cruel or unkind to anyone. She'll probably be delighted to welcome Lucy as her niece.'

'Can we wait until we see what Doctor MacEwan says?' Beth pleaded.

'Of course.' Fiona was contrite. 'You're tired and it's time I went home and let you get to bed.'

'Me too,' Conan announced, standing up quickly. 'I'll come tomorrow night, Beth, and we can decide what to do then.'

Outside he turned to Fiona. 'I'll walk you across to your house.'

'There's no need . . .'

'Yes, there is. I'd like to talk to you, and it's cold out here. What's more I could do with a stiff drink.'

'All right.' Fiona walked beside him, down the street and across to her own house. She had never seen Conan discomposed before, but she supposed it must be an awful shock to discover you had a daughter who was nearly thirteen and you didn't even know.

'Lucy has often reminded me of Bridie,' she said aloud. 'Now I understand why. She enjoys the same subjects at school, too.'

'Had you suspected then?'

'No, it never occurred to me that . . . that . . .' She floundered to a halt and was glad to concentrate on opening the door and flicking on the lights.

'It was only once! Just once . . .'

'Don't talk about it, Conan. It's all in the past now. It is Lucy we have to consider. Beth was right when she said Lucy gave Harry tremendous happiness. She did. He adored her. I often saw them together. Perhaps some good came out of your little indulgence.'

'For God's sake! You don't need to sound so superior. I don't suppose you ever put a foot wrong, Miss Goody Two Shoes.'

Fiona looked startled. She opened her mouth to reply, then closed it again. This was not her confession time and Conan Maxwell was the last man she would choose to confide in.

Twenty-Six

Fiona brought glasses and a crystal decanter half full of whisky.

'This suit you?' she asked.

'Yes, thanks.' He accepted the drink and swallowed a mouthful, and then another, feeling the fiery liquid warming his throat. 'I know we always seem to be arguing or striking sparks off each other.' He looked across at Fiona. She was eyeing him warily but she waited in silence. He realized she was not going to make things easy for him, but then he had not expected her to. 'The thing is, I can see for myself that Beth is seriously ill. She may not have long. I hope you'll be honest with me and let me know what Doctor MacEwan says after he has seen her tomorrow. I doubt if he will tell her the truth, but he might tell you if you explain that you are Lucy's guardian.'

'You mean I should ask to speak to him alone? Mmm . . . you may be right. Certainly I will tell you whatever he has to say. I think even Lucy realizes she may not have her mother much longer. I'm sure she will have questions to ask, but I think she is very considerate towards Beth, especially for her age. I don't think she will hurt her mother intentionally.'

'Well, I can't blame her for asking questions . . .' Conan drained his glass. 'I hope she doesn't hate me when she knows I'm her father.'

'Hate? That's a strong word surely? She may be wary, she may take some time to adjust and accept you as her father.

250

No one could blame her for that, but no, I don't think Lucy will hate you.'

'There's so many things to sort out. I'm certainly not looking forward to telling my father. We never did see things the same way and I can't expect him to understand how I felt at the time. Mother always was more understanding . . .'

'You surprise me, at least over this. I would have thought your mother would be the one to find it difficult to accept that you had cheated on Harry Mason when he was your friend.' Conan winced at her choice of words, but he had cheated on Harry that night he had made love to Beth. They must have been mad, both of them.

'Anyway I really wanted to ask if you think we could try to be friendly towards each other for the time Beth has left. It wouldn't be very reassuring for her if she thinks Lucy's guardians are forever arguing and bickering.'

'For once, Conan, I can agree with you on something!' Fiona gave a whimsical smile. 'In fact I would have suggested the same thing myself. I'm not sure how long we shall be able to keep it up, but for Lucy's sake I shall try not to argue with you in her company. She will need a lot of love and security.'

'Yes. That's another thing. I was out tonight when she came to the garage. She was waiting in the kiosk when I got back. I had been having a meeting with Turner Brothers. They have a small fleet of buses and I've struck a deal to take them over. It's more or less concluded except for the legal agreement your boss will be drawing up for me. Now I'm wondering whether I should cancel it. You'll have heard I paid Nick out?'

'Yes, Bridie told me. They both seem delighted with their plans for Nick to set up on his own.'

'Yes, but I still owe Nick three hundred and fifty pounds. He said I could keep it as a loan for a couple of years. The problem is that my flat is not a suitable place for Lucy to live. We only built one room above the kiosk. I've been thinking for some time I ought to build a small house but there's always some other deal which seems better for the business. Now Lucy must be my first priority and I shall need the money to make a proper home for her. It will take a bit of getting used to. I can't believe I have a daughter as old as Ewan . . .'

'I had hoped Lucy would move in with me,' Fiona said slowly, 'but of course that was before I knew . . . knew you were her father. Even so, it wouldn't be very suitable for her to live at the garage . . .'

'I don't see why not if I build a house.'

'Well, we're not going to argue, are we, Conan?' Fiona mocked gently, and lifted her expressive eyebrows. 'Are you going to tell the world you are her father, or only those most concerned?'

'Oh, only my parents! And Bridie, of course.'

'In that case don't you think people would gossip when you take a young girl to live with you?'

Conan scowled at her, then slowly he admitted, 'I suppose you're right. Maybe my mother will give her a home. Lucy has stayed with her on and off since she was a baby.'

'That's true. We shall have to wait and see, but in the meantime I have plenty of room here and I'm fortunate in that I can afford to keep her. Also I enjoy her company, so please remember, anything I offer to do is because I want to do it, for Lucy's sake.'

'I get the point all right. You're not doing it for Lucy's father,' he said dryly.

'Don't be prickly, Conan,' Fiona said with a sigh. 'We're going to have to pull together whether we like it or not. There's so many adjustments for Lucy before all this is over. I feel so sorry for her. I still feel guilty and sad when I think of my own mother dying, and I'm a lot older than Lucy is. I just hope it doesn't affect her school work.' She grinned suddenly, lightening the atmosphere between them. 'At least we know now where she gets her brains from. You always were top of the tree when you were at school, I recall.'

'If I didn't know you better, I'd think you were paying me a compliment.' He sighed and stood up. 'I'd better get home. The last time I came to see you I had a most enlightening visit, but I stayed all night then . . .' It was his turn to give a wicked grin now and he was delighted to see the blush which coloured Fiona's face to the roots of her hair. 'It would never do for me to ruin your reputation.'

'No it would not!' Fiona stood up and was glad of an excuse to hide her face from him as she led the way to the door.

Fiona saw the grave expression on Doctor MacEwan's face before he summoned a reassuring smile for Beth and told her he would give her some pills which would make her feel much better and ease the pain in her back.

'I think you should put away your bicycle for at least a month,' he told her, 'and if the Maxwells can manage without you for a few weeks the rest would do you the world of good.' He did not even mention an operation and Beth's relief and gratitude were profound. His eyes met Fiona's as they left the surgery and he gave an almost imperceptible shake of his head. She deliberately left her gloves behind and as soon as she had seen Beth safely back to her cottage and settled with a cup of tea, she made her way back to the doctor's house on the pretext of collecting them. She met Doctor MacEwan on his way between the surgery and the house and he greeted her without surprise.

'I am pleased to have a chance to talk to you, Miss Sinclair. Am I to understand that you are befriending Mrs Mason? She'll certainly need good friends.'

'I am Lucy's guardian, Doctor, so anything which concerns Beth naturally concerns me too and I have guessed for some time she was ill.'

'Very ill,' he agreed sadly. 'Life can be difficult. She has worked hard all her life and she adores Lucy. I wish there was something I could do, but except for trying to control the pain and giving her peace, there is nothing.' His tone was full of regret.

'I understand, Doctor MacEwan,' Fiona said quietly.

'Of course you do. It is not so very long since you lost your own mother with the same thing. It is impossible to say for sure but I don't think Mrs Mason will be with us for long after Christmas.'

'So short a time . . . ?' Fiona stared at him in dismay.

Later she went to see Bridie at the Glens of Lochandee to tell her Doctor MacEwan's verdict. 'It affects everyone, of course. Will you manage without Beth's help, Bridie? You must take extra care of yourself this time.'

'We shall manage all right. Poor Beth. She's so young to die.'

'I wonder . . . do you think I should tell your parents or will you?'

'I'll come over with you now, if you've time. We'll tell them together, but I think we shall only confirm what Mother suspects already.'

Fiona followed Bridie into the house unannounced. Neither of them had expected to see Conan at Wester Rullion in the middle of the afternoon and the atmosphere was electric as Ross and Rachel faced him across the kitchen table.

'I simply can't believe that you would do such a thing, Conan!' Rachel declared angrily. 'Harry Mason was your friend. Beth was his wife, a married woman. They trusted you! The shame of it . . .'

'Hush, Rachel, dinna upset yourself.' Ross put his arm around his wife's shoulders in a comforting gesture. 'What's done is done, and we shall all have to make the best of it. Lucy is a fine lassie, but she'll have a hard time ahead of her. Try to think about her . . .'

'How can I not think about Lucy, poor child. I'm surprised at you Ross, taking it all so calmly, and Conan . . .'

'Whatever's wrong, Mother?' Bridie asked, moving further

into the kitchen, but before Rachel could answer Fiona stepped forward.

'We came to give you Doctor MacEwan's verdict on Beth, Mrs Maxwell. He has told her she ought not to work for several weeks, or ride her bicycle.'

'Is that everything he said?' Conan asked, hope lighting his eyes.

'That is what he said to Beth.' Fiona met his eyes steadily. 'He's a kind man. He didn't want to leave her without hope. After . . . afterwards he told me he didn't think she would live long after Christmas.'

'So little time?' Rachel looked up at Fiona incredulously. 'Dear God above, where is mercy now? She's so young to die . . .' Bridie stared at her mother. She seemed distraught. She looked at Conan. He grimaced, then looked at Fiona.

'You haven't told her then?'

'It's not my place to tell anyone.'

'Fiona knows?' Rachel gasped, staring at Conan with hurt, angry eyes.

'Fiona is Lucy's guardian, Mother. Beth asked her after Harry died. Even then she suspected she was not well herself apparently. She wanted to make provision for Lucy's future. Who better to advise her than Fiona?'

'Yes, I suppose you're right,' Rachel said dejectedly, burying her head in her hands. 'I-I'm just so disappointed in you, Conan.'

'Will somebody tell me what you are supposed to have done, big brother?' Bridie demanded.

'It seems Conan is Lucy's father,' Ross said quietly, his arm closing more firmly around Rachel's shaking shoulders.

'He's what?' Bridie stared from her father to her brother in disbelief.

'I only found out last night,' Conan said defensively. His eyes moved to Fiona. 'I couldn't sleep when I got home, and I couldn't work for thinking about it this morning. So . . .' He took a deep breath and glanced at his mother's bowed head. 'I thought I'd better come and get it over with . . .'

'Over with!' Rachel's head jerked up, her green eyes, so like her son's, blazed with anger. 'Get it over with? You have a child the same age as your younger brother – a living breathing child! It is not something you get over.'

'Well I intend to face my responsibilities towards Lucy, now that I do know . . .'

'Oh yes? And where are you going to put her when Beth is no longer with us?'

'I-I can't believe I'm hearing right,' Bridie said, pulling out a chair and sinking into it beside her mother.

'Come and sit down, lassie,' Ross said to Fiona. 'It seems you're as much involved in all this as any of us.

'Yes, Mr Maxwell, I am, but I'm very fond of Lucy and anything I undertake to do I shall do willingly. I have already told Conan I think it would be better if Lucy lived with me after . . . when Beth can no longer look after her. I have plenty of room and we get along very well together.'

Rachel looked up then, her face white.

'You're a fine person, Fiona. Beth is lucky to have you as a friend but I feel Lucy is our responsibility now. It-it's just that it will take some getting used to the idea that we have a grandchild and a son, both the same age.'

'Well, well, well,' Bridie breathed, still astounded by the news. She looked across at Conan's white, strained face. 'Now that I know it seems so obvious. I mean, Lucy's musical talents, her looks and mannerisms . . . I just never thought about you . . . It must have been just before you went away to the war, Conan . . .' She suppressed a smile when she saw his face redden guiltily.

'It was only once,' he muttered.

'I should hope it was only once!' Rachel raged. 'Once was more than enough.'

'I think we'd better go,' Bridie said, sensing Fiona's uneasiness.

'Yes, your mother needs time to get over the shock,' Ross said gently, and gave Conan a signal to leave with them. He nodded and followed them with some relief.

'Phew! That was even worse than I thought it would be!' He sighed. 'I expected Father to be outraged, but it's Mother who is making the most fuss. She makes me feel like a criminal, and that's a bit unfair considering I'm illegitimate and all the doubts and confusion I suffered until I understood. She can't have been an angel either.'

'I think I'd better go,' Fiona said awkwardly but she had driven Bridie over and she couldn't leave without her. Bridie seemed more intrigued than shocked by the family skeletons tumbling out of the cupboard.

'I didn't know that!' she said. 'When did you find out?'

'Oh, once when Mother and Father were quarrelling and I jumped to the conclusion he wasn't my father and got all upset about it. Apparently the law is a bit different now, but at the time I was born the birth certificates couldn't be changed to the father's name if it was not on at the time of registration and if the father was not present. I was too young to understand but I overheard Mother and Father arguing about it. We went to stay with Aunt Meg for our holidays and I told cousin Polly. When Mother heard what had been worrying me she explained, well sort of. Of course I needed my birth certificate later and she told me then that she and Father had been separated and I had been born before they could get married.'

'Well, they certainly love each other, even after all these years,' Bridie said loyally, 'so I don't suppose they could help it. But it does explain why Mother gave me so many lectures about, well about waiting until I was married to Nick.' She blushed, remembering all the times Nick had wanted to make love to her, and how often she had been tempted, and always there had been her mother's firm injunctions at the back of her mind. 'It seems to me you're the one she should have been lecturing, big brother,' she teased. Conan didn't mind the teasing though. He was relieved to find that neither Bridie nor Fiona seemed to condemn him as his mother did.

Surprisingly it was Ross who reminded Rachel of their own situation and gently pointed out how unreasonable she was being.

'Oh yes?' Rachel flared with all her old spirit. 'You men are always in the right in matters of desire, but you d-don't know how much we women s-suffer in consequence.' In consternation Ross watched as she burst into tears. He gathered her in his arms as though she were a child and all the old protective love flared in him. He stroked her hair gently back from her brow, noting absently that there were scarcely any grey hairs yet amongst the red-brown tresses.

'We don't mean to make you suffer, dear Rachel. You know how much I loved you then, and how much I love you still.' She looked up at him through a mist of tears.

'I know, a-and we've been fortunate. But supposing Harry had ever found out . . .' She trembled at the prospect. 'Whatever would Beth have done then? She really loved him. It must have been Conan who . . .'

'But it does take two,' Ross protested mildly. 'I expect there were circumstances we shall never understand. Anyway, Harry didn't find out and Lucy gave him a lot of pleasure.'

'She did and . . .' Suddenly she leaned back in Ross's arms and looked into his face. 'You know I wouldn't be a bit surprised if Meg saw the resemblance between Lucy and Ewan and guessed there was something . . . At Bridie's wedding she made one or two comments I didn't really grasp at the time . . .'

'Well they do say an outsider often sees more of the game,' Ross nodded slowly. 'We saw Lucy almost every day so we never considered the resemblance, but now that we do know, I can't think how we could have missed it. The fact remains that Lucy is our granddaughter, and soon she will be an orphan. We must see Beth soon and reassure her that Lucy will still be as welcome here as she has always been.' He looked down into Rachel's troubled face. 'You do agree, my love?'

'Yes, Lucy will always be welcome. She's a lovely girl, but I still feel very angry with Conan.'

'I know, but what's done can't be undone, at least not in this case. I expect Beth will be worrying until she knows how we feel.'

'Yes, I suppose you're right,' Rachel sighed heavily. 'I will go down to see her soon, but not today. I need to sleep on it. It is such a shock and I need time to get used to it and think about what I shall say to Beth. Since she's so ill and has so little time, I wouldn't like to upset her.'

Twenty-Seven

R achel had pondered deeply on the question of Conan's involvement with Beth but in her heart, whatever her personal feelings, she knew she must do all in her power to ease Beth's mind during the time she had left to her. It must surely be the hardest thing in the world for a loving mother to know she was about to leave her child alone in the world and she resolved to do her best to offer reassurance for Lucy's future.

She decided they should all celebrate Christmas at Wester Rullion. It would be easier for Bridie, as well as having the whole of her family under one roof and it would reassure Beth of Lucy's place amongst them. She was a little hurt that it had already been decided that Lucy should make her home with Fiona. She knew she should not interfere but she was filled with misgivings. Fiona was attractive and intelligent and Rachel felt there was every likelihood that she would marry. Would Lucy still be welcome in her home with a new husband and perhaps children of their own? Yet it was plain to see the two of them got on well together and Fiona treated Lucy like the younger sister she had never had, and often craved.

Gravely, Lucy seemed to accept her circumstances must alter and Rachel's heart ached for her as she changed from carefree schoolgirl to responsible young woman almost over-night. She gave Beth all the care and consideration she could when she was not at school. In so doing she earned the respect of Doctor MacEwan and most of the people in the village, all of whom rallied to help in their various ways, once they understood the seriousness of Beth's illness.

Only with Conan did Lucy seem uncomfortable. The morning after she had discovered that Harry Mason was not her natural father she had demanded to know who her father was and whether her mother had truly liked him. She was shocked to discover she was Conan's daughter. Beth explained as well as she could but she knew Lucy was still too young and inexperienced in the emotions of men and women to understand the temptations, even less could she explain to her the stress of those wartime days, the grief of partings, the hunger and yearning, the fear, the confusion, the uncertainties.

It was a tremendous relief to Beth when Rachel called to visit and reassured her nothing would change between them. They had known each other too long and helped each other through too many trials to affect their relationship now.

'So you and Lucy and Fiona will come to Wester Rullion for Christmas, Beth? Bridie and Nick are coming, and of course Ewan will be there and Conan. We shall do our best to reassure Lucy that she will always have a family to turn to when she needs us. You know how proud Ross is of her musical talents. I suspect he will be more proud than ever now.'

'Ye're very kind,' Beth said wearily. 'We'll come for a wee while, and I thank you – I thank you from the bottom o' my heart for everything you've done over the years. I havena long now, but . . . but . . .'

'Hush, Beth,' Rachel said huskily, clasping the thin restless fingers in hers. 'There's no need for words between us.'

So the whole family gathered at Wester Rullion and each and every one of them made an effort to make it a Christmas to remember, hiding heartbreak beneath the laughter and teasing banter.

Fiona had changed her car for a new Austin so Nick and Conan were eager to examine it from front to back.

'If you'd asked me I could have got you a new Ford Popular at £390,' Conan said. 'I'll bet this one was a hundred pounds dearer.'

'Nearly, but not quite. I liked the Austin I had so I thought I'd stick to the same make.'

'Well, she's a nice little job,' Nick said admiringly. 'If I'd known you were thinking of selling your last car I'd have bought it for Bridie. It's time she had one of her own. When the baby arrives she'll not be able to go everywhere on a bicycle.'

'Oh, I don't know,' Conan grinned. 'Mother had a seat on the back of hers and a basket on the front and she took me with her when she delivered eggs and butter in the village – not that I can remember that, but that's what I'm told. As a matter of fact it was Beth's grandfather who fixed the seat so I could accompany her.'

'Well, I mean to buy Bridie a little car so if you see a bargain you can let us know.'

As usual Rachel had cooked a huge Christmas dinner with all the trimmings and two of the plump capons she had reared herself. The traditional clootie dumpling followed with silver threepenny pieces for lucky charms. Lucy got three in hers and Fiona and Bridie got two each. Ewan and Nick only found one and Conan got none but there was much laughter over it all.

Afterwards Beth fell asleep in the chair beside the fire while Lucy helped Fiona and Rachel clear the table and wash the dishes.

'Mum treats me like an invalid,' Bridie chuckled, 'and I never felt better in my life.'

'No, you're really blooming, lassie,' Ross declared, over-hearing her. 'When will the bairn be due?'

'About the middle of May.'

'Ah well, you'll miss the turnip hoeing very nicely then, but you'll be fit by haytime, eh?' He winked at Nick.

'I'll do my best,' Bridie promised with mock solemnity.

'Aren't any of you lazy bones going for a walk to shake down all that dinner?' Conan asked half an hour later.

'Not me,' Bridie yawned. 'Nick and Dad are outside discussing some changes to one of the tractors. You wouldn't think it was Christmas Day! Ask Fiona and Lucy. They're just about finished in the kitchen. And take Ewan with you. He got a Monopoly board for Christmas and he's pestering everybody to have a game with him.'

So Fiona and Lucy set out with Conan and Ewan to walk to the highest point of Wester Rullion and back, before it was time for afternoon tea.

'Nick and I will be leaving then to be back for the milking,' Bridie warned, 'so don't dilly dally on the way.'

It was a crisp clear day and Fiona enjoyed the brisk walk. The ground was not really steep and Ewan and Lucy were like a pair of young puppies let off the leash as they raced ahead.

'It's good to see Lucy putting her cares aside for once,' Fiona remarked. 'She's tremendously good with Beth.'

'Yes, and it's a relief to see Mother making them both so welcome,' Conan said.

'I never doubted your mother would do her best, however hurt she may be underneath.'

'You really think she's hurt? Are you wanting me to go on grovelling for . . . ?'

'No, no, of course that's not what I meant,' Fiona insisted. 'I do wish you wouldn't look for criticism where none is intended,' she sighed, putting a hand on his arm. He trapped it with his other hand and then held on to her fingers as they walked along, swinging her arm as they stepped out briskly.

'What are you two holding hands for?' Ewan demanded, running back down the path towards them.

'Och, Fiona's getting an old woman and she needed a pull,' Conan said grinning.

'Indeed I am not!' Fiona contradicted, 'and just to prove

it I'll race you all back to the farm, before Bridie and Nick leave.' She set off immediately, her long legs covering the ground with remarkable speed. She arrived at the gate into the farmyard, gasping for breath but triumphantly ahead.

'You cheated!' Conan accused laughingly. 'You had a head start.'

'No, you're too slow.'

'We'll see about that, one of these days,' Conan promised with a grin, watching the colour rise in her cheeks as she met his eyes. 'I must admit you can run faster than I expected though. Tell me, Fiona Sinclair, is there anything you can't do well?' To his surprise an awful bleakness came into her eyes.

'Yes, there is,' she said with a note of bitter regret.

'Oh? Are you going to tell me what it is? Maybe I can help you?'

'I doubt if anyone could help.' She shook her head vigorously as though wanting to empty it of memories.

'Not if you don't tell us what it is you can't do.' But Fiona just gave her head another vigorous shake and turned towards the house.

Bridie and Nick left soon after tea but Fiona, Beth and Lucy stayed on for the evening at Rachel and Ross's request. Conan decided he would stay too.

'In fact I might stay overnight if you've a bed, Mother? My flat is not exactly welcoming in this weather and there'll be nothing doing at the garage for the next few days.'

'You're welcome to stay whenever you wish, you know that, Conan,' Rachel said, 'but you're right about your flat. In fact you can barely call it that. I don't know why you don't build yourself a proper little house. You've plenty of land near the garage. It would be a good investment, wouldn't it, Fiona?' Rachel turned to look at Fiona and was surprised at the unhappy far away look in her wide grey eyes.

'Sorry?' She jumped as though coming back to the present was an effort. Rachel repeated her suggestion.

'Yes, I'd say a house would be an excellent investment if you ever wanted to sell the garage, Conan, or even for yourself.'

After supper Lucy and Ross played Christmas carols and they all joined in until Fiona felt Beth was tired and ready for home.

'It's been a lovely day,' Beth said, turning to Rachel. They both knew what was in her mind. Next Christmas they would celebrate without her. For a moment her new serenity deserted her and her eyes filled with tears. Rachael squeezed her hands in a warm grip, then gave her an unexpected hug. Lucy watched anxiously and Rachel turned towards her and embraced her too.

'You know there'll always be a place for you here, lassie,' she said softly.

Three and a half weeks later Beth slipped into a coma and two days later into the final sleep. Lucy, who had been incredibly brave throughout her mother's illness, sobbed as though her heart would break as she watched the coffin being lowered into the grave beside Harry Mason. It was the Scottish custom that the women did not go to the graveside but waited in the house for the men to return. Lucy had insisted she must go and not all Conan's persuasion could change her mind.

'In that case I will go too,' Fiona said quietly. Rachel nodded approval.

'I'll come with you.'

Later Fiona was glad of her help as they supported the sobbing girl back to the cottage. Doctor MacEwan had attended the funeral and he saw at once how Lucy's composure had cracked at last.

'It is better this way,' he said quietly to Rachel. 'I'll leave a draft, though, to help her get a good night's sleep.'

In the days that followed, Fiona helped Lucy sort through her mother's possessions and pack the things she wanted to keep. Conan came and helped them move the boxes and her own books and clothes to the little bedroom Fiona had prepared especially for Lucy.

'This is lovely,' he said as he looked around the pretty bedroom with its flower-sprigged wallpaper and pale pink curtains, with a bedspread made to match. Lucy gave him a wan smile.

'Fiona helped me choose the paper and the material. We sewed the curtains and the bedspread together,' she added proudly. 'But Fiona put the paper on the walls.'

'Mmm, you're a lucky lass. I shall have to come and ask the pair of you to advise me when I get a new house.'

'Are you going to build one then?' Fiona asked in surprise, knowing he had gone ahead with the takeover of the Turner family's buses and that money must consequently be tight, especially with his insistence on making her generous contributions towards Lucy's keep.

'Some day I'll get around to it,' he shrugged.

As the weeks passed and the days lengthened Fiona did her best to stimulate Lucy's interest in things beyond the village, hoping it would help to take her mind off her great loss, remembering all too clearly how bereft she had felt herself, and still felt when she recalled her mother's death. Sometimes Ewan accompanied them and Fiona enjoyed a visit to Edinburgh zoo almost as much as they did.

'I wish I'd known you were going,' Conan said when he heard. 'I might have come too. In fact, it would be a good idea for a day trip with one of the buses,' he added brightening. 'The next time you have any good suggestions, Miss Sinclair, perhaps you'd share them with me?'

'All right, we'll do that, won't we, Lucy?'

They visited the museum and the camera obscura in Dumfries when Lucy was doing a school project concerning local history, and the ancient ruins of the thirteenth-century Caerlaverock Castle.

'I'm so lucky to have you, Fiona,' Lucy said one night

when they were sipping cocoa before going to bed. 'You make ordinary things seem so interesting. You would have been a really good teacher.'

'A teacher?' Fiona considered the statement. 'I don't suppose I should have the patience. Not all students are as intelligent as you are, Lucy, and they don't all work hard either. As a matter of fact I think I'm lucky to have you too. It's far more fun doing things when I have company. Is there anything you would like to do in the Easter holidays?'

'Mmm . . . I don't know. I don't suppose we could go to a real live theatre, could we?'

'I don't see why not,' Fiona said thoughtfully. 'I'll enquire what's on in Glasgow and Edinburgh. We might need to stay the night though if we go to an evening performance.'

'Wouldn't that cost too much?' Lucy said anxiously. 'Do you think we should tell Conan? He might take a bus!'

'All right, we'll ask him. If he doesn't think it's a good idea we'll have a wee treat to ourselves,' Fiona smiled. She knew how sensitive Lucy was about money and being dependent on other people. She insisted on cycling all the way to Conan's garage every Saturday to work at the petrol pumps and earn some money herself. It was while she was there she mentioned the proposed trip to the theatre.

As a result Conan called to see Fiona the following Sunday evening.

'I think it would be a splendid idea to run a trip to the theatre if I can get enough bookings to make it economical. In fact I think I could do with you for an ideas and bookings manager. How about coming to work for me on the days you don't go to the Niven's. Of course I can't pay their rates . . .' He broke off and Fiona was touched by his sudden boyish diffidence. It was a side to Conan she was only just getting to know.

'The money isn't the problem, but your grotty little office would be. I don't know how you find anything in there. If you're serious I could make a list of suggestions though and make enquiries from here for the ones you approve?'

'I'd appreciate that,' Conan nodded enthusiastically. 'Things are going pretty well but the paperwork takes a lot of organizing and I end up doing most of it in the flat at night. I'm fairly certain I miss some bookings for trips if I can't get to the phone in time.'

'All right, I'll have a think about it, but it was Lucy's idea to go to the theatre so if that proves a success perhaps you could give her the credit?'

'Yes, I will. She's still a bit awkward with me. I don't think she feels I'm old enough to be her father. To tell the truth I don't feel old enough either.'

'I suppose it takes a bit of getting used to for both of you. You could try treating her as an older cousin, or something. You used to have such a good relationship, and after all it was you she ran to when she discovered Harry was not her real father. That must tell you something about her respect and affection for you.'

'Yes, I suppose you're right.'

'She is beginning to accept she's part of your family anyway. She was teasing Ewan the other day, calling him "uncle". She said he was furious. He seems so young in comparison to Lucy.'

'Yes, they're growing apart, but maybe girls do grow up faster.'

'Lucy has had a lot to contend with and it has made her more mature than she ought to be. I would like to bring some fun back into her life. What do you think to the idea of me taking her and Ewan on one of your bus tours? Do you do any to the seaside resorts? Something which might attract older children and young teens with their parents?'

'No . . . We usually have older couples and it's mostly to the Highlands or the Lake District,' Conan said thoughtfully. 'But if you can think of something which might appeal I'd be willing to give it a try. In fact we could make it a pleasant break for the four of us if I arrange to drive the bus myself. Maybe a week-long stay with a couple of bus

A Tangled Web

tours from whatever centre you decide on . . . Yes, I think that's a splendid idea.'

'You mean a combination of business and pleasure?' Fiona smiled. 'But I do see it has to prove economical to run the bus, and it may help you and Lucy get back on to your old footing if you are both more relaxed in other surroundings.'

'I do believe we could make a good partnership with your ideas and my transport organization,' Conan said on a note of surprise. He stood up to leave and held out a hand. 'Shake on it, partner?'

Fiona smiled and put her hand in his, but on the spur of the moment he bent and kissed her cheek. It was a light, friendly kiss, but long after he had gone Fiona pondered her changing views of Conan Maxwell. Beth had always insisted there was another side to him, hidden behind the confident and ambitious young businessman.

Twenty-Eight

B ridie had kept in remarkably good health and her excitement grew as the birth of her baby drew nearer. Nick was happier than he had believed possible a year ago. He and Conan had returned to their old easy camaraderie now that they were no longer in business together, and they helped each other out willingly where their business interests overlapped. Nick enjoyed his work and was continually improving his skills now that he had more time to experiment. The local farmers respected him for his fair dealing, while recognizing he was not to be trifled with. He employed a part-time driver for the cattle lorry and market days were proving increasingly hectic transporting all manner of livestock from farms to market and on to other farms.

'I think we shall have to employ a tractor driver for the ploughing and cultivation after all,' Bridie said one evening when Nick had been working late to catch up on his own work.

'Yes, I agree. Things have taken off better for me than I ever dreamed,' Nick grinned. 'How would you feel about employing Tommy for two or three days a week? A tractor driver for the War Ag, he was, before he came to drive the cattle lorry for me. He has a smallholding but it doesn't bring in enough money to keep his family. Six children to feed and clothe, he has.'

'Six! Goodness gracious, they will take some keeping. It's a good job the rationing is almost at an end. Perhaps you would ask him if he wants to work the rest of the week at the Glens of Lochandee? Otherwise you are going to end up with even less time for your wife and family than you had when you were working with Conan.'

'I've no intention of neglecting you, dear Bridie, or this little chappie,' he added with a grin and a gentle pat on Bridie's stomach.

'I hope you'll not be disappointed if your little chappie turns out to be a wee girl,' she said anxiously.

'Of course not,' Nick said grinning, then his expression sobered. 'Duw! All I'm asking is you both be all right. Overdue it is now I'm thinking?'

'Yes, by my reckoning,' Bridie sighed.

Two nights later Nick was wakened by Bridie's restless pacing of the floor. He wanted to send for the midwife immediately but Bridie persuaded him to wait until morning. The labour was a long one but nothing would persuade Nick to leave the house, or to go for a sleep. He had telephoned Wester Rullion as soon as it was daylight and Rachel had come over immediately, but the day wore on and night had fallen again. Still they waited.

'It is far worse waiting than it ever was having babies myself,' Rachel told Mrs Marsh, the midwife.

'Are you sure Bridie shouldn't be in hospital?' Nick asked abruptly. 'I thought more babies were born in hospital than at home now?'

'A good lot of them are,' Mrs Marsh said, 'but they can't hurry nature, even in hospital, and when the wee thing is born you'll be glad your wife and child are here, under your own roof.'

'But so long, it has been . . .'

'Aye, it's a big baby, I think. Probably a wee laddie.' She smiled at Nick. 'Laddies usually cause the most trouble.'

Two hours later Bridie brought her baby into the world. She was totally exhausted but almost delirious with joy and satisfaction as she cradled her son in her arms. Nick simply couldn't take his eyes from the child he and Bridie had created. He felt it was nothing short of a miracle and they were truly blessed.

A weary Mrs Marsh smiled with satisfaction at their happiness. She settled mother and child and promised to return first thing in the morning. It seemed to Nick and Rachel that the moment she had shut the door behind her the baby wakened and howled as loud as his tiny lungs allowed. Nothing seemed to calm him and Bridie was near to tears with doubts and weariness.

Gently Nick lifted the tiny bundle from her arms and began to sing to his son. There was a world of love in his eyes and his voice was soft and deep as he sang the Welsh lullaby 'Suo Gan'. Watching Nick rocking the child so tenderly, listening to the beautiful melody, Rachel felt a lump in her throat. Silently she tiptoed to the bedroom door. Bridie raised her eyes and smiled contentedly as her mother blew her a kiss.

'That was beautiful, Nick,' she said softly, as he laid the sleeping infant into his crib. 'Will you teach me to sing that lullaby?'

'In the Welsh? I'll try. Seemed to do the trick, it did,' Nick whispered. 'At least he's sleeping again. Noisy wee fellow though, isn't he?' There was a world of pride in his voice. He bent and kissed Bridie's lips. 'I love you very much, Mrs Jones.'

'And I love you too, "Daddy". I'm sure you'll be a wonderful father, Nick.' She smiled up at him, brimming over with happiness in spite of her exhaustion.

At the beginning of the school summer holidays Ewan and Lucy prepared excitedly for their first real holiday.

'You'd better come back ready to work, my lad,' Ross told his younger son gruffly. 'I'd left school when I wasn't much older than you.'

Conan grinned affectionately at his younger brother. 'I expect Father will blame me for being a bad influence if you don't turn out to be a farmer either, young Ewan.'

'Oh, but I do want to be a farmer. I want to make Wester Rullion the best farm in Scotland, and I've told Bridie I intend to beat her to winning the championship for the best dairy cow at Dumfries Show.'

'You may well beat her to it. Bridie has other priorities now,' Conan replied.

'She has,' Ross agreed, 'but it doesn't stop her keeping a close eye on her animals. She takes wee Max with her whenever she can, and she has at least two fine cows she's getting ready for this year's show. Nick seems keen to help her too.' He looked Conan in the eye. 'I'm glad the two of you split up the garage business. Nick takes a lot of interest in the Glens of Lochandee and he's proving a great support to Bridie now.'

'Is that a hint that you're still disappointed I didn't take up farming, Father? It's just as well when you think about it, you'd have needed to buy another farm for Ewan. Anyway, one day I intend to make you proud of my success too.'

'We're proud of you already, Conan,' Rachel assured him. She had seen the shadows in his eyes but she had long since given up hope of Conan and Ross seeing eye to eye about farming.

It had been Fiona's idea to take a coach tour to Scarborough, combining scenic tours of the Yorkshire moors and dales with the entertainment of a seaside resort. She had persuaded Conan to advertise in the local paper, making a point of attracting other youngsters with their parents. Conan had been amazed at the number who had wanted to book.

'We could almost have taken two coaches,' he said.

'Well, if it is a success you could arrange another a little later in the summer if the hotel can fit you in, or there may be other suitable hotels. This is a medium-sized, family-run hotel according to the person who answered my questions before I made the booking. I do hope it will be all right but the prices seemed reasonable.'

'I'm sure it will be fine. In fact I'm beginning to wonder

how I managed before you took over the bookings and arrangements.'

'My word, that is praise indeed, Mr Maxwell,' Fiona quipped. 'Can I have it in writing and signed, please?'

'Och, was I as bad as all that? You couldn't say much good can come out of anyone's death, but at least since Beth died we've been better friends.'

'Yes,' Fiona sighed. 'Lucy never grumbles, but I know she misses her mother terribly.'

'It's only natural, but I know she appreciates everything you do for her. She has told me so on several occasions after the two of you have been on some jaunt or other.'

Conan was a good driver and he had obviously read a lot about the area because he kept the interest of his passengers with local anecdotes and historical facts. Nick had fixed some kind of loudspeaker into the bus which Conan usually drove, and the passengers could hear him without difficulty. There were ten younger passengers on the coach and Ewan and Lucy had quickly made friends with fourteen-year-old twins from Lockerbie. There were four twelve-year-old boys and Fiona wondered whether they would be difficult to control when they all got together but Conan set out the rules from the beginning and his voice was pleasant but firm. He made it clear that he expected the parents to be responsible for the safety and behaviour of their own families. The other two fifteen-year-old girls had obviously been close friends before the holiday and were keeping each other company.

Fiona was relieved to find the hotel clean and comfortable and the proprietor and his wife gave them all a warm welcome and asked everyone to come to them if they had any difficulties or complaints. It seemed to strike the right note from the outset.

'It's so different from our sea,' Ewan said as they walked along the beach after they had all unpacked. 'The tide doesn't go out for miles and miles like it does on the Solway Firth.'

'No, but that's because it is a firth – a tidal estuary,' Fiona explained.

'There's such a lot of people here though! And all those things like the fairground. And Mr and Mrs Black say there's an orchestra plays in a park in the open air. And there's a café where you can eat the crabs and lobsters as soon as they're caught.' Conan grinned as his eyes met Fiona's. Ewan sounded very young and enthusiastic.

The following evening as they ate their evening meal Lucy told them that Mr and Mrs Black had invited herself and Ewan to accompany them on one of the steamers around Flamborough Head.

'They said we would be company for John and Jacquie,' Ewan added. 'We can go with them, can't we?'

'Only if you promise not to get up to any mischief,' Conan said sternly. 'Mother and Father would never forgive me if anything happened to either of you.'

Fiona was glad Conan had included Lucy in the caring and she knew by the flicker in her green-blue eyes that she had noticed and was pleased.

'Well I suppose you two could come as well,' Ewan said reluctantly, 'but we'd like to go on our own with John and Jacquie, wouldn't we, Lucy?'

'I don't mind so long as we can get to see what it's like on one of the big steamers.'

'I'll have a word with Mr and Mrs Black then this evening,' Conan promised. 'If we're getting a day to ourselves perhaps you'd like to take a picnic and explore some of the walks around the headland, Fiona? It would blow the cobwebs away.'

'Suits me,' Fiona nodded.

The following morning Conan had arranged to collect sandwiches and fruit from the hotel and the cook had added a flask of coffee. They set off together, feeling free and in holiday mood themselves. Fiona was wearing an apple-green pleated skirt with a white linen blouse and a dark green corduroy lumber jacket which zipped up to the neck if the weather turned cool. As soon as they got away from the shelter of the town and on to the open cliff tops Fiona knew her pleated skirt had been a mistake. Conan laughed aloud when a sudden gust almost blew it over her head.

'You might help instead of splitting your sides,' she told him balefully, her cheeks rosy with embarrassment, and the effort of controlling her wayward skirt in the wind.

'Just let it blow. I've seen your legs before, and very nice legs they are too . . .'

'Conan Maxwell! If you . . . if you mention that . . .'

'Mention what?' Conan asked innocently but his eyes were dancing with devilment. Fiona scowled and decided not to pursue that line of conversation. She still felt hot all over whenever she remembered the night of Bridie's wedding.

'I've seen a lot of women wearing slacks since we arrived here. My mother always disapproved of women who wore trousers, but I wish I'd had a pair for today.'

'Bridie has worn trousers ever since she left school, though I seem to remember she had a bit of a battle with Mother in the beginning, but she only wears them around the farm.' He eyed Fiona's trim figure consideringly, delighting in seeing her blush. 'I think you'd look very good in slacks with your long legs.'

'Looking good has nothing to do with it, but a skirt in this wind is just a pest. I think I might go round the shops when we get back and see what I can find.'

'Ugh, we'll not be back before the shops close. Mrs Black said the sail they'd booked didn't get back in until five o'clock so we may as well make the most of our day. Come and walk close to me then the wind won't be so bad.' He took her hand and moved to the side nearest the cliffs. 'There, don't I make a good shelter?'

After a while they headed inland a little way, climbing away from the sea and Fiona enjoyed the feeling of freedom and the wind in her hair. Conan sensed her mood and his heart soared too. He had never seen her looking so dishevelled and carefree. Her hair was neither blonde nor brown and today it looked almost silver in the sunlight, but she usually wore it in a smooth, shining swathe curving beneath her chin. Today it was blowing in the breeze, exposing her slender neck and oval face. 'I think you should wear your hair back more often,' he said, stroking it away from her brow with gentle fingers. Fiona looked at him and blinked.

'You're not at all like the Conan I remember,' she said.

'Maybe we've both changed since this business over Lucy, and Beth dying, and everything. It was such a shock . . .' He glanced at his wristwatch. 'It's a bit early for lunch but this wind has given me an appetite and there's a nice sheltered hollow just a bit further up that hillside. Are you ready to stop?'

'I am. I wondered how I was going to survive until one o' clock,' Fiona said grinning.

A little while later they settled themselves against a grassy hillock, sheltered on three sides from the wind and with an excellent view of the distant waves shining and dancing in the sunlight.

'There's something hypnotic about watching the ever moving sea, don't you think?' Fiona said dreamily, helping herself to a salad sandwich. After they had eaten, Conan leaned back, resting on his elbows, his long legs crossed.

'I thought you might have condemned me for . . . well, for giving Beth a child?'

'Condemn you?' Fiona frowned. 'It's not my place to condemn anyone. I must admit it was a surprise, a shock in fact, that you . . . that you . . . Anyway I don't know the circumstances. But I do know that Harry derived a great deal of joy and pleasure from Lucy. He really loved her and I'm sure Beth was right to keep her secret to herself, though it must have been an awful burden to her, especially when she suspected she had cancer and Lucy was likely to be an orphan.'

'Yes.' Conan sighed and plucked a stem of grass, twirling it absently in his fingers. 'It wasn't Beth's fault, you know. She . . . she didn't set out to tempt me or anything. Anyway I was so bloody green and innocent and confused then . . .' Fiona heard the anger in his voice and turned towards him.

'You don't have to tell me about it, or anyone else,' she said gently and laid her hand on his arm, feeling the hard muscles beneath her fingers.

'I know,' he said, 'but you see it all seemed so natural, so wonderful, not wrong or sinful . . .'

'Did it?' Fiona stared down at him, then she shuddered and closed her eyes.

'Yes,' he said defensively, 'it did then. I didn't plan it. I . . . I blundered into the scullery and Beth was stripped to the waist washing her hair. We . . . we both got a . . . a shock. I'd been washing at the pump so I only had my trousers on . . . and I hadn't a towel. It . . . it just happened. You've no idea how innocent I was,' he repeated wonderingly, 'or how much I'd dreaded all the questions and boasting of some of the older service men – and some of the younger ones. I was terribly grateful to Beth. You wouldn't understand that though . . .'

'Maybe I understand better than you think. Certainly I'm the last person to condemn anyone, especially the way things were, boys going to war . . .' Her voice was ragged and Conan looked up at her, his eyes narrowing against the bright light reflected from the sea.

'Fiona?' He turned his arm and clasped her fingers. 'I didn't mean to upset you, and there's only ever been one woman I really wanted since . . .' He was staring at the grass. 'But she certainly didn't want me.'

'Are you sure she didn't want you? Whoever she is, maybe she was uncertain too. Maybe she was frigid . . .' She shuddered again and Conan frowned.

'Frigid!' He gave a harsh laugh. 'I hardly think so . . .'

'But how would you know? How would she know?' Conan sat up then and turned to face her.

278

A Tangled Web

'You really don't know?' he asked incredulously. 'You haven't guessed you're the woman? The night of Bridie's wedding I damned nearly raped you. I've never felt so humiliated, so angry and frustrated in my life as I felt that night. I thought you'd led me all the way, like a lamb to the slaughter. Then slapped me down. You looked so beautiful . . . Then you turned your back on me, curled up and went to sleep. I-I felt I never wanted to speak to you again, or see you again. But you came to see me about Mother's vase and you carried on as though nothing had happened. So bloody cool! I couldn't believe it. Of course you made it very plain that you wanted nothing to do with me, probably didn't even trust me . . .'

'I didn't know . . . I didn't know.' Fiona snatched her fingers from his and buried her face in her hands. Her shoulders shook, but there were no tears, no sobs.

'Fiona? Don't be upset. I'm sorry . . .'

'It's not your fault,' she said in a muffled voice. 'I didn't know, I-I can't even remember much about the night of Bridie's wedding. I never drink much and even a little makes me sleepy and f-fuddled.'

'You mean you didn't deliberately lead me on, just for the pleasure of rejecting me?' Conan asked carefully.

'I wouldn't know how,' Fiona muttered dejectedly. She didn't raise her head, she couldn't look at him, but she began to speak slowly, her voice low and faltering.

'Do you remember Gerry?'

'Yes, yes I do. You were engaged . . .'

'Yes. We . . . we thought we were in love. We were so young. He didn't want to go away. He didn't want to fight . . .' She shuddered again and her voice sank even lower. 'He was sure he wouldn't come back. I-I tried to . . . I w-wanted to reassure him . . .' She was silent for so long Conan thought she was not going to say any more, then she said in a rush, 'We tried to make love and I c-couldn't even do th-that for him and it was horrible, horrible . . .'

She shuddered. 'I hated it. I knew then I would never get married. I d-didn't tell Gerry that, but in my heart I knew I would tell him when the war was over. But he never came back,' she said in a whisper, 'not even once . . .'

'Fiona, that was not your fault.' Conan reached out and pulled her towards him, smoothing her silky hair as though she was a child. 'You can't blame yourself. Thousands of men never came back.'

'B-but I couldn't give him anything worth remembering, anything to want to come back for . . . I c-couldn't love him!'

'But you were both so young, and it takes two, you know. I expect Gerry was just as nervous and inexperienced. That doesn't make you frigid.'

'That's what one of the men in Glasgow called me.'

'Did you sleep with him?'

'No! Certainly not. He was married. He thought I owed him a debt because he had helped me get promotion.'

'Good for you!' Conan said and felt a surge of relief. He felt her tremble in his arms and he put a finger under her chin and raised her face to his.

'I think it's time we both put the past behind us and started again. The two of us?' Fiona looked up at him then, her grey eyes scanning his face. 'Is that the one thing you felt you were bad at, Fiona? The thing you wouldn't tell me about?'

'Yes.'

'Then just for once I really will be delighted to prove you wrong . . .'

'Conan!' Her eyes widened and for a moment Conan glimpsed something akin to panic in their depths but he bent his head and kissed her mouth, very gently. Slowly his lips moved to her throat and back to her lips. He felt her begin to relax a little and he lay back on the soft turf taking her with him, sensing her resistance, her lingering uncertainty.

'I promise I will not do anything you don't like, Fiona. I've learned my lesson too. I'd no idea it was so easy to get babies

and if ever you and I have babies I would want to marry you first. Do you trust me?'

'Y-yes, but I-I . . .'

'Ssh . . .' He covered her mouth with his. Slowly, deliberately he unfastened the buttons of her blouse and slid his hand inside, pushing aside the lacy cup of her bra before she could protest. He heard her gasp, felt her breathing quicken against his lips, but slowly she gave herself up to the pleasure of his touch, he felt the firmness of her breasts and delighted in her response as her nipples hardened beneath his fingers. Only when he moved to draw aside her skirt did she open her eyes.

'Conan . . .'

'Trust me, please . . . ?' he said huskily and covered her face with kisses, even as his fingers released the suspenders from her stockings and he pushed aside the soft material which barred his way. He heard her gasp aloud but he did not stop. He had to prove to her once and for all that she had all the feelings, all the depths and passion of a real woman. Only when she reared up and clung to him with something between a groan and a gasp of pure pleasure did he pause to look down into her face. Her lips were parted and he held her tightly against him so that she could not fail to feel his own desire.

'Now, tell me you're frigid,' he whispered, but she just shook her head wonderingly. She became aware of his own desire. 'You . . . are you . . . ?' There was a question in her wide grey eyes.

'Yes,' he said gruffly. 'Yes, I want you, just as much as the last time, but this is not the time, or the place.'

'You're not angry with me this time?'

'No, my love, I'm not angry. A little frustrated maybe but if you would promise to marry me and let me have all of you, it would make the waiting more bearable . . . ?' He raised his dark brows in a question and Fiona saw the passion in the green depths of his eyes. She trembled against him.

281

'Can you be so sure I shall not disappoint you?'

'Oh yes, I just wish I could be as certain I shall not disappoint you, Fiona. I haven't much to offer a wife yet, but I intend to make my business a success.'

'All right, but can I just make one last bargain with you, Conan?'

'What is that,' he asked warily.

'Well, maybe two? The first is, will you let me build a house near the garage so that we can all live there together? Lucy and I can help when you need us . . .' His brow darkened. 'Please, Conan? I have the money, and you know it would be better for Lucy,' she pleaded. 'Please don't let pride stand in your way. I expect we shall argue enough over little things. We always have, but this is the most important thing in our lives, all our lives.'

'What was the other thing?' Conan asked before committing himself.

'Oh . . . er . . .' Fiona blushed rosily. 'I want us to . . . to make love, just once before we marry. I want to be sure I can please you, satisfy you . . .'

'Oh I can say yes to that!' Conan almost cheered aloud. 'But I know beyond doubt that you will more than satisfy me, my love.' He bent his head and kissed her and it was a long time before either of them spoke again.

Lucy was ecstatic when Fiona and Conan told her they were going to be married.

'It is the very best thing that could happen to me, the thing I want most in all the world,' she said gleefully and hugged them each in turn.

'And will you be my bridesmaid, Lucy?' Fiona asked, still scarcely able to believe in her own happiness.

'Yes, please! Mum would have been so happy. She always thought you made a lovely couple.'